## "What is your desire?"

Raiven asked in a throaty whisper that was pure nerves. . . .

Quynn's husky reply settled her mind on the success of her efforts. "Might I perchance get to view what lies beneath the bathing linen?" he asked, pointing to the wrap she still wore about her.

The air between them had definitely changed quickly, but Raiven couldn't back out now. Her hesitation was fractional. She went on in what she hoped was a teasing manner.

"A tiny look, a wee look, but no more."

"I promise 'twill pass so quickly you will scarce believe I have looked at all." His tone warned he would tolerate no procrastination.

Raiven's heart was slamming against her chest as she slid with natural grace to her feet. She took a deep breath and prayed that her courage did not desert her now. With her back to Quynn she slowly dropped the linen. . . .

For orders other than by individual consumers, Pocket Books grants a discount on the purchase of **10 or more** copies of single titles for special markets or premium use. For further details, please write to the Vice-President of Special Markets, Pocket Books, 1633 Broadway, New York, NY 10019-6785 8th Floor.

For information on how individual consumers can place orders, please write to Mail Order Department, Simon & Schuster, Inc., 200 Old Tappan Road, Old Tappan, NJ 07675.

# When I Give My Love

## ANTOINETTE WRIGHTON

POCKET BOOKS
New York London Toronto Sydney Tokyo Singapore

This book is a work of fiction. Names, characters, places and incidents are products of the author's imagination or are used fictitiously. Any resemblance to actual events or locales or persons, living or dead, is entirely coincidental.

An *Original* Publication of POCKET BOOKS

POCKET BOOKS, a division of Simon & Schuster Inc.
1230 Avenue of the Americas, New York, NY 10020



ISBN 978-1-9821-5291-8

First Pocket Books printing May 1996

10 9 8 7 6 5 4 3 2 1



Printed in the U.S.A.

***This book is dedicated to***

Don, for all the hundreds of things you do, and the millions more that you are . . .

. . . and to my parents, James and Louise Wrighton, who taught me to expect the best and give nothing less . . .

. . . and last, but certainly not least, to Jaime, Don, and Christopher. I really couldn't have done it without you. You guys are the greatest!

To Linda Marrow, for entering my life but a brief moment—and changing it. And Catherine Collins, my editor; I don't know which I value more, your endless enthusiasm and encouragement or your unique ability to make work a lot more fun than it has any right to be. Thank you both.

# When I Give My Love

# Chapter 1

## England 1154

Innkeeper! Another skin of wine for my friend!" The masculine voice, though slurred, was clearly heard despite the noise of the tiny roadside inn.

The innkeeper nodded his gray head once in acknowledgment of the demand. If he secretly thought these men had had wine enough, he kept his thoughts to himself. For a certainty, *he* was not about to chastise the four warriors who had entered his inn a goodly while and four skins of wine ago. Even in their inebriated state, the innkeeper was sure they would be able to crush him and ten others of his stature without missing a swill of their spirits. He sighed heavily and hurried to the back to fill their request while muttering a quick prayer that they were not the sort moved to violence by much drink.

Unaware of the innkeeper's disquiet, Perevil Dunkirk lowered his voice to a companionable roar. "So, Quynn, how does it feel to be the most fortunate man in all England?"

There was a round of hearty laughter as the one addressed frowned and said nothing.

In truth there was very little left for Quynn St. Crowell to say. He had already, quite volubly, let his feelings on the matter of his upcoming marriage be known. His younger sibling, James, who resembled his brother to a great degree except he was fair where Quynn was dark, turned and loudly whispered to their companions that despite his full score and two years, his ears burned nigh on an hour as Quynn had lamented his fate.

More raucous laughter ensued as Quynn cast a derisive glance over his brother and friends. His expression condemned them as being so far in their cups that they'd laugh at anything at this point, humorous or not, and said he was not about to add to their lack of sense.

Still, he had to admit that the flush that bloomed in his cheeks was probably as much the cause of their laughter as James's words. If his ire was not sorely piqued, he probably would have found amusement in their reaction, realizing as he did that it was something they had never seen before.

"Ah, come now, Quynn, there's naught to fear." Douglass, one of Quynn's knights, roared while slapping him aggressively on his back. "You may even reach the point where you can bed the wench wi'out a full skin of wine to make the deed more palatable." He guffawed loudly, and Quynn winced, not from the blow to his back, but the verbal blow he was certain was coming. He was not to be disappointed.

"However, it comes to my mind that the *act* is the least of your worries. If 'tis truth Perevil speaks about the comeliness, or lack thereof, of your betrothed, 'tis a fortunate man ye'll be if ye can even *think* like a man around her."

He pounded the table with a mighty fist in his humor, causing the near empty tankards to rise and fall with a disjointed clatter. So consumed with his mirth, he gave no heed to the cool gray eyes that sliced over him with such a vengeance that it was truly a wonder blood did not begin to seep through the links of his mail.

Quynn, seeing he was being heartily ignored by his knight, sighed. Another would have long since had the good sense to be quaking with fear, but Douglass, resting in the confidence of their long friendship, knew Quynn too well.

Despite Quynn's being a baron and Douglass a mere knight, Douglass was the closest friend he had—next to Perevil, whom he had known practically from swaddling—and had earned the right to tease him thus. Another would never have been allowed to do so, either by Quynn or Douglass himself for that matter.

Quynn looked away toward Perevil and was slightly surprised to have his steady gaze returned unwaveringly—proof that Perevil had not consumed as much wine as he had previously assumed. At the very least he was not in the same condition as the men who sat to Quynn's right and left. He also had not, now that Quynn reflected upon it, made sport of the situation as avidly as the others. This was a sure indication that Perevil was aware of how much Quynn truly hated what he was being forced to do. The king had decreed his marriage to a woman unknown to him—a Frenchwoman at that.

Quynn, who had meant to ask in a quiet manner, was annoyed to hear his voice, which was usually deep and vibrant, crack slightly. "'Tis truth then? The wench really is lacking?"

Perevil looked uncomfortable. "Naught but rumors and speculation are known about the lady." His eyes slid away from Quynn's. "'Tis best you wait and see for yourself. Unless you feel able to dissuade the king from his course?" His voice ended on a hopeful note.

Quynn shrugged his shoulders, then ran his hand through his dark shoulder-length hair. Although he was unaware of it, there was more than one female present, respectable and not, who sighed heavily in their hearts, wishing it had been their hands that so caressed his dark locks as well as the endless breadth of those magnificent shoulders.

And Quynn St. Crowell was magnificent. His height, which was intimidating even while he sat, was an impressive six feet and six inches. Yet he had none of the awkwardness usually associated with one so tall. His movements were fluid and graceful. Those massive arms, which could have, as the innkeeper assumed, crushed the life out of many men, did not move in uncoordinated jerks and starts, but instead with a sureness that caused many a woman to wonder how it would be to feel so crushed. His legs were well muscled and firm from years of training and many hours astride a horse.

All of these things were enough to assure he'd not be a lonely man, but when coupled with a face even the imagination could never have conjured, the effect was totally devastating. He had night black hair of so deep a hue that it glistened blue. His forehead was broad, and his eyes were the clearest silver gray over a well-shaped nose and sculpted lips that had the most appealing natural curve to them.

Usually Quynn was very aware of feminine perusal. One did not live twenty-five years and not realize that there was something in one's possession women found extremely tasteful. But tonight he was completely oblivious to all lures being cast his way as he shook his head slowly to Perevil's inquiry.

"It does not seem likely, my friend. Henry may appear to be too affable for any to take seriously, but he's a monarch through. Once his mind is set, none can change it, especially on a matter such as this, where substantial lands are involved." His sigh was laced with bitterness. "I'll be marrying Raiven de Cortillion one month from the day, and on that you may be sure."

# Chapter

# •2•

James St. Crowell eyed his older brother through what was left of his vision after a night spent in his cups. Both were silent as they broke the fast. In truth the silence suited them well. Quynn's expression said that words would not be welcome, and the incessant pounding in James's head said that words would not be appreciated. Still, contrary to the dictates of his sore head, James's mind was working furiously, trying to decipher his brother's mood. He was almost willing to let the matter lay, uncertain whether his mounting confusion was due to the overindulgence of spirits or had some basis in reality. He kept stealing glances toward Quynn in search of an answer. Each time he did, his brother's expression was the same.

Nay, the ale may not be aiding his clarity, but it was most certainly not creating a problem either. It was unlike Quynn to be so silent for so long, especially if something displeased him. And it was clear that his upcoming marriage displeased him greatly.

Usually Quynn did not resist this strongly something he knew he was incapable of changing. That had been one of the first lessons Quynn had taught him. James could not count the number of times when Quynn had told him that a true man did not fight the inevitable. Rather, he showed his strength by his ability to prevent the circumstances from altering him. For the better part of yestereve and now this morning, James could scarcely recognize the sullen individual across from him.

What could be so horrible about marriage to the little de Cortillion woman? It would do so much good for the St. Crowells. She had an extensive estate in the region of Poitou and another sizable one in Gascony. Her lands were reputed to be extremely fertile, if underworked, and the estate in Gascony would bring a small treasure to their coffers from the wine it produced. All this should have had Quynn a mite more accepting of the position in which he now found himself. He had always been the one to think of Havilland first.

The St. Crowell estate, located southeast of London and north of Canterbury, enjoyed a moderate temperature and sufficient rainfall, which, along with the stream that ran through the estate, accounted for the richness of the soil and the lushness of its appearance. However, its geographical beauty could not camouflage the spartan interior and it was clear that it was far from equal to that of the young heiress's. And unlike hers, their heritage was not an old one. She would bring much to the house of St. Crowell. These facts, added to the knowledge that James knew Quynn was not in love with anyone else, made his brother's intractable attitude exceedingly difficult to understand.

James again looked to his brother. Only this time, to his surprise, he found Quynn staring back at him.

"How slept you, Brother?" James rumbled self-consciously, at a loss for being caught staring.

Quynn laughed sharply. "'Tis a question you would be better suited to answer than to ask. Your eyes this morn are a unique host of color, a little green, a little white, a lot of red."

His amusement grew as he watched James flinch at the sound of his laughter.

"Do not try to waylay the true matter."

"Which is?"

James was undaunted by the hint of threat in Quynn's tone. Many times he had seen seasoned warriors become weak at the knees when Quynn used that particular tone with them; however, upon him, it had no effect.

"Since your wits seem to have grown soft with a night of drinking, I'll remind you. You are betrothed by Henry's order. In less than a sennight you are to send word to your betrothed about your arrival so that within the moon you can be wed. Remember?"

Quynn's jaw went rigid. "Remember?! 'Tis all I've thought about since the king's messenger came and gone. Blast! How could he do such a thing?"

"Why, with a wave of his royal hand, Brother."

Quynn's massive fist slammed down on the table as he stood, causing the dishes to rise and fall in a discordant clatter. James closed his eyes against the increased pounding in his head. When the spasm of pain had passed, he opened his eyes, looking surreptitiously at the wood to see if it had splintered.

"What ails you, Quynn?" he asked softly. "Surely you knew there was always the responsibility of your marrying to provide an heir whether 'twas your wish or not. 'Tis the two-edged plight of being the eldest."

As this prompted no response and Quynn continued to stare out the window onto the grounds, James went on. "It is not as if these things are not done. In truth, 'tis more the case than not."

"Not in this fashion," Quynn growled.

"Betrothals are arranged all the time," James began slowly. His brows lowered in confusion.

"Aye. Forced betrothal is usually the case for a reluctant *bride.*"

James could feel it coming, even though he knew he should not dare. As hard as he tried to control it, equally in fear of the pain it would bring to his head as of Quynn's reaction when he heard it, the temptation was irresistible. His lips began to twitch, and a suspicious cough escaped his throat. Quynn's gray eyes narrowing slightly was the final additive.

Laughter burst forth from deep in James's chest.

Deep, melodious laughter that grew more compelling as the moments passed and he noted the expression on Quynn's face.

Quynn waited until James calmed, then spoke. "Call to my mind, youngling, how ale affects you next time I offer you a drink. I did not realize how *long* so *little* spirits could affect one of your years and inexperience."

Instantly the humor on James's face fled, and his eyes sparkled dangerously. He surged from his chair to hurl himself at his brother as he'd done so many times in their childhood, when suddenly he smiled and sat again.

"Be glad, Brother, I find no true offense at your words, seeing behind them your intent." His smile grew. "You'll not use me to vent your frustration about this situation." He almost laughed again at the expression on Quynn's face, but this time he controlled himself, although it became increasingly difficult as Quynn cast him a baleful glance.

Quynn knew that he was behaving the fool, but he couldn't seem to stop himself. James's broadening smile was not sitting well with him either. Last night, he had endured all the jibes he was going to about his upcoming marriage. Now, when he was ready to vent all his considerable frustration, his lackwit of a brother picked this time to pay heed to his many lessons. Quynn had taught him early on that you never allowed your tormentor's words to push you into a rash move, that you hid all weaknesses well. Naturally Quynn knew of James's sensitivity about his youth. Heretofore, it had never failed to stir a reaction from his brother. His jaw clenched in irritation. Part of him was proud, whereas another part became aggravated, seeing the opportunity for confrontation slip away.

Despite the troubling thoughts vying for attention in his mind, he took a moment to look at his younger sibling in a new light. James was three years his younger, and because of their age difference, Quynn had always been extremely protective of him. Naturally three years was not that much, but when you had lost parents and sister in one frightful summer, and a younger brother was all that remained, it seemed to Quynn that James would forever need him to protect him.

For the first time in a long time he allowed himself to think of the horrid summer when his mother, father, and then his twin sister had died. During that time, because he was heir, all responsibility had fallen to him, and he'd had to develop a will of iron. That was the first year he had discovered his protective and possessive streak. In those first months after his parents' death, he would have absorbed James into his flesh to spare him any more hurt. It was that emotion as well as the conviction that his parents would want it so that had led to his intractable stance that James have no hand in the many problems that had plagued Havilland and its young baron. He could see the sincere desire in James's eyes to help, but he had remained adamant. James had erroneously thought his brother held his youth against him, and his sensitivity over the issue had steadily increased over the years. Quynn was aware of his feelings but refused to relent.

Alone he had managed their troubled estate through great financial want and barely managed to keep a roof over their heads. His father's enemies had been strong. He had had to be stronger. There was no time to lament over the fact that the men who decried his family's honor were not acting honorably. There were only the seemingly unending life-and-death decisions to keep Havilland from their greedy grasp and his desire to protect his brother at all costs. He had seen to James's training and had provided counsel not only to him, but to the serfs that depended on him to steer them through the troubled times.

Things had changed slightly when Quynn had come to the rescue of a young man who was set upon by thieves while riding through their property. The man had turned out to be the future king of England, Henry Plantagenet. Although he had not stayed long, he had promised Quynn he would not forget his debt. For once since the death of his parents when he was three and ten, Quynn had felt he could breathe easily. Henry had been grateful, and it would seem that the stigma of dishonor that had plagued their family for three generations was now about to pass. Then one of his father's enemies had craftily pointed out that the attack on the future king had occurred while riding through St. Crowell lands. There had been no outright accusation or else Quynn and James would have been placed under arrest. But enough suspicion was cast, and the supposed old treacheries, which were seemingly never far from anyone's mind, were again brought to the fore.

It had been of no use to argue that he had saved Henry's life. Quynn's detractors had said his actions could have been merely a ploy to garner Henry's favor and escape the block when he saw his plan might go awry.

Quynn's eyes narrowed in frustration as he thought of his family's enemies. None had the courage to come forward and decry him openly so that he might face them openly and clear his name. Nay, their way was to make accusations that were truly not accusations and to deal in gossiping half-truths spoken on the wind, lacking substance but still leaving much damage in the way of suspicion and distrust.

Those few individuals whom he confronted only claimed their concern was for the future king. As usual, no direct accusation was made and Quynn was astute enough to know that too much protest on his part would have only worsened the situation. After all, claimed Baron Langford, a supposed supporter of Henry and one who never bothered to hide his contempt for Quynn, *if* he were innocent, then he would not object to a thorough inquiry. His scorn had been clear when he added that 'twas no rumor that threatened Henry's life.

Quynn had been more than a little disposed to do more than threaten the arrogant baron, but he controlled himself. It mattered not as long as the king knew the truth. But then that had been the rub. When next Quynn saw Henry, he had been made king, and although Quynn couldn't say he saw distrust in his eyes, there was a certain wariness.

Quynn had tried to control his anger at the king. After all, Henry was a rather young monarch, with much tribulation of his own. After the debacle of Stephen's reign, in which there had been a civil war between him and his cousin Mathilda, who was Henry's mother, Henry needed to prove beyond a doubt that he was strong enough—unlike his uncle Stephen—to wear the crown of England. Any threat had to be immediately addressed. Still, knowing this, it did little to ease Quynn's sense of betrayal at Henry's reaction.

Quynn had avoided court from then on, not wishing to be looked upon with suspicion that he could neither confront nor deny. He had thought that Henry had forgotten him until he received the missive from the king that stated he was to wed Raiven de Cortillion within one moon at his family's ancestral seat.

As he'd read, Quynn had nearly turned purple with rage. He knew his limited marriage prospects were due to both his lack of coin and the scandal that refused to die. However, that was not sufficient cause to thrust a shrew of a bride upon him. It was well known that no one else, except those hungry for estates, would even think of wedding the de Cortillion heiress. Why, 'twas said that the woman covered herself when dealing with others for fear of the effect her appearance would have on them. 'Twas no wonder then that her father had done the unthinkable and left her in control of the two massive estates after he died. Obviously he knew that without the inducement of that much land, no one would ever marry his daughter.

And now ironically, he, Quynn Alexander St. Crowell, was to wed her without so much as moue of protest. It was humiliating. Secretly, he had always envisioned falling in love—naturally with an heiress but falling in love nonetheless. Despite the lessons his father had thought to teach him through harshness, he had learned by way of his dealings with his tenants, serfs, and even his knights, some of whom were wealthier than he, that the path to true happiness began with love. He was not about to wax poetical with sonnet and song, but although he felt a responsibility to Havilland, he felt an even greater one to his heart. From the age of three and ten, he had done nothing for himself; always it had been the estate, his brother, his people. Now, the one thing he had harbored for himself was no longer his to control. He had never admitted these feelings to any other, including James.

As his eyes again fell on James's broadly smiling countenance, his irritation grew.

Despite the menace in Quynn's eyes, James's expression said he was not the least bit repentant. "You are attempting to divert me from the issue of your wedding to the little heiress and to keep me from understanding your real feelings."

"Which are?"

James sobered slightly. "For some unfathomable reason 'twould seem you are ashamed."

Quynn looked away and flushed.

"By God, that's rich! What is the shame? She'll provide you with an heir for Havilland and much-needed funds for this place. Marriages have started with less."

Still Quynn said nothing, hoping James would allow the subject to drop. He did not.

"Could it be that you preferred to select your own bride and then have *her* be forced into marrying you? I suppose 'twould be just in those circumstances?"

Quynn's voice was a growl. "'Tis how 'tis done. At least my wife would come to me subdued. Now I must go begging like a waif with tattered pride."

James could well see his point. Yet, it did not matter. His brother had no option, and he felt compelled to try to talk him round. "She most likely does not know of our circumstances."

Quynn grunted.

"Perhaps she will take one look at that visage of yours and faint dead away, begging you to take her and her lands," James said lightly, trying to bring a little humor into the depressing situation Quynn had forced him to see.

Quynn gave him a narrowed look as he strode to the door. "'Tis not so far from the way 'twill be, Brother. She may come with the advantage, broad bovine that she is, but she'll know soon enough that she married a man and not some milksop who will jump to do her bidding for fear of the loss of coin. That I vow!"

James's hands went to his head as the door swung shut with enough force to tremble the stones. This was not an auspicious beginning to be sure, but as much as he loved his brother, his sympathies were entirely with his yet unknown sister-in-law. He could agree with Quynn's estimation—due to the meager knowledge of her they possessed—of her looks. But he stopped to consider, as his brother did not, that lacking beauty, she probably also lacked the confidence and courage that usually accompanied fairness of face and form. It would do her confidence no good to confront the snorting fury of Quynn's anger. No one, absolutely no one, should have to withstand the siege of rage of which Quynn was capable. He fervently hoped that whatever his sister-to-be lacked, she possessed the fortitude to endure what lay ahead.

# Chapter
# •3•

Had James been able to miraculously whisk himself across the Channel, he would have reevaluated his assessment of his sister-in-law. He would have seen not only that the female in question had the stamina to endure, but an equal part aggression of her own that would have given Quynn pause and shaken slightly his assertion of certain success in subduing her.

Elaine, Raiven de Cortillion's chambermaid of the last six years, would have wished she could be as far away as England. Instead she stood outside her mistress's closed portal, listening to the violent rumblings from within. She and Raiven, both nineteen years of age, had, in a way, grown up together—as much as a lady and a servant could. Elaine understood Raiven better than anyone—with the exception of Jacques, Raiven's younger brother.

So she knew that now was not the moment to approach her mistress about her morning toilette. Best let her have an hour—Elaine jumped again as a tray crashed to the floor—or a day to digest the news she'd just received. Nodding to herself about the wisdom of her decision, Elaine backed away from the door, only to collide with something just as solid. Startled, she jumped and gave a small yelp when a firm grasp spun her around to meet the laughing green eyes and handsome face of Jacques de Cortillion.

Elaine quickly regained her composure. Casting a furtive glance in the direction of Raiven's door, she waited to see if her small exclamation had been heard. The enraged muttering continued, making it clear Raiven was unaware of her presence beyond her door.

Jacques smiled. "I see she received her message," he said, tilting his head toward Raiven's door.

Elaine, like nearly all the serving women above- and belowstairs, near swooned at the sound of that deep melodious voice lowered to affect a conspiratorial tone. She flushed from that almost as much as the fair good looks of the young man before her.

It really should have been indecent for one family to be so blessed. Not only did they have the most fertile land in Poitou and Gascony, nature endowed them with a physical beauty that made an onlooker's heart stop. Raiven, with her tawny mane of hair; sharp, clear green eyes with dancing topaz flecks that glistened to a compelling gold when she was angry; and full-lipped mouth over a feminine but firm chin, was a vision to behold. For all her height—the de Cortillions were tall people—she had a figure that was neither gangly nor uncoordinated. Her every movement had a sensual appeal enhanced yet further by high, firm breasts, a tiny waist, and shapely legs that seemed endless.

Jacques, three years younger than his sister, could have been her twin but for the fact that where Raiven's features softened, his hardened into manly lines. He possessed the same magnetic green eyes with gold flecks, the same tawny hair and appealing sensuality. Already at ten and six his body was fulfilling its promise to be large and strong, and his shoulders were of a span difficult to measure. Despite his youth, Jacques already stood at six feet four inches, making him only half a head taller than his sibling.

Their only marked difference, besides their sex, was Jacques's merry disposition compared to Raiven's more serious one. Jacques was slow to anger, whereas Raiven's temper flared quickly and often.

Today was a glaring example of the difference between brother and sister. Observing the slightly bemused expression on Elaine's face, Jacques laid the blame for it at Raiven's feet. Surely it was his sister's surly attitude that had rendered the girl practically speechless. He was not any more fond of the contents of the letter they'd received than Raiven, yet he accepted the news. He saw the futility of resistance. Sighing inwardly, he knew that Raiven eventually would also, but only after she blistered a few ears, broke a few jars, and railed about the injustice of it all. He knew that Raiven considered him to be little more than a lad, but on this matter he felt his sister could learn from him. His way was easier. 'Twas useless to fight what one could not change.

Taking in Elaine's flustered expression, he added to himself that it was not only easier, it was also better for the well-being of the servants. Stirred to compassion by the girl's plight, Jacques set out to soothe the maid, never dreaming that his reaction would cause her consternation to worsen.

Reaching out, he patted Elaine on her arm and urged her toward the stairs. "Never mind Raiven, Elaine. You know 'twill not last, and then she'll be sorry for her lack of control."

Elaine surprised him by blushing even harder at his most gentle tone. *Good Lord, what had Raiven done?*

Taking the tone of one trying to gentle a skittish mare, Jacques said, "Go below. I'll talk to her."

Elaine turned automatically and left, cursing herself inwardly for her foolish behavior. Jacques would believe her a total thickwit when he discovered she had not yet seen Raiven this morn. She flushed again to think of how he would eye her when they next met, and castigating herself even more, she went belowstairs.

At the moment, Elaine was the last thing on Jacques's mind as he foolishly entered Raiven's room without knocking. The earthenware vessel she threw with amazing accuracy missed his ear by inches when he ducked from its path. The crash of the jar against the wall in the hall caused a momentary quiet belowstairs. On the heels of the silence came a loud resumption of noise as one and all ascertained what had happened. Today was not the day to bring any attention to themselves through conspicuous silence.

"Good morning, Sister." After glancing at the shards of shattered pottery, Jacques turned back to his sister. "And how are you?" he inquired with a chuckle.

Raiven ignored his humor and his question. "Have you read this? This, this thing?" Viciously she swept the parchment from where it lay and flung it violently at Jacques. The letter's soft landing on the floor midway between them gently mocked her irate gesture.

"Aye. I have read it."

Raiven eyed his calm demeanor critically. "That is all you have to say? Do you not realize what this means?"

Jacques had long since learned how to handle his sister. He knew Raiven was waiting for the words from him to encourage the rebellious course he knew she was plotting. This was not their childhood, and this was no naughty prank played against the tutors their father had hired to teach them. He could not encourage her to defy a king's order.

He sighed. "It means you will soon be married."

Once he quietly uttered these words, he waited for the violent explosion he knew was coming. It came with a vengeance. Raiven ranted and raved the likes of which he had never seen or heard before. She went on for a full fifteen minutes while Jacques stood by and watched silently.

When the tirade finally ceased, he asked patiently, "When do we leave?"

Eyes like molten gold turned on him, and her voice was a mere whisper, a sure sign of danger. "Have you not heard a word I've said? I will not marry some English upstart, no matter what his title. Just because Eleanor decided to barter away her country and lands by marrying that English brat, I will show them we are not a land of harlots to be bought or sold to the highest bidder or the man with the biggest—"

"Raiven!" Jacques stopped her, certain she was about to say something exceedingly vulgar. He knew it was just her anger speaking, especially when she had mentioned Eleanor as she had.

Raiven spoke of Eleanor of Aquitaine, who had married Henry II just that past May, making him the duke of Aquitaine and all the lands pertaining. An estate that by any definition could not be considered minimal. It extended south from the Channel to Gascony, west to the Bay of Biscay, and east as far as Île de France.

As owners of vast estates in both Poitou and Gascony, the de Cortillions owed double fealty to Eleanor. Under the usual circumstances this may not have been noteworthy, but the circumstance was hardly "usual." In 1154, peace was hard won, and when achieved tenuous, for Aquitaine was riddled with division. Each subdivision was ruled and governed by the baron, viscount, and so forth, of that region. Unrest was strong throughout the land, and only through the ruling house of de Cortillion was there any semblance of peace between the Poitevins and the Gascons. A delicate balance existed, and it took skill and extreme diplomacy to maintain it.

Surprisingly, this was the problem that weighed uppermost in Raiven's mind when she considered marriage to an Englishman. Her father had defied the convention of the day and named her his heir despite the fact that he had a son. He had seen in his daughter an ability to continue to maintain not only the peace, but, of greater importance, their lands. Most of the people in both regions had known her since birth and were grudgingly accepting of Émil de Cortillion's decision. Raiven had painstakingly won their respect, and she did not want to risk losing it by marrying a foreigner, especially an Englishman. His lack of understanding of them and their ways would make the situation very difficult.

Relations had been strained ever since Henry had become duke. In the past months he had made it clear that he was not fond of the natural anarchy that pervaded the region. He was trying to assert his rulership—something the Williamses, the line through whom Eleanor had been born, had never done. Throughout the centuries they had ruled strongly only in Poitiers and Bordeaux, where they had their fortresses and estates.

This latest idea of Henry's was no more than a scheme to inflict his rule over Eleanor's people. It was his attempt to peacefully, yet inexorably, enforce his will. He was shrewd. Raiven could already see his plan to retain and solidify the province so as not to lose it as Eleanor's first husband, Louis Capet, had done when they divorced.

*Well, it won't work!* Raiven thought vehemently as she paced in front of Jacques's stunned face. All of Eleanor's subjects loved her dearly. Raiven was no exception in this. However, she meant every word she said.

Jacques, recognizing the determined slant to her jaw, tried to reason with her. "Raiven, this is a royal decree. You cannot just disregard it. There will be consequences for you and our people."

"No worse than with the insensitive heel of an Englishman upon them. He does not know of us or of our ways. Am I to just hand our estates and people over to him without any discussion? I think not, Brother. Nay, I know not! There is none who can force me in this. Father has passed, and there is no other ruling male. He left everything to me. I'll not disappoint him by yielding to an English pup of a man who needs to have a wife found for him."

"What of the king of England?"

"What of him?" Raiven's voice dripped with venom. Clearly any affection Raiven had for Eleanor did not extend to her husband. Here again, Raiven was not the exception. Most of Eleanor's subjects despised the new duke. Henry's wishes were of little account.

"His retribution will come," Jacques said sagely. In his heart he shared his sister's opinion, but his concern was for her and their people.

"Again I disagree," Raiven asserted stubbornly. "He

has not made a great start with Eleanor's people. He may want us unified, but not against him. Surely that is what will happen if he forces himself against a lone female."

Jacques burst out laughing at Raiven's description of herself. Even Raiven had the grace to look sheepish. Both knew how ludicrous that description of her was.

"Besides, dear Brother," Raiven continued, "what of you? Father left me to see to the estates, but he knew they'd also be secure for you. If they're given like Viking booty to this Englishman, what do you think will be your fate?"

Jacques shrugged. It was not that he did not have similar worries. It was just that the consequences were more distasteful than the situation. Raiven could be endangering herself, and that possibility alone was enough for him to deny himself anything. Yet, knowing her, he could not tell her these things. If he did, she would never retreat and do what they both knew to be the sensible thing. So, he instead feigned injured pride.

"I will manage. I am a man, Raiven. You must remember that. It is up to me to make my own way, and Father knew I could. You speak as though he left me naught when you know well that he left me very fertile land at the edge of Gascony. The revenues alone will see to my needs for the rest of my life."

"Not if it falls to English hands. I'll not do it, I tell you," Raiven continued stubbornly.

Jacques's eyes widened incredulously. They both knew her inheritance did not entail his land. As such, he would lose nothing in the event of her marriage. She was simply refusing to relent.

Unlike his sister, Jacques knew when the time to retreat came, so he left her alone, but he was ill at ease. This Henry was not a man to take lightly.

With a clarity that Raiven could or would not see, Jacques knew that her refusal was not the end of the matter. Nay, it wasn't the end at all.

# Chapter 4

## One month later

James knew that his brother had a fierce temper. Yet, even he was unprepared for Quynn's reaction to the contents of the king's new order, delivered by royal messenger. As Quynn heard the words, his face had at first gone white, then blue, as rage coursed through him. James did not know how Quynn had restrained himself enough to listen quietly to the entire message. There was an awful moment when James had thought he would attack the man, but he did not, instead giving only a terse response to the man's queries. When the messenger left unscathed after giving Quynn a separate private note, James breathed a sigh of relief for Quynn's control because it meant death to attack an emissary of the king.

Quynn, however, after reading the note, showed no more restraint. He had smashed tables and literally torn chairs asunder, frightening the servants so badly that none had dared venture forth to clean the debris.

Although James could allow Quynn the cause for his anger, he was more worried over his brother's health. Quynn's rage—the likes of which James had only seen Henry duplicate—showed no sign of abating.

Just minutes ago, Quynn had slammed out of the hall,

and James hoped the ride he knew his brother would take would calm him. He climbed the stairs, his tread heavy as he walked to Quynn's chamber.

At first his mind refused to accept the scene that met him. There was chaos everywhere. Quynn had broken all the breakables and smashed and ripped all that could be smashed or ripped. The feather down mattress that once lay upon his bed was now—bits and pieces of it—adorning every corner of the room.

"My God," he breathed before he caught himself. Never had he seen Quynn in such a rage or exhibit such destructiveness. Usually he was meticulous to a fault with his possessions. He never ever forgot how hard it was to obtain and retain them. If his anger had been too great, he always rode it off, not trusting himself to be confined. But as James cast another unbelieving glance about the room, he understood his brother's motives. In this sort of state, Quynn most likely would have killed his horse. Undoubtedly, that would have only increased his anger, if such a thing were possible. A knight's horse was better than his arm. They were a true partnership, and Quynn and Khan had been together so long it seemed the horse knew Quynn's commands before he gave them. So, instead of riding immediately and possibly killing his horse, he stayed to wreck his home, then he had flung himself on Khan's back and rode away.

James took hope. Quynn's actions showed that he was not totally beyond rational thought. Still, as he took another look around his brother's empty chamber, he shuddered inwardly, honest enough to admit that he was glad that, for the moment, Quynn was absent.

He knew he would have to speak to him, but later was just as good as now. As if repetition could make him believe what he was seeing, he looked around the room again before closing the door, thinking that, in this instance, later was even better than now.

It was late when Quynn returned to the hall. There were only vague recollections in mind of what had happened after the king's messenger had gone, but he knew he had lost control. He also knew that James would be waiting to speak to him. He wasn't sure if he was ready to face that. He didn't trust his emotions. Despite his vigorous exercising of Khan, he had barely exorcised his rage. It was still there, only in abeyance, waiting for the right incentive to bring it back to full-blooded life. And a discussion of the woman he was to marry was definitely sufficient incentive.

When he at last entered the hall, all was quiet. Only a lone candle burned at the dais to illuminate the room. Irritated by the near darkness of the place that was usually well lit and cheery, he had taken only two steps when he felt something sharp pierce the sole of his shoe. Swallowing a harsh word, he bent over to remove the offending object from his foot, reaching out for support from the table by the door. Too late he realized that it was not there. He fell in an ignoble heap, venting his anger and frustration.

Suddenly, the door to a smaller room on the far side of the hall opened, and James rushed into the room.

"What happ—Quynn?" James's voice ended on a surprised note.

"Aye."

James could feel his lips twitch as he made out his brother's form lying amidst the debris he had created. He brought the candle he held aloft a little closer.

Quynn's eyes clouded with a rage that even through the near darkness seemed to at once burn and freeze James to the spot.

"Do not, as you value your life, even smile at this situation."

James swallowed and tried to cover his surprise. "I would not dream of it. But I must ask," he went on, not hiding the amusement in his tone, "if you intend to lie there for what is left of the evening or if you will eventually rise? I would like a word with you."

Quynn's glare increased. "If you would but use your head for some chore other than a separating device for your ears, you would see I am trying to dislodge something from the sole of my shoe."

"Oh."

That response satisfied Quynn no better than James's former ones. What was going on in his hall? The place, besides being dark as a cave, was, from what little he could see, a mess. The suddenly loud and insistent growl of his stomach made him also note that there was no trencher of food awaiting him as there usually was when he returned home late.

"Have the servants all gone daft? This place is a sty. There is no food, and 'tis as dark and gloomy as a chamber for the dead." He regained his feet by the end of his tirade, and his brow lowered as he looked about. "Where, in the name of thunder, is everyone?"

James was suddenly beset by a bout of coughing. When he could speak, his voice had a strangled edge to it. "I believe the serfs gave themselves an eve of rest. I believe they thought you wished it so."

Quynn's stare would have melted rock, but James studiously avoided it.

"Come. There is a dish of food and a tankard of ale awaiting you in the small room. While you eat, we can talk."

He followed James into the other room, and his mood improved at the sight of food, drink, and enough light by which to see.

For the first few moments, there was nothing but silence as Quynn attacked the food and ale left for him. James watched him, undecided how to proceed.

Quynn took the matter from his control. "Do you have a ken what she has done? Know you how much trouble she has caused—this viper that is to be my wife?"

Now that Quynn had opened the subject himself, James was at a loss for words. He looked away into the hearth, saying nothing.

Quynn continued as if he had not expected a response. "By her blatant and public refusal to wed, which has all England in titters at my cost, she has now brought the wrath of Henry upon us. *I* obeyed the order. *I* humbled and humiliated myself by sending betrothal gifts to her.

She sends them back! What was I to do?! Steal her?" He shook his head at the suggestion. "My pride has its limits."

During his speech, he stood and began to pace the floor. Suddenly he stopped and looked at James again. "Do you ken what day this was to be?" Again he went on without James's response. "Our wedding day. No one believed she would continue to refuse a royal decree. We both could have gone to the Tower for her stubbornness. Henry blames me. He feels I could have nevertheless gone—"

Finally James spoke. "Henry knew of your intent, Quynn. He knew, despite your not liking the matter, you would have acquiesced."

Quynn, who had resumed his pacing, paused to give his brother his full attention. "Intent does not signify in the mind of any sovereign when the end of the matter is that his will is being ignored. Besides, knowing the history of the St. Crowells, this particular 'request' leaves me doubtful."

"You think the king intends to trick us?"

"I would not put it so strongly, and neither should you," Quynn reprimanded his brother. The king had eyes and ears everywhere, and it would be foolish in the extreme to think that their hall was any different. James's words could be repeated out of context or in, for that matter, and it could prove very damaging. "'Tis only that I believe that the king offers a gift with one hand and a test with the other."

Quynn was silent a moment. "In that instance, he is right. I could have journeyed to France to get her. I was so enraged over her public rejection, I did not think clearly. It doesn't matter now. Henry has personally sent one of his ships from Southampton for her, and 'twill be here in less than a sennight. From the time of her arrival, we have less than a day to do the deed else we both lose our lands and titles."

James's brow darkened. If there was one thing Quynn had taught him well, it was that any threat to Havilland was intolerable. The circumstances were of no account. "What say you? I heard no such condition."

"It was in the private message the king sent to me. And that is not all. Upon Henry's order, due to what he deems our intractableness, we must produce an heir within one year or else the same forfeiture still applies. He is making sure that the union is consummated and unbreakable."

Abruptly, the expression on James's face changed. Quynn raised a brow in question.

"You must allow, it is rather an ingenious plan. An Englishman will still have claim to the region, and should he ever lose it, which is doubtful, there is the possibility of regaining it due to the inflow of English with valid claims. Why, it is superb! What an interesting way of making war—by making love!"

Quynn stared at his brother as if his senses had finally abandoned him. "I, too, would be able to applaud Henry's tactics if I were not one of the instruments he was using to bring about this population." He ran his hand through his hair. "The union would have been difficult enough without this to heap upon it. What if the woman is barren? What if I—?"

"Prove to be incapable?" James teased, for which he received a slicing look.

"What if I find her so unattractive, the desire is not there? I have heard she is everything from an Amazon to a dwarf, but the one unchanging trait has been the issue of her manliness. In such case, I would not wish to subdue her every night."

"It may not be for many nights, only until she is impregnated. Try to see the good of it, Quynn. Henry's order may work for your benefit. At least your wife cannot deny you her bed as many other wives have done. In any event, Brother, there's naught for it but to wait and see."

Quynn grimaced and turned away. It was easy for James to be philosophical. Henry was not playing chess with his life.

* * *

Quynn was not the only angry one. Raiven knew she had lost, and as usual, when she let her temper rule, the end situation was well worse than the former.

*When will I learn?* she thought, then slammed another of her precious gowns into the coffer containing her clothes. *Who would have thought the king would react the way he had?* On the heel of this thought, another gown met the same mistreatment. Each gown she so abused was, in her mind, either the heart of her husband-to-be or his sovereign's head. So intent was she upon her imaginary mayhem interspersed with short bouts of self-recrimination, she did not hear the door open. When she looked up, it was to see Jacques staring quietly at her.

Pain tore through her heart as she watched him smile at her. She hadn't yet told him of the contents of the private message Henry had sent to her. Looking into Jacques's smiling face while knowing what she must do caused a feeling of deep hatred to form in her heart for her new sovereign, her new home, and her new husband. Unknown to her, her sadness showed for the briefest instant on her face.

Jacques's response was immediate. He came forward and wrapped his sister into his massive arms and softly kissed the top of her head.

"It is not as bad as all that, Raiven. England may not be like France, but we will survive. *Nous sommes de Cortillions, n'est-ce pas?*"

Raiven felt the prick of tears behind her eyes as he uttered a portion of their father's favorite phrase: "We are de Cortillions, is that not so? There are none better!"

Taking a deep breath, Raiven began to pull away slowly, putting distance between her and Jacques. Until this very moment, she had not realized how much she had come to depend on the strength of her younger brother. She could now see with astounding clarity that all the while she had assumed she was supporting him through this and other tragedies of their lives, he had been holding her up in return. Now they were to be separated indefinitely because of that cursed English king. There was no way to know when or if her future husband would allow her to visit her brother or vice versa. Raiven swallowed a huge lump of awareness that said had she not publicly shamed her betrothed, he might see her way in this one event.

For the millionth time she cursed her temper. If she had not provoked Henry, he would not now hold Jacques and her land in virtual ransom against her cooperation. Unless she left—without Jacques—on the ship that had arrived for her, and the other Frenchwomen of a similar fate, she would lose her titles, her lands, but most of all her beloved brother.

She could not bear the thought. Henry was tearing at what remained of her family. She would be in England alone, without friend or ally. The only person permitted to accompany her was Elaine. Total isolation, coupled with the stipulation that she must bear an heir within a year's passing or still face the same odious consequences, made her prospects seem bleak indeed.

He was smart, this English king, for how could she cause a breath of problem when she didn't know what the consequences would be for her brother? Jacques would not be allowed to control the de Cortillion affairs in her absence. An English steward, chosen by her betrothed, would oversee the vast estates.

There were moments when she thought she'd swoon with the rage she felt. Yet she had to banish such thoughts. For once, her temper could not rule. Her lack of forethought was what had brought them to this distasteful pass. Raiven was determined not to worsen the situation.

Tears of futility and impotent rage began to stream down her face. Through her tears, she saw Jacques approach, but she shook her head and held up her hand to halt him. She couldn't allow him to comfort her now or she'd totally lose control. As much for the glimmer of worry she could see in his eyes as for her own need to maintain her crumbling control, she adopted the authoritative tone she used to use when he was a child caught in some act of devilment.

"We must talk."

"Why do you cry?" Although he would never admit it, being a man of sixteen, Raiven's tears frightened him. Raiven never cried. She might rant and rave, but tears were never shed. To see them now, just before they were to leave for England, was a bad sign.

"It is a bit of selfish foolishness on my part, naught else." Raiven sniffed and wiped away the moisture on her cheeks. "I am thinking I should be taking you with me, but that is wrong. You are needed more here. Guirlande must have a de Cortillion in residence. It has been so for generations, and I cannot break the tradition no matter that my heart bids me otherwise."

Jacques's eyes widened incredulously. "What nonsense is this, Raiven? You know well that Simon can look after this place. Your need is greater. You will be alone with no one but the enemy around you."

This was the first time he had referred to the English as their enemy, and again Raiven cursed herself a stupid fool. She should have discerned that he was being calm only to settle her. His feelings were no different from her own. He had reacted as he had solely to prevent her from acting rashly, which, given the present situation, was absurdly laughable. Jacques really was a lot more mature than she had guessed. Now she faced the disagreeable task of trying to persuade him to remain behind, and Jacques was intuitive enough to know that it was not of her own design. Her options were gone. There was no time to convince him to stay or explain the English steward's arrival.

Raiven walked to the trunk that had clothes lying at every conceivable angle and now folded a golden bliaut with extreme care. It looked ludicrous when placed beside the other crumpled garments.

"I'll not be alone," she began slowly. "Elaine will be there to see to me. I trust her with my life."

"Do you trust her more than your own brother?"

Inwardly Raiven groaned. It seemed she could say nothing right this morn. She took a deep breath. "Certainly not. It is why you must stay here. None other can look to *our* interests better."

By the end of her speech, she had glanced away, unable to meet Jacques's stare any longer. After folding another bliaut with painful care, she chanced a look. At his expression, the bliaut slipped from her nerveless fingers to fall on the pile of clothes in the trunk. For the first time in her memory, Jacques's eyes began to smolder to the yellowish gold that spoke of rage. His anger took Raiven so unaware that for a moment she did not hear his thundered question.

"Whose thought was this, to leave me behind?"

Raiven was struck dumb with shock. She stared blankly at him until his large hand, which had always been so gentle with her, began to encircle her arms and shake her, causing her to wince with pain.

"Henry's," she managed to whisper.

Jacques pushed her away, and Raiven could only watch in amazement as his body began to tremble with emotion.

"Jacques, listen to me," she began softly. "It is best. In this way you can care for the people, and they'll not be totally bereft with the both of us gone and only a cold, pinch-faced Englishman to answer their—"

He turned slowly back to her with eyes now a boiling yellow gold. "Repeat your words. I could not have heard aright. Are you now saying that low-born charlatan is sending someone here to oversee de Cortillion lands?"

The words Raiven was about to speak became lost beneath his roar of indignation and rage. By the time she collected her thoughts after the shock of his reaction, Jacques had already gone.

In a daze, she resumed her packing, and this time it was not rage that made her place her clothing in disarray. It was worry over her brother and the situation she was leaving behind.

Raiven saw Jacques only once more. He came to the port to bid her farewell. His hug was warm, his words were a comfort, but when Raiven leaned back to stare at his face, his eyes were still that violent yellow gold.

# Chapter 5

Raiven's first glimpse of England was not an impressive one. Just off the English coastline they'd encountered a storm that stayed with them until the dreary shores of England had come into view. Elaine, suffering severe mal de mer, was still below, writhing in silent misery, leaving Raiven alone to watch the dismal gray banks of her new homeland draw closer and closer without anyone beside her to tell her things were not as bad as they seemed.

Raiven turned away from the uneventful vista, feeling her despair sharpen apace with the growing of the coastline. She could not blame the deepening desolation she felt on her silent solitary vigil. Even if others stood with her, their presence and words of encouragement would mean little. She felt despair beyond the cure of mere words. Despondency settled upon her like a cloak as gray as the brooding English sky. Her despair tempered all she felt and saw with an unattractive drabness. Yet Raiven knew her mood was not a result of the weather. The sun could have beamed brightly from a cloudless sky and England would still have looked the same to her.

Suddenly the deck teemed with seamen readying the

ship for docking, and Raiven knew she should return below to pack her belongings. Since the onslaught of Elaine's sickness at the start of the voyage, Raiven had had to do everything herself. The servant still had not regained her feet despite the calmness of the sea after the storm, and Raiven held no hope that Elaine would already have the chore done.

Raiven had just reached the door to the smallish cabin she shared with Elaine when a familiar voice called to her. Turning, she watched Fleurette Deveaux come toward her, and an automatic smile of welcome lit her face.

Fleurette Deveaux was the one friend Raiven had made during the journey from France. The other noblewomen from different regions in France kept their distance, but Fleurette had logically informed Raiven that it did not matter now that she was from Bordeaux and Raiven from Poitou. What mattered, she stated matter-of-factly, was they were both on their way to England.

Raiven liked this woman's straightforward manner, and in the days that followed, she gained respect for Fleurette, who was three years her senior. Their conversations had been intriguing, and Raiven learned many things from the lively, petite redhead with the soft brown eyes. Fleurette's views were different from any Raiven had encountered, but this difference had only made her enjoy her new friend more.

There was one unusual attitude that Fleurette held that Raiven could neither accept nor tolerate with laughing camaraderie. She was shocked when she heard Fleurette speak of her husband-to-be without animosity. Fleurette had philosophically stated that she had always known that a husband would have been chosen for her, so she was determined to make the best of it even though he was an Englishman.

The quiet logic Raiven respected so much in her friend was now igniting her temper as Fleurette began to try to convince her that her betrothed deserved more than her hostility. Fleurette believed that his pride had withstood enough damage, having been laughed at in two countries.

Raiven's eyes darkened at that, and her response had been a tart, "There is no best of it to be made." Before Fleurette could counter with another argument, Raiven had demanded to know how she knew the man had been ridiculed.

Fleurette had been unaffected by Raiven's show of temper. Instead, she shrugged daintily and proceeded to ask with calm logic how he could have avoided it. Supposedly, a man controlled everything in his life, especially his possessions. Raiven was, whether she liked it or not, now considered his possession. Private humiliations were one thing, but Raiven had humiliated him publicly, and that would be a hard thing to overcome. Throughout her speech, Fleurette did not raise her voice but, instead, maintained her composure as if self-control would make Raiven understand.

Raiven could not fault Fleurette's reasoning, but her emotions were less impressed than her mind. Her response had been acerbic. "If one barters for a wife, one has to take what is given." After all, *he* was still with his family; she was not. *He* was still in his homeland; she was not. Ultimately, his king had supplied him with all he desired. She had nothing. She would give him no more. They might be able to make her wed, but they could not compel her heart to love. Her heart was a possession of hers that neither he nor his king could control.

The subject was dropped after that, both Fleurette and Raiven feeling discomfort for the first time over their dissimilarity. Raiven thought she had spied a look close to pity in Fleurette's brown eyes and that made her hackles rise even more. They had parted then without another word being spoken.

That conversation had taken place a day before the storm hit, and Raiven had not seen her friend since. She had been afraid that she had angered Fleurette irreparably until she heard the soft voice calling her name. There was nothing but welcome in the petite redhead's eyes as she came closer.

"Fleurette, what are you doing about now? Surely you know we will dock soon. You must prepare."

Fleurette gave a characteristic dainty shrug. She was such a fine-boned, tiny woman that if Raiven did not possess confidence in herself, she would be excessively uncomfortable being in her company.

"I have already seen to that—most of it anyway," she added. "If my betrothed has to wait a moment, an hour, a day, what matter? I will be his wife forever, and that is surely worth the wait, no?"

"Very much so," Raiven agreed. The twinkle in her eyes increased, and her smile became impish. "I, on the other hand, have pressed the matter to the boundaries of the king's patience. So, just when they least expect it, I shall be most cooperative."

They both laughed.

"It is good to see your change of heart, Raiven. Now I need not worry over you."

Immediately Raiven's expression sobered. "I have not changed my mind, only my tactics. I will not give them reason to harm me or my brother further."

Fleurette's brow darkened, but she let Raiven's remark pass. "I shall miss you, my friend," she whispered softly.

"And I you. It saddens me to think that there is something for which I must be grateful to Henry. If it were not for him, we never would have met." Raiven's eyes took on a faraway look. "I have learned much on this voyage that would benefit my people, only I will not be there to share the knowledge with them. Things should be different in France. We should not be fighting among ourselves."

"Things are what they are," Fleurette replied reasonably, "but since change begins gradually, perhaps things will be different in the future." She hugged Raiven fiercely. "Be happy, my friend, and remember, do not allow your temper to rule your heart. When all else is gone, what have we except love?" Fleurette did not wait for Raiven to respond. She hugged her tighter, then gave her a light kiss on the cheek, going back the way she had come.

When Raiven entered her cabin, to her surprise, Elaine was up and bustling about, packing their belongings. It was then she realized the ship was no longer moving. As she helped her maid, she could not help but think of Fleurette's words.

Her temper would not rule her heart because her heart was not in danger from what awaited her in England. No danger in the least.

Quynn delayed long enough. He knew if he stalled any longer, he would be late to greet his betrothed when the ship docked. Somehow the thought of her waiting for him was not enough to hurry him along. Scorn was the only emotion he felt at the thought of standing there with the other nobles to await their betrotheds. It was not the fact that these men had laughed at his humiliation that kept him from his task, but rather, the fact that he found it degrading to stand around as if he was eager to meet the woman who had publicly scorned him.

Before his anger could fully take root, he gathered himself and left the inn where he had procured a room for himself. He wouldn't be returning. Once he met his future bride, they would journey directly to Havilland. His conscience rebuked him for his plan to drag a travel-weary woman across many more miles. A wry smile crossed his face when he thought of what his mother's reaction would have been to his action. No doubt, she would have boxed his ears soundly for his lack of gentlemanly concern if she were still alive.

Quynn's smile faded as the image of his mother dimmed, replaced by the formless visage of his betrothed. *That* woman had done nothing to deserve a kind thought. She did not deserve the concern he would have shown anyone else. As he drew closer to the dock, already crowded with various conveyances, horses, and carts, Quynn decided that he would spite his bride-to-be and make her wait until everyone left before he collected her. It was probably *her* intention to keep *him* waiting on the docks until the very last.

A chilly smile crossed his handsome face. There was a

considerable amount for his new bride to learn. He saw no reason to delay the beginning of her much-needed lessons.

At first, Raiven had been pleased when there had been no immediate discreet tapping on her door to inform her that there was a conveyance with either a servant or her "lord" waiting for her. She did not want to pass through a crowd of smirking faces. Faces that would watch avidly while she went to meet her betrothed and then crow with delight when she was led away "subdued."

An agonizing hour passed, during which there was a great commotion in the passageway. Then another hour elapsed, and the activity level greatly decreased. A soft tap on her door sent her heart racing, but it was only Fleurette coming to say good-bye and trying one last time to persuade Raiven to see reason.

"You are very beautiful, Raiven. Your husband will want you immediately. It should be your goal to make him care for you. Do not, I beg you, make things more difficult than they need be."

Raiven smiled softly, and a muted sparkle lit her eyes. "You do not know me very well. According to my brother, Jacques, being unreasonable is my shining accomplishment. Nevertheless you must not worry. Although I care not for his wants or feelings, I have come to accept what cannot be undone. I will make the best of it," she added with amused emphasis, causing Fleurette's smile to widen. "*He* must realize that he is not the one who has truly suffered. His humiliation will pass, if it has not already. My life will never go back to what it was."

She was quiet for a moment before continuing softly. "I will tell you something, Fleurette, that I have not mentioned to another soul. I am tired of confrontations. It would seem all I've known this past year. First, the struggle to prove myself after my father's death and then this. I've told no one that one of the reasons I objected so vehemently to this marriage was because there would be more hostility and more struggles to prove myself. I do not want that. I only want peace. I've had very little of it recently. When my father died, I could not take the time to grieve properly. I simply had to endure."

Fleurette's eyes filled with understanding compassion. "Then tell him so, Raiven. It will make all the difference."

Raiven slowly shook her head. "I cannot. There is my pride to consider. I will not lay myself vulnerable to him. He has taken enough from me already. First let me see the ilk of this man who would claim me for wife."

Fleurette left then, and Raiven continued to wait.

Three hours later she was still waiting.

Raiven's thoughts had long since ceased to be peaceful. It was clear no one was coming for her. Her humiliation deepened. She began to pace like a caged tigress, unable to bridle either her anger or her anxiety. Elaine wisely stayed out of her path, saying nothing to ignite the simmering anger.

The sudden knock on the door startled both of them. Elaine felt relief that they would leave the ship and that Raiven's anger would now cool. She was partially right.

Raiven's anger reached its zenith. Angrily she jerked open the door without asking the identity of the person on the other side. Her hot gaze settled on the captain. Another time Raiven would have laughed at his alarmed expression, but she had long ago lost her sense of humor.

Henry Masterson, a seasoned captain of several years, again found himself thinking dark thoughts of his sovereign as he stared into the yellow hot gaze of the woman before him. He had to clear his throat twice before he could produce a voice, and even then, to his horror, it squeaked. Manfully, he tried not to be in awe of her beauty and size, but his attempt failed. It both infuriated and stimulated him that she literally looked down on him by two inches.

When he had first espied the lovely lady, envy filled his heart for the baron of Havilland, who would possess her. Now, at the end of this seemingly never-ending voyage, he felt none of his former envy. This woman had done the unthinkable to him. She had shown him a strength and presence of mind that revealed the weakness in him. Nay, he wouldn't wish her on anyone—especially an Englishman. Her ways were too haughty, and though he knew he was not the man to subdue her, he was glad someone would be. His only sorrow in seeing her leave was that he would not be around to see her subjugation.

In his opinion, she was not smart enough to feel trepidation at her situation. However, he felt a vicarious strength that the baron had kept her waiting. The captain would never voice his laughter or his satisfaction, but he allowed himself a small smirk of a smile, waiting for Raiven to question him.

Raiven read the venomous thoughts Masterson was incapable of hiding. The man was contemptuous. He was the type to lord over those he felt were weaker than he. She had detested him on sight, and she knew the feeling was mutual. She would not ask him anything despite the depth of her desire to know what was happening.

Raiven continued to glare at him, waiting.

Finally, he grunted, "'Tis time for you to leave."

Turning to Elaine and effectively dismissing the captain without a word, Raiven told her to gather their things so the seamen could speedily collect them.

They were standing on the docks alone when Raiven thought to ask one of the seamen about her escort.

"Sir, excuse me, but did the captain inform you of the whereabouts of our escort?" She put on her brightest smile to cover her embarrassment.

"Nay, milady, he did not," the man said with a smile of regret while staring in awe at the winsomeness of the lass before him. "We must make final port upriver a bit. Ye were to be met here, so 'tis my guess 'tis why the cap'n's letting ye off." With that, he bobbed once, then turned and walked up the plank to the ship, hoping they'd reach their destination soon. The lady had stirred feelings in him that demanded attention, and while his wife was not nearly as comely, she was woman enough to satisfy his hunger. His step picked up in anticipation, and he whistled jauntily as he rejoined his mates.

Raiven watched him and enviously wished she had cause to whistle without a care, but under the circumstances, she was finding it increasingly difficult to maintain her composure, let alone adopt a carefree attitude. Surely someone would come! The only question was when. She glanced around the dock, noting that it was not large. There were the usual inns and such, but not much activity. Of course, that could all change and probably would with the onset of night, which was not far away.

It was unthinkable that she and Elaine try to procure lodgings for themselves here, yet what else was there to do? One could get in just as much trouble merely standing on the dock, as they were now, as sleeping in one of its seedy establishments.

Raiven decided to wait a little longer, her nerves beginning to fray. With each hour that passed, Henry's threats began to take on new meaning. He had been explicit in his demand that she wed on the day of her arrival. She had finally resigned herself to her role in this farce, and now it would seem that her effort was for naught. She was no closer to being married than when she was aboard the ship—and the day was passing.

By the sun's setting and the continued absence of any escort, Raiven reached the conclusion that this was a filthy plot to divest her of her lands. Fantasizing about all manner of mayhem she would wreak should she ever chance upon her supposed betrothed or his king, Raiven noticed a man approaching on a beautiful black stallion.

Surely it was the magnificence of the horse that gave him such stature. He was tall—taller than Jacques, it would appear—and his bearing was such that Raiven knew who he was even before he stopped in front of her. His voice was deep and vibrant when he announced, "You, no doubt, are Lady Raiven de Cortillion. I am Baron Quynn St. Crowell of Havilland, your future husband. Welcome to England, milady."

# Chapter
# ♦6♦

There wasn't an ounce of welcome in the clear gray eyes that ground through her. If Raiven foolishly harbored any remaining doubt about her reception, the chill in his voice swept away any such fancy.

She was about to tell him her thoughts when, of a sudden, a strange sort of weariness besieged her. What did it matter if he truly did not welcome her? She did not want his welcome. So, she merely stared up at him, feeling empty and sensing both his and Elaine's curiosity over her silence. If she had felt anything, it would have been amusement for the way they were beginning to stare, but she felt . . . nothing. She didn't care about anything. Her only emotion was soothing apathy. Her emotions, having careened wildly from one extreme to the other, were now numb. Raiven thought it truly would be a gift of mercy if the hollow feeling never went away.

Tense seconds passed, and as they continued to gaze unwaveringly at each other, Quynn took a moment to study the tall woman whose unfocused gaze seemed locked on his face. She was tall, aye, very tall for a woman, but not so tall as to be uncomfortable for him. Indeed, as he viewed her proportions—what little he could see beneath the voluminous cape she wore—he decided that she looked to have been formed just for him. Her green eyes, now clouded and distant, had, only a moment prior, sparkled with crystal fire. Her mouth, deliciously formed, was a sensuous curve. Her chin was strong in the delicate oval of her face. Her forehead, high and wide, gave way to a rich tawny mane of a thickness such that the braid that hung down her back was as wide as his wrist. Even with her delicate nostrils flaring like Khan's when he had run too hard—here he smiled softly to himself with the thought that she would probably little appreciate being compared to his horse, no matter the magnificence of the beast—she was beautiful, exquisite, more than he had allowed himself to hope she would be.

The thought that perhaps Henry had not done him such a disservice after all quickly died when his mind fiercely reminded his racing heart that this woman despised him and had done all she could to shame him.

The warmth that had begun to replace the icy stone in his heart scattered. He lifted his gaze from the oval perfection of her face with regret. When he caught the knowing look in the eyes of the pretty woman who was obviously her maid, any lingering remorse fled. He collected his thoughts and turned back to Raiven, wanting to make sure she was under no illusion that her beauty would bring instant accord between them. He had to make himself believe it, too. With each word he spoke, he thrashed out a warning to them both.

"I realize, milady," he began in a tone even colder than before, "that your beauty may far outdistance your mental power, but we cannot stand here any longer if we are to fulfill the king's demands. Havilland is a long ride from here, and I would see the deed done with all haste."

Quynn was pleased to see that shock had wiped the smugness from the servant's face; however, her mistress's face had gone totally blank.

Despite what Quynn thought, Raiven was not completely unaware of what was going on around her. She had not missed his thorough perusal, and she had not missed the sudden smile that fleetingly softened his features. It had come and gone so quickly she almost wondered if her mind was not teasing her, crumbling beneath the stress. Because she had said nothing to him, his increased hostility was a mystery to her. However, she couldn't dwell on that bit of strangeness because she reeled beneath the jolt of his declaration.

"We are riding to your home tonight?" Her voice lost its naturally husky timbre, and the question came out more of a squeak.

Quynn smiled devilishly. "So you do speak. I had begun to wonder. Alas, I knew there had to be a flaw somewhere." He nodded curtly. "Aye, we ride to Havilland tonight. Yon cart is for your possessions." He pointed to a large conveyance drawn by a sturdy-looking horse and an even sturdier-looking driver that had, until this moment, gone unnoticed.

Hoping to hide her intimidation at the prospect of being married in his home, Raiven tried to inject a little asperity in her question, "Where, milord, am I to ride? In the cart with my cases?"

Quynn's frosty smile widened. "Nay, milady. 'Twill be your pleasure to ride before me. We shall be wed directly, and in what little time there is, we should begin to know one another."

Raiven did not move. Her mind, which, just moments ago, had been fretting over the consequences if they did not marry, was now recoiling at the idea that they would. Either option offered odious results, but she knew which she would take. On a level deep within herself she had always known. In fact, she had known from the very first day that hateful message from Henry had come. However, in spite of that inner knowledge, Raiven couldn't make herself take a step toward him.

"What of my servant Elaine? I see no transport for her."

The tightening of his jaw was an indication that her stalling tactics were not unnoted. His voice deepened with his ire. "She will journey with Gunthar and the cart—in the cart, on the cart, or below it if 'tis her desire. I care not. Come, milady," he finished, extending his hand to her.

To delay any longer would be outright cowardice as well as futile. Raiven only dared to give Elaine a quick quiet word of instruction, then reached up to place her foot in the stirrup. Suddenly she found herself lifted as if she were a small child and placed before Quynn. His breath had not caught at his exertion. He allowed her a moment to adjust her modesty. When she finished, she turned to tell him so, but before she opened her mouth to speak, the stallion gave a great lurch and with a thunder of hooves pounded down the road.

Raiven never heard or felt him give a command to his steed, yet the beast was definitely under control, and their ride, though swift, was not unsettling. For the first time the thought that there might be more to him than a fortune-seeking, handsome face began to form as she experienced a begrudging admiration for his strength and horsemanship.

Just as abruptly as the thought came, a warning went off in her head. She would have to move cautiously. Her betrothed was not what she had expected. This was not some soft baron who needed to have a wife found for him. Lord, his face alone would have assured him of the wife of his dreams. Yet he possessed something Raiven found more alluring than superlative looks. He had inherent strength that was above and beyond the physical. She sensed it immediately. It was in his bearing. He exuded power like the most potent aphrodisiac. Raiven had been taught to respect strength all her life. Above all the other faults she had assumed her husband-to-be would have, it was weakness that she had held against him most. She had thought that he would have come for her himself if she had been what he truly desired or if he was man enough. But instead he chose to send gifts to her from afar, like some spineless boulevardier, as if she did not merit more attention.

Only a mere half hour's time had passed since their meeting, and Raiven had to change that perception. The man behind her was man enough for anything.

There was much here for her to consider. Her thoughts running apace with the horse's racing hooves, she began to rethink her situation as she settled in for the journey to her new home.

A few hours later, Raiven was no longer admiring either the man or the beast. Although he had long since slowed the horse, it was becoming clear that he had no intention of stopping—even for the most basic needs. He had not said anything further, and Raiven, still unsure of him, did not know how to breach the silence.

*So much for our getting acquainted,* Raiven thought dryly. Getting to know each other or not, there was a matter of some delicacy she needed to discuss, and for the life of her, she could not find the words.

Another hour passed, and by this time, Raiven had convinced herself he was not human. She, an accomplished horsewoman in her own right, was beginning to feel the strain in her legs. Perhaps it was because she was riding sidesaddle, something her father had encouraged, but she had rarely done when riding at Guirlande. Or perhaps it was nature's needs pressing so firmly upon her she could think of nothing else. Whatever, it was time the warhorses beneath and behind her realized they were not alone. She could endure no more. Turning to Quynn, she kept her eyes level to his chest.

"Stop!"

Quynn's eyes narrowed dangerously. Other than that he gave no indication that he heard her command.

"Please, milord," Raiven gritted out, knowing he was not going to consider her request unless she softened it. Hoping the darkness fully obscured her embarrassment, she explained, "I—I have need of privacy."

In the same fluid motion that had begun their ride, they stopped. Raiven slid to the ground and, to her horror, felt her knees begin to buckle. She would have sunk ignominiously to the ground had Quynn not dismounted and caught her as she swayed. It was the first time they stood face-to-face, or rather chest-to-face, because Raiven found she still had to look up to see his face. She could not make out every feature distinctly, but her memory burned with the image of him.

Raiven recalled how clear a gray his eyes were, the strength of his jaw, the deep blackness of his hair that now blended with the darkness around him. Her eyes traveled leisurely down to his shoulders, across an endless expanse of chest, to sweep to narrow hips and long, well-formed, superbly muscled legs. He was, as she had thought before, a man of a maiden's dream.

The realization came that she would have liked meeting him under different circumstances, where they would not have had to see each other as a cause of bitter resentment. She was certain his fierce resentment spoke of a deep ability to hate and, conversely, to love. To her amazement her heart constricted with the sensation of loss. She was certain that the gentle side lying beneath the potent virility, latent strength, and aura of supreme power and authority was one she'd never see.

"Had I known 'twas only your desire to devour me with your eyes and not nature's call that prompted your request, I would have refused." Quynn's words were dry. "I am what I will be. And as your husband, you'll see enough of me. Move along."

Raiven could feel herself flush throughout her entire body. While it was true she had been staring at him like a love-struck maid, he could have allowed it to pass. Had she just thought there was tenderness in him? Aye, he was tender, about as tender as a blade of steel. Berating herself for being a fool, she started toward a thick copse of trees for the privacy she requested, again wondering why she allowed his taunts to go unanswered.

Where was the ire that used to flare so easily, devouring any who dared to raise it? "I must be tired," she muttered to herself, unable to name any other reason for her behavior.

When she returned to Quynn, he had already remounted. Without a word he reached for her and settled her in her place in front of him. Again they were off without either a visible or audible signal, but this time Raiven was too weary to appreciate his skill. In time it took a great effort to maintain the rigid posture she had adopted so she wouldn't touch him. As furlong passed furlong, her eyelids began to droop, lulled by the rhythmic cadence of the horse's hooves churning away at the ground. Several times she awakened to find herself resting against his broad chest. Each time she would jerk forward.

The moon was a high white ball in the night sky when she finally admitted defeat. With a heavy sigh, she leaned back against him. She was fully asleep in moments.

Quynn knew the exact instant the bewitching bundle in his arms gave up the struggle and relaxed against him to take her ease. He had watched her, his anger growing, as she refused to touch him. Then he had noticed that her posture was loosening. Her back was no longer rigid. He had thought he had prepared himself for the moment when she would rest softly in his arms—without the jerks and starts—but when it happened, it was a jolt to his senses, causing his body to tense.

Immediately Khan broke stride, sensing the difference in his master's body. A softly whispered word reassured the agitated stallion, and once again his gait was smooth.

Now Quynn turned his full attention to the beauty sleeping in his arms. Her eyelids did not even flicker at the disruption, so deep was her sleep. He inhaled deeply, and his nostrils became filled with her scent. It was not just the soft perfume she wore, but a clean, fresh fragrance that he instinctively knew came from no bottle. The smell was at once strange and familiar. In his mind, he knew until a few short hours ago he had never beheld the lovely vixen now lying intimately against him. However, in his heart, he felt an eerie sense of acceptance and satisfaction that left him uneasy.

When he had first seen her, his heart, unruly organ that it was becoming, had slammed against his chest, seemingly frozen and suspended on nothing. Then when she had recognized him, it had begun to gallop at speeds Khan would envy. Despite the best of exertion of his will, he could not suppress the excitement within him that said in mere hours she would be his wife, and then he would be able to peel away the layers of cloth that concealed her body from him.

Raiven turned gently in his arms, snuggling closer to his warmth, interrupting his musing. Quynn brought his stare to rest on the full lips that had parted in sleep. Unbidden, a frown creased his brow as he recalled how tightly she held her lips when he'd taunted her. Somehow he had expected more fire from her instead of quiet rebellion. He had come to expect from her adamant stance prior to their meeting that she would be a feisty and formidable adversary.

He knew he left her unbalanced. He could read the confusion in her eyes. However, for the first time in his adult life, he was unsure of the exact impact he was having on a member of the fairer sex. The only thing he knew for certain was that she was keeping herself tightly contained. Like a glimpse of the sun in a cloudy sky, he realized that there lay the reason for his displeasure. He didn't want her tightly contained away from him. He wanted her—all of her. Henry had given him her lands and her body. He decided he wanted more.

Grimness settled about his features as he let his eyes rove over her fairness, and possession rose in his heart. He would have it! She would share all with him and leave none locked away. He would tap into the woman she sought to hide, the one lying beneath the exterior. Then her surrender would be total, and he would be content. He would not be deterred from his goal. Nothing else would satisfy him. Why this should be so, he did not know, but feeling more the Quynn of old, whose attitude James would have recognized immediately, he accepted it without rancor.

"Henry may have brought this strange enigma to my door, but I will not rest till I solve its meaning. This I promise," he vowed softly.

It was almost as if Raiven heard his words, for she stirred slightly as if giving a subconscious protest of his avowal, causing Quynn to smile in the darkness.

"Very well then, milady. The challenge has been issued and well met. Let the match begin."

He urged Khan into a faster gallop. Suddenly he was eager to be home.

# Chapter 7

Raiven was being nudged awake. Although her bed felt strange, she had no desire to awaken. Truth to tell, this was the best rest she'd had in weeks. She definitely didn't want to awaken to all the problems she knew she'd face. Problems with her people, worries over Jacques, and the overwhelming weight of the death of her father. She made to roll to her side, feeling slightly stiff, when she experienced the sensation of falling. Her eyes flew open at the same moment strong hands caught her.

While her feet were suspended a foot or more above the ground, her eyes were held by a set of laughing gray ones. "Careful, milady, I appreciate your haste. I, too, would see the deed done with all speed, but you must have a care that no injury come to you."

Raiven struggled in his grasp, embarrassed and angry. "Your concern leaves me touched."

He frowned at her sarcastic response, then lowered her to the ground. "Concern?" He hesitated, seeming to give the matter careful thought. "Nay. 'Tis only that it would grieve me greatly to delay the ceremony whilst your wounds are tended."

Raiven managed to keep her features deliberately blank.

Quynn's smile became mocking. "We are to wed," he said with the exaggerated emphasis and tone one would use when speaking to someone of slow wit. "The king has commanded we wed on the day of your arrival. Though it is not day still, I feel he will allow a certain amount of room for interpretation. Surely you have not forgotten the reason you are here?"

"I have thought of little else, milord," came Raiven's bitter response.

In an instant the smile vanished from his face. "Nor have I. Shall we commence?"

"Can it not wait a few more hours, milord? I've scarce arrived. You have not shown me your lands." She swallowed, looking around nervously. "The grounds look as extensive as Guirlande—my home."

Quynn silently stared. He would not point out that it was too dark for her to see anything or for a tour of the grounds. Besides, he knew she had no desire to see his land any more than it was his desire at the moment to show it to her. He continued to say nothing, giving her time to compose herself.

Raiven continued to prattle on. She talked about everything from tenant farming to the serf problem. Just what views did he have on the use of a short spear as opposed to a lance in the joust? Of a hawk as opposed to a falcon in the hunt?

Despite the pace of her tongue, Raiven was aware of Quynn's disturbed look as he watched her go on about the subtle differences between the two birds of prey. She wanted to stop, but she couldn't. She knew she must sound the total idiot, but her nerves had snapped, and the words tumbled out, of their own accord, senseless and unending.

While her mouth proceeded to sprout inanities, inwardly her mind begged him to say something to make her cease.

Quynn stared at her disbelievingly, his only thought not for her sanity, but to wonder if her stream of words would ebb to a trickle long enough for her to speak her vows.

When she realized that Quynn intended to maintain his silence, Raiven gathered herself in hand and took a deep, steadying breath. "My belongings are with Elaine. I would prefer to wait until they arrived."

Sliding with fluid grace from Khan's back, Quynn said firmly but not unkindly, "I am sure you would, but I do not. Come." He spoke with quiet authority, making her instinctively want to obey. However, her fear of the situation overrode her awe of his authority.

Quynn had already begun to mount the three wide steps that led to the double door of the hall, confident that Raiven followed, when her voice halted him.

"Why are you doing this?" Raiven detested the pleading tone her voice had taken. Her pride was suffering, but what price pride when compared to what was about to happen to her? Since meeting this man, she saw that a forced marriage was not necessary from his standpoint. That knowledge coupled with the fact that he clearly did not want this marriage either shook her self-confidence, chasing away all noble thought of her sacrifice. She needed a reason to go through with this. She needed support. Raiven could not remember ever feeling so alone or helpless.

It was to this unspoken need of hers that Quynn responded. He walked back, stopping a few inches from where she stood. He studied her face as best as he could in the darkness. Her face was pale in the torchlight of the outer yard. Her fear touched him, raising in him a desire to soothe her.

"I don't mean to taunt you. Like you, I am bound by more than a decree from the king. Would that things were different. I, too, would be happy."

His tender words caused hope to burgeon in her heart. "Surely if you spoke to your king, he would listen. If you told him that you did not desire this marriage, mayhap then he would relent."

Quynn's hand came up to brush a wisp of hair from her brow. "You are hoping on dreams, little one. Henry will not relent and I will not tweak his ire further by asking what I know he will not give or delaying what must be done. By the sunrise you will be wife in every way," he said with such quiet finality that Raiven knew further discussion would be useless.

He turned away again, and though he did not add the imperious order to come, he assumed that she would.

Raiven's last hope died, and her temper, never the best, finally snapped. She could feel the anger course through her, and she did not even try to control it. It felt too good to be finally reacting to him in a way she could understand, in a way that was familiar to her. The inconsistency of her reaction, she did not consider. It did not matter that when he spoke tauntingly, deserving her anger, she had fallen silent. It did not matter that now when he dealt her a kindness, she returned it with anger.

Without thinking she replied, "I will not."

His back stiffened, but he did not turn. "You will. The alternatives are not pleasant. You may, in your obstinacy, be prepared for them; I am not."

He did not elaborate on whether the retribution would come from him or the king or both, but the renewed threat was enough.

Raiven could feel her anger deflate. How could she have, even for a second, allowed her fear to make her forget her brother and her people? Curse her temper! Even if it killed her, she was going to learn to think before she acted. Too much depended on it. She could not think only of herself.

Raiven felt drained. For the second time that day, her emotions had run the gamut from nervous fear to stinging fury to despairing defeat in the span of only a few seconds. Her emotions seemed to be as beyond her control as everything else, and she could not recall another moment of her life when she was as tired as she felt now, standing in the dim light of the strange courtyard. Lifting her hand wearily, she pulled the tangled mass of her hair away from her face and walked to where Quynn waited on the stairs.

When she looked up into his eyes, he saw the apathy she had displayed at the docks, only it seemed worse, as if it pierced through to her heart.

"I am ready."

Now Quynn hesitated. He could not ignore the raw pain and frustration on her face. After a long moment, he said softly, "You must love your brother very much."

Fleeting surprise that he knew of Jacques' existence flashed in her eyes, then it disappeared. She shrugged. "Aye, I love him very much. He is all the family I have left. I promised my father I would see to his welfare, and it is the one promise I have every intention of keeping, no matter the cost. Would you not do the same?"

"I am a man" was all he said.

"Well, I am a woman, and my word is no less precious to me." Raiven grew weary of the conversation and the strange way he watched her. "Is there something else you want to discuss? You have already pointed out, milord, that delay of what must be done is useless."

"If you wish," he said, forcing himself to ignore her tone, "I can show you to our chamber where you might repair yourself before the ceremony begins."

He made the offer in such a way that Raiven knew he expected her to jump at the chance.

She smiled for the first time since she had met him. She knew she looked travel worn. The wind had snarled her hair and her bliaut, once a pretty green, was covered with dust from the road. Perhaps there was dust on her face also. It was funny that he thought she would care when her looks were her last concern. Mayhap it was important to him. If it was, he was in for a disappointment. She was no shallow self-centered miss in need of constant perfection in face and form. There had been times at Guirlande when the pressures of responsibility had been so great that she had gone from sunup to sunset without combing her hair. Elaine had been outraged, but Raiven hadn't cared. She didn't care now.

She was no hypocrite. This was not a love match. She would not be a radiant bride coming to her anxious groom. He would marry her now, as she was, worn and dirty, or they wouldn't marry at all.

Despite all the threats to her brother and her people, she had found to her horror that her courage had chosen this day to desert her when she was most in need of it. If she did not do the deed now, she feared she would not be able to at all. Already, in a manner totally foreign to her, she had swung from one decision to the other.

"Nay, milord," she said quietly. "We marry now, travel stained and dusty be hanged. I will not seek to evade my fate any longer."

Raiven turned to walk away, and she could hear Quynn's step behind her. She could feel his guiding hand in the small of her back. However, she couldn't see and wouldn't have been able to decipher the strange light that shone brilliantly in his eyes.

An hour later Raiven sat in the middle of a tub soaking away the grime and grit from the road. She looked around the candle-lit room, not too different in size from her room at Guirlande.

That was the only similarity.

Compared to the opulent appointment of her room at home, this one was spartan. Through the daze that had descended upon her during and after the brief ceremony, she had noted that the same stark appearance was prevalent throughout what little of the hall she had seen.

Strangely, she found that the thought did not bother her as it once would have. If Quynn had been a different man, she would have been immensely uneasy; as it was, she merely accepted the fact that her husband had less in a material way than she.

Even if the sour-faced woman, whom Quynn had called Ella, had not told her, Raiven thought she still would have recognized the room as Quynn's. The tapestries were a dark sienna with a deep dark orange running throughout in fanciful swirls and whorls. The furniture was the same deep brown color, causing Raiven to hope that when the sunlight filtered through the massive windows above the desk it would relieve the rather somber effect. She examined all her surroundings from floor to ceiling, while avoiding the main feature of any sleeping chamber: the bed. Yet the longer she avoided looking at it, the larger it seemed to grow, until she could no longer resist. She stared at the place where her hus—where Quynn, she could not call him husband, would soon come to her. The bed was massive—larger than any she'd ever seen. Quynn no doubt had it made especially to accommodate his huge form. Furs and pelts covered it, and Raiven knew it would be warm beneath them. Then she thought of Quynn coming to her there, and she grew cold.

Rising from the tub, she used the linen left beside it for drying. With one end she wiped her body, then she wrapped herself in the whole length of it when she was done. Almost gingerly she sat on the bed. Picking up the brush she had been given—after asking a mere two times—she began to pull the tangles from her wet hair.

A quarter of an hour later she was glad she'd followed her mind and saw to her toilette herself. Either Elaine had not arrived or had not been told where she was. Certainly no one else here wanted to help her in any way. The bathwater she had used had yet to be emptied, giving her an adequate estimation of the servants' lack of desire to help her.

Not knowing what else to do—she couldn't even dress because her clothes were with Elaine and Ella had taken away the ones she had worn—she brushed her hair thoroughly dry while watching the flames leap and dance brightly as they devoured the logs.

Raiven never knew when she fell asleep, and she definitely did not know Quynn had come. Opening her eyes slowly, further disoriented by the strangeness of her surroundings, she saw a shadow standing next to the bed. Just when she would have screamed, she recognized the form of the man who was now her husband for all eternity, his dark hair sparkling with drops of water from a recent wash. She could not see his face because the fire was to his back, but the rest of him was all there for her to view. He had shed his clothes before coming to stand next to the bed, and Raiven could see it was not the bulk of his clothing that added width to his massive shoulders.

To see that he had no hair curling on his chest was a surprise but not unappealing. His skin covered firm muscles, which due to the fire, glowed with an orange copper hue, and the shadowed ridges of solid muscle across his abdomen tapered to a narrow waist. Quickly she skipped the section of his body that she feared most, bringing her gaze to rest on his long legs, which like his chest, did not have much hair. Raiven prayed the shadows concealed the blush she could feel in her cheeks when she returned her eyes to his face.

Although Raiven couldn't see the expression in his eyes through the darkness, she still felt trapped by the stare she knew was upon her, and she couldn't look away. Absorbed in the strange pull he was exerting on her, she didn't even notice his hand move toward her until it pulled at the linen that was still wrapped about her body. Her stiffening was immediate.

Quynn gave a soft chuckle. "Am I not to have the same pleasure of viewing your body as you have had of mine?" He did not pull on the linen, but neither did he remove his hand.

Raiven stared mutely at him, not even attempting to hide her surprise at the mildness of his response to her slight rejection. Perhaps had she known that while the firelight behind him did nothing to illuminate his features, it left hers clearly defined, she would have tried harder to mask her responses.

"Relax, little one." His voice was gentle, as if he was trying to tame a skittish mare. "I will not hurt . . . You need not fear me."

No sooner had he said the words than Raiven found herself crushed in his arms as he lay beside her.

Then there was only sensation.

His chest was damp, yet warm, seeming to burn with a hidden fire rivaling the one glowing a bright orange in the hearth. His hand was slowly touching the pale gold of her hair, sweeping the tousled mass from her face to place a soft kiss where her hair had been.

From that small embrace the heat of his body began to

invade hers. It entered through the place his lips caressed and settled like warm coals in the pit of her belly.

Quynn's breath was gentle on her face as his lips moved to her ear, taking little nipping bites that forced a tiny groan from Raiven's lips. Raiven didn't know if her reaction was from pleasure or dismay, but she was aware that the heat in her lower body intensified with every teasing nip he took.

Another groan she couldn't seem to suppress tore from her lips, and she moved her head back and forth in denial of the new feelings that were surging against her wishes and beyond her control.

"What is it, little one?" Quynn asked just before his lips found the pulse in her neck and began to caress it with tiny, darting flicks of his tongue.

The heat within turned to fire.

Raiven knew she had to make him stop. Innocent of men she might be, but she was wise enough to know where these burning kisses would lead and what would be the result.

It was an effort to produce a voice, and she was afraid that she would never achieve one that would appear dispassionate to the magic his lips were weaving. She knew only she could not let him continue.

"Why do you call me little one? Is it only to mock me, or are you lacking in wits?"

To her dismay, Quynn ignored her taunt, and despite the darkness, she could see the flash of white teeth as he smiled. "Ah, but for a man of my dimensions you are."

His words were both an invitation and a potent caress, nullifying the tension she had tried to create. To her distress, Raiven found she couldn't ignore the invitation. Of their own volition, her eyes skimmed his body, not missing any of its magnificence. Her throat tightened at the sheer beauty of the man. Her fingers tingled with their desire to explore the endless breadth of chest, flat stomach, muscled thigh, and all else her eyes beheld. With a sinking feeling in her chest, Raiven knew she was yielding to him. Without her consent, she found herself wanting him.

The situation was too new. The feelings he evoked were unexpectedly powerful. Raiven felt as if she were drowning, being pulled under by feelings she had not known could exist. Against the urgings of her mind, her body was making its desire known. And, at the moment, the fact that this man was her enemy did not concern it in the least.

The war taking place between her mind and her body tore her apart. She practically suffocated beneath the feeling of self-betrayal. Why did he have to use her own weakness against her? Her mind would have accepted it better had he come in like a beast, pounced on her, and took what he wanted. It was no less than she had come to expect from him and his people. Now he was attempting to make a lie of what they were doing by giving it a tenderness it did not deserve. What they were doing was ugly, a thing of duty, and she didn't want the pretense. In truth, she didn't believe she could bear it. Had he not said she would be his wife in every way by morning? This was only his way of seeing it done. Raiven had not missed the fact that his every action since she'd awakened to see him standing over her had been deliberate. He wanted to calm her into not resisting him. He had nearly succeeded.

Gathering her fleeing will, she forced herself to remember her vow to give this man nothing more than his king had already taken from her. Now when his lips and hands caressed, she felt a different kind of fire, the kind that burned because of the pain she had suffered due to him and his king. Each new thought fanned the flame of her shame.

The suffocating feeling intensified, bringing with it mindless panic. For the second time that night, Raiven thought of fleeing. But again Henry's threats held her still. ". . . Must be married and the act must be consummated on the day of your arrival. I will brook no more disobedience. Your brother shall be my guest until at such time I am satisfied that all is well. Heed my words well. No other warning shall be given." "Act must be consummated." *"Must be consummated."*

"I cannot." The torturous words were out before she realized it.

In her anxiety, she gripped his face to make him cease, and when she felt his jaw tighten, Raiven knew he was not pleased.

"You can."

Raiven looked away, staring into the fire. "I do not think so, milord." Her next words could barely be heard above the crackle of the fire. "I would feel too much the whore."

Quynn stiffened. "What do you mean, whore? We are properly wed."

"At the king's command."

"It matters not how," he said sourly, giving a fleeting thought to his own ruined plans.

Raiven shrugged. "It should not matter. I have tried to see this"—she waved her hand to encompass the two of them—"as mere duty, but it still reeks of whoredom. I am to give myself to you not from desire or from my heart's urging, but from the lips of another man." She turned to look directly into Quynn's face. "What would you call it, milord?"

Quynn found himself uncomfortable under her unwavering gaze and the modicum of truth in her words.

"We do what we must" was all he could manage, only to watch the green eyes beneath him sparkle with anger.

"Like rutting dogs? Nay, not even that. Even those lowly animals have honest urges to impel them. I feel nothing for you. You feel nothing for me. How can we *do* anything?"

Quynn's burst of laughter was ugly. "Is that what bothers you? That we do not love? Did you really think we would after all that has passed?"

"Nay, I did not," Raiven replied tightly, disliking his laughter and the derision in his tone.

"Then what is it? And do not tell me there was nothing between us. I could feel you begin to relax in my arms. What happened? Did you remind yourself that you were bedding the enemy?"

His words were so accurate Raiven could think of no

answer to give him. No words were necessary. For the first time since she had met him the facade of coldness had cracked, and she was seeing the molten emotion that simmered beneath.

"Nay, not that?" he taunted. "Are you sickened then at finding yourself abed with—if I remember your description—'that English pup of a man who needs a wife found for him'? Aye, that was it." His hand, which was still enmeshed in her hair, clenched convulsively, pulling the soft locks painfully.

His voice was softly dispassionate, causing a spurt of fear to travel down her spine. "If memory serves," he went on with distant coldness, "and I believe it does, you also wondered if Henry would have to 'prop me up to see the bedding done aright.'"

He was almost snarling now. Suddenly he released his grip on her hair, then thrust her violently away from him as if he couldn't stand to be near her, let alone touch her.

Quynn jumped from the bed, his anger fully aroused as he recalled the full extent of his humiliation.

"Have you come to the conclusion that I can perform without the king guiding my strings?" He bit out the words.

Raiven was still grappling with the mortified awareness that he had heard those things. She had said them in the heat of the moment when she had first discovered the king's intention. She had never dreamed that her words would be repeated to him. Yet, she found she could not apologize, even in the face of his obvious rage. One apologized when one said something one regretted. She regretted none of it. She felt justified. He and Henry had pushed her to it.

Quynn read the mutinous emotions on her face. His rage grew when he realized that he waited in vain for her to say something either in denial of or atonement for the horrible words. Black fury burned every thought from his mind except the desire to hurt in kind.

So be it. He had tried to be decent with her under the circumstances. He had tried to make this something she would not have to view with disgust. During their brief ceremony, his insides had twisted at the look of pain and terror in her eyes she couldn't hide. He had almost defied Henry himself, wanting to call a halt to the proceedings. Only the thought of Havilland and looking away from her had enabled him to go through with it.

He had understood himself no more then than he had when they were journeying to Havilland and he had held her sleeping form in his arms with such gentleness. Nevertheless, he had made up his mind to add no more pain to the haunted look in her eyes. One night with a wench was much the same as any other to a man, but when the wench was your wife and that night was her first . . .

The rage distorting his mind caused an ugly thought to form. Unfathomable menace entered his eyes. Quynn's fists clenched at his sides. Knowing he was perilously close to losing all restraint, he took a deep breath to regain control. The air hissed through his nostrils as he tried to put the ugly images from his mind. Of all the humiliations he would endure, *that* was not one of them. If there had been another man before him, he would kill her and gladly await Henry's justice in whatever form it would come. In any event, he would know soon enough. The wench had had enough her way. It was time for her to learn that there were other things in life besides what she wanted. Her lessons would begin tonight.

Raiven was not privy to Quynn's thoughts, but she felt something chilling enter the air between them. She knew he had changed toward her, and it wasn't only the words she had rashly spoken so long ago that were responsible. There was a calmness about him that was in itself more terrifying than his rage. He was again cold and in control, and his demeanor said he had had enough, and he would be carrying out the king's demands whether she said yea or nay.

Her heart plummeted as she realized that here was the beast she had wished upon herself. Unbidden, strains of an old proverb ran through her mind, *Do not ask for what you will wish you had not got.* Raiven deeply felt the sharp bite of her own folly. If this thing must be done—

and from Quynn's menacingly aggressive stance, it did—then she would much rather live with the pretense of tenderness he had offered in the beginning. She had been a fool to think she would rather have had him pounce on her like a crazed animal, which was now what she was afraid he would do.

Raiven's mind raced to find a way to recapture the moments past. She couldn't bring herself to ask for it, and she didn't believe for an instant that Quynn would respond favorably to mere words at this point. As much as her pride rebelled at the notion, the only option left to her was to show him. She would have to calm him not with words, but with actions.

Another quick glance at his rigid posture was enough for her courage and resolve to flee. There had to be another way to calm the beast within him. However, deep inside, she knew there was not.

Quynn placed a knee on the bed and began to reach for her. Raiven pulled away and, without thinking, blurted the first thing that came to mind. "I concede, milord."

Quynn stopped, baffled at her words and the near-hysterical tone of her voice. He had truly begun to think that there was no fear in the woman. He certainly never expected to hear anything sounding remotely like surrender coming from her lips. Hadn't he just given her the chance to apologize and make amends for publicly shaming him and she had stubbornly tilted her chin and remained silent? What trick was this?

Raiven could not see the surprise on his face because of the darkness, and even had it been light, she probably would not have noticed. She was so overwhelmingly relieved that she had gotten him to halt that she was aware of nothing else except how she should next proceed.

From somewhere in the corner of her mind came the memory of the way the young village girls at Guirlande had behaved in Jacques's presence. She had, at the time, thought their antics to be silly, but now remembering the way Jacques had responded to their attention, she was not sure.

Quynn had not moved since he placed his knee on the bed and Raiven knew he waited to hear what else she was going to say. Her voice came unnaturally high.

"I concede that for a man of your size, I might be considered little."

He continued to half crouch, half stand above her. Raiven could feel his curiosity, yet he remained silent and still. It took only a moment for her to realize he was still waiting, intending to test the extent of her sudden change. His words confirmed it.

"What else might you 'concede' me?" he challenged, though his voice had lost some of its previous harshness.

"What is your desire?" Raiven asked in a throaty whisper that was pure nerves. If the situation were not so dire, she would have laughed aloud at herself. Of the many skills she possessed, playing the role of a seductress was not among them.

Quynn's husky reply settled her mind on the success of her efforts. "Might I perchance get to view what lies beneath the bathing linen?" he asked, pointing to the wrap she still wore about her.

The air between them had definitely changed quickly, but Raiven couldn't back out now. Her hesitation was fractional. She went on in what she hoped was a teasing manner.

"A tiny look, a wee look, but no more."

"I promise 'twill pass so quickly you will scarce believe I have looked at all." His tone warned he would tolerate no procrastination.

Raiven's heart was slamming against her chest as she slid with natural grace to her feet. She took a deep breath and prayed that her courage did not desert her now. With her back to Quynn, she slowly unwrapped the linen. When it was ready to drop, she caught it and turned, not realizing how teasingly seductive her movements appeared.

Quynn had lain down when she stood, and although

the firelight revealed his features, Raiven couldn't read them. His position, legs crossed casually at the ankles, hands propped nonchalantly behind his head, said he couldn't care less. But as Raiven continued to watch him, she suddenly knew he did. An abrupt birth of woman's knowledge told her he was greatly anticipating the sight he would see when the linen fell from her body. That certainty made her feel heady with a different sort of power than any she had ever known.

Warming now to her role in a totally new way, she gave him a slow smile. "Remember your promise, milord."

"Madam, you speak to a knight of his majesty," he said with a gruffness she didn't believe for a minute. "Proceed."

Expectation and unfulfilled promise hung between them as Raiven slowly lowered the towel, her movements unconsciously seductive.

The only sound in the room was that of Quynn's breath arresting in his throat. Raiven could feel his approval and desire. His pleasure warmed her. It wrapped around her as securely as the linen towel she had just discarded. His obvious enchantment was a balm to her ego, and she couldn't resist taunting him just a little.

"What now of your vow of a fleeting glance, milord?"

Quynn rose to his knees, causing the bed to dip as he advanced toward her. "You have me at your mercy, little one, and I pray you release me from my vow. In truth 'twas a fool's promise, and I have no choice but to recant, because I am not nor have I ever been a fool."

His eyes lingered on hers for a full minute after he spoke to let the full meaning of his words sink in. In that instant Raiven knew that Quynn had seen through her scheme and that he had allowed it. With her eyes still on his, she nodded slowly, silently acknowledging her agreement.

With that gesture from her, Quynn gave in to the impulse that had seized him from the first time he saw her. Groaning in relief, he brought his lips to hers, half expecting her to retreat from the passion of his ardor. To his extreme satisfaction, she did not.

Raiven met his kiss haltingly, then with boldness. When his tongue sought entry into the moist haven of her mouth, she opened her lips willingly to allow him the access he demanded.

Slowly, through the mating rhythms of their tongues, he enticed and gave her glimpses of the act to come. When he leaned back to fall on the bed, he didn't remove his mouth from hers nor allow her body to move away from his. Raiven experienced the delicious thrill of having the entire length of her body pressed against his. Even then, he did not break the kiss but continued to mesmerize her senses with his lips and tongue. Raiven felt his arms tighten as he rolled with her on the bed, and only then did he pull back to look into her eyes.

Raiven's fingers trembled with wonder as they lifted to touch her lips that still had the feel of his upon them. She was in awe that something as simple as putting one's lips on another's could cause such wondrous pleasure.

Quynn had kissed her with the finesse of a master. He knew what he wanted her to feel, and he knew how to make her feel it. Raiven did not know of men and their passion, and she did not want to appear any more ignorant in his eyes than she already did.

Nervously her tongue darted out to lick her lips, still swollen from his kiss. She couldn't bring herself to look at him while she said the words, so instead she fixed her gaze on the area between his chin and his chest. "If there is more to this game than this, milord, I do not know it," she admitted softly. "Again I ask what is your desire, only this time I ask you to teach me of mine as well."

Quynn let out an agonized groan before his lips fell to hers again. Now his hands joined the passionate assault as they began to roam feverishly over her body both teaching and pleasing her at the same time. His passion soared when she left off the passive role and began to touch him as he had her. His innocent wife seemed determined to know his body as intimately as he was coming to know hers. When he could endure no more, he rose up, then paused just before entering her. Her very innocence compelled him to warn her.

"Raiven"—he waited until her eyes lifted to his—"'twill hurt. I do not wish to cause you pain, but it cannot—"

Gently her fingers pressed to his lips, silencing the rest of what he was about to say. Her eyes sparkled with unfulfilled passion and a bit of reluctant humor.

"Nay, my lord. It is one time I will not relent. Come to me and finish well what you have so ably allowed me to start."

Quynn's mouth covered hers before she finished speaking. He kissed her like a man starved for food and drink and she was all the nourishment left in the world. His groan of satisfaction at finding her truly untouched enveloped and drowned her cry of pain as he thrust fully inside her. The sensation was so acute, he wanted to lose himself immediately into her welcoming flesh with a force that would bring the release that was only breaths away. Her tightness and warmth was almost more than he could bear. Only by making himself remember her delicate state could he find the willpower to endure. Perspiration beaded his forehead, and his muscles trembled at the effort he was exerting to stop for a moment to give her body time to adjust.

As the pain began to subside, Raiven wondered dispassionately if this was all there was to lovemaking. She had heard it was so overwhelmingly simple to please a man, and now she was learning that it just might be. Quynn was lying so still. Didn't men do that when it was over? It must be, and she couldn't help feeling a little sad. Was this what all the fuss was about? It was pleasant enough she supposed—if there was no more pain—but worth all the trouble? Hardly! After all, here it was finished and done before she scarcely knew it had begun.

She realized then that he was still inside her, and upon the heels of that realization came feelings she hadn't felt since Quynn had first kissed her. These feelings, however, were stronger and centered at the core of her being where his flesh met hers. She closed her eyes, reveling in the pleasure that was building inside her. When the desire came to move, she did and gasped aloud, her gasp and Quynn's agonized "Don't" mingling together.

Raiven opened her eyes, thinking she had done something dreadfully wrong. Quynn's voice had almost sounded pained.

"Why?"

"'Tis too soon," he ground out. His breathing was harsh. "You are not ready. I don't want to hurt you any more than I must."

Was that what this stillness was about? He didn't want to hurt her? It finally occurred to Raiven that the perspiration on his face and the tightness she could feel in the muscles beneath her fingers came not from extreme pleasure, but from the mighty effort of self-restraint. Again, her woman's knowledge took over and told her he was waiting for a word to proceed from her.

Wrapping her arms and legs around him, she raised her hips to surround him more fully and was thrilled by the warmth he was causing without and within.

"Milord, you won't hurt—" The rest of her words were cut off in a gasp as he began to plunge madly into her welcoming body.

Reacting purely on instinct, Raiven wanted to give him the greatest pleasure imaginable. She wanted to return some of the wonder he was sharing with her. She wanted to give to him, and she wanted him to know that her offering had naught to do with the king's demands. What she gave here no one could order. It was hers to give freely or withhold, and she prayed Quynn would know it. How else could she accept without guilt the marvelous pleasure his body was giving hers?

His every movement spiraled sensation higher and higher until the aura of their lovemaking blazed with a brilliance beyond description. Certainly it was beyond anything Raiven had ever imagined could exist. When the pleasure became too acute to bear, she could feel her insides unfolding, reaching for something they instinctively knew was in Quynn's power to give.

Then it came. An explosion of sensation so marvelous that she couldn't contain it. Her cry of pleasure filled the room. Although lost in the rapture of her own fulfillment, she still felt his body tense with exquisite torture before giving him the release she had experienced mere seconds ago.

In the quiet moments that followed, Raiven pulled away, and Quynn, already lost in thoughts of his own, silently released her. There seemed to be nothing for either of them to say. There was no underlying feeling of closeness or warmth between them. And likewise, there were no words to erase the demeaning sense of mockery each felt at what they'd just shared.

Raiven, for all her inexperience, knew there should have been more. There should have been some soft word or gesture—a true climax to what they had shared. But knowing what should be did not change what was, and so she also knew there would be no tenderness forthcoming. The false aura of warmth that, like a cloak, had shielded them from the darker motives was gone.

Once again the room reeked with the stench of duty and the stark awareness of an innocence lost in more ways than the physical. It was done. Her husband had seen to the fulfillment of the king's demand to the letter.

It would appear that tonight was truly the night for learning of powerful emotions never felt before. Self-loathing over her willing part in what had taken place held her tenaciously. As Quynn left the chamber, Raiven turned away, curling herself into a tight ball, trying to stave off some of the pain, but it was no use. It overwhelmed her, washing relentlessly over her in a seemingly unending tide. And that's when she felt the totally foreign wetness on her face. Another new experience.

For the first time in her adult life, Raiven wept herself to sleep.

# Chapter

# •8•

Raiven awakened to the cheerful and familiar sound of Elaine humming as she went about her morning chores. Without opening her eyes to see, she knew exactly what Elaine was doing, and the beginning of a smile started across her face.

Fighting her way fully conscious, Raiven was happy to begin the day. After the horrible nightmare she had had last night, anything would be better. She knew it was silly to allow a dream, even one as bad as the one she'd had, to affect her so strongly, but the dream was a true nightmare. That in itself should have given her a clue. No one's life could change that much for the worse. However, the terror of the dream had done one good thing for her: it had made her grateful for her life as it was. No longer would she complain about the pressures of overseeing Guirlande and the rest of the de Cortillion lands. Sighing happily, she began to roll over, chiding herself for her foolishness.

She stopped midroll, her eyes suddenly flying open, and the wonderful delusion shattered. Her movement made her aware of a curious, yet distinct soreness in her lower body. With the pain came the memory, and

Raiven groaned slowly, firmly closing her eyes to banish the images of last evening that flooded her mind.

Raiven had almost forgotten Elaine's presence until she heard a soothingly quiet voice from behind her. "It cannot be so bad."

"Not now, Elaine." Anguish and self-recrimination was rife in those three little words.

Elaine's voice was soft, compassionate. "You must arise, milady. Your husband arose hours ago."

When Raiven did not move, Elaine continued. "Already his servants snicker as they pass. They feel you have been severely chastened and subdued."

Raiven rolled to her back to look into Elaine's troubled face. Fresh guilt assailed her. She had not spared a thought for Elaine's welfare.

"How fared you, Elaine, during the journey here and last eve?"

Elaine gave a typical French shrug. "'Tis not France, milady, but I did not expect it to be." She turned away to pick up the linen that had wrapped Raiven's body.

Raiven's cheeks burned a bright red, and she was glad the servant had her back to her and couldn't see her reaction.

Without another word, Elaine walked to the garderobe and gave Raiven a robe. Raiven felt her face burn even brighter as she accepted it, mumbling an indistinct "Thank you."

Raiven was uncomfortable with the sudden awkwardness that sprang up between the two of them. Elaine had seen her bare more times than she could number, but now, in the span of one night, things had changed. For the first time since they were together, Elaine gave her a robe to rise—and Raiven took it.

As she struggled to wrap the robe around her without losing the sheet, Raiven also struggled to find a way to soothe the discomfort of the moment. Deciding a sense of normalcy was the solution, she stood up, asking Elaine for garments suitable for inspecting the hall and grounds. The words froze in her mouth, her hands ceased the motion of belting the sash of her robe, and her eyes were riveted to the dark red stain on the bedsheets.

Somehow the evidence of her loss of virtue made the night's happenings more shameful. Seeing that stain was all it took to make her humiliation complete. Despite her avowals to the contrary, she had married and, after a fashion, enthusiastically bedded a man she barely knew. The situation worsened as she considered that the man in question had no feelings for her other than antipathy. She could have been anyone, and the night would have been the same for him. His only emotional link to the act had been a determination to see the deed done.

Suddenly the spot disappeared from view, and a harsh voice rapped out, "Milord will be needing these. 'Tis small enough comfort, but leastways he'll know he wedded a virgin."

The look on Ella's face was scornful. Obviously Raiven's virtue meant nothing to her. She still hated her new mistress.

Raiven watched the servant's uncompromising face, saying nothing. Behind the woman she could see the horror on Elaine's face, both at the woman's unannounced entry and her acid words. Elaine looked ready to commit an act of violence, and Raiven smiled over her loyalty.

Strangely, she felt no anger at Ella. While it was true that were she in France, such a thing would never have happened, she had already been rudely jolted to the awareness that she was not in France.

She observed Ella's sullen departure, and she couldn't prevent her smile from deepening. Her situation was truly ironic. In France, not even a noble, let alone a servant, would have spoken to her thus. A noble would have refrained from doing so out of respect, and a servant out of love and affection.

All her life she had been surrounded by loving people, from her father and mother to the youngest of the servants. Now she lived in a strange country, in a strange home, surrounded by hostility that started with her noble husband and ended with the lowest of his servants. Undeniably, her life had taken a bizarre unforeseen twist.

Elaine's snort of displeasure broke through her thoughts, causing her to turn away from the now closed door.

"'Tis glad I am that you can be amused by such a servant. I wanted to box her ears. If we were in France—"

"But, as you have said," Raiven interrupted softly, "we are not. Although it pains me to admit that the servants are not more gracious in what they consider my defeat, I must accept their rancor. For now."

Elaine smiled at the tiny hint of returning fire in Raiven's eyes. "Perhaps they follow the lead of another."

"Whose?"

"Their lord's."

"I do not think so."

Raiven's quick denial caused Elaine to pause. She noted something in her mistress's gaze she couldn't decipher.

"As you say, milady."

Raiven ignored the puzzlement in her maid's tone and moved over to the basin sitting on the washstand. She could feel Elaine stare at her as she went about her chores. She counted the seconds, knowing the silence would not last. She had not gotten to ten when Elaine's voice came again, her tone carefully curious.

"How fared you last eve, milady?"

Raiven splashed water on her face in an attempt to hide her reaction. She continued to splash water on her face as Elaine continued to stare. It was her thought that if Elaine did not relent soon, she would have the cleanest face in all England.

Elaine's voice was soothing, sensing her mistress's discomfort. "Milady, 'tis no need to speak of intimacies. Even had I not seen the proof of what happened here, I would have heard what Ella said to you. I do not mean to step beyond my place, but I have a care for you, and Milord Jacques is not here to see to your welfare."

Near the end of her impassioned speech, her voice trailed off and her eyes lowered to the floor.

Elaine and Raiven had been together for a long time. As such, Raiven allowed her certain liberties that other servants did not have, but never before had she spoken to Raiven in this way. It was clear by her stance and downcast eyes that she was not sure of what her mistress's reaction would be to her boldness.

Her fears were for naught. All Raiven heard in Elaine's voice was concern, and her eyes unexpectedly filled with tears. More than anything else, right now she needed to have someone express affection for her, any kind of affection. She felt so alone. After last night she also felt something else. She felt vulnerable. Feeling so, Elaine would never gain her censure for her concern when it was what Raiven needed so desperately.

Without thinking or stopping to dry her face, Raiven rushed over to envelop Elaine in an embrace that shocked the already uncomfortable servant.

Elaine's arms were slow to return Raiven's embrace, so stunned was she at this great show of affection by her mistress. When she pulled away, Elaine's astonishment increased at the glisten of unshed tears in Raiven's eyes.

"I would like to thank you, Elaine, for your care now and of the past years." Raiven paused. Elaine began to speak, but Raiven held up a hand to forestall her. "My husband was cold to me, but not cruelly so." Raiven walked back to the washstand and unfolded a drying cloth, patting her face as she spoke. "Later he just did what had to be done. As am I, he is bound by the king's order."

Elaine nodded. "Perhaps it will be different once you conceive."

Elaine's practical statement left Raiven completely unbalanced. She lifted her face from the cloth, her mouth agape as she stared at her maid for a full minute before she recovered. "You know the full circumstances of my marriage?"

Now it was Elaine's face that colored red. "Milady, I

did not mean to read your letter, but it lay upon your coffer . . . and I could not help it."

Raiven smiled, breaking the tension. Then she laughed, her first real burst of amusement in days. "Father said I'd rue the day I taught you to read. But, as you already know, there's no need for pretense. In truth I am happy you know. I would not like you to think I have so little morals as to fall into bed upon such short acquaintance, regardless of the situation. As you have read, I must bear my husband a child within a year or else"—Raiven swallowed heavily, the last vestige of her smile disappearing with her thoughts of Jacques—"the consequences will not be pleasant."

"You should have told your brother."

"Nay!" she shouted, then lowered her voice. "'Twould have done no good. I'm afraid things are bad enough in that quarter." Jacques' angry face as she had last seen him appeared clearly in her mind, and she rubbed suddenly sweaty palms in the cloth before placing it back on the stand.

Neither said anything else as Elaine helped Raiven with her toilette.

Three-quarters of an hour later Raiven descended the stairs to her husband's hall, noting the quiet, efficient manner in which it was run. There were already fresh rushes on the floor, and the tapestries had been beaten to clear them of the ever-present dust of the hall.

At the bottom of the curved staircase Raiven found herself in what appeared to be the center room of the hall. There was a large wooden trestle table set on a dais a safe distance from the hearth. She moved closer to examine the table, noting by its size and its elevation from the floor that it was the baron's table. Raiven approached it, drawn by the large bowl of various fruits that graced its center.

Raiven was about to take an apple when she heard someone come up behind her. She turned abruptly to see a slight red-haired, brown-eyed lad watching her with interest. The intensity and duration of his open-mouthed stare brought a smile to her face. The boy seemed even more baffled when she did so. Raiven guessed him to be about ten years old. His unblinking stare certainly identified him as being at that age when lads discovered the world was filled with things other than horses and the knights who rode them.

"Good day," Raiven said when it seemed the boy was not going to speak. "I am Raiven of Guirlande, the baron's new wife."

The boy continued to stare silently.

Raiven's smile broadened. "And you are?"

"Thomas, milady," he rasped, remembering belatedly to bow.

Thomas was in complete awe of the woman before him. He had been at rest yestereve when she arrived, and this morn he heard his mother's irate mutterings about the "shrew" of a woman the baron had been forced to wed. Ella had rambled on about everything. She had condemned the baron's wife for her height, saying she resembled an ugly, awkward stork. Thomas did not agree with that. Ella had called the baron's lady haughty. Thomas would have disagreed if he knew what that meant, but he was sure it wasn't anything nice. His mother's anger had almost frightened him when she told how the baron's bride hadn't even deigned to look at his lordship during the ceremony, only staring ahead as if the hall and everyone in it were naught but dirt, to which Thomas couldn't form any opinion, because he had not been present. He did not, however, think she looked the shrew or that she'd meant any harm. She seemed nice. She smiled at him.

The lady's pleasant voice brought him from his musings.

"Well, Thomas, as you seem to be the only one about, may I trouble you for something to break the fast?"

He found his tongue, recalling his mother's words about her probable laziness. "But 'tis long past the hour for—" He stopped abruptly, his face turning practically the same carroty hue as the hair on his head when he realized what he was saying and to whom.

Raiven ignored the look of guilt she read so easily on

his face and squelched the laughter that threatened to erupt at any second at his comically woebegone expression. She went on as if she had not heard his outburst.

"You would not believe how tired one can be after journeying so far. Even though 'tis late, cannot something be found? I would appreciate it mightily."

Typical of either the young or the unsophisticated, all his emotions were reflecting clearly on his face, and his relief was almost as amusing as his chagrin. However, it was not his concern for her feelings that made Raiven feel an instant liking for the boy. It was his eyes. The rich brown orbs were full of friendliness and acceptance. It was the first nonhostile gaze she had encountered since coming to England.

Thomas, for his part, was going through a certain amount of adjustment. Although the lady's words were not an apology, her tone was not one of demand either. He began to wonder in earnest if his mother could be wrong in her opinion this once. His last doubts as to the lady's nature fled when she added, "And afterward, if it is not too much trouble, I would like it if you would guide me about the hall and the grounds. I am sure you would know everything I need to be told."

Thomas felt his face heat beneath her solemn gaze, and the smile he gave her was shy.

"'Twould be a pleasure, milady. I'll see what Cook has left."

"My thanks, Thomas."

Raiven watched him practically stumble over his legs in his haste to fetch her meal.

"Another male heart hopelessly ensnared."

The sound of that deep masculine voice caused her heart to hammer. *Please, God,* she prayed quickly, *don't let me blush when I face him. And please, if it is not too much to ask, don't let me quake and stammer like an idiot.*

Raiven turned slowly to look into the cool gray eyes of her husband. Lord, he was big. He seemed to have grown larger with the night's passing. Anyone who could dwarf her had to be huge, and he most certainly was that. As he approached, she noted that his shadow totally consumed hers. This disturbed her on an instinctive level. The complete absorption of her shadow into his was like an omen of things to come. A chill skittered down her spine, warning her that this man and his way of life would consume her completely if she allowed it. Nay! She was not willing to accept it! With resistance came the strength to lock eyes with his and answer his hailing retort.

"Another, milord? Does that mean perchance that yours was the first or at least among the many?" Raiven smiled with forced brightness that turned genuine when she saw the crackle of gray fire in his eyes telling of her barb's accuracy.

"Many have been the times, madam, when I have labored in what had been called a foolish cause, but as God is merciful, I've learned quickly the merit of any venture 'ere 'tis started." Quynn raked his eyes down her slender form. "My heart is safe."

Instead of becoming insulted by his reference that she was not worth any effort on the part of his heart nor a threat to it, Raiven's amusement grew. She watched Quynn's expression, and she couldn't contain the laughter that escaped her throat. It tinkled merrily about them, bringing a sparkle to the green of her eyes.

Despite himself, the sound captivated him. It also irritated him. He didn't want to like anything about her. He didn't want to think about her moods, which were unpredictable. He didn't want to think about her when she wasn't around. And now that he heard it, he didn't want to crave the sound of her laughter. The woman was tying him in a confused knot, and he didn't like that at all.

Raiven sobered, but her magnificent smile remained. Although she knew she shouldn't, she couldn't help adding a small taunt. "Safe only for now, milord."

The moment the words were out, her smile faded, and her eyes dimmed before she looked away, cursing her witless tongue. Why did she say something like that? She didn't want his heart or anything else of his. Would he now think she wanted him? She hoped not.

Chancing a glance at his face, she waited to hear what he would say, but just then his gaze shifted beyond her, and Raiven knew they were no longer alone. She turned to see Thomas coming with the meal she had requested.

"Here is yer food, milady. I am sorry it took so long, but Cook . . ." He trailed off, looking miserably in Quynn's face. "She was . . ." For the second time Raiven watched his face suffuse with red.

"Already occupied with preparations for the evening meal?" Raiven supplied helpfully when it seemed Thomas could find no diplomatic ending for his sentence.

Thomas grinned in relief. "Aye, milady. That she was. I have stable chores to do, but when ye are done, I'll be able to take ye about like ye asked."

Quynn's voice interrupted her answer. "That will not be necessary."

Both Raiven and Thomas stared at him in surprise.

Quynn's gray eyes were unreadable. "It will be my greatest pleasure to show my bride about. I'll return for you in half an hour's time." With that he left them.

When Thomas had also departed, Raiven sat down to eat and found her appetite had fled. She barely touched the porridge and warm bread Thomas had brought. Her inability to finish the meal was more disappointing when she considered what Thomas obviously endured to get it for her. Clearly, Cook, whoever that was, had no more liking for her than any of the other servants she had met. Still, her appetite had been ruined by her husband's strange announcement, and there was nothing for it.

Leaving the uneaten food on the table, she arose and walked to the entryway of the hall.

As soon as she stepped out in the late morning sun, she saw Quynn standing across the courtyard, conferring with one of his vassals. Immediately she became aware of a fluttery sensation in her stomach. It took a second to realize that it was anticipation for the time she would spend with her husband. Again she admitted that here was a man who need not barter for a wife. True, his home was not excessively impressive, but if he had stood before a maid in nothing save a loincloth and a smile, that one would gladly give up the treasures of the kingdom to be with him.

Raiven's innate honesty forced her to admit that she was attracted to him. However, the same honesty also compelled her to admit that attraction was not enough. She didn't know him. She didn't know if he'd be good for her people. Guirlande and her other holdings had to come before any feelings she could or could not have for him.

To make that decision, she would have to come to know the man beneath the appealing face. Her situation was beyond her control but not totally ruined. She would have to tread cautiously because there was much at stake. If she allowed herself to think with her heart and not with her head, she could lose everything. The most difficult task would be to exercise self-restraint in the face of all the animosity she encountered here. Nevertheless, the first order of procedure was to get to know the man who was now her husband.

Raiven's spirit lifted somewhat when she considered that her first opportunity to do so was at hand. She promised herself she would not waste it.

It turned out to be a glorious day. The sun was high in a blue sky filled with puffy white clouds. It was the first clear sky Raiven had seen since her arrival in England. A breeze blew with gentle warmth, taking away the chill that was wont to linger in the air, and the land before her was an endless verdant panorama.

Quynn's deep voice as he pointed out certain facets of his land was a soothing addition that did not disturb the quiet tranquillity of the day. Pride rang in his voice when he told her of his father and grandfather and their dedication to the land—this land. He spoke of the land in living terms that let Raiven see his deep attachment to it.

They had made a complete circuit about his property when he dismounted beneath a tree, letting Khan's reins drag on the ground. Raiven dismounted from the fine white mare she rode. She had admired the beast when Thomas led her out of the stables. She had watched her spirited antics and felt the depth of muscle in her sleek frame. Her husband owned magnificent horseflesh.

With her thoughts turned back to her husband, she watched him walk to the shallow stream that he had pointed out earlier. Quynn had told her that it ran the width of his property and was partly the reason for the fertility of his land. Now, Raiven watched him bend low and take a drink, after which he liberally splashed his face and hair. He shook his head to free it of the excess water, and Raiven found herself mesmerized by the black waves glinting in the sun.

When Quynn turned to her, she quickly averted her eyes, not realizing what an entrancing picture she presented with the sun creating a brilliant ring around her fair head. Her eyes, before she had glanced away, had sparkled like emeralds, and her full, pink lips parted slightly, giving a glimpse of pearly teeth. Though the bliaut she wore was an ordinary one of dark green, the gold girdle and long blond hair that framed her slender body made the garment seem richer.

Nothing escaped Quynn's hungry gaze. He noted her heaving breasts—caused by either excitement or nervousness—and the urge formed within him to discover from which source the movement sprang. He did not bother to ask her to come to him. He rose and walked to her.

Raiven knew what he would do when he reached her. His eyes had boldly signaled his intent when she glanced back at him. There were many things she wanted to say, things she wanted to know, but despite coherent thoughts forming in her mind, her tongue suffered the delay of confusion. Her lips were parched, and she licked them, unknowingly sending an invitation it would have taken a strong man to resist.

Quynn had no such strength. He did not even make the attempt. His mouth descended to Raiven's. Even before contact was made, his lips were feeling the pleasure of meeting with hers.

Raiven, for her part, could not tell whose groan it was that filled the air between them. It did not seem to matter. For a brief moment she wondered about the strange, wanton woman she was discovering inside herself whenever Quynn touched her, but that, too, was insignificant. She did not care that no words of protest formed either on her lips or in her mind. It suited her just fine that no anger or indignation at being all but sold to this man flared up to disrupt the magic of the moments in Quynn's arms. She knew those feelings were still there in spite of her attraction to him. They merely became inconsequential whispers in the wind when he turned to her with the fire of passion in his eyes.

Hadn't she known that this would happen again between them when she rode off with him? Isn't this what that strange tingling sensation had heralded? It hadn't mattered then, and it didn't now.

Raiven did not realize that they had laid down and was not aware when Quynn had removed both their clothes. All she knew was sensation upon glorious sensation, the joy of being held and loved so intimately, and she reveled in it. She knew that, like the night before, when his arms withdrew, so would this wondrous illusion, but that thought was pushed away. Somehow that pain seemed minuscule compared to the pain of pulling away from him now.

When they had both regained their senses, Raiven again was the first to move away. Hurriedly she dressed, keeping her back to Quynn while she tugged on her clothes and prayed he said nothing to break her fragile control.

She knew when he came to stand behind her, and she sensed the precise moment he reached out to touch her.

"Please do not."

Quynn's brow lowered. "Why, madam, when I have been allowed to do much more than touch?"

Raiven bit her lip, trapped between the truth of his

words and something she couldn't explain satisfactorily even to herself. Anger at herself made her defensive and her words bitter.

"That is precisely why."

Quynn spun her about quickly, his eyes narrowing dangerously. "You will explain."

Raiven raised tormented eyes to him, swallowing hard. Telling him of her loss of control at his touch was unthinkable. "Your king stripped away my rights along with my lands. Only my will is my own, and it is not subject to command. I have no choice in the matter of my body," she ended, praying that he did not know how much of the truth she spoke.

Quynn's eyes turned into gray shards of ice. "Do not say to me 'tis only because of Henry's words that you respond to me. I know when a woman wants me, when she is hungry for my love, and you, madam, were starved. I will allow your disappointment over the loss of your home, but I will never allow you to lie and excuse what takes place between us with the convenience of Henry's order."

Raiven was unprepared for the vehemence of his response. "I was not—"

"You were, and we'll not speak of it further. 'Tis over." His words were curt.

"It is not 'over,' milord. You speak of this thing between us. What is it? Have you a name besides lust for this thing that flares and dies so suddenly? Nay, milord, it is not over." Misery expressed on her face, her eyes probed his for an answer to her questions. "I fear it is only beginning."

Quynn shook his head. "It is over because I say it so."

Raiven's temper ignited. Her eyes began to simmer a golden green as she spat, "You are a fool if you believe that."

Quynn's eyes darkened dangerously at her insult. If any other than his wife had said those words, they would not have lived long enough to regret their error.

Unmindful of his reaction and growing fury, Raiven continued, long since past the point where caution could persuade her to take note of his warlike demeanor and thus soften her tone and words. "Things cannot be so merely because you speak it. You are no better than your king. Words do not make deeds. Is a man strong because he says it? Are his deeds just because he says it? If that is your reason and rationale, my people will never accept you and neither will I. You, milord, are in for a struggle from which you cannot hope to emerge the victor."

Quynn momentarily forgot his anger in the face of her determined declaration. "Am I not now your husband?"

"What does that matter?" Raiven asked, losing patience with him and his refusal to see what lay before them. She had come with him in the hopes of knowing him better. She was not liking what she was finding. Her fleeting hope shriveled and died in her chest.

"Have you not accepted me as your husband by law as well as by action?"

The flame in her eyes leaped to burning yellow as Raiven began to see the bend of his mind. That he should throw that up to her. The man was a swine, a stupid one at that. Did he really think that was all it took?

"I *tolerate* you, milord. Your king has taken away other options. My people are not obligated to produce your heir."

Her voice lashed him with quiet scorn. Instinctively Quynn knew she was more dangerous now in this quiet fury than the unrestrained explosions for which she was known. In addition, he knew he had somehow diminished in her estimation. He immediately brushed that thought aside, telling himself that he didn't care about her opinion of him, as he studied her with new awareness.

"Are you not their lady, left in that position by your father?" Quynn did not miss the grief that clouded her eyes at the mention of her father, but he went on. "Do you not rule? Or is it different from the way I have been told?"

Raiven sighed, her anger blunted. "Can you not see that it matters naught? Aye, I am ruler, made so by my father. Yet even *I* had to prove myself to my people. They did not just accept me. I fought long and hard to win their approval. The de Cortillions have ruled not solely by right, but more importantly by merit. That is something my father labored mightily to teach me."

"I concede the wisdom in your father's words, but I do not anticipate any extreme difficulties."

"As you say, milord," Raiven said, tired of trying to get him to see reason. He would know the truth of it soon enough. She started back toward her mare, but she did not miss his words or the amusement in his voice when he replied, "'Twas what I tried to get you to see from the beginning."

# Chapter

# 9

By the time they reached the hall, dusk was settling and Raiven's fury was not. It was hot enough to refire the day anew. When they arrived at the stable, young Thomas hurried over to assist her even before helping his baron. This gesture served to assuage a great portion of her rage. That her demeanor had not changed entirely was evident by Thomas's hesitant question.

"How was yer ride, milady?"

Raiven favored the boy with a smile, her first of the afternoon. "I would have enjoyed it more had you been my guide. 'Twas pleasant enough with milord." She caught Quynn's frown, and her humor lightened further. She laughed. "Perhaps next time, when you've no other chores to take your time, we can ride together?"

Thomas hesitated, and Raiven wondered if she had embarrassed him because he could not ride. Then she saw the direction of his gaze.

"If it is permitted, milord," she asked Quynn, knowing Thomas would not. For the first time the thought occurred that mayhap here at Havilland, as at several other baronial estates, servants were not permitted to ride the master's horses. Raiven was not merely trying to annoy Quynn; her liking for Thomas was genuine. His was the first friendly face she had encountered in England. There was no one else to ask. Elaine hated riding. She hoped Quynn would not deny her this small thing.

Quynn nodded curtly, and Raiven released the breath she had unknowingly been holding. Looking down at Thomas, Raiven smiled at his face-splitting grin. The boy hurriedly promised to take the best care of her horse. He disappeared with an excited whistle inside the stable and reappeared just as quickly, running back to Quynn, his face flushed.

"Oh, and thank ye too, milord." He bowed quickly, then ran back to the stables.

Raiven wanted to laugh at his exuberance, but instead she looked at Quynn asking, "Is he not a bit small to be doing such hard work?"

The faint smile that hovered about Quynn's lips disappeared. "What would you have him do, madam?"

"I do not know. He just seems small to me, and caring for horses is hard physical labor."

Anger was clearly visible on Quynn's face. "Do not ever again intimate that I am cruel to those in my care. To set it aright, madam, my squire takes care of the horses. Thomas helps him because he wants to one day become a squire. I have consented to this, and I have also told him he must learn to do all things. Therein lies true strength and ability, not the mere brandishing of a sword and the might to slay one's foes."

Raiven's face colored guiltily. She was spared, however, from responding when the thundering hooves of an approaching horse broke the silence between them.

A handsome young man on a chestnut stallion rode to a quick stop beside them. He had laughing gray-green eyes and golden hair. Although his body did not meet the dimensions of the man beside her, the proportions were similar. He was tall, yet his figure was not as imposing as Quynn's had been when she originally viewed him mounted on that black beast of a horse he rode. His thighs and calves were long and strong. The spurs on the back of his heels signified his knighthood.

When Raiven looked back to his face, she found herself subjected to the same intense inspection she had given him. The young man was oblivious to the glower coming from Quynn, and Raiven had to fight the urge to smile. It was to no avail. His face was too open, his smile too friendly. His first words were tinged with laughter.

"Has no one told you, milady, that it is rude to stare, especially in the presence of what I must assume to be your husband?"

Raiven did not take offense at his words. "In this instance, sir, I feel it is a case of the pot calling the cetel, don't you agree?"

He nodded his blond head, sliding lithely to his feet from the great height of his horse's back.

"I am Raiven, late of Guirlande, now of Havilland, and you, sir?" This she added when Quynn did not seem prepared to speak.

Neither of the men missed her stumbling over her name. Both had different reactions. Unexpectedly the blond one laughed uproariously, and the other scowled more deeply.

The amusement of the fellow was totally disproportionate to the situation, and Raiven wondered if perchance he was not in full control of his faculties. When he sobered, he flashed her a look that said he knew what she was thinking. Then he turned to her husband.

"Well, Quynn, neither dwarf nor Amazon, though I would say closer to the latter than the former. Have you written Henry to thank him yet, or shall I?"

Quynn's jaw flexed in irritation. "'Tis fortunate she did not meet you first, Brother. Else she would think we are all a family of half-wits."

"Brother?" Raiven echoed to Quynn in surprise.

He said nothing, leaving his brother to respond. "Tell me you will not hold it against me. I assure you 'twas none of my doing. He was here when I arrived, and I had no choice but accept him."

Bowing before her with smooth grace, he said, "I am James Malcom St. Crowell at your service. Welcome to the family, Sister." Then he kissed her gently on the cheek, earning a warning glare from his elder sibling, at which he laughed.

"Ah, Quynn, 'twas naught but a gesture of affection. There was no need to slay me with your eyes."

With the two standing side by side, Raiven began to see a familial resemblance. Despite the fairness of James's hair next to the ebon darkness of Quynn's and the flecks of green in his eyes that made them seem more hazel than gray, she could see definite similarities. They shared the same high forehead and angular face. Even through the beard James wore, Raiven could see a sameness in the strength of jaw.

She turned to Quynn. "I did not know you had a brother."

"Nor did you bother to ask."

James stepped between them before Raiven could retaliate to Quynn's attack. "There's time enough to learn of us. It must be unsettling enough to be married so suddenly." Beneath the lightness of his tone there was unmistakable intent. "Give her time, Quynn. We'll grow on her."

Raiven liked this new brother-in-law. When he turned back to her after rapping his horse on the hindquarters to send it toward the stables, the smile she gave him was warm and sincere.

James blinked twice at the sheer brilliance of it. Then he offered her an equally bright smile of his own that heightened the twinkle in his eyes. Taking her arm in his, he started toward the hall.

"I suspect," he began slowly, "that there is more to you than your beauty, Sister."

His comment disconcerted her so because one of Quynn's first remarks to her had been so different—exactly different. Raiven laughed at the irony of it. "And I am beginning to think there is more to the English than threats and orders."

"I shan't dare to ask what is meant by that statement," James returned with feigned disdain. He looked back at

Quynn then and gave an all too good imitation of a shudder.

Raiven laughed again, Quynn glared, and James shrugged in mock innocence as they walked into the hall.

From the aroma permeating the room, Raiven knew dinner was not far off, but as the hour was early and the men had not yet come in from their drills, the trestle table where she had tried to eat her morning meal was clear. She was surprised then when James said, "'Tis glad I am not to be waiting for dinner. My appetite is such that 'twould make naught of an entire boar, tusks and all."

Accurately reading the silent question in her eyes, he added, "Come with me, fair damsel."

Raiven's curiosity would not be denied. She followed him to a wide door near the hall stairs. Once she stepped through the door, she saw the reason the scent of the unseen food had been so strong.

A mouthwatering array of food laid out in three place settings on a table smaller than the one in the center room of the hall met her gaze. The entire room was a fraction of the center hall. Scattered around the fireplace she had now grown used to seeing were chairs covered in tapestry of the same colors she had seen in Quynn's bedchamber. In a corner near the window stood a hearpe, a musical instrument that made entrancing sounds when the strings were pulled.

Raiven walked over to the instrument, admiring the quality of its workmanship. Absently she plucked a few notes, and even her untutored hands produced a lovely sound.

"Do you play?"

"Nay," Raiven responded softly to James's query. "I have always been fascinated by it. My mother used to try to teach me. She was sure there was some ladylike ability lying beneath the surface. Alas," she continued ruefully, "'twas lying so deep 'twas not worth the effort to bring it up."

"Darrielle used—"

"No one plays here. 'Tis more for decoration than aught else."

James looked to Quynn with amazement. An unspoken communication passed between them.

"Let us eat."

At Quynn's brusque command, an oppressive silence fell over the room, and Raiven knew it would be futile to ask anything further. Still she was curious about this strange hall. She had never seen one like it.

"What room is this?" she asked James as he held her chair.

James shrugged, and Raiven sensed a strange reluctance in him to speak. From his expression, she almost didn't expect an answer, but he surprised her by saying, "For naught better a name, you might call it a family room. No other but members of the St. Crowell family are allowed to enter."

Raiven gave this some thought. "How unique. I have never heard of the like."

Most halls had only a large central room where the baron and his knights, all seated at various positions according to rank and importance, partook of the meal in one place. Naturally there was the buttery, the pantry, and, at a farther distance from the house, the kitchen.

"Whose thought was this?"

"'Twas our mother's," James provided, pausing between bites of bread and tender venison.

Quynn ate on, seemingly unaware that they were present, let alone that conversation was taking place around him.

Raiven took a dainty bite of bread as she considered the other unusual things she had noted. "That passageway on the other side of the stairs, what is that?"

"'Tis only the servants' passage. Mother had it done after she once had to go to the kitchen in the rain."

Raiven nodded, admiring the woman's wisdom. "Your mother must have been a remarkable lady. She seemed to have a strong sense of family and feeling for others."

James stopped eating. A smile of remembrance curled his lips. "She was that. She also had Father instruct his men to build the fireplaces you see. Father ranted on about the dangers of the contraption, but Mother would not relent. She detested the cold and insisted that no one should be so inside their home."

James smiled fondly in memory. His gaze fell back on the woman across from him. "I feel you would have liked her, Raiven, and she you. I may call you Raiven, may I not? 'Tis foolish to constantly say milady."

"I insist that you do, and I thank you for your kindness."

Ignoring the burn of Quynn's gaze at his wife's soft tone, James leaned over to lay his hand on Raiven's, giving it a gentle squeeze. One part of his mind registered that finally Quynn was at least acknowledging their presence, while another part sought to tweak his attention even further.

"I spoke truth, not kindness."

They both jumped at the thunderous sound of Quynn's chair falling back to the floor.

"Perhaps 'twould be better if I took my meal elsewhere." The icy venom in his voice was unmistakable.

Raiven stared, at a loss for words. James, on the other hand, was not having any difficulty understanding his brother.

"If you wish, Brother."

Quynn's eyes sizzled with fire that he dispensed equally between them. Leaving the remainder of his meal untouched, he left the room without another word.

Raiven's expression showed her worry and confusion when she looked at James. "Is there something mayhap I should know about your brother, James?"

James smiled at her unconscious use of his Christian name, especially since he had not heard her use Quynn's name once. "If you're asking if there are any loons in our family, 'tis safe to say there are none."

Raiven sighed in relief until he added, "Until now," and looked toward the door where Quynn had just departed.

Raiven looked away uneasily, and James's shout of laughter rang out. "Ah, Raiven, no matter the beginning circumstance, I am glad you are here. 'Twill be good for my brother to be married to one such as you."

She knew he teased her to put her at her ease, and she was grateful. Nevertheless the smile she gave him was still weak. "I do not know the merit in it yet. Neither of us seem to be capable of finishing a meal when the other is about. In a moon's time we may both be so weak from lack of sustenance that *we* dissolve long 'ere our marriage."

James's laughter burst forth again, causing Raiven to wonder at his attitude toward her.

When he sobered, Raiven questioned him. "I thought you would resent me as Quynn does. Even the servants share his feelings. Why are you different?"

Instantly his smile vanished. "Has anyone said aught disrespectful?"

"None," Raiven replied quickly, distrusting the sudden quiet tone of his voice and the stillness of his body. "It is only I thought that you would blame me for the ire of your king."

"Shall I point out that he is now your king as well?"

The look on Raiven's face gave him his answer.

"Nay, I thought not," he said with a laugh, then became serious. "For a time I did blame you, especially when I discovered that Havilland might be at risk. Then I tried to see things from your view, and I understood. I might have acted in the same way, not caring of the consequences to another. In the end you did what was needed. To my mind that is all that counts."

"I begin to think Henry forced her on the wrong brother. Had I known of your instant attraction, James, I would have, until my last breath, tried to persuade the king to serve her up to you like the main dish at a royal dinner instead of to me."

Quynn gave no chance for response, leaving as silently as he had come.

Raiven glared at the now empty portal, while James sighed ruefully.

"Do not worry overmuch, Raiven." His smile was

devilish as he went on. "'Tis only the sorrowful plight of any loon on an eve when a full moon is due."

Quynn did not seek their bed that night. To Raiven's astonishment, when the full blush of dawn crept through the window, she had to admit that she missed his presence. In just two days he had made himself a part of her life. She accepted that realization uneasily, disliking the truth of it. Despite her anger at his cruel words in front of his brother, she had still wanted him beside her. Her reasons were unclear and too unsettling to examine closely, but she did know it was more than a simple desire to know what had irritated him.

Rising, she wondered where Elaine was as she pulled her chamber robe about her. It was at that moment that Quynn entered the room without knocking.

"Do you always enter a room unannounced?" was Raiven's surly greeting to him.

"Good morn to you, too, madam," Quynn replied sardonically. "In answer to your question, the only room I enter unannounced is my own." He raised a black brow, daring her to speak further on the subject. When she did not, Quynn moved over to the basin and splashed water on his face and hands.

"Milord," she began, missing the darkening of his brow, "if you would have Elaine—"

"My name is Quynn. Remember to use it. 'Tis easy enough to say."

Raiven took a deep breath, set back by his rudeness. "Very well then," she nodded, "will you send Elaine to me? I do not know where she sleeps, and usually she is here when I awaken, but this morn she was not."

"She was here, but I sent her away."

"For what purpose?" she started, then remembered that *he* had not been here last night. "When?"

"When what?"

"When did you send her away?"

"Earlier this morn. She was awaiting you, and I told her you would call when you were ready for her services. You no longer sleep alone, madam."

Without thought, Raiven replied with rancor, "I did last night."

Quynn's look of surprise gave way to a burst of laughter, which made Raiven cringe. "So you missed me, little one? Now that I know of your craving for my company, I'll not stay away at night anymore."

Raiven was about to deny her desire for his company when he interrupted her.

"I came in early this morn. You were asleep, and I sent away your maid, not wishing for either of us to disturb you. Now that we speak of it, I must admit I do not wish to face a gawking girl every morn when first I open my eyes."

Raiven opened her mouth to say that she and Elaine were the same age, then thought better of it. She had already made enough of a fool of herself. Her lips tightened into a straight line, and Quynn tilted his head to the side in silent invitation for her to speak her mind, his face still reflecting traces of amusement.

Raiven held her temper and her tongue. Finally he nodded, then started to leave. "I shall send your servant to you." He stopped at the door. "If 'tis your desire to see James before he leaves, I would suggest you proceed with haste."

"James is leaving? I thought he had only just returned home last eve."

Quynn spoke slowly, measuring his words, knowing what his wife's reaction was going to be. "That he did. Now he is leaving again for a longer duration. He will be leaving for France within the hour."

Raiven's heart clenched. "Why is he journeying to France?" she asked, deliberately ignoring the only possible answer to the question.

"Do you always have ceaseless questions?"

Raiven was not put off by his apparent exasperation. She heard something else behind it.

"It is rude to answer one question with another. Tell me please, why does he go to France?"

Quynn saw how distraught she was, and he gentled his

answer. "I fear you already know why. He goes to assume stewardship over our lands there."

"Our lands? I was not aware *your* family had property in France." Raiven knew she was acting perversely, yet she couldn't stop.

"Know you well to which lands I refer." The hard edge was back in his voice. "You knew a steward would be sent to oversee the estates."

"You must jest! Surely you do not think to send a boy to manage such a troublesome region?!"

Quynn frowned at her reference to his brother as a boy. "Do I mistake the matter or was I not informed that *you* managed the estates?"

"We have had these words before. You know you are not in error. But it is not the same." Why would he not see?

"Am I now to understand that you are a man?" Quynn asked, his eyes roving over her in search of evidence to his preposterous question.

"You play at words! James is a foreigner. He does not know our ways or customs. Does he even speak the tongue? The people will never accept him. He is too . . ."

Quynn waited for her to finish her thought, but Raiven could not. She had been about to say that James was too young. If Quynn had not listened to any of her other arguments, he would surely laugh at that one. James was three years her senior.

Feeling the futility of it all, she ended instead with "They will never accept him."

The look that now came to Quynn's face was hideous to see. His eyes narrowed dangerously, and his body radiated venom. "Are you saying they will seek to slay him?"

Quynn's angry face was superimposed by the vision of Jacques as she had last seen him.

Unfortunately, Quynn took her silence for defense, and in two strides he came to her, shaking her roughly. The image of her brother shattered, replaced with her husband's angry visage.

"I tell you now they had *better* accept him, and no treachery had best befall him or they will all rue the day of their birth. They will either accept him or my vengeance."

Raiven's face whitened, her thoughts still of her brother and his anger. "They are my people," she whispered through the terror constricting her throat.

"And he is my brother," Quynn countered with deadly quiet. "'Twould do them well to remember that."

When he left, slamming the door behind him, Raiven's knees weakened with dread. There would be trouble, of that she was sure. A cold chill frittered up her spine, leaving in its wake the assurance that tragedy would come and the torment of not knowing how it would come or to whom.

# Chapter
# •10•

James had mounted his horse by the time Raiven stepped from the hall into the outer yard. His smile was warm and appreciative of her appearance. Deep understanding reflected in his eyes and said he knew of her disagreement with his brother. Instinctively Raiven knew that Quynn had said nothing but that James's intuitiveness coupled with his knowledge of his brother had given him that insight.

Raiven's expression was wary as she watched him approach. She did not want to talk about Quynn. She did not want to talk about their differences. By the time James halted his horse beside her, Raiven did not want to talk at all, and she regretted her decision to come tell him good-bye.

She glanced away, uncomfortable beneath James's penetrating stare. She didn't like the fact that he seemed to be trying to discern her most intimate thoughts, but protest required words, and she couldn't trust herself to speak.

*Why won't you just leave?* she screamed inwardly while waiting for him to speak or to go. Unable to endure his mute scrutiny any longer, Raiven finally blurted out, "What is it?"

Although it looked as if he were trying to hold back a smile, his eyes were solemn when he replied, "I have been trying to decide whether I should speak my mind to you."

"Well?" Raiven prompted when he fell silent again.

James stared at her a few minutes longer, then he seemed to come to a decision. After looking around and spotting Quynn talking to another of his knights, James leaped from his horse saying in a low voice, "I have much I would say to you and little time to say it. Walk with me apace."

Strangely, Raiven followed him without thought. Here was another shared characteristic of the St. Crowell men. They both could be commanding when they wanted. Of course, to Raiven's mind, Quynn had this trait in an overabundance, whereas James tempered his.

They walked a few feet away from where the men were still performing a few last-minute preparations for the journey. Finding a quiet spot along the outer wall, James stopped.

Raiven now had her back to the frenzied activity, whereas he faced it. She thought he did this deliberately, and his first words confirmed her suspicions.

"'Tis about Quynn," he said, looking past her shoulder to where his brother stood, then back to her. "I want you to understand that I speak now not in defense of my brother, but that you may understand him."

When Raiven realized he was waiting for her acknowledgment of his motives before proceeding, she nodded, saying nothing.

"Very well. There are certain things you should know about the man you have married. Things I do not believe he will tell you. He would probably run me through for what I am about to say, but Quynn is not as hard as he appears. Aye, he is strong. However, only his enemies need fear his might. For those he loves, his strength is naught but a comfort. Since the time he was three and ten he has single-handedly managed this estate, with its many problems; supported and defended the serfs, tenants, and all others under his care; raised a younger brother; and tried to cope with a grief no young person should have to suffer alone.

"Our parents and sister died twelve years ago. 'Twas particularly hard on Quynn because all the burden of responsibility fell to him. Our father had always prized strength and detested weakness of any kind. He made it clear to Quynn that only a strong man could maintain Havilland. He felt emotion made men weak and interfered with the manly execution of duties. He felt it a hindrance to be stamped out at all costs. There were no exceptions."

James's eyes took on a faraway look. "When they died, Quynn did not allow himself to grieve. I think he thought it would mean he was weak. I never saw him cry. But I cried. Oddly enough, Quynn encouraged it, but he never gave in to the pain. 'Tis strange that although he adheres to Father's principle, he did not foist it upon me. He taught me the value of strength, but I was allowed to know and feel other things that I am certain Father would have forbidden had he lived."

His eyes focused on the stunned look on Raiven's face, and he quickly added, "'Twas not that Father was a cruel man. He was just one of . . . definite opinion."

James said no more, giving Raiven a chance to reflect on what he said thus far. His words certainly clarified a few things. She had already noted the vast difference in personalities between the two brothers. Now she understood why. She had surmised that Quynn held his feelings in constant control, saying nothing, sharing nothing. True, it was evidence of great internal strength; however, it was also a lonely existence. It was as if he lacked or ignored the knowledge that when pain is shared, it lessens, and when joy is shared, it increases. In her heart, she began to grieve for the young boy whose life had never permitted him to be a child. Inside, she shed tears not only for his loss, but for him.

With shock, Raiven realized what she was doing. "Why have you told me this?" she snapped, resenting this sudden revelation about Quynn. She didn't want to feel any understanding or pity for him.

James was not fooled by her outward hostility. He could see the compassion she tried to suppress. "I feel you will be a challenge for him. I feel you will be the one to break through the shell he has erected to protect himself from us all. You can give back to him what he has been denied."

"In one day's time you know all this?" Raiven asked sarcastically. "I do not love him," she denied emphatically.

James's eyebrow rose. "Does it take love to be compassionate?" he returned, ignoring her question. "Need you love him to be understanding? Must love be there before you can share with him of yourself? 'Tis odd, I always thought those were the things that led to love and not the other way around."

Raiven heard the rebuke in his voice and tried not to feel chastened by it.

"It is different for us."

"Why?"

Raiven made a rather unladylike snort. "You know the why of it better than I. We were not brought together because of anything as noble or lofty as love or compassion; we were given to each other because of the ambitious greed of your king."

"Whatever the reason," James continued doggedly, "you are now wed. Is that not reason enough to try? Do you not want to love him?"

Raiven squirmed under the directness of his question and his gaze. "That is not a fair question. This thing between us rings more of war than of love."

"Well, didn't someone once say that love is a kind of warfare?"

Raiven sighed deeply, looking above his head to the sky. James's words made her confused. Since coming to England, nothing was as it should be. She didn't have answers to James's questions. He was relentless in his pursuit of . . . Of what? She didn't even know precisely what he wanted from her. Did he want her to love his brother? She doubted the possibility of such a thing. Besides, her loving Quynn did not, in itself, assure

Quynn's happiness. He would have to love her in return. If she doubted the possibility of her loving him, one thing was certain, the love of Quynn of Havilland was something she'd never have. She didn't know if she wanted it.

"Tell me of your sister. Was she the youngest?"

James did not blink an eye at the abrupt change of conversation. "Nay, she was not. She was a special person. I suppose all brothers say that of their sisters, but I truly mean it. A smile would come to your face when she entered a room. She was kind. She was loving. In many ways she was a little replica of my mother. She and Quynn were extremely close. I suppose that was only natural. They were twins."

Raiven's surprise was genuine. "Twins? What was her name?"

"Darrielle. She was the one I mentioned last eve. The hearpe in the family room was hers and my mother's."

The subtle shifting of James's gaze alerted Raiven to the fact that her husband was approaching. She had more questions she wanted to ask, but the time was lost.

She could feel James tense beside her, and in a soft voice she answered his unspoken question. "I will give thought to what you have said."

He smiled at her in gratitude, and it came to her mind that she would miss him. In the span of one day, a rapport seemed to have sprung up between them. He possessed the ability to understand her without words being spoken. He had only to look at her, and he knew things about her.

What was even more disconcerting was that she understood James, too. Raiven found this feeling almost as unsettling as the fiery emotions Quynn evoked. Nothing was proceeding the way she had thought. She had never expected to care for anyone she met in England. Yet that was exactly what James was asking of her and what was happening on its own. Since arriving, she had become aware that it was not just her life Henry had disrupted. This revelation left her open to acceptance, and acceptance left her open to caring.

Impulsively she reached out to embrace James regardless of Quynn's presence. Before she pulled away, she whispered in French, "Take care. Return to us safe and sound, my new brother."

James stiffened. When he looked down into her eyes, he read the turmoil there. He knew she'd spoken in a language that she assumed he did not understand, but he did not so much as bat an eyelash to reveal that he understood her words. However, he could not hide his confusion.

Raiven smiled softly at the question in his eyes. "I could not say the words in English. Good-bye, James." She gave no other explanation. Excusing herself, she started back to the hall.

Quynn stared after her departing figure with a scowl on his face, her words of that morning still ringing in his head.

"What did she say to you?"

"'Twas naught," James replied absently. He, too, watched his brother's wife walk away. "Quynn, I have something to ask of you."

Quynn said nothing, but he gave his brother his full attention.

"Would you allow Raiven time? I feel you will not be displeased."

"Leave my wife to me." His tone brooked no further discussion.

"Very well then. I only pray you have a ken what you are doing. Many men would be happy to have her—without her lands."

Quynn's scowl of a moment ago seemed mild in comparison with the expression on his face now. "How do you know so well a woman you met only a day ago?" he demanded, unknowingly echoing Raiven's words.

James shrugged. "She reminds me of Darrielle," to which Quynn's only response was a snort.

"As you wish, Quynn. But do not say you have not been warned. Remember my words."

Quynn's voice came harshly. "Is that a threat? Do you speak from your own desire, James?"

James stiffened. "I will not dignify those words with an answer. I am glad to be leaving. It has always been a particular sorrow of mine to see my brother, who I respect and admire, behave the fool. Throughout the years you have not sought my counsel nor heeded my words in many things, but I tell you this: if you persist in this lunacy, you will lose her, king's order or not. You are well familiar with loss, but I tell you that that loss will be more tragic than any other."

Taking Quynn's continued silence for obstinacy, James turned away to mount his horse. He was seated when Quynn came to him, grabbing his horse's reins.

"We should not part in anger." Again he echoed his wife's words. "I will give thought to your words."

James nodded, satisfied. "I will guard your trust with all my strength."

"See to your back. Godspeed."

As James galloped away, Quynn started for the stables. He stopped when he noticed his wife in the entryway of the hall. He had not observed her return. Changing the direction of his steps, he headed toward her, wondering if she had heard James's words. He himself felt so inhibited by the weight of his brother's proclamation that when he finally stood before her, he didn't know what to say. He was surprised to see a gentle flush suffuse her face as they continued to stare into each other's eyes. For the briefest instant, her gaze wavered.

Raiven's voice was quiet with uncertainty. "I wondered if we might ride awhile. I have need to speak with you so none would overhear."

Ignoring his initial eager response, Quynn asked, "Can it not wait? There is much I must do."

"It is important to me. I shall try not to detain you overly long."

Indecision warred within him until Raiven added softly, "Please."

Stopping his squire as he passed, Quynn called out, "Have my and my lady's horses saddled."

With a quick "Aye, milord," the young man was off to do as Quynn ordered. By the time he and Raiven arrived at the stables, the stablemaster had saddled the giant black, and Thomas was leading out the white mare Raiven had been using.

Raiven smiled warmly at the boy as he checked the cinching of the straps of her saddle. "You have done well, Thomas. You do your baron proud."

Thomas's face lit up at the enthusiastic praise. "Thank ye, milady, but truly I did naught but help."

From the corner of her eye, Raiven saw that Quynn had already mounted, but she took a moment longer to speak to Thomas.

"You only increase your worth with your honesty," she added, then, realizing that her words were embarrassing the boy, quickly changed the subject. "She is a fine beast, is she not? Tell me, Thomas, how is she called?"

"Sunstar, milady."

Raiven inspected the horse. "It suits her."

Khan took a snorting side step, and Raiven knew that was Quynn's way of telling her to come along. She was certain the great war beast would have stood still as stone for an eternity until he received a signal from Quynn.

"I shan't keep you any longer, Thomas. Again, my thanks."

She'd barely sat in the saddle when Khan surged forward. Raiven prodded Sunstar into a gallop to follow, not overtake. The mare, though swift, could not achieve the fleetness of the stallion her husband rode, and today Quynn rode as a man tormented.

After a distance of about a furlong, he seemed to recall her presence, and Khan slowed. Raiven spurred Sunstar to gain his side. The mare blew softly, whereas Khan showed no evidence of exertion at all. She patted the mare's neck, whispering a word of encouragement before turning her attention to the path Quynn had chosen.

He was leading them in a westerly direction, and Raiven looked at the splendid landscape around her. They halted by a hilltop overlooking a low-lying valley. They seemed to be at the highest point of his property.

From this spot, everything could be seen. The green carpeting of the lush field of grass was even more striking because of the array of various autumn blossoms. The trees, tall and straight, had their branches spread luxuriantly, and the crisp green, yellow, and orange leaves created a delightful canopy.

Raiven was content to merely look in silent wonder at the beauty around her until she realized Quynn was waiting for her to speak. Despising herself for her lack of courage, she decided to talk about the scenery rather than the issue close to her heart.

"It is beautiful here. It feels as if we are perched atop the clouds with the world as our window."

Quynn grunted. He, too, stared at the multicolored vista below and around them. When he spoke, Raiven shifted in her saddle to gaze at his profile, and suddenly an entirely different spectacular view claimed her attention. In relief against the blue of the sky, his facial outline was unspeakably beautiful. His nose, long and straight; his lips, full and sensuously curved; and his jawline, strong and firm, looked like a statue hewn with perfect precision by the hands of a master sculptor.

Raiven was so absorbed in watching him that she almost missed his words.

"Aye, the view is awesome. I believe 'tis one of the reasons my great-grandfather chose to settle at Havilland over any others."

"Where were your people from before then?"

"Does it matter? England is my home. I am as loyal to it as anyone whose family has been here for generations."

There was a strange note to his voice, a near defensiveness to it that Raiven found perplexing. The question was a simple enough one. Why was he reacting as if she had insulted him?

"I did not question your loyalty, only your origin. If I have trespassed, I apologize."

Quynn's gaze shifted abruptly to hers. "My great-grandfather was Norwegian."

"Oh," Raiven replied quietly.

Quynn shook his head, amused at her reaction, or rather her lack of reaction. For so long he had experienced distrust and suspicion when the subject under discussion was his ancestry that he had come to expect it as normal, which was why he usually responded defensively to any questions about his lineage.

"You truly do not understand, do you?" he questioned.

"Was there something I missed? I asked where your family had been before they came here, and you answered that they were from Norway. I *did* know that Norwegians came from Norway."

Quynn's lips turned up slightly at the corners, and for the first time since she had known him, Raiven saw a twinkle in his usually brooding gray eyes.

"How well do you know the history of the invasion by the Normans?"

Raiven shrugged. "About as well as any other. William the Conqueror of Normandy felt cheated that Edward the Confessor named Harold II king of England when it had been agreed previously that William would be king upon his death. He later invaded England to seize the throne. He and Harold met in battle at Hastings, Harold was defeated, England was forced to bow to William as king."

Now Quynn did smile. "You speak so dispassionately, as if you were merely reciting facts from history."

"Am I not?"

"Have you not yet realized that those long-ago events shaped the future of two countries not only on a political level, but on an individual basis as well? Henry Plantagenet is a descendant of William the Conqueror. Ever since that time, your country and mine have been irrevocably entwined, and always bloodshed has been the result."

Quynn continued. "All thought that the problems were solved when William was crowned on December 25, 1066, but this was not to be. In reality, the problems were only just beginning. I make no pretense at being a scholar. However, one need not be to know that the newest turn of events—Henry's marriage to Eleanor—

will not bring about a peaceful existence. Perhaps generations from now, they will know peace, but definitely not in our lifetime.

"Many lives were irreversibly changed because William felt cheated. You are here because William felt cheated."

He watched her face, searching for a reaction to his words.

Raiven thought over all he said, certain there was some point of particular import that he felt she missed. "What has all this history done directly to you?"

"Am I not now married to a woman who hates the ground upon which I tread?" he asked.

Somehow Raiven was certain that was not all of it. She chewed her bottom lip in thought. "What else has it done?"

Quynn gave a burst of ugly laughter. "Is that not enough?"

"Aye," Raiven answered slowly, "but there is more. Why do I feel that you have paid your own personal price for that moment of history?"

"I do not hold the exclusive right to suffering. My family has been cast into an unsavory light because of things beyond their control. During that time, you either chose a side or one was chosen for you. My family was not different. We were loyal to Harold II and would have fought beside him. However, Harold had other plans. He recognized the threat from the north—from the Norwegians. He knew that Tostig, his rebellious brother, had allied with Harold III of Norway. He had hoped to weaken the forces from the north, and he felt our family was the way to achieve that."

In spite of herself, Raiven was captivated. "How?" she asked when Quynn fell silent. "How could your family's being Norwegian help to weaken the threat from the north? You were only one family. What could you do?"

"Ah, but we were not just any Norwegian family. My family was allied with Magnus I of Norway, who until 1047 co-ruled with Harold III."

"I begin to see." Raiven sighed, truly intrigued by the

story unfolding before her. "Harold of England probably felt that your great-grandfather would be able to supply aid in the form of men."

"Or, at the very least, in the way of splitting the unity of the invading Norwegians. Recall that Harold of England went from the battle of Stamford Bridge in Yorkshire straight to his defeat at Hastings. Many feel that if he had had more men to deploy, things would have been different. They feel William was victorious only because he fought a wearied king whose forces were sorely stressed."

"What happened to your great-grandfather? What happened to Harold's plan?"

Quynn's face hardened. "I do not know. Treachery abounded then as it still does. According to my father, Harold had my great-grandfather awaiting word from him. He did not want any to know of his plan until the last moment, then there would be no counterplan. He and the men he amassed waited, but there was never any word from Harold. Next he knew, Harold had died, and England suffered an ignominious defeat at William's hand at Hastings."

Quynn looked down into the valley, his voice harsh. "When my great-grandfather finally returned to England, a cloud of suspicion plagued him the remainder of his life.

"None realized that there was naught else for him to do but return here and continue on. The stench of death and the sting of loss put any such thought from their minds. During a time when all were being stripped of lands to satisfy the greed of the men who fought with William, Great-grandfather was allowed to maintain his. Only those who had betrayed England or played the harlot for William at the expense of their country were granted such a privilege. You can imagine the bitterness directed at our family by those who had been stripped of their lands and those who felt that, through their treachery, they deserved to take possession of Havilland.

"Father once speculated that William purposely permitted Great-grandfather to keep his possessions because it gave the Saxons something to chew. It served as a distraction to keep them occupied with things other than the Normanizing of their country. To my mind that seems a bit extreme, but who can say what another's thoughts were or were not at the time? Who can say why Harold, after conceiving such an ingenious plan, never implemented it?"

His jaw flexed, his hands tightened on the reins, and Khan immediately began to shuffle and jerk his head back and forth at this treatment.

Raiven's eyes moved from his tightly clenched fists to the iron outline of his jaw. "Has the cloud disappeared?" she asked softly.

"Nay. It lingers still, ever ready to burst above our heads like the worst storm, leaving us devastated and bereft of home, pride, and honor. By all that's good, I vow, 'twill not happen as long as I breathe."

Raiven believed him. The ferocity of his words left her stunned. A threat to his home would not be taken lightly or tolerated. She well remembered her reaction when she learned she might lose Guirlande. She also remembered that she had not cared that Henry had issued the same ultimatum to her betrothed. She now realized what it was that he held most strongly against her. Quynn would have been able to accept her forced intrusion into his life. However, her obstinacy had almost cost him the home and pride of his family name, and that was unendurable.

No wonder Quynn had refused to ask anything of Henry, especially her request that he reconsider their marriage. His position was worse than hers. Raiven cast her eyes around the beauty and deceptive peace of the scenic view, recalling a favorite phrase of her father's: Things are rarely as they seem, and even when you think you know the way of it, you do not.

That certainly applied here, but where did that leave her?

Quynn's deep voice broke through her troubled thoughts.

"I'm sure that neither the beauty of the land nor my

ancestry nor the desire to understand political machinations was the reason you wished to speak privately to me. We have already wasted more time than I intended. What was it you wished to say to me?"

At the moment, so powerfully drawn into the picture he had painted, Raiven had forgotten what it was she wanted to speak to him about. Now that he had brought the topic abruptly back to its beginning, she found she didn't know how to word her request.

Quynn looked over to her and sighed. "Do not hedge. I have come to expect a directness from you that I have found in few men. Even though there are circumstances where it is unappreciated"—his eyes flashed briefly, and Raiven knew he was thinking of her public denial of him as a fitting mate—"your directness has my admiration."

Raiven swallowed hard. She had not expected him to speak to her thus. She was unable to speak with the directness he claimed to admire, because his backhanded compliment tied her tongue in knots.

She opened her mouth to speak, then closed it. She did that twice, and still she was no closer to broaching the subject. All the while she was aware that Quynn watched her and that the slow sensuous smile that lifted his mobile lips was one of amusement. The effect of the smile was so devastating that what little thoughts she had gathered fled.

Raiven turned to him ready to burst forth with her petition when one dark brow rose, and he smiled at her again, as if he knew the turmoil she felt.

If the other smile had been heart stopping, this one nearly made Raiven slide bonelessly from Sunstar's back. She at once hated and loved it. She hated her reaction to it. Yet she loved the fact that he could look so gently at her and smile as if her presence was not something terribly unpleasant that had been thrust into his life.

However, her tongue still refused to obey her mind's dictates, and Quynn tired of the wait. Sliding effortlessly to the ground, he walked over to Raiven and, lifting her by the waist, set her on the ground between his broad chest and Sunstar's side.

His arms, wrapped so possessively about her waist, brought forth memories Raiven would rather have left undisturbed. She could feel herself blush, and she was certain Quynn was successfully reading her thoughts when his smile broadened and a wicked twinkle lit his eyes. Aggrieved, she tried to pull away only to find herself held fast.

"I would give much to know your thoughts at this moment." The laughter in his voice caused her blush to deepen.

Raiven responded tersely, "I have the feeling you already hold more information than I am comfortable with."

Quynn's amusement grew apace with Raiven's agitation. "What say you? I am no seer. How can I know unless you *relent* and tell me? Even then I would not know if 'tis truth or fabrication."

Raiven's voice thinned as Quynn's thickened with merriment. "So you trust my honesty to an extent."

"Do you throw out challenges, milady? If so, be warned that I pick up all gauntlets."

Something in his eyes told her that it would not be wise to pursue that vein of conversation, but Quynn would have none of her silent diplomacy.

"Shall we test this quality of honesty? If I ask what your thoughts were, would I receive the truth?"

Raiven smiled slyly, seeing a way to trap him by his words. "One would not know until the trial was undertaken. Are you now throwing down the gauntlet?"

Her sweet laugh rang out at his perplexed expression.

Quynn's eyes flashed. "It now lays at your feet, madam. What were your thoughts when your face blushed like a white rose at dawn?"

"It is an easy challenge: my thoughts were of us."

"Is that all your answer, your thoughts 'were of us'? No explanation of such obviously torrid thoughts?"

Raiven tutted in feigned woefulness. "Now you attempt to change the nature of the challenge. The substance of my thoughts was not in question, only the subject. It was an honest answer to a direct question." The light of triumph shone from her eyes.

After a moment of staring, Quynn burst out laughing. "I am glad women are not, as a rule, my adversaries. I would cry unfair, madam, but 'twould make me appear the resentful loser. I bow to your quickness of wit and your honesty."

He released her waist, taking a few steps away from her. Raiven watched him closely, fascinated by this flash of yet another facet of his personality. His moods changed so swiftly, from dark and pensive to sensuous and teasing to calm and relaxed. Now seemed a good time to introduce the reason she wanted to speak to him.

"I have a request to make of you."

Like the mist before the heat of the sun, his relaxed mood vanished. Had she not seen the startling metamorphosis, she would not have believed it possible. When he turned to her, there was a hardness in his eyes she had not seen since the day he had come for her at the docks. He stood aggressively, braced for attack and ready to do battle.

"Why do you stare at me like that? Is it impossible to believe my request would be a simple one, well within your power to grant?" Raiven hated the defensive edge in her voice, but his attitude brought out that side of her.

"At last we come to the meat of the meal. No more teasing games to distract. No more paltry compliments or false interest in family for the purpose of disarming, just the truth. What do you want?"

For some reason it hurt Raiven to think that in his mind all that had transpired between them was a ploy to disarm him into agreeing to whatever insane idea he imagined she'd propose.

"Your request, madam?" Quynn repeated. "I grow bored with delay."

Raiven's anger fired. "It is right you are, milord," she snapped, forgetting his command to use his Christian name. "I had hoped to distract you with false concern and pretty words. Since that ploy has failed, I shall be forced to change my request. Originally it was my design to ask you to overthrow your king. However, your mood has soured toward me. Therefore I'll save that petition for another time. Instead I shall ask if a letter from me can be delivered to my brother in France. I know it is not major political news—certainly not on par with old family intrigue—but it is all my feeble mind could concoct since you saw through my former plan so quickly."

Quynn felt the sudden urge to laugh again. Squelching it, he maintained his stern expression. "'Tis not possible."

Raiven blinked. "What is not? Not possible for me to write? I assure you I can both read and write very well in several languages."

*Why does that not surprise me?* he wondered. Quynn knew she was a unique woman. Still, her request could not be granted. It amazed him that he felt saddened to refuse her. He sensed what it cost her to ask anything of him, especially when she was so unsure of him and their situation.

He tried to phrase his refusal gently. "Unfortunately your talent shall be wasted. Your letter cannot be delivered to your brother."

Raiven's voice was a whisper in the stillness. "Are we at war? Has the Channel been blocked? Speak plainly, milord. Why can not a simple letter be delivered to him?"

Again he was taken aback by her rage. *'Twill take time to become accustomed to her true anger,* he mused. *Her voice softens like a serpent's sigh, the only true indicator of her turmoil being hot yellow flecks that brighten her eyes.*

"Perchance have you been struck dumb, milord? Answer me!" Raiven snapped heedlessly, angered and hurt at his refusal to grant so small a favor.

Quynn stiffened, no longer enchanted by her reaction. "There are many things I have tolerated from you, but do not ever again speak to me in that tone. I shall not permit it, madam, and you will sorely regret it. Have I made myself understood?"

Raiven checked her anger. She soothed her pride with the rationale that she did not do so out of fear, but because he held her and her brother's fate in his fist. He could either open it and extend leniency or close it and crush the life from them both. His pride was great and, as Fleurette had said, seemed to have endured enough. Recognizing this, Raiven realized that retreat was not only expedient, but necessary.

"I meant no disrespect. Please understand, Jacques is all the family I have remaining. I only wished to write him and let him know I am well and tell him of James's arrival."

Quynn's gray eyes lost some of their heat, yet he did not relent. "There is no need for your letter. 'Twould not arrive before James, and as for the other, James will inform your brother of your well-being."

"It does not matter that 'twill be later. 'Twill be from me, and there is the issue. Jacques will not believe that I allowed anyone to speak for me, just as James would not think it proper if another spoke for you."

Raiven knew she was pleading, but she didn't care. It was important that she write to Jacques. The real reason was not something she could disclose to her husband. She wanted to tell Jacques not to do anything to anger her husband or his king. In the last few days Raiven had seen enough of Quynn to know that neither action would come with a light consequence—a consequence she didn't want Jacques to pay. Her life had been decided. Jacques had other options.

Yet how could she tell her husband that? What if something happened in France? By her own words, she would cast suspicion on her brother. She couldn't. She would just have to maintain her silence and try to find another way. No matter what, she had to protect Jacques.

Quynn watched the different emotions displayed on her face. He had to harden his heart when he saw indecision and then fear. He could not allow her to unman him. She had done it before, and he didn't know her well enough to say she wouldn't do it again. Nothing she had shown him worked to convince him otherwise. Still, the soft look of pleading and the depth of emotion in her voice were almost his undoing.

"Why? It is such a small thing. Why are you doing this?" Her eyes searched his for an answer to his arbitrary cruelness.

Quynn looked away. "The king has forbidden contact between you and your brother out of fear for what plans you might brew. He suggested a period of adjustment for you both. In light of your previous behavior, he cannot be blamed for his caution."

Raiven's eyes narrowed, and her voice was filled with bitterness. "I should never have married you, no matter what the threat. 'Twould have made it much easier for you and your king to continue your unusual alliance without the disruption of my presence. Perhaps, seeing that the two of you are in such accord, *you* would have done well to marry your king. Then mayhap both of you would have left me alone. As it stands, three in a marriage is a crowd. Since you do not object to the king's presence and he appears to have no intention of bowing out, it seems I must. Never fear, milord, henceforth I shall make my presence felt as little as possible, and I shall not ask anything else of you. Good day."

Raiven jumped on Sunstar's back and galloped away, leaving Quynn staring after her.

"Make her presence felt as little as possible?" he repeated to himself, stomping over to where Khan stood. "That will be the day of days."

From the day he had first heard her name, Raiven had done naught else but make her presence extremely known until he now reached the distressing conclusion that a burr in the seat of his chausses would be felt less and with a smaller degree of pain.

Shaking his head ruefully, Quynn set off for home, mentally preparing himself for the next confrontation with his firebrand of a wife who had actually deluded herself into believing she could make her presence be as "little felt" as possible.

# Chapter 11

Aye, 'tis perfect, milady."

Raiven nodded agreement, adding nothing more to Elaine's enthusiastic words.

"'Tis hard to believe so much has been done in just one moon," Elaine went on, ignoring Raiven's silence. She stared around the room with amazement at the changes they had made.

Raiven could scarcely believe them herself. Pride in their accomplishments was shining brightly in her eyes. The somber effect of the dark browns and burnt oranges was lightened by rich and thick tapestries of cream and yellow. The earthenware washbowl was now replaced with one of fine porcelain. A thick fur of the gigantic white bear covered the bed in the place of the pelt that had once been there. On the bed atop the great white fur were several colorful bolsters. The heavy brown drapes that hung about the four posters of the bed were now complemented by lighter material of white and cream. Not only did the lighter material add beauty, it also served the more practical purpose of being cooler on days of warmer weather. Sparse wooden chairs now had homemade cushions upon them, cushions that Raiven and Elaine had labored long to create by sewing scraps of material together and filling the middle with goose feathers.

The thick rugs scattered across the floor and the new ink and quill on Quynn's massive desk all bespoke of comfort and luxury, giving the room a pleasing effect.

Raiven sighed in satisfaction. Until now she had felt like a visitor within her husband's house. There was not much for her to do. The servants were already well organized and supervised by the ever-vigilant Ella. Raiven had felt useless. The feeling was not only unfamiliar, but unwelcome. There had been many things Raiven had been raised to be, but idle was not among them. Once or twice she had tried to offer her services, and though she could not say any of the servants had dared to be overtly rude, a fool would have seen that her ideas were less than enthusiastically received. It chafed that her services were so unwanted. There were many things that she saw, both in and outside the hall, that, had she been at home in France, she would have changed. However, it seemed that no one, including her husband, wanted her help. Their unenthusiastic attitude announced that the only thing they wanted of her was to be as inconspicuous as possible.

Trying to broach the subject with Quynn had been a waste of time. He had informed her that he knew nothing of women's work, and his home was fine as it was. He saw no need for her to do anything.

At the time, Raiven had nodded, her pride stiffening her spine so he would not see how his attitude had hurt. Quynn's position left her occupying only a single part of his life—his bed.

In bed he came to her with a zeal that was startling. No matter what happened or did not happen during the day, the nights were always the same. They were filled with a passion and sharing that mocked the sterility of their lives during the day. Despite Quynn's reticence in allowing her to fully participate in his world, alone in their room, he shared the universe with her. He taught her the complete side of physical intimacy with a vigor that left Raiven breathless and totally satisfied.

That his attention was fired not from passion but from the need to see the king's edict fully met had occurred to her more than once. However, Raiven continuously pushed that disturbing thought away, unable to accept it.

The crux of the problem was she didn't know anything about being married. Her only example was her parents' marriage. Since becoming an adult and especially since coming to England, she had begun to believe that what her parents shared was a rare thing. Émil had honored Genvieve and respected both her and her opinions. Her mother had been a necessary part of her father's life. Perhaps that was not what most husbands wanted. As distasteful as she found it, Raiven had had to consider that her marriage might not be as unique as she thought. Perhaps, no matter whom she had married, he would expect her just to bear his child and do very little else. Whereas Raiven had known her father loved her and Jacques dearly, she also knew that his love for them had been an extension of his feelings for Genvieve. They were the living proof and not the cause of the force of his devotion to his wife.

Those thoughts had only made her more melancholy, and she chided herself for thinking them. She was a fool if she expected her marriage to even resemble her parents' relationship. Outside this massive chamber, Quynn barely noted her existence.

A knock sounded on the door, breaking her sudden despair.

Elaine opened the door to admit Thomas, who carried in each hand a bucket filled with the water for Raiven's bath.

Watching Thomas perform the task he did for her every evening, Raiven suddenly realized it was dusk. She had not once left the chamber the entire day. Time had passed speedily while she occupied her mind and her hands with her project of redecorating.

When her dowry furniture and materials had arrived earlier in the week, Raiven had felt the first stirring of excitement. Mixed with her excitement, however, was a liberal dose of caution. She had somehow known it would not be wise to inundate Quynn with change. So her additions had been subtle, the vase, then the water basin, then the likeness of her mother and father. When Quynn's only reaction had been a slight pause in step as he passed the new items, Raiven took heart and decided to add the remaining things.

Her initial trepidation returned, however, as she looked about the room. Perhaps it was too much too soon. She didn't know her enigmatic husband well enough to assume what his reaction would be.

Young Thomas, however, left her in no doubt as to his opinion. When he finished pouring the water into the tub, he turned to look about the chamber with delight.

"Oh, milady, 'tis a room fit for the king himself. 'Tis beautiful, every bit o' it."

Raiven's eyes lit at the sincerity in his voice. "You like it, I assume?" she asked unnecessarily, laughing lightly when Thomas's head bobbed up and down.

"Would that I could have a room half so nice."

The wistful tone in his voice was unmistakable. However, Raiven hesitated before responding. Her feelings for Thomas were not in question. She liked him immensely. He was one of the rare persons who had shown her any kindness since her journey to England. However, his kindness had been curtailed recently.

Thomas was Ella's son, and when Ella heard of his penchant for being around the mistress, his visits suddenly stopped. Raiven did not know what Ella said, but now Thomas was too busy to talk. When he did any task for her it was either "Aye, milady," or "Nay, milady," his natural friendliness and acceptance restrained. His eyes would meet hers for only a brief moment before he hurried away—until today. His awe at her handiwork would not allow him to maintain the mask of indifference.

Ignoring the warning voice in her head, Raiven offered, "If you like, I can make some of the same things for you, Thomas."

"Truly, milady?" His eyes grew brighter with disbelieving joy.

"'Twould be my pleasure." Any lingering worries she had faded at the pleasure on Thomas's face. Impulsively Raiven turned to her coffer and pulled out a white bear fur, smaller than the one that covered the bed she shared with Quynn. Holding the fur out to Thomas, she said, "You can place this on your bed, and then once I've made your pillow, it can have a nice place to rest."

Thomas's eyes widened more, and he stared, trance-like, at the fur Raiven held out to him.

Finally he reached out to take it, holding his treasure gingerly away from himself and the water that remained in the buckets he held.

"My thanks, milady. I do not know what to say," he murmured.

"Ye can say that 'tis not necessary and return it at once." Ella's sharp tone rang from the doorway. Both Raiven and Thomas jumped at the harsh sound of her voice. Guilt swamped his features, and the care he'd used a moment ago vanished at the sound of his mother's harsh voice. Heedlessly, he swung about, causing the fur to slip from his hands into the bathwater he had just filled for Raiven.

The mortification in the eyes he slowly raised to Raiven's face was heart-wrenching. He tried to apologize, but words that would have been difficult under the best circumstances now froze when he correctly read the fury in her eyes.

However, Thomas was not the recipient of Raiven's anger. When he began to mumble an incoherent apology, Raiven collected herself enough to assure him it was all right. In the softest tone imaginable, she asked him to take the ruined fur and dispose of it. Thomas had barely disappeared when Raiven turned to the stiff-faced woman standing in the door. She didn't know which was greater: her anger or her bewilderment at Ella's cruelty.

"Why? Why did you have to spoil it for him?" Raiven asked, her anger pulsing through her.

Ella took in the fury on her face but did not back away. "He is my son. I have sole responsibility for him now that his father died. I will not have him spoiled."

"How is giving him a cover for his bed spoiling him?"

Ella looked at the fur on Raiven's bed as if it were vermin ridden. "Surely milady is aware of the cost of such a cover. I want my son to learn the value of people, not possessions."

There was such derision in her voice, Raiven felt as if the woman slapped her. The pain from Ella's words cooled her temper. In a milder tone she asked, "Is that how you see me, Ella?"

The woman said nothing, but her eyes were eloquent enough as they wandered about the chamber, resting on each of Raiven's additions.

Raiven walked over to Quynn's desk and toyed with the ivory elephant she had placed there a few hours ago. A slow, sad smile lifted one corner of her mouth. "You do not know me at all, any of you. The pity of it is that it appears you lack even the desire to know or understand me. What have I done to set your hearts so hard against me?"

Ella watched Raiven closely, a niggling suspicion that she may have misjudged the lady beginning to form in her mind. Then she remembered Raiven's previous actions and the pain they had caused Quynn, and her mind rejected her heart's softening.

Quynn held a special place in Ella's heart. She had practically raised him when she was no more than a child herself. When his parents had died, it had been Ella to whom he had turned. She had soothed his unspoken uncertainties. She had comforted him and given him confidence in himself and his choices. She loved him as her own.

When her husband, Thomas the senior, was alive, he had taught Quynn all he knew of horses and other animals, teaching him to hunt wild game and survive well in the woods. When her son had been born, it was Quynn who had made him a fine wooden cradle despite his many other duties. It was only natural then that throughout the years, Ella had developed a fierce protective streak for him. His pain was hers. His enemies were her enemies. As yet, this new wife of his had shown herself to be nothing but an enemy. All her prattle about not marrying Quynn if he was the last man created still fired Ella when she thought of it. The woman could have done no better than he.

Raiven's ridicule of the king Ella had taken in stride, but when she humiliated Quynn, that was past bearing, and no softly spoken, pretty-sounding words were going to change that. The lady would have to prove herself. To Ella's mind, she had not started well. How could she be so insensitive as to bring her finery here and flaunt it in Quynn's face, all but telling him that he was nothing? Telling him by her things that he could not provide for her as well as she could provide for herself? Was the woman aught else save an attractive face with naught a brain betwixt her ears? Had she no ken to the pride of a man like Quynn? Had she no ken how mightily she had already damaged that pride? And now this?

Again Ella looked around the room, resentment building in her breast. Mayhap the lady was not lacking in intelligence after all. Perhaps she knew precisely what she was about. When Quynn saw this room, he would again realize what she had and he did not. She would hurt him—again. Ella's heart hardened further.

Raiven stood silently, watching the expressive play on the servant's face, and noting that Ella's eyes were growing harder and harder, Raiven knew she would not find a listening ear. Whatever it was she had done or Ella thought she had done, the woman was not of a mind to forgive her.

Ella moved to leave, and Raiven thought she would not answer her question at all when she turned back.

"Milady, may I speak with openness?"

Raiven suppressed the desire to laugh. When had the woman spoken in any other manner? However, if Ella now felt the need to ask permission . . . Raiven mentally began to brace herself. She nodded reservedly, hating herself for the haughty gesture but momentarily at a loss for anything else to do.

Ella's hesitation was fractional. "Milady inquires what she has done to harden the hearts of those here? Well, I'll tell ye. 'Twas bad enough when ye refused to marry milord, but then was heard that ye thought he was beneath ye: an 'upstart pauper' I believe ye called him. We here at Havilland love our own. From the day milord's parents died, he has taken the best of care of his people. I do not know of any here from old man to young child who would not die to keep him from a moment's pain. Ye, milady, have caused him much more than that. So do not think that a few pretty smiles will set to right the wrong ye have done in our eyes. I know I have taken a great risk speaking thus to ye, but should ye tell milord, I will not deny it. I will say I only answered a question asked of me."

With a last disparaging glance around the chamber, Ella left.

"Well, now I know my crime," came Raiven's droll undertone while she stared at the door that had been slammed shut in her face.

Elaine, whom Raiven had forgotten during her confrontation with her husband's servant, rushed forward. "Give no heed to her words, milady. They do not know of what they speak. How could they?"

"That is not true, Elaine," Raiven said softly. "I took no thought of what my actions and public refusal would have wrought for the baron. In my stubborn, open defiance of the king of England, I publicly flayed my husband's pride, leaving him unable to retaliate." Raiven smiled ironically. "It is an excellent stratagem if one is at war but a supremely stupid one if you're not, for now I've created an enemy rather than conquered one. No matter my actions, the baron was still bound by the king's order to wed me. This made him look even more the laughingstock. Men find things like that hard to forgive or forget."

Elaine said nothing, and Raiven continued. "I remember Father saying to me that a man's pride is both his most invincible and yet vulnerable shield. He asked that I never forget that. In making me his heir, he knew he was placing me in a position usually held by a man and that the majority of my dealings, therefore, would be with men. He wanted me to know how to deal with care with those who would seek to befriend or oppose me.

"In this instance I have failed my father, for I'd forgotten that important rule. I not only forgot in dealing with my husband, but with his king as well."

"Your father would also have said, 'What's done is done,' milady," Elaine countered, unable to bear seeing Raiven so despondent. "Do not let that Ella's words cause you to doubt yourself."

"Damage may be done, but I can repair it," Raiven spoke softly to herself, then, louder, to Elaine, "Ella's words would not cause me a minute's pause if I did not recognize some truth in them."

Whatever Elaine was about to say was forestalled when Quynn suddenly entered the room. Despite Elaine's brave words, she still did not know the measure of her new lord. Whenever he appeared, she disappeared, as she did now, leaving Raiven alone with him.

Quynn stared at the changes in the room, saying nothing, while Raiven's heart took up lodging in her throat. She waited warily for his response, Ella's bitter words having sounded an alarm she was powerless to ignore. Raiven knew her motives for the alterations had not been malicious. Her only offense had been that of not thinking.

Cringing inwardly, she could hear her father's gentle voice as he instructed her, "Thinking is something all creatures inevitably do, Raiven. A wise one does it before he acts, a foolish one is forced to do it after." Looking at Quynn's stony expression, she admitted which of the two she had been and prayed that he would not see this as another ploy to unman him.

Finally he looked over to her, his gray gaze riveted to the ivory elephant she still held before moving on to the elaborate ink and quill set. His words came, dry and emotionless. "All the comforts of home, madam?"

Raiven swallowed twice. "Nay, milord." Although she could understand what he might be feeling, *her* pride would not allow her to explain what it was she was trying to accomplish. Having lost what little hope she'd had that he would understand, Raiven waited for his explosion.

However, he shocked her by calmly stating, "Your bath cools. I suggest you hurry. 'Tis hard work for Thomas to tote that water up those stairs."

Already on the defensive, Raiven heard only that he was calling her insensitive. "I realize that," she snapped, forgetting her resolve to undo the existing animosity. "I intended to see to it quickly, but I was detained."

"By your delight in your regained treasures?"

"By my desire to share something other than my body with my husband."

That got him. Quynn stopped for a full second, then he continued on as if there had been no pregnant pause. "I see the wealth you have at your disposal. I trust that 'tis enough to satisfy you."

Raiven remained silent, not fully understanding his cryptic response. She turned away from him to look out the window at the magnificent grounds beyond the house.

Quynn's rough voice grated over her. "Tomorrow you can send it back—all of it."

Raiven spun around. "You do not mean that."

"Pray, madam, do not begin to tell me what I do and do not mean. I can assure you I do. On the morrow you can pack these things away. Send them back to France or cart them down to the cellar, I care not, but they cannot remain here."

Green eyes widened into gray ones, disbelievingly. "In the cellar, where it is damp? These things will be ruined."

His voice was cold. "You had another option."

"I cannot send them back to France."

Quynn's black brow rose in question.

Raiven lowered her eyes. "These things were a part of my dowry."

Quynn nodded curtly. "I can see your pride would be wounded under such a condition. Nevertheless, the cellar is below. Your pride should not quake overly much at that."

Raiven stared at him a full minute while she wondered why he would try to be considerate of her feelings. Again she felt the sting of self-censure as she recalled that she had returned all his gifts with no such consideration for his feelings.

"Please, milord," Raiven began humbly, "I ask when I know I have no right. May I please keep my things here with me? With these things, my new life does not seem so strange to me."

"What if all this now seems strange to me? 'Tis my home." The angry edge was gone from his voice.

Raiven's voice was a whisper. "I was of the mind to make it mine as well."

Doubt flashed across Quynn's face. He could feel his heart begin to soften toward her, and he was not ready for that. The struggle to keep her detached from his life was hard enough, especially when she responded with such warmth to his touch. Now she was hinting that she wanted to be a part of his life.

Blast her! Her responses—in and out of bed—were building in him a flame that, once extinguished by their passion, smoldered like a fiery coal in his loins only to blaze again at the slightest thought of her. He spent his days alternating between fury and captivation at his unwilling response to his wife. He grew angered at himself when he realized that for her there was no indecision. She could care less if he came or went.

Now she seemed to be changing, and instead of making him happy, it angered him. She had no right. She had no right to make him feel guilty because he was now abiding by the rules she set. Yet, as he was becoming increasingly aware, there were no simple answers with Raiven. He could only hope to keep her at enough of a distance so as not to become ensnared by her until she revealed that her heart had really changed toward him.

In these sorts of confrontations with her, his confidence in his ability to carry the day in the contest of wills between them without looking more of the fool than he already did began to waver. He had known from the moment she spoke he would not be able to carry out his petty act of vengeance.

Looking again around the room, Quynn noted that she had done what she said. She had made the room hers as well without overshadowing the fact that it was the lord's chamber. His personality was still vividly there, only softened by the addition of a woman's touch. Were things different between them, he could not have asked for better. Now, he was left with the peevish thought that she was besting him again. What made his ire worse was the knowledge that, as with the other times, he could stop it, but he would not. He didn't care to acknowledge his reasons for it. Quynn only knew it made him equally angry with himself and her.

Muttering that he did not care what she did with her cursed dowry furniture, he slammed out of the room.

For a long time Raiven stared blankly at the place where he had stood. Her thoughts were not on her actions when she slowly undressed and slid into the now cool water. The water's temperature did not register. She could think only of the contrariness of Quynn's behavior. While she was happy and grateful that he had acquiesced, she was sharply cognizant of the fact that something else had just taken place—something beyond the words spoken. Yet, even if her life hung in the balance, she could not have said what.

# Chapter
# •12•

I would have a word with you if you have a moment to spare."

Quynn's stride was unbroken as he moved to the garderobe, leaving Raiven unsure if he'd heard her request.

*Remember your promise to come to some kind of agreement with him. Anger will not help. Besides, he may not have heard you,* Raiven reasoned to herself, trying to assuage the anger that brewed close to the surface—anger that had been brewing constantly over the last days.

It had been a week since their unusual conversation about her dowry furniture. That was the first of many "unusual" happenings. Quynn hadn't returned to her bed that night, nor had he been there since.

The week had been strange in other ways, too. Whereas before there had been a chill whenever the servants were in her presence, now there was a downright frost. If she made a request and the servant's back was to her, he or she feigned not to have heard. If she made the request to their faces, the response was slow in coming. They never spoke a voluntary word to her, making it seem that for them, she didn't exist. Thomas's behavior had again altered. Before when he had not lingered to talk, his eyes had always been warm with the desire to please. Now he never looked at her directly, and when he spoke, it was quick and mumbled. That particular defection hurt the most, no matter how Raiven tried to pretend that it didn't, but there was nothing she could do about it. Despite what Ella thought of her, she did not want to cause trouble for Thomas with his mother, so as Thomas's demeanor changed, Raiven's followed.

Her facade of indifference almost fell when one day he had brought the water for her bath, and he didn't lower his eyes quickly enough. Raiven almost gasped at the expression of hurt within the warm brown eyes. She had taken two steps toward him when Ella's disapproving visage appeared in her mind, stopping her.

To Raiven's mind, the coincidence was entirely too large that Quynn's abstinence and the servants' severe disrespect could be unrelated. In halls such as this, though one would wish it otherwise, it was difficult to keep troubles between the lord and his lady a secret from the other occupants or the servants. Especially the servants.

For the first time Raiven gave credence to Elaine's words. Perhaps the servants but followed the lead of their lord. When it had been assumed that Quynn was sharing her bed, she could be tolerated. When it became known—through the servants' system of information, which rivaled that of the king's counselors—that Quynn no longer shared her bed, for whatever reason, they followed his example. They would not tolerate her if he did not. Ella had told her something similar. As she thought of the unrelenting disapproval of the dour woman, Raiven became certain that Ella was responsible for the servants' change in behavior.

With acute discomfort, Raiven realized her thoughts had been on Quynn's absence from her bed more than anything else. *How could it not,* she thought defensively. *Has he not told you that he would not watch his family lose all they'd held dear if 'twas in his power to see it secure?*

His ferocity when he had uttered those words, almost as if he was speaking for the assurance of someone not there, had confused her. His voluntary abstinence confused her all the more.

Raiven did not have much knowledge of child conception, but she knew that Quynn would need to play a more active part if a child was to be made. Since she had not told him that a child was coming, why was he staying away? He may not have *liked* her, but he certainly gave the impression that he *liked* making love to her.

By no means did she believe that she knew Quynn, but if there was one thing she had come to know with a certainty, it was that Quynn was a man of definite, ah, amatory appetite. It had not mattered the hour, the circumstance, or whether she feigned sleep or put up minimal passive resistance. Quynn made certain that neither of them shirked the duty of making a child that Henry had thrust upon them. His vigor in performing what he termed his "reluctant duty" made Raiven wonder how he would behave if his heart were involved instead of only his honor.

In her mind's eye, Raiven saw him as he would be then: passionate, giving, tender, and relentless in his pursuit of pleasure not only for himself, but his woman as well. The surprising clarity of her mental images caused a warm blush to cover her cheeks.

Unfortunately Quynn chose that moment to come back into the room. He was about to speak when he noted the high color in her cheeks. A knowing twinkle—the first she had seen in days—lit his gray eyes, and a sensuous smile curved his lips. He stared at her a long moment, watching the color in her face heighten, and his smile widened.

Raiven shifted uncomfortably, telling herself he did not, could not, know the nature of her thoughts, while praying he would not question her.

Quynn's smile grew to near face-splitting proportions, but he did not remark on her fiery countenance.

When the uncomfortable silence had stretched to its limit, he asked, "You wanted a moment of my time?"

Quynn read the exact moment her expression changed from the muted flame of embarrassment to the blazing fire of anger.

"You heard me yet did not answer?" Raiven asked softly, hissing the words from lips stiffened in anger.

Her sharp answer brought a startled expression to his face but no alarm at her obvious ire.

"I fear one of us has grown daft, for surely I heard myself speak a reply to you just now. What more of an answer do you desire?"

Raiven was not appeased in the least. "You walked by me as if I had not said a word. I know it is difficult for those here to accept my presence. However, simple courtesy does not seem too large a request," she finished bitterly, thinking of the many slights that she'd received from him and his servants.

All traces of amusement in his eyes fled, and Quynn's voice was steady. "I answered you."

"If that is what you see."

"What I *see* is that you make no sense. If there is aught the matter, speak plainly. Making veiled accusations solves little."

Raiven faltered briefly beneath his directness. He had certainly put the matter squarely before her, but she could not bring herself to ask why he suddenly found her so distasteful that he had to sleep elsewhere. Besides the humiliation of it, she would seem like a child begging for attention.

Seizing on the safer topic of his servants, she asked, "Have you noticed how your servants treat me?"

Quynn blinked. "My servants?"

His tone made her uneasy, and a warning went off in Raiven's head to proceed with care. She did not want him to think she was carrying tales or trying to elicit his sympathy.

Taking a calming breath, she continued carefully. "I do not know how to proceed with them. Already their minds are set against me. If I attempt to take my place here, I am met with suspicion. If, because of ignorance, I make an error, it is treated not as a mistake, but a deliberate insult."

"And you would blame servants for your admitted ignorance?"

"Nay, I blame you for their response," Raiven retorted without thinking.

Quynn's gray eyes widened in surprise, then narrowed. Raiven recognized the warning, but this time she refused to give ground. In any event, a graceful retreat at this point was not a possibility.

"You anger too quickly. I only attempted to explain a situation to you and seek your counsel."

Quynn made a rude snort. "I doubt you would 'seek my counsel' on anything. Is it so strange that I should take your *telling* me I am to blame as accusation instead of explanation? As for my quickness to anger," he explained, accurately reading her bewilderment, "I perceive a large portion of the pot remarking on the cetel's blackness."

A smile flitted across Raiven's lips before she could stop it. Quickly putting her head down so he would not see her amusement, she nodded. Her words were nearly indistinct when she said, "I apologize."

She darted a quick look up at his face, and his expression of astonishment was too much. Raiven's smile became a full grin. "Surprised? Is it beyond your comprehension that I could and would apologize? Never mind," she went on briskly, not allowing him to answer. "Your expression is enough." Her smile faded as she continued. "What I meant earlier was if I am to live here, I need to find my place. I do not wish to unduly upset things"—she ignored Quynn's choking cough—"but I need to do more than arise in the morning and retire at night. I'm used to activity and responsibility. I have none of that here."

"You have a responsibility," he returned blandly.

"What is that?"

"The responsibility of bearing the next baron of Havilland."

Raiven's eyes flashed. "It is odd that one of your years has not learned the difference between a responsibility to be carried out with pride of accomplishment and an edict that is to be carried out under threat of punishment and shame."

Quynn smiled suddenly, and it was not pleasant, causing Raiven a spurt of regret that she had rashly provoked him, especially when it had been her aim precisely to avoid that. Now, after their moment of almost amused camaraderie, his displeasure seemed somehow more acute. Sighing heavily, she opened her mouth to begin again when a totally irrelevant and distracting thought sprang into her mind. It was miraculous that he could look so furiously violent and spellbindingly attractive at the same time.

Quynn's cold voice snapped her back to full attention. "You must allow that only since your entrance in my life have the two become so confused for my befuddled wits. I had always expected to carry out my responsibility of creating the next heir for Havilland with pride and dignity." He allowed silence to fill the space before he finished in a voice that lashed her with its venom. "Now there is only you. Pray, madam, what makes you think these recent occurrences are any less distasteful to me than they are to you?"

His words hit her like a physical blow, leaving her unbalanced. She had been behaving as if he had all the things he wanted. She had made no attempt to hide her contempt for any of the events that brought them together. Although she responded to him, it was after he pushed through her defenses. Perhaps . . .

"Is that why you avoided our bed these last nights?" The words were out before she gave thought to what she was saying. They fell baldly between them, shocking them both.

The anger drained immediately from Quynn's face. His stance ceased to be aggressive, and he studied Raiven with thoughtful eyes. Raiven flushed deeper under his steady gaze, a part of her mind wondering if she was doomed to spend the rest of her life in constant embarrassment around this man. She knew he waited for her to speak, to fumble her way through either a retraction or denial, but she could not. Instead she firmly closed her mouth, which had dropped open in unladylike shock at her boldness. She had said enough.

Every lesson her father had taught her about men and how to deal with them logically and with a cool head seemed to evaporate like mist beneath the heat of Quynn's gray gaze. He constantly left her unbalanced, causing her to act the fool.

*Well, it ends here,* Raiven thought mutinously. Quynn could stand there with that expectant look on his face until his flesh rotted from his bones, and she would say no more. Slowly she rose from where she sat on the edge of the bed and walked to the window to look out at the beauty of the grounds and the day.

She saw nothing.

"I needed time to think," came the soft reply, without a hint of boast in it over her admission that he had been missed. "I did not feel my absence would cause any undue alarm."

Raiven held herself stiffly while she waited for him to go on.

"You feel as if you have no place here. I felt as if you did not want to take one. I realize things have not been easy for you, but can you say that you have honestly tried? How was I to know that you wished for things to be different? 'Twould seem from the time I first heard of you, all I have received is the sharp side of your tongue."

Surprised, she turned to him. Despite his implacable expression, Raiven knew he was, in his way, asking why she had said the humiliating things she had. She recalled the other time he had questioned, and she sensed the difference. This was a desire to know or understand, not a demand for an apology. She also instinctively sensed that he would not ask again. This was her genuine and last opportunity to set that aright.

Raiven opened her mouth and lost the words. What could she say? Could she tell him she had never meant to hurt him? What would such information do to their relationship? Where would that leave her? Then a soft inner voice taunted, *What relationship? What do you have now? Are you prepared to live the remainder of your life this way?*

Until that moment, she had never truly considered the permanency of their relationship. The thought of living with constant animosity for the rest of her life was overwhelming. Raiven raised her hand tiredly to comb it through the heavy blond mass of her hair, unaware of the sadness in her eyes reflecting her inner turmoil. She was also unaware of the way the simple movement outlined the shape of breasts against the bliaut she wore or caused her hair to ripple down her back like golden silk. Most of all Raiven was unaware of the effect that her movements were having on Quynn. As he watched her, pity warred with sudden voracious hunger for the sweetness of her within his arms. His hunger, as passionate as it was, gave way to frustration as concern for her plight overrode all else.

"Raiven?" he called softly, only to receive no response.

Raiven had heard him. It was only that she was too preoccupied by the other disturbing thoughts that slipped into her mind through the crack left by her uncomfortable admission. She saw herself as Quynn must have seen her. She heard Ella's words again. Only this time instead of anger, she felt the pain she had caused. She understood now what had puzzled her about her conversation with Quynn over her dowry furniture. He had shown a kindness to her. He had been considerate of her feelings. He had set aside the revenge that was well within his grasp and instead allowed her to have her pride. He had no way of knowing she genuinely wanted to share. In his way he had allowed her to wound his pride further by setting up her finery.

Quynn did not call to her again as he watched the different emotions flash across her face: surprise, worry, revelation, and then sorrow. He could not move when he saw her eyes soften with compassion. He did not know what to expect when Raiven came to stand quietly before him. When she laid a soft hand on his chest, he jumped involuntarily, his hunger of a moment ago resurging almost uncontrollably.

In quiet shock, he listened to the apology she wouldn't give the night of their wedding as it fell from her lips with gentle and sincere honesty.

"I am very sorry for the pain I have caused through my thoughtless temper. In truth, 'twas more a raging against your king." Raiven went on in guileless innocence, not realizing that to some, those words would convict her of a more serious offense. "I cannot honestly say I ever put a face and feeling to the man that was to become my husband. If I had"—her full lips quirked in self-derision—"it is sad to say, I do not know if I would have behaved differently. I would like to think that I would have, but"—she shrugged helplessly—"I do not know.

"When I brought these things"—her free hand waved to encompass the room—"my only thought was to share what I had—to try to make this room not mine or yours, but ours. I had long since arrived at the conclusion that you could not possibly be the sort of man who needed a rich wife found for him. I was only thinking to blend our two lives in a small way besides the physical. The room was rather harsh."

Quynn stiffened beneath her hand, and Raiven, not wanting any more angry words, went on before he could speak. "Harsh, not unattractive. Masculine, with no evidence of a feminine presence. I only thought to give it that, no more. I realize you have done your part to be fair under the circumstances, and I apologize for my intractableness. Whether you believe or not, it is my word I give you that, from the first day we were wed, 'twas never my intent to cause you shame."

Raiven searched his eyes while she spoke, but there was no expression in the gray depths that were neither warm nor cold. She could not tell whether he accepted her words or not. Thinking that perhaps he needed time to consider what she had said, Raiven turned to move away and was held fast as he gripped her hand and brought it back to his chest.

"Are you saying that you now want to make the best of what Henry has forced upon us?"

Raiven hesitated a moment, then nodded slowly.

"Then no longer will I be made to feel a beggar in my own house?"

"I never knew . . . " she began. "Nay, I will try my best not to make you feel that way. If this is too much for you, I will send it back."

Quynn's smile was warm. It also held another element Raiven couldn't define. "'Tis not necessary to send it back. I like to think myself a man with an eye for beauty in nature as well as objects."

An alarm sounded in Raiven's head at the turn of the conversation. She hoped Quynn did not think she was offering more than what she said. Other than her remorse at humiliating him, things had not changed. She and her brother were still virtual prisoners of him and his king.

Although the words clamored to be said, she hesitated to break the tenuous first bond they had made. Gently, she tried to free her hand. The alarm intensified when not only did he not release her hand, but gathered her waist in the steel band of his arm. He began to kiss gently her forehead, her eyes, the tip of her nose, and then rain featherlike kisses on her mouth, asking without speaking for entrance.

Turning her head, Raiven managed to get out, "Milord, please."

His breath was hot in the shell-like crevice of her ear. "You know my name, Raiven; use it." The tenor of his voice and the heat of his breath combined to create a potent caress.

Knowing what would soon happen, Raiven made another attempt at diffusing the situation. "Please, we still have other matters to discuss. This was not what I had in mind—"

"'Twas what I had in mind. Why think you I returned to this chamber midmorning?" He groaned and said something that sounded like, "I could not stay away any longer."

Quynn caught her face and held it still, making her look into his eyes. "Did you not think it strange, my being here at this hour?"

Now that she thought of it, his appearance was rather unexpected. Usually Quynn practiced vigorously with his knights until noon. After the noontime meal, he met with his sheriff to see to complaints and inspect the progress of his tenants on their various tasks. When he returned, Raiven merely assumed he felt a need to use the garderobe. She realized now how little sense that made. He could easily have availed himself of the plentiful woods. Her belated knowledge caused her to stiffen even more in his arms.

"'Tis morn. Surely you cannot mean—I have washed and dressed for the day."

"Things put on can be removed"—this was said as he undid the silver girdle at her waist—"and then put on once more."

"I—I would prefer not."

"Why?"

"This does not sit well with me—"

"'Tis not sitting we'll be doing." The look in his eyes became downright wicked when he added, "Unless you have a preference."

Raiven, busy with trying to reattach and retie everything he was undoing, could do no more than mutter, "I have already stated my preference." Her exasperation grew as she began to see the futility of her resistance. The man seemed to have hands everywhere. Soon, despite her best efforts, she was naked in the morning sun before him.

"You cannot do this. You do not want me," she cried, frustrated at his easy accomplishment and hurt at the truth in her words.

Quynn's smile widened as he deliberately misunderstood her meaning. "I assure you I can."

"Why now?"

"Why not now?" Quynn sighed. "Raiven, what is the matter? I know you enjoy our lovemaking as much as I do. When I came from the garderobe, your expression was inviting. Had it not been, I would have left to return to my men regardless of my desire. Your eyes said you wanted my touch. Your questions concerning my absence let me know you miss my attentions. What is all this coyness now?"

Raiven colored, unable to deny his words and ashamed that she could not. How could she explain to him that those feelings were not enough?

"It is not coyness! Don't you understand? There has to be more than this. I will not deny you can make me feel things, but that is all. We cannot stay abed. There are other things besides breeding your heir that mean something to me."

Quynn sighed again, louder than before. "Are we back again to talk of responsibility and courtesy?"

Despite her nudity, Raiven held herself with dignity. How could he be so blind? She had all but asked him to give her more than his body, and he did not see it. She would not ask again. Her pride had been squelched enough. Grabbing the opportunity he had inadvertently given her, she shrieked, "Aye, we are back to that. I understood your way, can you not try to understand mine? Haven't you heard one thing I've told you? Since my arrival here, my actions and words have been misunderstood or under suspicion. You have done it, and it is easy to see how the servants, following your example, act the same. Is it too much to hope that I might be given a chance?"

The boyish animation that had momentarily brightened Quynn's face disappeared. His voice was lifeless. "Things have not changed all that much, have they?"

Raiven was about to speak when he raised his hand. "You have said enough. Your position is clear. I shall talk to my servants on the morrow."

Without another glance at the body he had playfully undressed, he left her standing there. Raiven sank onto the bed, not bothering to cover herself. The maelstrom of emotions within her chest roiled about without relief or answer. A sad, self-derisive smile crossed her face. Now that Quynn had left, she couldn't decide which was more humiliating: making love in the middle of the day or having Quynn walk away from her naked body as if she were less than nothing. But wasn't that what she wanted? She honestly couldn't say. She had wanted him to understand, but she didn't know if she had wanted him to leave.

Absently, she pulled on her clothing, trying to sort through her confusion. By the time she dressed, Raiven was certain of only one thing. In some way, despite all her resolve to end bad feelings between them, she had just hurt Quynn—again.

# Chapter
# •13•

"This is my wife."

That was it. That was all he said the next day to the assembled serfs, servants, tenants, and knights.

Raiven stood beside him with a frozen expression on her face, torn between overwhelming humiliation and absolute fury. Defiant pride made her stand tall as all eyes turned to her after her husband's brief speech. They waited expectantly, but she couldn't bring herself to smile at them or to speak.

In the next few awkward moments before Quynn nodded a dismissal, she caught the eye of more than a few of the serfs and villeins. Their eyes were blank, reflecting neither warmth nor coldness, neither like nor hatred. A short formal bow was their only acknowledgment before they turned to leave.

Quynn's knights were a little more gallant. All the same, behind their flowery compliments to her beauty and words of welcome, Raiven recognized the same sense of apathy.

She nodded curtly to one handsome young man bending over her hand, unaware of his words. Pulling her hand away, she excused herself and returned to her chamber to bask in the full burn of mortification. The hot tears she had held back within view of the others began to chart a slow, scalding course down her cheeks. No sooner had they fallen than they dried quickly beneath the heat of her building fury.

How dare he humiliate her like this? "This is my wife," indeed! Who did he think they thought she was?! And what was that to prove? What had been resolved? Better he had said nothing at all.

Raiven dashed at a wayward tear just as the door to the room swung wide. Quynn stood tall and menacing, but Raiven, in the throes of her own overpowering anger, did not care.

"Look, it is my husband," she taunted. "To what do I owe this honor? Since it is not quite the noon hour and you have not made tracks to the garderobe, I must assume you have come to complete what you started yesterday. Shall I disrobe now and save you the effort of my laces and girdle?" She frowned in deliberate concentration, then put on a falsely bright expression as if the answer finally came to her. "Forgive me, milord, I have mistaken the situation. Humiliating me here by bearing your weight and eventually your seed," she sneered venomously, her green eyes glittering savagely, "is not your favorite pastime."

Rashly, Raiven walked over to him and tried to leave through the still-open door only to have it swing shut in her face, missing the tip of her nose by inches.

The gleam in her eyes brightened as she turned back to slice Quynn with a sideways glance. "Is there aught the matter, milord? Surely I could not have mistaken the matter twice? You have come here to drag me belowstairs to further my education in the wonderful art of being publicly humiliated, have you not?"

Quynn's voice was dry. "'Tis a unique gift you have in your ability to always attack before being attacked, to charge blame before being accused. This time, however, 'twill not work. You will explain yourself now, madam."

Raiven sniffed and turned away from him. She had nothing to say to him. He could wait for an answer until the steel of his sword melted to butter, and she would not tell him anything.

Without raising his voice, Quynn managed to achieve a terrifying tone with just one word: "Explain."

Shaking off the chill his voice had induced, Raiven answered coldly, "There is naught on my part to explain. Clearly you are too dim-witted to see how you have just humiliated me."

In a tone that matched hers, he said, "Since I am so sorely lacking in wits, perhaps you can tell me what I have done."

"How could you stand me before your serfs, servants, tenants, and knights and announce only that I am your wife?" she burst out. "How could you think that was what I wanted you to do? What was the purpose of it? This may surprise you, milord baron, but they already have a fair idea of who I am."

The last word had barely escaped her lips when he was standing in front of her, clasping her by the arms in a grip that was not gentle.

"Would you have me say to them, 'I demand that you respect her' when all know you have done naught to earn it? Not even for James did I do such a thing. What respect he has, he has earned. I thought you understood that. Your father labored to teach you such a lesson, so you carp. Maybe he did not labor long enough. Or do you feel that stupid Englishmen have no right to demand you earn their respect? Could it be you save your high values for those of your kind?"

Stunned by what she saw as an unfair assault, Raiven opened her mouth to reply. However, Quynn was not through, and he shook her into silence. His next words hissed at her like a whip's cracking, and like a whip, they flayed.

"I have done more for you than any other, including my own brother, who has love and respect for all here. The simple words with which you find so much displeasure are enough to ensure that all here give you the respect due you as my wife. I bade them respect you, and you in turn expect them to swallow your contempt. I have done all I will. For even if I could, I would not force my people to accept your disdain. It is now your turn, madam, to show your worth. Expect no more from me. You have insulted those who stayed to know you, and you have humiliated me for the last time. From now on I care not what you do, though I warn you freely, do not ever," he ground out, his hands tightening painfully on her arms while his eyes shot gray shards of ice, "humiliate me in public again, or you will surely wish you had not."

Raiven had never seen him this close to losing control. She could feel his fingers tremble in their fierce grip, and she realized Quynn wanted to do more than spit fiery words. His eyes darted compulsively to her throat, and his hand gave an involuntary squeeze.

He waited for her to speak, but Raiven could not find the words. Everyone must have noted her less than enthusiastic response to Quynn's brief speech and had taken it for scorn. Her disappearance so quickly afterward only reinforced that opinion, she thought miserably.

Seconds passed, and still no words came. For the first time in her life, Raiven was subdued by the enormity of both her error and the anger she saw in another. Besides, what words could she say to alleviate embarrassing him in front of his men?

Swallowing heavily, Raiven nodded, praying that would be enough and he would go away.

Quynn was not appeased. "Have you heard me?" he ground out.

"Aye," Raiven managed through the tightness of her throat.

Finally, Quynn released her and started for the door, then stopped as if remembering something.

"In the future, be assured that I will exercise my husbandly rights only as I deem necessary to fulfill the command of the king. Therefore, there will be no need for more of your derision of my touch than is merited. You need not waste your insults at a time when the farthest thing from my mind or my body is desire for yours. My suggestion to you is to save your insults. You will have ample chance to use them when there is no doubt of my intent."

Over the next few days, the truth of Quynn's words was borne out. Although the servants were not happy with her presence, the outright disrespect ceased.

Raiven would have been loath to admit it, but something else he had said was also being proven. Their disrespect might have vanished, but the resentment remained. If anything, it seemed to have increased. It was as if everyone knew the reason for Quynn's uncharacteristic behavior. To their minds, she had repaid his kindness by being rude to his knights and men-at-arms.

The poor fellow from whom Raiven had walked away while he was praising her beauty and delighting in her presence at Havilland was Douglass, Quynn's second-in-command.

Raiven colored anew as she remembered that particular fact. At least it couldn't be said of her that she did anything half measure, she thought with wry self-derision. In the short time she'd been at Havilland, she'd insulted her husband, the woman who ran his hall and was like a second mother to him, his second-in-command, and, not least, his king. In a way, Raiven thought with gloomy self-disparagement, it was fortunate his parents were not around. Heaven only knew what insult she would give to them.

Her appalling lack of sensitivity left her unsettled. Usually she was not so insensitive to those around her. She couldn't afford to be. Her position as chatelaine would not allow it. Yet, ever since she had heard of her upcoming marriage to an English baron, she had made more mistakes and errors of judgment than the smallest child fresh out of swaddling.

Her father had always told her that others could afford a loose tongue and thoughtless deeds; she could not. Everything she did, every word she spoke, he'd warned, would be under close scrutiny. She flinched inwardly when she thought of what her father's reaction would be to her thoughtless behavior. She could hear him say, "Ah, Raiven, *petite,* why do you work so hard at playing the fool when it is so much easier to think first and thus be given the role of the wise? To be a fool, one must learn nothing, do nothing, and speak always. To be wise, all one must do is be aware of others, listen, and know when to be silent."

Weighed down by the increasing discomfort of her thoughts, Raiven walked to the window of her room that overlooked the portion of the bailey where Quynn and his knights practiced. Her eyes found him immediately. He had removed his tunic, and his bare chest glistened in the sun while he swung his massive sword back and forth as if it weighed nothing. Watching the glint of the heavy steel, Raiven absently admired the workmanship while thinking of her father's sword. It had been Émil's pride. Now it belonged to her. She did not wield it with the precision and dexterity that Quynn displayed, for the sword was heavier than the one her father had had made for her, but nonetheless, she felt a sense of pride that her father had left it to her.

Quynn's well-muscled body moving in a graceful parry of his opponent's lunge brought her mind and her eyes back to the practice area. The air had a chill to it, making gooseflesh rise along her arms, but Quynn moved as if he did not feel the cold against his bare torso. It was not the first time Raiven had seen him work thus, impervious to the elements.

Suddenly, with the instinct of the warrior he was, he glanced her way, sensing her gaze, impaling her on his. Even over the distance, Raiven could see the sparkle of his steel gray eyes and the empty expression in them. The change in her face alerted him that he had allowed his attention to stray too long from his opponent, and he turned back just in time to thwart the blow his overeager squire was about to deal him.

Raiven had learned that Quynn allowed no mercy in practice. Whether sparring with a knight, one of the men-at-arms, a squire, or the baron himself, if one saw an opening, he was to take it. "For a certainty," she had heard him warn, "the adversary on a battlefield is not going to allow for a momentary lapse." It was this sort of rigid discipline that had made Quynn and his men the most formidable warriors in England.

Not wanting to interfere anymore and not wanting all to think she was just staring at her husband, even if that had been what she was doing, Raiven backed away from the window.

Assailed by unrelenting restlessness, she sat beside the now cool fireplace. In the months that she had been at Havilland, she had spent the majority of her time inactive. What was worse, she had spent the bulk of her time in this room, looking at the walls, almost as if she expected them to supply her with the answers she sought. The only time she left the room was to take her meals. Then she scurried back to it like a mouse to its hole. What was the matter with her? Raiven knew she had not made a great start with Quynn or his people, but it was unlike her to hide away like a scared rabbit, barely eating or speaking, barely living.

She had always viewed her marriage and forced residence in England as a sort of prison. Raiven was now seeing that the prison was of her own making. It was her fault she stayed cloistered away. She was serving a self-imposed exile in this room, not even going out for her daily rides as had been her custom.

It had to stop!

Raiven felt like someone awakened from a long sleep. Along with the reawakening came the resurgence of pride and determination that had made her father choose her to succeed him and made the people she ruled come to respect her. In retrospect, she could see that even Elaine had allowed her cowardly retreat. The loyal servant had consoled her, albeit from love, when a stern hand was what had been needed.

Raiven cringed in shame when she thought of how she must have sounded when she spoke to Quynn—like a spoiled child begging people to be nice to her. Then when he had obliged her, she didn't like the *way* he had done it. How could she expect to change their minds or their feelings when all she did was hide away in this room and behind Quynn?

With new awareness, Raiven looked around the room. The truth suddenly came to her that she had not been honest with herself or Quynn. She had not remodeled the room to share with him. She had been trying to make a haven—a place where she could be and not face the overwhelming changes in her life. She had made a little replica of the home she adored and thought to hide in it until . . . Until what? She did not know. All Raiven knew was that she wasn't going to hide anymore. Like it or no, this was her home, and there was no going back.

For the first time since her marriage, Raiven felt free. Rising from her chair, she laughed aloud, giddy with the pulsing feeling of confidence and the excitement it brought. It had been too long. She did not know how her husband or the people at Havilland would react to the real Raiven de Cortillion, but she didn't care. The real Raiven was back, and never again would she let circumstances scare her away.

# Chapter
# •14•

The sun was shining crisply when Elaine made her way to the lord and lady's chamber. She did not like this new arrangement. However, she thought tartly, as was the case with her mistress, she had no choice in matters since her arrival in England. She would have adapted had she not seen the toll it was taking on Raiven. Elaine's ire began to rise, making her knock on the stout wooden door a bit more sharply than she'd intended as she thought of the loss of sparkle in her mistress's flat green gaze. It was as if all Raiven's joy in life had evaporated since coming to this cold country with its even colder inhabitants. Elaine shivered as a draft swept the corridor, thinking that it was no wonder the people here were cold. Having warmth of *any* sort seemed an impossibility in England. This chilly, barren place probably made it so. If Raiven's new appearance was any indication, certainly this "beloved" England was not the place to be.

It suddenly occurred to Elaine that she was muttering fiercely to the door and had yet to receive an answer from within. Knocking again, this time louder than ever, she felt the first twinges of alarm. Tentatively, she tried the door. It was unlatched. Walking in, she looked around the room, surprised to find it empty, even the garderobe.

Elaine's brow knit in concern. 'Twas early still. The baron had left the night before on an expedition of some sort, and Elaine assumed that she could attend to Raiven at the usual time. If they were in France, she would have no worry, but here—where would Raiven go? Where could she be? Should she wait silently for her to return? What if she was in danger? Could she be harming her mistress if she kept her silence?

Elaine had never been more miserably aware of the difference between Havilland and Guirlande. Here, there were no normal steps to take. Of late, she had watched silently as Raiven closeted herself more and more in this room. She had understood that. She knew it had made her feel closer to home and things familiar. Nibbling on her bottom lip in growing worry, Elaine acknowledged the many times she had wanted to come and hide away here with her.

Shaking her thoughts back to the matter at hand, Elaine again bemoaned the fact that there were no usual steps to take. In France, Raiven's absence would be no problem. First, Raiven would never have closed herself away, making her sudden disappearance a cause for concern. Second, if she had, Elaine would have known what to say and would not have hesitated to say it. Here, understanding her mistress's plight had made her hold her tongue.

Guilt overwhelmed her. Had she in some way failed her lady? Life was so topsy-turvy in England. Things that should be weren't, and things that ought not to be were.

Rousing herself from growing self-recrimination and the paralyzing grip of indecision, Elaine again tried to focus on the immediate problem. Likely, she should tell the baron, but even if she found the thought less than traitorous, to her knowledge, the baron had not returned. Should she tell one of the baron's men in the event Raiven was in danger? What if no danger existed and Raiven only sought escape from an intolerable situation? On the other hand—

"Where is your mistress?"

The deep voice caught Elaine off guard, effectively quelling her rising hysteria but increasing her fright as she spun around to face the man she did and did not want to see.

"Ah, milady, milord?"

Quynn entered the room, casting the servant a derisive glance, giving a fleeting thought to the strangeness of her behavior.

"Aye," he repeated slowly, "milady. Your mistress, my wife?" He pointed to her and then to himself to emphasize the point, his agitation growing at the look of shock and then bewildered concern on Elaine's face. "Do you ken where she is?" he barked, losing all patience with her when she continued to stare at him in openmouthed silence.

Elaine looked about the room as if Raiven would be hiding beneath the furnishings and she expected her to materialize at any moment. Accurately noting the growing anger of the man who was not only Raiven's husband, but her lord, she summoned the courage to speak past the dryness in her throat.

"Nay, milord."

"Nay what?" Quynn's voice had a hard edge.

"Nay, I do not ken where she is. I arrived here only moments ahead of you. When I entered the room, 'twas as you see it."

Elaine swallowed heavily, hoping she had not spoken too impertinently. Watching the storm gather in the baron's gray eyes, she wondered if the freeness of speech Raiven allowed her was such a good thing after all.

Elaine could have rested easy, for Quynn was not paying her manner any attention. His thoughts were all on the meaning of her words. In an instant he considered and discarded the idea of asking any of the other servants if they knew of Raiven's whereabouts. If her own trusted Elaine did not know, Raiven most certainly would not have told another.

Throwing a fulminating glance Elaine's way, he swept from the chamber without another word. Belowstairs he sat at the great trestle table, then, too agitated to sit, stood to pace. His thoughts kept returning to the same improbable—but as time passed and she did not appear—inescapable conclusion. Raiven had run off. But where? She knew no one here. Could she have attempted to go back to France? Quynn's eyes narrowed apace with the growing fury of his thoughts as the notion solidified that that was where she had gone or was attempting to go. There was nowhere else. Surprisingly his first thought was not of the shame this would inevitably cause him when it became known. The thought uppermost in his mind was the danger to her. Times were unsure; a lone female, a lone *French* female, would be a bitter target.

Snatching his sword and shield, he went back out into the courtyard where his men were beginning their drills. He noted absently how tired they were, and his anger grew. His wife had planned well. She had chosen to bolt on a night when he and his men had been busy attending to other matters.

One of the tenants on the farthest reaches of the estate had had his cottage looted and fired. The brigands were about to make off with the man's young daughter when Quynn and his men arrived. Despite their quickly dispatching the miscreants, the fire had already damaged the cottage beyond saving. Hours passed while they ensured the fire destroyed nothing else. Then the task of finding the man and his family a place to stay had taken the remainder of the night.

Quynn and his men had only just returned home, tired from their activities, and now he would have to have them mount again to seek his errant wife, who had obviously used his absence to flee.

Quynn froze as a thought, long since relegated to the back of his mind as not being important, came rushing to the fore. When he and his men had engaged the brigands at the tenant's cottage, a few had made a cowardly retreat rather than face him and his vengeance. They had fled into the darkness of the surrounding woods while yelling curses at him—in French. With the swiftness of a lightning bolt, his mind wondered if there could be a connection between that unusual occurrence and his wife's sudden disappearance.

Slowly, Quynn shook his head, unwilling to believe such a thing or to consider that the wrenching he felt in his vitals at the possibility was pain. 'Twas too horrible to contemplate, he thought brusquely, becoming angered with himself for thinking something so foolish.

Raiven would not betray him in such a foul way. Of all the petty vindictive things she had done, she had never tried to see him or any of those belonging to him harmed.

*There is no connection, only overwhelming coincidence,* he vehemently declared to himself. And most assuredly that coincidence stretched to encompass the fact that he had only had such trouble once, years before when Henry was passing through his lands.

In spite of his desire to the contrary, his thoughts caused him to falter as he went automatically toward the stables. Hadn't that nagging suspicion been the reason he had gone directly to his chamber upon returning? Hadn't he wanted to assure himself that things were as normal as they could be since his disastrous marriage two months ago?

Quynn's teeth clenched as the ebbing rage surged to the surface again. He would find her no matter where she was. And if he could control his hands long enough, he was going to get the answers to the questions that plagued him. The extent of his control would be determined by the strength of his belief in her answers.

Only a few feet from the stables, his attention was caught by the unnatural quiet of the courtyard when, only moments ago, it had been buzzing with the noise of men at practice. Looking back to his men, he saw they were all staring at a sight beyond his shoulder. He turned to see the cause of their unprecedented distraction from their practice, and the breath left his chest as he watched the vision approaching on the back of a white horse.

Raiven, his wife who had ridden so stiffly before, was riding the white mare. She rode as one with the animal, the mare a natural extension of her grace. She rode—and Quynn squinted in disbelief, thinking the sun played a trick with his eyes—astride and bareback!

Her hair was unbound and flowing like a glorious banner behind her. She was bent low, the whip of the horse's mane almost blending with her flowing tresses, and as she drew closer, Quynn saw the reason for her unusual posture. Raiven was riding—Father in heaven!—without reins, guiding the animal solely by a handful of mane. She rode at full gallop to the stables, coming to an abrupt halt that caused Sunstar to rear up. While standing on her two hind legs, the horse emitted a whinny that sounded eerily similar to the shout of triumphant laughter from the golden-haired nymph that rode her. When Sunstar righted herself, Raiven slid gracefully to the ground, walking to the front of the horse, speaking soft words. Her steps made no sound, and it was only then that Quynn noticed she wore no shoes. Her feet were dangerously close to the horse's hooves, and his heart, which had just relaxed, clenched in terror, realizing that one brush from those hooves would cripple her.

Words strangled in Quynn's throat, and he could not bring himself to call out. He, like his men, was entranced at his wife's horsemanship and graceful beauty. He was in terrified awe.

Quynn was still standing mute when Raiven disappeared in the stables, totally oblivious to the spellbound audience she had left behind.

"Have ye ever seen aught like it, milord?"

Quynn dragged his bemused eyes from the stable door to look down at Thomas's face beaming up at him with incredulity and amazement. He had not even heard the lad approach.

"Nay, Thomas. I have never seen aught like it." Looking at the expressions on the faces of his men, Quynn realized that their thoughts were not too dissimilar from Thomas's. Glancing back down to the boy, he added, "Should you not be about your duties?"

Thomas nodded and turned away, still preoccupied

with what he had seen. Quynn watched him and smiled. The smile, however, evaporated when he saw his men still gaping like speared fish at the door through which Raiven had disappeared. He cleared his throat loudly enough to gain their attention, and that was enough. Before he had taken two steps, all had resumed their activity.

Quynn approached the stables slowly, suddenly remembering his anger and the reason for it. Strangely, it was gone. Once he had seen that she had not used last night's activity to flee from him, another emotion that uncomfortably resembled relief replaced the anger. Then he remembered her antics on the horse—riding without even a rein—and anger of a different sort coursed through him. When he entered the stables, he fully intended to berate her for her foolhardiness, but in the time it took his eyes to adjust to the darkness of the stable, he heard her voice speaking softly, and again his anger was forgotten.

"You are not as well trained as Tonnere—*mais non,* do not become disturbed. Tonnere is a bad-tempered black brute of a horse, but I love him immensely. I have had him since he was foaled, and he has known only my hand, so it is natural that he respond well to me, *n'est-ce pas?"*

When Quynn's eyes had fully adjusted, he could see Raiven was grooming the horse herself, a chore he had never seen a woman perform. She spoke in a quiet conversational tone as if she expected the beast to answer her. When Sunstar turned her head at the sound of her voice, Raiven stopped brushing and went to stand before her, resting her head on the horse's nose.

"There is no need to be jealous, *ma chérie.* You did well. I was proud, and in a month or two, Tonnere will have much to be jealous of in you. That is better, no?"

Quynn did not want to believe the movement of the horse's head signified a response to her words. Shaking himself from such fancy, he was about to announce his presence when Sunstar shifted and Raiven turned to see what had disturbed the horse.

Raiven was startled to see Quynn standing there. She had not known that he was back, and it was only now that she noticed Khan was in his stall at the rear of the stable. Fighting a growing apprehension, she watched him, saying nothing. Although she had wanted him to come to know the real her, she didn't want to shock him unduly. Even her father had found her early-morning rides without reins or saddle a bit unconventional, and *he* had been tolerant. Quynn was anything but.

Too late, she lamented the urge to ride that had overcome her. Raiven had thought today was a good opportunity to at least begin one of her former habits, because Quynn had not returned to the hall last night. She had thought he wouldn't discover what she had done until she had the chance to gradually make him aware of her rather unorthodox habit. *So much for best-laid plans,* she thought glumly, watching him draw nearer. If his expression was any indication, he was not pleased, though his opening words were neutral.

"Good morn."

Raiven decided to follow suit. "Good morn to you. When did you return?" she asked, hoping he would say he had only just done so.

"Perhaps half an hour's passing," Quynn replied, watching her face and noting the sudden jerk of her features. The movement was telling. Abruptly, he changed what he was about to say, instead asking, "Did you enjoy your ride?"

Raiven's answer was soft. "Aye. When I was at ho—Guirlande, I would ride before the start of each day. It clears my mind."

Quynn made no comment to that. "Have you yet broken the fast?"

"Nay, 'twas too early. I did not wish to disturb anyone."

*More likely you didn't want anyone to know what you were doing,* he thought in amusement, a ghost of a smile flirting around his lips.

"Would you join me?" he asked aloud.

Raiven didn't trust the look in his eyes or that half

smile that played with his sensuous mouth, but she wasn't going to retreat again. She had done enough of that to last a lifetime. Dropping the curry brush she still held in her hand in the tray beside Sunstar's stall, she answered, "But of course, mi—"

Quynn's smile became full-fledged. "You were saying?" he prompted, knowing what she had almost said and not willing to let it pass.

"I was saying, 'twould be a pleasure," she remarked smoothly, refusing to be baited. Without giving him an opportunity to reply, Raiven stepped through the stable door into the bright morning sunlight.

The sight of Raiven gliding gracefully along on Sunstar's back became common over the next few days. Just as Quynn was becoming accustomed to that, he noted other changes inside and out of the hall. In the past few days something about the hall had perplexed him. When he realized it was a more pleasant smell, he remarked on it to Ella, only to be told, "Milady brewed a mixture of flowers from the garden, then ordered the dried petals mixed in with the rushes, and the result is what you smell." Quynn could see that Raiven's ingenuity did not sit well with Ella, but he said nothing.

A few days later, at mealtime, he became aware of another change. The fare, though the same, had a different taste to it. All of his men noted it, some even jesting that they would marry the woman who could cook like this. When the meal was finished, Quynn called for Mildrede, the woman responsible for the cooking. When he complimented her on a meal well done, he was again shocked to discover that his wife was responsible.

Flustered at having gained the baron's attention when she had not before, Mildrede made an awkward curtsy and replied, "Milady showed me herbs to use tha' I hadna known. Why right 'neath ma' nose they grew, and never I dreamed they could be used for such." Her annoyance at Raiven's interference did not appear as harsh as Ella's, or perhaps she only hid her pique better. In either case, Quynn was again surprised that his wife was responsible for yet another improvement in his hall. Sending the cook away with an absent gesture, he pondered the strange events that had been taking place recently.

While his men groaned lazily over the amount of food they had consumed, Quynn held himself back from partaking in the conversation and good-natured jesting that was as much a part of mealtime as the food itself. With a deceptively attentive smile on his face, he leaned back to give his full attention to his wife's sudden change.

If her behavior had puzzled him before, now he was truly perplexed. First, she had stayed in her room like a sequestered nun; now, she was about the estate, her influence being felt far and near. None of her changes were overbearing. They were the types of things he would have expected from his wife, and that only confused him more. Now that Raiven was giving him all he wanted—well, almost all he wanted—by improving his home, taking away the need for his attention to the trivial matters of running the hall, complementing him in all ways, she confounded him all the more. What was she trying to do? What was her purpose?

Had it been any other marriage and had it taken place in any other way, he would have assumed she took on these responsibilities lovingly, out of her earnest desire to improve his house. However, this was Raiven, and if there was one thing Quynn was sure of, it was how his wife felt about him *and* his house. Perhaps if she had done these things at the beginning, he would not suspect any ulterior motives. Initially, he had been secretly overjoyed with Raiven. She had shown herself to be a woman of strength. Once he allowed himself to forgive, if not forget, her humiliation of him, he had realized that Havilland would need a mistress such as she.

Then once at Havilland, his perception of her began to alter. She had done none of the things he expected. She had been almost mousy in demeanor, hiding away in her room—a room she had changed into a luxurious bower to remind herself, to Quynn's mind at least, of her wealth and all she had given up to marry the "English upstart." Despite that acrimonious thought, he had not been able to say her nay. He also had not, even with Henry's order burning in the back of his mind, been able to bring himself to return to her bed. He knew that time was passing, and he hated himself for his reluctance. The only thing he hated more was the idea of the quietly resisting woman he would meet there. The woman whose passion he knew existed, lying there beneath the surface, taunting him. The passion about which her body lied, but her eyes always spoke. The passion that would erupt to leave him gasping from its intensity only to disappear before his thirsting eyes like the illusion of water in a desert.

And what of the absence of fire in her eyes? That disconcerted him. His vow to get to know the woman beneath the surface was being met with nothing but frustration. Unwilling to admit that he missed their verbal sparring, he had made attempts to engage her in debate, only to have her fix him with a blank, lifeless green stare. Her eyes no longer changed to the golden fire that warned of her anger, and instead of rejoicing at her docility, stupid fool that he was, he lamented its absence. Deep down, Quynn had long since admitted that Raiven's disagreement did not stem from mere peevishness, but a strength of assertion. He had admired that, or so he had thought. When her moods abruptly changed, he had to reevaluate his opinion, coming to the bitter conclusion that he had been in error before. Her malcontent was just that: malcontent with no underlying motive to give it any justification.

With those thoughts crystallizing in his mind, he could no more go to her bed than he could force himself to fly. He had prayed that the times he had come to her had been sufficient to produce an heir, but while he waited impatiently, the realization came that no word was coming because there was no news to tell. And this left him no choice but to return to her bed. His heart had sunk lower at that prospect, and he began to try to see ways to extract himself from the torture his life had become.

Just when he thought he'd finally ascertained her real nature and would adjust accordingly, Raiven's personality had reshaped itself again. Now, when he saw her gallivanting on Sunstar's back with her hair billowing behind her, instead of dread, he found himself feeling pride and awe. She moved freely among the servants with her back straight and head high despite their veiled animosity, winning the reluctant approval of a few of them. Her beauty, which had been dulled by her lackluster personality, was now, conversely, enhanced by the sparkle in her eyes, the sureness of her stride, and the confidence of her wisdom.

This was a woman he could desire. This was a woman who might someday possess his heart. But was this finally the real Raiven?

Quynn gave an inward sigh and pulled himself from his thoughts to look about the room for his wife, starting slightly when he saw that she was not present. Slowly, so as not to attract attention, he eased himself from the table while his eyes scanned the hall gradually. His casual glance confirmed it. Raiven was not here. Stretching slowly, as if to take the knots out of tired muscles, he made his way over to the door and slipped outside.

Once outside, he allowed a little of his concern to show. His first fleeting thought was perhaps she had gone for an evening ride. Then he discarded that idea as foolish. Raiven would not leave without telling anyone, would she? He knew she was a more than competent rider, but even she could have an accident in the dark, especially at the speeds he'd noted she liked to ride, and Raiven was certainly smart enough to realize that.

Nevertheless, Quynn walked toward the stable, unsure if his wife's logic would be as sound as his own. When he reached the door, he stepped silently inside, instant relief flooding his chest. There, perched elegantly on a high stool, as if it was the throne of England, sat Raiven, talking to Thomas while the lad pitched hay. Neither was aware of his entrance.

"I dunno, milady. Milord said he himself would train me to be a squire when the time is right, but I don't think even with his help I'll ever be one."

Quynn did not mean to eavesdrop, but Thomas's sorrowful tone caught his heart, and he stepped forward, thinking to comfort the boy, when Raiven spoke.

"What ails you, Thomas? Surely you know the baron is the fittest knight in Henry's realm. If he will train you, and I'm sure he shall since he's given his word, none will be able to deny your competence. Have heart. To a child, many things seem impossible, but as time passes and he grows, he sees things differently."

Quynn could tell Thomas did not appreciate her referring to him as a child, but the boy listened. His next words were a shock.

"But I am no noble's child. My father was a tenant here. My mother is a servant. I may not be thought of as worthy because of that."

Quynn could see another emotion flash across Raiven's face before it disappeared behind indignation. "What nonsense is this?! How came you by such prattle?" Her face lost a little of its vehemence, and her words were careful. "A man's worth," she said, gazing directly into Thomas's eyes with not a hint of a smile showing on her face as his chest puffed with pride at being inadvertently called a man, "is not founded purely on his ability to claim kinship to great men dead long past. His *worth,*" she stressed, "comes from what he is within. A man's greatness lies in his heart, in his capacity to love, to be strong, and not to intimidate those who are weak. To have compassion and know when to show it, to be understanding without fearing such makes you weak, are an accurate showing of a man's worth. Worth lies in the ability to be firm yet fair to those who have entrusted their lives to you. To stand firm when you think you are right, even when no one else is of that opinion. Is that not the essence of the vow of knighthood?"

Thomas nodded.

Raiven slipped off the stool. "Well then, Sir Thomas,

you shall be a great knight indeed, because all I have said are things I already see in you."

Thomas's eyes grew embarrassingly moist. "In me, milady?" His voice cracked, and he cleared his throat manfully. "How do I do those great things?"

Raiven smiled in the torchlight, and Quynn thought she had never looked more beautiful than she did at that moment. "I shall tell you a little story, Thomas. It is about a very scared and lonely lady. She was cast adrift from family and friends—from everything she held dear and had known. She was told to sail far away. Her fright was like nothing she had ever experienced before. In truth, 'ere that time, she had never really known true fear.

"She and her servant went to a faraway place, and once there, she met a man who was to be her husband. He was a giant of a man, and the lady's fear increased tenfold. She felt that she could show neither her fear or her loneliness. Instead, she pretended that nothing was amiss. She met no new friends, and people were as suspicious of her as she was of them—all but one. He was a fine lad. He smiled at her not only with his lips, but, more importantly, with his eyes. The smile said, 'Welcome.' He made the lady feel a little less scared and a lot less lonely. He didn't care what others thought. He did what he felt was right and fair. His name is Thomas, and he's a fine young man."

Quynn smiled softly, his throat unexpectedly clogged at the soft poignancy of her tale. He was not the only one affected. Thomas's face turned a bright red.

"Truly, milady? I did that?"

"Truly." Raiven's smile was dazzling.

Thomas's face lost some of its animation. "'Tis more to it than that, milady. May I tell ye something?"

Raiven nodded solemnly.

"I've watched the baron practice with his men. I've seen what they do." He swallowed audibly. "I've also seen what happens when they make a mistake. I don't think I could take milord's displeasure."

Raiven paused for a moment. "I don't think 'twould be so for you. True, the baron is exacting. It is only because he cares, and he wants his men to be the best. Is that not what made you want to be trained by him?"

Thomas nodded agreement, but the worry was not eased from his brow.

"I will tell you what. What if you trained by yourself so that when the baron begins his training, you will know many things, making it impossible for him to be displeased with you."

"'Twould be nice, but none of the men have time, and if I ask the baron . . ."

Raiven smiled wryly. "I see your problem. Well, what about me? I am not so busy. I could—"

Quynn surged upright from his indolent leaning against a support beam. His incredulity was equally expressed in Thomas's "Ye, milady? 'Tis not stitchery or hearpe playing, but swords and bows."

Raiven laughed. "It is glad you should be that it is not stitchery or hearpe playing. My stitches resemble anything but, and my hearpe playing is second only to my stitchery."

A puzzled look came over Thomas's face. "Are not ladies supposed to do those things?"

A delicate shoulder lifted to fall back into place. "I suppose it is what people expect. I have learned not to give what people expect, but, rather, do the things I do best."

Thomas considered her words, then he asked, "Can ye really show me the manl—er, uh—a few things?"

"Aye, I can. However, because of your reaction to my, er, . . . uh"—from across the stable, Quynn could see the glint of laughter in Raiven's eyes—"manly ways, I know you'll understand why I would not like anyone else to know of this."

A wisdom beyond his years visible upon his face, Thomas asked, "For the same reason ye only speak to me in here while everyone else takes their meal?"

It was evident Raiven hadn't known that he noticed.

She replied softly, "Aye, for the same reason. I know all here do not approve of me. I would not wish to get you into trouble because of befriending me. Also, I would not like the extra criticism because of my rather unusual talents."

Again Thomas nodded.

"I shall meet you here 'fore dawn. We will practice before any arise. Agreed?" She held out her hand.

Thomas, although being only a boy of ten, already was showing what dimensions he would achieve. When his hand grasped hers in warm agreement, Raiven's hand was nearly swallowed.

"Agreed, milady."

Quynn slipped out quietly when he saw Raiven turn away. He barely heard her say, "On the morrow then."

Knowing he could not make it to the hall without being seen, he stepped into the shadows around the stable and watched her make her way back to the hall.

Thomas had long since emerged from the stable when Quynn stepped from the concealing darkness. His steps were slow and aimless, and his face had the look of one in deep thought.

Early the next morning, Raiven and Thomas were making their way across the meadow beyond the house to the woods on the other side. It was not the best place to practice, but they could not have passed the sentries Quynn kept stationed about the main gate without answering questions, and to practice in the front court where they might be seen was unthinkable.

They walked in companionable silence to a tiny circular clearing in the forest. Trees ringed about them, concealing them from the casual eye, while providing excellent targets.

"I think this is a good place, don't you?"

Thomas, still a little wary of his mistress's ability to help him but loath to hurt her feelings, nodded silently.

Raiven set down her quiver with the arrows on the cool, damp ground, then lay her bow beside it.

"What shall we do first?"

"I do not know, milady," Thomas whispered, causing Raiven to laugh.

"It is not necessary to whisper, Thomas. There are none about to hear." Her eyes sparkled a brilliant green in the early morning light. "I ken. You still have doubts about my ability. Did not want to hurt my feelings, I take it?"

Thomas colored, and Raiven laughed again.

"Well then, that is the place to start, is it not? I must prove my competence." She glanced about. "There. See you that tree with the large gnarled knot there on the edge of the circle? I shall pierce it squarely in the center with my arrow."

Raiven reached down to grab the quiver and extract an arrow. "Watch."

Quicker than Thomas was prepared to look, her arrow whistled cleanly through the air, making a loud *thunk!* as it pierced the very same tree in the same spot she said it would. Expectantly, Raiven turned to look at Thomas's face. She was not disappointed. There was such an expression of awe on his face that Raiven laughed again.

"Just to prove 'twas my arm and not good fortune that directed my bow, I shall do it again. Only this time I shall split the arrow already there in two."

Raiven knew she was vaunting her talents shamefully, but she didn't care. It felt wonderful to be herself, to laugh out loud in real amusement and not cynical disbelief. Pushing aside all her careful tutoring on the consequences of a lack of modesty, she took aim and let her arrow fly.

True to her word, her second arrow sailed unerringly to pierce the first in half. By now Thomas was grinning even more than she.

"I shan't be doing this often," she warned him in a rueful tone. "I've only a limited amount of arrows with me, and 'twould not do to take from the baron's supply. I brought my knife along, but I do not like killing for killing's sake, so I will demonstrate its toss only when what I pierce can be slipped into Cook's store after the baron's men have returned from a hunt." Her words allowed for no argument.

"May I see it, milady? I've never seen a lady's knife."

Raiven smiled, and reaching inside the quiver, she extracted a long-bladed, light-handled hunting knife. She unsheathed the blade and turned the handle toward Thomas, who took it gingerly. He touched it as if he expected it to break. "'Twill not break, Thomas. 'Twas made especially for me by my father after I had successfully learned to throw accurately."

By now Thomas's confidence was high, and with exuberance he had not shown before, he asked, "When did ye learn? Do ye have yer own sword?"

Raiven resheathed the knife. "He taught me when I was not much older than you are now. And aye, I have my own sword."

Bright brown eyes flashed to the quiver.

"It is not in there, nor is it at the hall. I could not successfully bring it as I could these. On that you will have to take my word."

"I believe ye," Thomas breathed fervently.

"Good." Raiven smiled. "Shall we begin?"

"Aye!"

And so began many a pleasant morning for a lonely lady and a servant's son. They trained, they played, they cavorted, totally oblivious to their different stations in life and the warm gray eyes that watched them from a distance.

# Chapter
# •15•

Elaine, please hurry."

Raiven fidgeted in her seat, making Elaine glance at her in exasperation as the bandage she was trying to wrap securely about Raiven's hand slipped. Without a word, she continued her task.

"I'm already late, and I did so want to be inconspicuous. If I'm any later, they'll all be there and no doubt will notice my hand. I'll have the devil's own time explaining it," Raiven urged, this time remaining still and barely flinching when Elaine wrapped the long white cloth about her bleeding hand. Beside her on the floor lay three bloodied cloths. Elaine's head did not move from its bent position over Raiven's injured hand.

"I am moving as quickly as safety allows. 'Tis no mere cut you have here. 'Tis long and deep."

Raiven made a face. "Well I know it. I still cannot believe I was so inept."

That made Elaine's head dart up. "How came you by this?" Just as quickly she lowered her head to keep from smiling into Raiven's expression of sudden shame.

"I was trying to show Thomas the proper way to throw a knife," Raiven began disgustedly. There was no need for subterfuge with Elaine. She knew of Raiven's early-morning excursions with the boy. "We were using our favorite tree for practice. I went to retrieve the blade. 'Twas stuck and required a stronger tug. At that moment I thought I heard something, and I turned, no longer giving my full attention to the task. Unfortunately, I placed this hand too close to the blade, and when I pulled, this was the result. It sliced through the skin 'ere I knew it. In truth, 'twas Thomas's gasp that made me realize my stupidity."

Elaine sighed, shaking her dark head. "I must tell you, milady, that you must be very careful. The bleeding has slowed, but it has not stopped. I fear if 'tis struck or pressed in any way, what little mending has been done would open anew. I fear you need more than a stitch or two."

Raiven looked down at her bandaged hand lying limply in Elaine's lap. "I agree with you. Unfortunately, I could not do it myself, even if my stitching was better than passable, and you were not available earlier. I have no choice. This will have to do. If I don't go downstairs, I fear poor Thomas will blather the whole of it in his worry. His face was as white as chamber linen when he saw the damage. Besides, to stay here, I would need a reason and that would again call attention to this thing." Raiven grimaced toward her wounded member.

Raiven could see Elaine was not convinced. Effectively stopping further protests, she stood and moved with fleet grace to the door. "I will allow you to attend it later. For now I will have a care. I promise." She slipped from the room, leaving Elaine alternating between a stern frown and vicious muttering about the stubbornness of certain people.

Elaine and her disapproval had fled Raiven's mind completely by the time she rounded the bend in the hall stairs to see that everyone indeed had already arrived for the evening meal. Tucking her hands behind her back to conceal her wound brought a reflexive groan to her lips and an immediate loosening of her grip.

Raiven practically ran to the table. By the time Quynn turned to bid her good evening, she was already seated, her left hand hidden beneath the table. Smiling quickly at Quynn and his men seated with him, she began to eat.

As the meal progressed, she ate automatically, not really tasting the food. The throbbing in her hand was becoming practically unbearable. Her body's natural pain suppressant was wearing off, and as the blood surged to the wound, Raiven made an art form of chewing the venison, which, in truth, was so tender chewing was practically not necessary.

Once or twice when Quynn glanced her way, she gave him a weak smile and ground her teeth together in what she hoped was an adequate imitation of someone enjoying her meal.

Her conversation was abysmal. While she was not rude, she was not nearly as animated as she had been recently, and her tacitness did not go unnoted.

Raiven's smile weakened to the point where it was more of a grimace. She no longer cared. It was all the response she could manage. As if she read Quynn's thoughts, Raiven knew he was surely thinking that she had changed—again. Although she didn't like the look gathering in his eyes after the surreptitious pleasure she had gained from the slight thawing she had observed in his gray gaze recently, she was powerless to change it.

Once again Raiven met the questioning look in Quynn's gray eyes, and once again she gave the smile that was no smile at all and looked away.

*Oh, blast!* she thought angrily, cursing herself roundly for her stupidity, which was causing her to lose all the ground she had gained with him. *Why did this have to happen now?*

During the past days, Raiven had noticed Quynn staring at her. When she met his gaze, the look she saw in his eyes made her feel warm throughout her entire body. At those times, she smiled shyly at him and turned away, hoping the flush she felt was not as evident on her face yet, strangely, not caring if it was. Those were the moments that made her certain he would return to her bed soon, and it was those moments that made her lie awake at night, remembering and waiting. Nevertheless, her wait had been for naught, because although the frequency of his stares increased, he still had not sought her out at night.

Now his expression chilled instead of warmed, and she longed to reach out and soothe the frown gathering on his brow but could only sit silently. The pain in her hand was so intense she was afraid if she opened her mouth, the only thing to emerge would be a groan.

By the end of the meal Raiven's sparse comments had trickled to a halt, and it was all she could do to remain seated while the utensils were removed. She was about to excuse herself, not caring what Quynn or the others thought, when Thomas entered the hall. His appearance made her momentarily forget the throbbing in her hand as he came straight toward her, and she did her best to will him away.

She knew he came to ask about her hand, and she couldn't talk about it now. With Quynn now watching her constantly, she knew he would pick up on anything out of the ordinary. Helplessly Raiven watched Thomas approach, give his greeting to Quynn, then turn to her.

"How are ye faring, milady?" he asked solemnly.

Raiven could have wept with relief that he had asked such a neutral question, and a strained smile crossed her face.

"I am *well,* Thomas," Raiven replied emphatically.

"I came to see about—"

"Do you not have chores?"

Thomas looked stunned. "Yes'm," he began, clearly confused by her manner, "but I—"

"I would not want to keep you from them. I was about to take my rest," Raiven interrupted again. Then, because she was unable to bear the look of hurt gathering in his eyes, she added, "On the morrow we can talk." She glanced about nervously, well aware that Quynn was paying close attention to the most words she had spoken since she came to the table.

Raiven's discomfort grew when Ella chose that unfortunate time to return to the hall. Immediately her eyes took on the customary frown she reserved solely for when she saw Thomas and Raiven together.

To Raiven's relief, understanding finally dawned on Thomas's face, and she felt safe to exit the growing unease of the main hall. She began to back away from the table, grateful that no worse damage had been done, when Thomas gasped, "Milady, it bleeds still."

Although it was barely a horrified whisper, Raiven knew immediately that Quynn had heard. Now she did groan, whether in pain or anxiety she could not be sure.

Casually, as if he did it all the time, Quynn's arm bumped the remaining goblet in front of him on the floor. When Ella made to rush forward, he allayed her with a glance while he leaned to his right to pick it up. When he was righting himself, his eyes went to Raiven's lap and he blanched.

Raiven looked down to see what he and Thomas saw, and she gasped. The white bandage was crimson. Her eyes slowly rose to meet Quynn's, and she was paralyzed by what she saw there. Gray fury engulfed her, and his condemning eyes turned to Thomas.

To his credit, the lad stood his ground, though he shifted lightly from one foot to the other.

"I can explain," Raiven began softly, still trying not to attract undue attention. "It is not what you think, really."

One ebony eyebrow rose, and Thomas ventured to redeem both himself and his lady. "Milord, 'tis my fault."

Quynn's eyes snapped to his, and whatever words Thomas had been about to say died in his throat.

"In the morning, Thomas. For now my lady needs attention."

Swallowing heavily, the boy turned and ran from the hall. Raiven rose to go after him, but with one glance, Quynn dared her to set foot from the hall. If her acquiescence was due to his wordless threat or because from the corner of her eye she saw Ella look at them strangely and then follow behind her son, Raiven did not know. She did, however, remain where she was, allowing the tenseness of aborted flight to leave her body. At least someone would look to Thomas. There was no one to look to her. Quynn's closed expression gave no indication of his emotions. The fury she had glimpsed had been tamped back. He merely waited, his eyes blank, for her to explain.

Raiven swallowed heavily. "Mi—please, 'twas only an accident . . . a little thing. Elaine shall mend it, and all will be well. Please do not blame Thomas. He's only a lad."

Quynn's eyes narrowed thoughtfully, but his only response was, "I suggest you find your servant quickly." He rose in what Raiven thought was dismissal, but instead he walked around to her and, effectively blocked from view of the others, pulled back her chair, and escorted her to the stairs.

Raiven had mounted the first step when she turned back to him. "Thank you for saving my pride."

Quynn smiled softly, his first genuine smile at her of the evening. Again, Raiven forgot the pain in her hand.

"Your thanks are not necessary. I saw your dilemma. In a moment more, your secret would have been out, no matter your wish otherwise. Good night, Raiven."

His deliberate stress of her name was all the admonition he gave.

"Good night," she whispered before turning and running up the stairs, impelled as much by the remembered pain in her hand as by the enchanting snare of Quynn's gaze.

A long time later, Raiven slipped into the comfort of her bed, glad that the ordeal of stitching her hand was over. Her eyelids were beginning to droop, partly from exhaustion due to the day's activity and partly from the elixir Elaine had forced her to take for the pain. She was about to succumb to the welcoming arms of oblivion when a disquieting thought snapped her eyes back open.

Quynn had not asked how she had sustained such a wound. Even if he didn't care about her, she knew Quynn was unusually protective of those entrusted to his care. That he took that responsibility seriously she did not doubt. Hadn't he been ferocious in his defense of James's safety? If that was not enough, there had been a few incidents since her arrival at Havilland that had wiped any question from her mind—the most outstanding being Quynn's fury at the attack on his tenant the night before the morning he saw her riding. That night, as she watched him, Raiven had been glad that for once his rage was not directed at or caused by her. That particular situation had cemented in her mind Quynn's unbreakable loyalty to his people or any who were his own.

Obviously, she was not one of them. After a moment of shock at the sight of her blood, he was unaffected. He hadn't really cared that she was wounded. Raiven became aware of an unfamiliar tightening in her chest, which she attributed as a side effect of the strong tonic Elaine had forced upon her.

Despite the best of her will, Raiven found she couldn't fight off the sudden depression that overcame her. The rationale that she wouldn't feel this way if the drug had not lowered her inhibitions did no use. The one depressing thought that Quynn did not consider her one of his own was the crack in her emotional dam, and she relived every hurt, imagined and real. She spent the next moments alternating between laughing and crying. In a corner of her mind, Raiven knew she was behaving the way she had seen her father's guests react when they had had too much wine at table, but just as quickly as reason came, it fled, replaced by euphoric paranoia. This was different. They had just been silly, and she was . . . not. She was . . . Raiven sighed, her mood shifting abruptly again, leaving her cheerfully confused over her loss of thought. She didn't know what she was feeling, but whatever it was, it hurt and it was everyone's fault, she thought with undue woefulness, her mood altering once more.

For the next few minutes, Raiven alternated between exaggerated self-pity and unexplained merriment. When the full effect of the drug took hold and she had finally fallen asleep, neither emotion had the upper hand. Yet beneath it all, determined to be addressed and recognized, that unfamiliar and unnamed sensation lay waiting quietly in the shadows of her heart.

The next morning, when Raiven awoke, she was groggy from the depth of her slumber. The rest, however, had had its desired effect. The pain from her wound had subsided greatly. Unfortunately she also discovered that she had overslept. On the heels of this realization came thoughts of Thomas. He would be worried. After the way she and Quynn had behaved toward him yestereve, he would no doubt be feeling guilty.

Rising quickly, Raiven washed and dressed, hoping that in spite of the lateness of the hour, Thomas had stayed around to see her. Although they would not be able to practice, they could talk. She needed to speak to him privately to make sure that he understood why she had spoken as she had and that none of this was his fault.

By the time Raiven stepped out into the courtyard, Quynn's men were already hard at their drills. She looked around quickly, but there was no sign of Thomas. She set off for their rendezvous spot anyway, hoping that he might have seen her and would soon appear.

He did.

Raiven became aware of someone approaching, and when she turned, she looked into Thomas's sad brown eyes.

"Milady, 'tis sorry I am about yer hand. If I hada knowed that ye would be hurt on 'count of me, I would never have let ye show me things, no matter how much I needed the help," he blurted immediately.

Ending his obviously rehearsed speech, he fell silent, looking at her with beseeching eyes.

"I thank you, Thomas, for your concern, but you did naught. 'Twas my own stupidity that caused my injury. I did not give attention to what I was doing, which is a perfect example of why I have always stressed to you that you must maintain concentration. Losing it only serves to bring wounds to yourself, perhaps worse than those given by your opponent. And, of course," she added, a twinkle in her eyes as she tried to alleviate the sadness in his, "you only make his job the lighter, for he need never touch you, because you will have done the deed for him."

A reluctant smile crossed Thomas's face, which Raiven returned.

Happy with her success at lightening his mood, Raiven smiled widely. "That's better. Now as for my unfortunate *accident,"* she stressed, "we'll speak no more of it."

A little of the shadow returned to Thomas's eyes. "What of milord? What did he say?"

"Rest easy, Thomas. The baron has said nothing. That should let you know how trivial it is. Had it been worthy of note, you, knowing the baron as you do, would know that for a certainty he would have had something to say. Milord barely noted a scratch such as this one."

Fleetingly, a remembrance of sadness crossed Raiven's mind, but she could recall no reason for it, so she merely shrugged away the feeling a moment before a voice interrupted them.

"While 'tis true, Thomas, you may rest easy, 'tis equally untrue that 'milord' barely noted that *gash* on your hand," said a quiet deep voice behind them.

Despite his seriousness, Quynn quelled the desire to smile at the astonishment on Raiven's and Thomas's faces. He waited a full minute, not releasing either from the weight of his stare. The urge to laugh was getting stronger as both continued to gape mutely at him, so Quynn decided to speak again lest he burst out laughing and lose the graveness of the situation altogether.

"Instead of barely noticing as you assumed, I was only waiting for a better moment to speak of it. 'Twould seem the moment is here. What have you to say?"

Quynn stepped forward into the clearing, and Raiven observed that he was dressed for the lengthy drills that he undertook daily with his men. Tearing her eyes away from his imposing stature, Raiven glanced down at Thomas. Quynn's sudden appearance, in spite of his words of assurance, left the boy unbalanced. Clearly if 'twas answers Quynn sought, Thomas would not be able to supply them. Nervously, Raiven cleared her throat and tried to speak. When no sound came forth and Quynn's brow arched quizzically, she tried again.

"We are, that is to say, we were . . . Is it time for your practice with your men?"

Quynn's lips gave a telltale twitch. "Your pardon, but did I not pose the first question?" The threat was mild. "I trust I shall not be forced to repeat it?"

"Quynn, there was no real harm," Raiven began, speaking quickly. "Thomas needed a little practice, and I had naught else to do. We helped each other, for I knew none of your men would practice with me. Yesterday, the knife became stuck in a tree, and as I pulled with my right, I accidentally cut my left. But I tended it quickly as best as I could. Elaine was off helping another, which was why 'twas in such poor condition at the evening meal. Later, as *you* instructed, she mended it, and now I scarce know it is there. Please do not be angry with him. 'Twas none of his doing."

Unconsciously Raiven laid her hand on his chest as she pleaded with him not to take his anger out on Thomas. For herself she asked nothing. He would do as he would, she was well aware, but Thomas looked up to him, and the lad's feelings were still tender. She did not want that to be shattered. Already he blamed himself. Quynn's anger would only make it worse.

Raiven searched his face to see any sign of relenting, but she could not decipher the look that leaped into his eyes. She was not to know that he was having the greatest difficulty following her oration after her first word and gentle touch upon his chest. She had, in her earnest desire to allay his anger from Thomas, used his name, and the sound of it falling from her lips captivated him more than a caress. His name on her lips, then her touch on his chest, along with the pleading look in her sparkling green eyes, caused inappropriate feelings to suddenly envelop him, feelings that had no place in a clearing with a young boy watching them. 'Twas Thomas's face that lent Quynn the strength of control. Now 'twas he who cleared his throat to produce a voice.

He pulled away from Raiven and walked to the center of the clearing, standing with his back to them while he regained control of himself.

Thomas and Raiven waited. Quynn's silence did not bode well, and Raiven, seeing Thomas wilt before her eyes, was about to speak again when Quynn finally turned.

"So, what is it my wife has taught you?" His voice was strained slightly.

Raiven's sigh was audible, and the grin on Thomas's face threatened to split it in two.

"She has taught me much, milord." His face grew momentarily puzzled. "That is, much for being only a girl."

The last of the strain left Quynn's face, and his smile was brilliant. "'Twould seem she is full of surprises, eh?" His words were directed toward Thomas, but his eyes were upon Raiven, causing her to feel extremely warm.

"To be sure," Thomas crowed, echoing one of the phrases he had heard Quynn use repeatedly, totally innocent of the look and the increasing undercurrent between the lord and his lady.

"Since milady is injured, would I do as a replacement?" Quynn asked gravely. "I may not be full of many surprises, but I believe my skills are adequate."

Happiness radiated from Thomas's face as he nodded eagerly. Then he turned to Raiven. "Ye do not mind, milady?"

Raiven's countenance was sufficiently serious as she replied, "Not in the least," but inwardly she admitted that she did not think Thomas would care if she objected or not. She turned away, about to return to the hall, when Quynn's voice stopped her.

"Where do you go? Surely you know that any knight or knight-in-training," he added, glancing at Thomas, "desires the audience of a beautiful woman. Stay while we attempt to regale you with our talents."

Raiven perched on the stump of a long-dead tree and waved for them to begin. If she but knew it, her face rivaled Thomas's for brilliance as she watched Quynn showing Thomas new things and augmenting what she had already taught. He was not brusque, but he was stern, telling Thomas that he must always be aware of the situation.

"Sometimes," Quynn warned solemnly, "'tis a man's ability to know what is about to happen that saves his life."

Thomas listened and absorbed this and everything else Quynn said like dry earth taking in precious drops of water. He did not demur when Quynn made him try things again and again. He took criticisms as well as he took compliments, and Quynn commended him all the more.

Raiven watched the two and felt a special kind of joy. Quynn was good with Thomas. He did not speak down to him. He did not deliberately miss a mark so that Thomas would win their contests. Therefore, when Thomas did something well, he could feel full achievement because of his own merit.

When Quynn called a halt to their practice about an hour later, again both Raiven and Thomas had identical expressions: that of disappointment. It was only after they had started back that Raiven realized that Quynn had found them seemingly without any trouble. His ease at locating them seemed to answer the question of his calm acceptance of her injury even before they had explained. Since he knew of this place, he obviously knew of their activities and had come to a reasonable conclusion about her injury on his own.

Raiven felt her chest fill with a warm feeling as she thought about the way Quynn handled the situation. He could have confronted her last night, but he did not, allowing her to get the attention and rest she needed. Today, he came along to stand in for her so that Thomas would not miss his practice.

The thought occurred to her that she was not the only one full of surprises. With only half an ear, she listened to Thomas and Quynn arrange to meet again tomorrow.

As she cast a speculative glance up at Quynn, a smile shaped her lips only to disappear hurriedly when he turned to her.

Raiven flushed and looked away from his stare. However, her thoughts of him were not so easily set aside, and the warmth in her chest enveloped the rest of her body, and when the small smile came to her lips this time, it stayed.

# Chapter
# 16

The events of the next day irrevocably changed Raiven's standing with Quynn and his people. The day started normally, giving no indication of the momentous events to come.

Raiven and Thomas had again met with Quynn to resume practice, and again, she was given the uninhibited pleasure of watching her husband without having to pretend that she wasn't. She was no longer disturbed by her desire to watch him. Raiven had decided that her decision not to hide from situations included facing the deepening attraction she felt for her husband. She didn't know where things would lead, but it was silly to continually pretend that she still hated her husband and her marriage.

Her way here was easier, and if the people did not like her, at least she had gained a grudging respect.

Watching the sun glint off Quynn's dark head as he bent to help Thomas steady his bow, she wondered if his opinion of her had changed. There were times when she caught him staring at her with an expression that was no longer cold, though it couldn't exactly be termed warm either. Reflective, Raiven decided, would be a more apt description.

Yestereve had been a prime example. After the evening meal, she had been walking about the hall when she discovered—to her delight—a chess set. The board and pieces were exquisite, carved from mahogany and ivory, with each piece being at least six inches tall.

Without thinking, Raiven began to move the pieces in their strategical planes, becoming more involved in her one-man game. As she became more absorbed in her contest, the presence of the others around her faded. Therefore, she had not noticed when an increased hush began to spread through the usually rambunctious hall. One by one the men became aware that she was really playing a game of chess with herself and not idly moving the pieces about the board.

Raiven had progressed to the point where she had the mahogany queen in danger, but to take the piece would leave her vulnerable for the next move or two until the ivory bishop and knight could maneuver to close her left flank. She was pondering deeply the feasibility of it all when a deep voice interrupted her musings.

"Surely, milady knows that to take the queen, although tempting and accessible, would leave her own defenses assailable to an attack that may not be worth the risk."

Raiven looked up, her eyes revealing her absorption in the game. Douglass, the same knight from whom she had rudely walked away when he had been paying homage to her beauty, was watching her game with acute fascination. Douglass smiled. The baron's beautiful wife was still preoccupied with her dilemma. Without waiting for an invitation, he asked, "May I?" pointing to the chair on the other side of the chess table.

Raiven nodded, and he slid into the seat across from her. Realizing his intent, her eyes focused fully on him, and a winsome smile crossed her features.

"Obviously you play the game, sir. If the move were yours, what would you do?"

Douglass's dark brown brows furrowed. This time his smile was slow as it crossed his face, and when he spoke, it was not about the intricacies of the game.

"If milord minds not my speaking thus, I would concede the match, never before having met an opponent so fair."

"Fiddle faddle," came the instant and laughing response. "I'm sure you did not get to be a knight of your stature by being fooled by the appearance of the enemy. Your move, sir?" she invited, turning aside his compliment smoothly. She hoped she had not offended him again, but she really didn't want to hear about her looks if what she suspected—that she had found someone to challenge her chess skills—was true. Her father had once told her what he deemed to be high praise: that she played chess with the cleverness of a man—as if a woman could not possess such a virtue.

Douglass inclined his head, accepting her challenge, but when Raiven made to realign the pieces to their original positions, he stopped her.

"I prefer to continue this match. I find your strategy most intriguing."

The board was attached to the table much like a wheel to a cart, allowing the player or players to turn it to best advantage before making a move. Douglass shifted the board so that the mahogany pieces were in front of Raiven, and as he said, he did not risk taking the queen at that moment. However, Raiven was not free from danger. Three moves later he was threatening her defenses again. She had barely escaped the capture of her king before he was being hotly pursued again.

By this time quite a crowd gathered to watch, and both Raiven and Douglass were oblivious to them. Douglass was beginning to realize that his baron's wife was a very worthy opponent, and Raiven was engrossed as always when she played chess.

Raiven made a series of expected moves, and she could read the disappointment in Douglass's eyes until he realized she had him outmaneuvered. A spark lit his eyes, and only quick thinking saved him from being checkmated for one of the few times since he began to play the game. Suddenly he slid his chair back slightly and bent forward to the table. Raiven recognized that as the signal that the game would now begin in earnest.

An hour later it was Douglass who made Raiven aware of Quynn standing behind her when leaning back, rubbing his ear, a disbelieving grin on his face, he said, "It pains me to admit that I must concede the draw. I see no way to win the round. Your wife is a master player."

Raiven flushed, turning around to see that Quynn stood close behind her chair. His speculative gaze held hers, and Raiven detected something else stirring in the depths of his eyes. To her shame, as in the days past, she lacked the courage to return his stare.

Mumbling her consent to Douglass's request for a rematch, Raiven had hurriedly excused herself from the room where she was the center of many stares, most especially the disconcerting one of her husband.

She had almost made it to the stairs when Quynn fell in step beside her. To her delight and terror, he had accompanied her to her chamber, stepping aside when she opened the door. For one heart-stopping moment, Raiven had thought he was going to come in with her. Her cheeks had pinkened as she recognized the truth of her own eagerness for him to enter her chamber *and* her bed. She had been disappointed then, when his eyes lingered a long while on her face as if reading a message there, and finally he had turned and walked away after a soft "Good night."

Raiven had closed the door quietly, leaning against it, with her face pressed against the cool wood. At first she had been mortified that she had been too obvious in her desire, and then she had been equally chagrined that perhaps she had not.

As she had slowly undressed for bed, Raiven had pondered her sterile existence. She wearied of sleeping alone. She wasn't ready to face whatever she felt for Quynn, but she knew she wanted him here beside her at night. Her problem was, she had admitted, punching her pillow in frustration, that she didn't know how to go about getting him there.

Raiven was still thinking of her husband when Thomas's shout of exultation brought her back to the present. Turning, she saw what had caused his excitement. There, still quivering from the impact, was his arrow in the center of their target. Forgetting herself, Raiven rushed exuberantly from her perch on the stump to give him a hug.

"You did it! Did I not tell you that time and patience are the best teachers? Time and patience and lots of practice, that is. Now see there! In the center, Thomas. Congratulations! I am so proud of you."

"Thank you, milady," Thomas replied somewhat stiffly, making Raiven aware of Quynn's watchful gaze.

Awkwardly she pulled away from him, embarrassed enough for them both. "Forgive me, Thomas. I forgot that one of your years has no need for such a display. It is unseemly for someone almost a man and a knight."

Thomas nodded curtly, but it was Quynn who spoke.

"'Tis precisely why such things are necessary, lad. Why, I cannot call to mind any tourney or contest where a beautiful lady did not present the prize. One with the developing skill you have shown had best grow accustomed to 'such displays' because I'm sure 'tis only the first of many."

Raiven looked up at Quynn and smiled warmly. He had managed to erase Thomas's discomfort and embarrassment while praising him for his budding talent. He really was a remarkable person. In truth, the more she saw of him, the more she found to lo—like. Raiven knew he would be wonderful with his own children.

Immediately her face burned red when she recalled that she was to be the means by which he would get those children.

As always, Quynn chose that unfortunate moment to return his gaze to his wife. His smile widened, and Raiven, not for the first time since knowing him, had the strangest sensation that he knew the bend of her thoughts. Whatever the case, she lacked the courage to answer or even acknowledge the unspoken question in

Quynn's eyes. Instead she hastily removed herself back to her stump and watched as Quynn and Thomas resumed their practice.

*"That's the way it is done, Raiven,"* she muttered to herself in disgust, *"at the pace you proceed, why, you'll have him in your bed, and no mistake—by the time you're three score and ten."*

Later that afternoon, Raiven and Elaine set out to visit the tenant whose family had suffered in the raid. The family, who had been lodging with another of Quynn's tenants, had recently moved into a new cottage, but they lacked furnishings, having lost all to the fire. Raiven had a few things she wanted to take to them. When she told Quynn of her desire, at first he hesitated. He could not accompany her. The extra time he spent with Thomas in the morning tightened his schedule in the afternoons. However, Raiven insisted, and at last he relented after making her promise to return before nightfall. Since the attack, he had set extra guards, but he wanted to take no chances.

With Quynn's admonition to return home by nightfall still reverberating in her ears, Raiven and Elaine started off. They had not traveled far when they heard strange sounds coming from the direction of the stream Quynn had shown Raiven her first day in England. Elaine, immediately fearful, suggested they return and summon help.

"And what shall we tell them, Elaine? That we thought we heard strange sounds coming from over the hill? Nay, I don't think that will do. Let's ride to the rise and peer over. If there is trouble, we'll be close enough to see but far enough away so as to be in no immediate danger."

"I don't think the baron would approve," Elaine argued.

Raiven shot her servant a curious look. "When did you become concerned over what the baron would or would not approve?"

"Well, he has been kind," Elaine began defensively

only to end in a screech as Raiven turned the cart toward the rise. "Milady, I do not think—"

"Cease your talk of what my husband would approve. In fact cease your talk period, else you will alert whoever is there to our presence. You don't want that, do you?" Raiven hissed.

Elaine closed her mouth, her eyes wide and round, and Raiven thought she saw her ears twitch from the strain of trying to hear. She would have laughed, but her words had not been merely a ploy to frighten Elaine. If there was something amiss, it certainly was not wise to announce their coming.

When the stream came into view, there was no one on the shore, and the strange garbled noise had stopped. Raiven stood in the cart looking around the area, but she saw nothing. Frowning, she looked about again when Elaine said, "You see, 'twas naught. Let's leave here."

Shaking her head over the strangeness of it all, Raiven sat back down, as puzzled as Elaine was relieved, when the sound came again, and this time there was no mistaking it.

Elaine's eyes widened anew. In unison two pairs of eyes, one questing, one fearful, turned to the grassy bank along the stream. Still there was no one and nothing beyond the ordinary visible.

Raiven knew there were swift eddies and undercurrents in the stream. One could hear the water's constant surge against the rocks that made the bed, but that would not be responsible for the distorted sound she and Elaine heard.

Scanning the water instead of the shore, Raiven saw a faint movement quite a way out. From this distance, she could not make out what it was, but she was sure she saw something.

Elaine's renewed protests went unheeded as Raiven jumped from the cart and began to run down to the shore. As she drew nearer to the water's edge, she saw what it was, and calling back over her shoulder to Elaine, she cried, "Someone is drowning! Elaine, go quickly to the hall and get help! He may be too large for me to carry back to shore by myself."

Elaine had barely dismounted from the cart before Raiven had pulled off her bliaut, rolled back her hose, and dived cleanly into the water to search frantically for any sign of the person she had glimpsed from the bank. Had the situation been less dire, Raiven would have laughed when she heard Elaine shriek at the top of her lungs while running back to the hall. Raiven well knew that Elaine could neither ride a horse nor direct a cart. So she must have opted for the only things she could do: scream and run.

Elaine might not be as fast as a horse, Raiven thought as she hurriedly scanned the water, but she was certainly louder than one and would probably attract attention long before she even entered the inner courtyard of the hall.

Raiven dived beneath the surface, certain that help would be coming quickly if only she could locate the person and keep him afloat. After a few moments, she resurfaced to take in air and search the top of the water to see if she could detect anything. The water was smooth and undisturbed.

Uttering a frantic prayer, Raiven dived again. Already her limbs were becoming numb from the chill of the water and her eyes were beginning to ache from the strain of looking underneath the cool surface of the water. She swam underwater, heading in a direction parallel to the one she had been traveling in the cart. At last she spied a sluggish movement ahead and swam toward it. When she closed some distance, Raiven saw it was a boy, not a man. When she reached him, her shock was so great at discovering that it was Thomas she made the near fatal mistake of taking in air where there was none.

Grabbing at Thomas's head, she shot to the surface, her lungs burning intensely. Clutching Thomas's head to her breast, Raiven breathed slowly, trying to lessen the pain in her chest. With determined precision, Raiven warded off the hysteria nibbling at the edge of her consciousness. When she gathered her control, she tried to swim with him to the shore. Her strength was failing, and neither of them would survive much longer in the water. But Thomas would not budge.

Mindlessly she tugged on him, terrified to admit that something under the water held him anchored. Irrational fear began to assail her at the thought of returning below the water's surface to try to free him. Her lungs and nostrils still ached, and her mind rebelled against the thought. A few more futile, strength-sapping tugs assured her that that was what she would have to do. The bank was quite a distance away, and no one had yet to appear over the rise. Raiven tried to beat back the fear that said if she didn't do something now, they would both drown before help arrived.

Breathing as deeply as she dared, Raiven let go of Thomas's head, dismay overwhelming her at how quickly he sank beneath the surface. Without further thought to enhance her fear, she dived below to see what held him.

A piece of vine or rope of some sort had wrapped itself around one of his legs. Obviously Thomas in an attempt to free himself had created a knot of sorts. Raiven could feel her nails snap and tear as she almost hysterically tried to release his foot, all the while lamenting the fact that she had left her dagger on the bank with her clothes.

Her lungs burned, and she was crying with frustration by the time the rope finally released Thomas's limb. Grabbing the boy by the throat in a grip that surely would kill him if she tightened it but a fraction, she headed for the shore.

Raiven was crying and coughing when they finally reached the bank. For a few precious moments, she was content merely to take in sweet air. Then she noted that Thomas was not breathing.

"Oh God, nay," Raiven moaned. Surely they had not endured all that for Thomas to die.

Forgetting the exhaustion weighing down her limbs, Raiven leaned over and placed her ear to Thomas's chest. His heartbeat was so faint.

"Naaay," she moaned again. Seized by violent stomach cramps, Raiven doubled over as the water she'd swallowed surged up from her lungs. Raiven almost collapsed from the force of her retching, but suddenly her eyes snapped back to Thomas. He, too, had swallowed water, much more than she. Could there be a way to make him expel the bulk of it as she had just done?

Raiven crawled over Thomas's still body. Pushing the heavy tresses of sodden hair from her eyes, she said a fervent prayer that what she was about to do would help and not finish what the water had started. A quick look back to the hill again only increased her distress. No one was coming. All was still silent. She couldn't wait any longer. Thomas could not wait.

Using the heels of her two hands, she applied pressure to Thomas's stomach in an attempt to imitate the same violent sensation that had rid her stomach of its unwelcome contents. She pushed once, twice, three times. Each time Raiven pushed harder than the last.

Suddenly Thomas's body began to jerk, and water spewed from his mouth at the same time he began to cough. He alternated between coughing and retching. Seeing that the pressure was no longer needed, Raiven rolled Thomas to his side so that he would not choke himself and the water could exit freely. When it finally stopped, a few weak coughs were all that remained, but Thomas was breathing on his own, shallow breaths, but breathing nonetheless.

He began to shake, and Raiven noted his skin had a bluish tinge to it. He was far from out of danger. Grabbing up her discarded bliaut, she ripped the seams and made a small blanket of it, absently noting that her exertions had reopened her wound. Pulling off his wet chainse, Raiven wrapped Thomas in the ripped bliaut, then dragged him against her body for whatever meager warmth she could offer while praying for help to come soon. She prayed for Quynn.

Raiven watched the fire roar in the hearth. She was sitting in her bed wrapped snugly in the fur throws she had brought with her from France. She had already sipped about as much broth as she was going to, and she rather acidly informed Elaine of that when the woman tried to urge her to sip a little more.

Elaine had harrumphed that, despite the hoarseness of Raiven's voice, if she could be that irascible, Raiven would be fine.

Raiven did not miss her smile, and one of her own softened her features. She knew Elaine had been truly worried about her. Elaine had fussed and cried over her so much that Raiven was certain that half her bathwater had been Elaine's tears. Tears had flowed while she restitched Raiven's hand, washed her hair, and settled her in her bath. The only time Elaine's tears had dried had been when Raiven refused to go to bed for the rest she declared she needed.

Fortunately for Elaine and unfortunately for Raiven, Quynn had entered the room and had given Raiven the choice of either returning to bed on her own or being carried there and restrained if needed. And despite the kindness of his manner, there had not been an ounce of compromise in his gray eyes.

Raiven capitulated and went to bed.

In truth she was happy to be able to do nothing but rest. In those long moments of holding Thomas's shivering body, she had never been more terrified and exhausted. When she had heard the blessed sound of hoofbeats and had opened her eyes to see Quynn standing over her, she had wept with joy, knowing Quynn would take care of everything.

In the next moments things happened so quickly she didn't have room for any thought at all. She was swiftly lifted to Khan's back, and Thomas was wrapped securely in the rear of a cart.

When they reached the bailey, Ella had been there to meet them and had started crying softly when she saw her son. Quynn had ordered them to take Thomas to his cottage where his mother could tend him, and he carried Raiven to her room and bade Elaine to follow.

While Elaine had begun the preparations to care for her, Quynn had built a fire in the room and ordered a hot broth for her to drink.

Now she sat, stuffed, pampered, and still weak but curious to know about Thomas, and all Elaine would say was "He is being given every care."

When at last Raiven threatened to go find out for herself, Elaine relented and went to seek out information. Within minutes, she returned with Quynn.

"You wish for something?" he asked quietly, standing at the foot of the bed.

Raiven shot Elaine a murderous look that branded her a traitor, then replied, "I want only to know how Thomas fares. He was so cold, and his skin was blue. He was much worse than I. Who is tending him?"

"His mother."

Raiven nodded, vaguely remembering Ella's following behind Thomas's body as Douglass had carried the boy to their cottage.

"Does she know the herbs to use to bring down the fever that will certainly come? Has she treated this sort of malady before?"

Quynn shrugged. "She is his mother. She will do what must be done."

To the astonishment of the two people watching her, Raiven swung her long, shapely legs from beneath the furs and struggled unsteadily to her feet. She had swayed only once when Quynn lifted her back to the bed.

"What do you think you're doing?" he snapped.

"I must go to him. He will need me. Don't you understand? He can still die. He was in the water much too long. He needs to drink a potion for his fever. I only want to help, to make certain he is cared for properly."

Quynn studied her agitated face. "You cannot go," he said implacably, although his tone was quiet. "Does Elaine know how to concoct this brew?"

Raiven nodded.

"When done here, she may go."

Quynn stepped away, and Raiven sat impatiently while Elaine examined her. The instant she was done, Raiven bade her hurry. Elaine grabbed her satchel containing her herbs and potions and hurried away without another word, leaving Quynn and Raiven alone in their chamber for the first time in weeks.

# Chapter 17

Silence stretched between them, growing and enveloping them in an awkwardness Raiven could not find the words to break. Glancing at Quynn, Raiven was astonished to see that he was not immune to the stress of the situation.

It occurred to her that for people who were married they had never *talked* to each other. She didn't know anything about him, and he knew nothing of her. Grasping for something—anything—to end the silence and make him stay, Raiven said, "It is a lovely estate you have here."

As soon as the words were out, she winced. Did she really just say that? Raising her eyes to Quynn's again to see his reaction to her idiotic remark, she thought she detected a twinkle in his eyes. Raiven looked away when his lips began to twitch. Then her eyes snapped back to his, glittering a warning that Quynn did not heed. He threw back his head and laughed, great gusting fits of laughter that made tears roll down his face.

Raiven colored miserably while waiting for him to regain control of himself. Between blushes, she shot angry looks at him that should have melted him on the spot. Finally, when she tired of the whole of it, she said waspishly, "Oh, come, Quynn, 'twasn't that amusing."

Quynn's laughter subsided slightly. "It wasn't? Pray, when did you get to see the estate? Was it before or after your dip in the stream?" he asked between chuckles.

"Nothing is that funny," Raiven returned. "And if you're that much of a thickwit to know that you shouldn't laugh at sick people, then I—"

Quynn's renewed shout of laughter cut her off, and Raiven's eyes began to smolder dangerously.

This time, however, Quynn heeded the sizzling message in her eyes. After a few more chuckles, he sat on the edge of the bed and said solemnly, "I am sorry."

"You should be," Raiven retorted.

Quynn's smile grew dangerously wide. "Surely you must allow that was a rather, er . . . common thing to say."

"At least I said something," Raiven said sullenly.

"I cannot argue that point."

Raiven turned her back to him, furious with herself and with him for ridiculing her attempt at conversation. "I am tired. I'd like to rest if you don't mind."

None of the humor left Quynn's face. "Am I now dismissed?"

Grinding her teeth to hold her temper, she decided not to answer him, but his next words efficiently doused her anger and captured her full attention.

"Do I make you that uncomfortable?"

Slowly Raiven turned to face him. "What makes you ask that? Just because I made one inane statement does not mean that you, that I—I am not uncomfortable."

Quynn smiled another lazy, relaxed smile. Leaning back against the bedpost, he lifted his knee to rest on the bed. Raiven had never seen him more at ease or look more handsome. She started when he reached out and unclenched her fingers from the bear pelt and then began to play with them while he spoke.

"'Tis not the statement, Raiven. For the past week, perhaps longer, every time I look at you, you look away.

When you do look at me, your eyes . . . never . . ."—he paused between each word while reaching out with his other hand to place a gentle finger beneath her chin, raising it—"look . . . into . . . mine." When he finished, he had raised her chin enough for his eyes to lock onto hers.

Raiven couldn't remember how to breathe. "That's not true."

"It isn't?" he asked softly. "Then why are you now staring at my nose?"

Her lips twitched involuntarily, and Raiven could feel the tension leaving her body. Raising her eyes to his, she bluntly said, "I do not know. I suppose it is because we're so close and yet so distant. I do not know you. I do not know what to say. I know naught of your thoughts or what you feel."

Quynn's eyes darkened. "Would you like to know what I feel at the moment?"

Raiven shook her head quickly, and Quynn's smile took on positively lethal proportions. "I did not think you to be a coward," he taunted softly.

Raiven laughed softly. "Until I met you, neither did I."

He looked surprised over her honest answer, but Raiven refused to look away.

"I like that."

"What?"

"I like it when you are boldly honest with me. I like it when you show me the real Raiven with no pretense."

"How could you know me well enough to know which is real and which is pretense?"

Quynn studied her face before answering. "Would you believe me if I said that you tell me?"

The look Raiven gave him patently said she did not.

"'Tis there all about you. Some have expressive eyes. Their eyes always reveal what their lips do not. Some have expressive faces, and their true emotions are slashed across them. Others have bodies that talk. Aye, bodies that talk," he affirmed as Raiven's gaze grew more incredulous. "Their bodies announce their thoughts, telling all what they have done or are about to do."

"To be sure that's an unusual theory you have there," Raiven teased softly.

Quynn took her jibe in stride and unobtrusively moved closer to her. "Scoff all you like, madam, but my 'theory,' as you call it, is what makes others think me to be a nearly invincible foe." He said it without the least bit of vanity.

Raiven was intrigued. "How so?"

"Because," he said, inching a little closer, "if you can read your opponent, you know what he is about to do at all times. In truth they beat themselves because they reveal what they plan, thus giving you the ability to counterattack."

By the time he finished, his hips were next to hers and his left hand was now planted on the other side of her hip.

Raiven drew in a deep breath. She had not seen him move, yet now he was so close. Her first instinct was to back away, and then she remembered his taunt about her cowardice. Forcing her eyes to remain on his, she asked hoarsely, her throat suddenly dry, "What kind am I?"

"Ah, sweet Raiven," he murmured, his mouth lowering to hers. "You, my sweet, are all."

His lips seared hers, and Raiven could not answer. She wanted to ask if he meant she was all the kinds of people he described or if she was all to him. But as his lips continued to caress hers, she didn't want to know anything except that the wonder of his kiss would not cease. With a sigh that was more of a groan, she raised her arms around his neck, shivering with delight when his arms encircled her waist, crushing her to him.

Quynn deepened the kiss, his tongue invading her mouth's inner moisture. Raiven became aware of his hands moving feverishly over her body, and she cried out against his mouth in response to the sweet agony of his hand upon her breast. The cool rush of air on her back was the only indication she had that he had removed her gown. Then he tore his lips from hers to spread tiny heated kisses along her face, her neck and shoulders, and then to the full breasts he had bared.

Raiven's head fell back, and her teeth bit into her bottom lip to keep from screaming aloud. She found herself being pressed gently back onto the bed, and the thought came that finally her long wait was over. She would not sleep alone this night. Then as Quynn's hot breath caressed her ear before moving on to claim her mouth, she amended that thought. Sleeping would have little to do with what would take place in this bed.

Abruptly she became aware of the fact that Quynn was no longer caressing her. The sudden cessation of keen sensation was startling, and disappointment swept over her in a cold wave, blunting her budding happiness. Raiven could feel his stare upon her face, and she knew he was waiting for her to open her eyes and look at him. Slowly, she opened her eyes.

Despite the heat that blazed from Quynn's eyes, he was perfectly still, watching her, as if he sought or waited for something.

"What is it?" Her voice was a strangled whisper. "What is wrong?"

Quynn shook his head slowly. "'Tis naught," he replied, his usually deep voice thickened. "'Tis only that I want to be sure that you want this as I do."

Relief flooded her features. She was about to say, "I do," when his finger on her lips silenced her. Already sensitized to his touch, this simple contact was too much. Moaning softly, she began to caress his finger with her lips, flicking it with her tongue and finally taking it inside her mouth, sucking on it with passionate fervor. Lost in sensation, she closed her eyes again, emitting another tiny groan.

"Raiven?" Quynn's voice was almost unrecognizable.

"Hmm?" she asked, rubbing her breasts against his bare chest, not even giving thought to when he had disrobed, only loving the feeling of his skin against hers.

"Look at me."

Long moments passed as Raiven slowly opened her eyes to stare into his, and even then her gaze was dull and unfocused. The passionate expression in them wrung an answering groan from Quynn, and this time it was he who looked away, unable to maintain the contact.

"Don't," he muttered, extracting his finger from her mouth and lowering his forehead to hers.

Raiven's smile was slow, warm, and sensuous. "Don't what?"

"Don't look at me."

Her smile disappeared as a slight frown creased her brow. "Did you not just ask me . . . ?"

Quynn made a noise between a grunt and strangled laughter. "I know. I know what I said. 'Tis only I never dreamed you'd look at me the way you do now. 'Tis too much."

He shifted slightly, laying full between her legs. "I need to know, need to hear, that you want this, too. When 'tis done, I want no blame, only the shared beauty of the moment." Lifting himself slightly, he stared down into her eyes, searching their depths for any doubt.

Bringing his hands to cradle either side of her face, he went on. "I care not for Henry's order. I care not if we make a babe at this time or nay. I . . . want . . . you, and I want you to know it. All I ask in return is the same knowledge. I want to know that you want me. I want to know that what you see before your eyes is not that 'English upstart' or the 'pup of a man.'" He drew a deep breath. "Henry forced me upon you. That I cannot change. But I want you to see me, all that I am and am not, and then I want you to wrap your arms around me, open your lovely mouth, and say, 'Aye, Quynn. I want you.' 'Tis all I want, but no less will satisfy me."

His words left her breathless. For a moment Raiven only stared at him, too caught up in their beauty to do anything more. Then she stared deeper into his eyes and thought she glimpsed his uncertainty, and her heart melted completely.

Lifting fingers that trembled from the force of the emotion he'd evoked, she traced the outline of his finely chiseled lips.

Quynn did not move.

Raiven's fingers began to trace the path of his brow while her lips nipped at his chin and followed its line to caress his ear.

Still he did not move.

Lying back, Raiven once again stared deeply into his eyes while her fingers entwined in his hair. Reaching up again, she kissed him full on the mouth and wrapped her arms around his neck and started to whisper, "Aye, Quynn. I want . . . ," but her "you" came out on a gasp as he finally moved to plunge deeply within her. Each thrust was an echo of her submission. Each caress a repetition of his request. Raiven was moved past description by the beauty of it all. She wrapped her arms tighter and tighter about Quynn's neck, her breath coming faster and faster with each meeting of their bodies.

Like a litany, his asking her to want him played over and over in her mind, bathing her senses, heightening her pleasure. Unaware that she spoke aloud, Raiven uttered her desire, telling him of her pleasure. The intensity of sensation surged sharply beyond enduring, and her mind ceased to function, giving over to the dictates of her body, which hurtled her forward to fulfillment that could not be denied. When it came, Raiven cried out, vaguely recognizing Quynn's answering cry as he drove into her one last time, groaning her name.

The next few moments were lost on Raiven. She must have slept because when she opened her eyes, she was lying on her side, with her head on Quynn's chest, wrapped securely in his arms.

Giving her a wicked grin, he said, "Welcome back," in a deep, soft voice that Raiven felt down to her toes. "Or should I say welcome home?"

Raiven stiffened slightly. "Is it?" she asked softly. "Is it my home?"

"It is what you want it to be, all that you want it to be." He sighed, kissing her atop her head. "Ever since your arrival here, you have said that no one asked you what you want, that no one has given you the opportunity to have a say in your life. I give that to you now. What do you want, Raiven?"

Now that someone was finally asking, all the words that Raiven had stored up to say vanished. She had wanted to be the mistress of her own destiny—Henry had taken that. She had wanted to be mistress of her hall—Quynn had been pushed into taking that. The only other things she wanted were to see Jacques—Henry would never allow that—and to be loved for herself—she could never ask for that. So where did that leave her? With naught to say.

Burying her face in Quynn's chest, she said, "I want nothing."

Quynn chuckled. "Typical woman. You cry and cry for your own voice, and when asked, you do not speak. Very well then, perhaps this is something you can answer. Do you want this to be your home?"

Slowly Raiven raised her eyes to his. After a long moment, she nodded.

Quynn gave her a squeeze and an engaging smile. "Good." Then, after a moment, he asked, "Aren't you going to ask what I want?"

Feeling suddenly lighthearted, Raiven quipped, "I know what you want."

He quirked one night-dark brow at her. "Really?" he asked dubiously.

"Really," she replied with certainty, her green eyes sparkling like twin jewels, "and I truly want to give it to you. But," she stopped him as he growled possessively, about to capture her lips, "first you must tell me what sort of person I am."

Her question made him freeze in puzzlement, then he remembered. Laughing heartily, he pulled her tighter into his arms. "As I said, sweet, you are everything and all."

He laughed again as the look in her eyes told him he had not said any more than he had before. Not allowing her the opportunity to protest his still ambiguous answer, he claimed her lips and then her body, not relenting in his quest until he had tantalized her to the depths of her soul.

# Chapter 18

A heavy weight on her hair awakened Raiven as she attempted to roll over. For an instant, she didn't know what had entrapped her. Turning her head gingerly, she saw that the blond tresses were locked beneath Quynn's arm. It took the barest second for memory to return to explain why he was there, and in memory's wake came a warm feeling.

He had stayed with her!

He had never done that before. That horrible first night he had left while she slept, and the few times he had been with her following, he had left immediately after.

Relaxing now and easing her head back onto his chest, Raiven was just letting out a contented sigh when a deep, dry voice said, "Had I known you fidgeted thus, I would have insisted upon separate chambers."

Raiven forgot her entrapped hair and jerked upright only to wince when the strands pulled painfully.

Seeing her dilemma, Quynn moved his arm and released the long blond locks.

"You're awake," Raiven said unnecessarily while rubbing her scalp gently. "I did not know. I thought you slept still."

"With all that thrashing about like a boar in a thicket?" Quynn asked, his voice filled with humor.

"I wasn't thrashing about," Raiven defended herself. "You were on my hair."

"Hmm, I see. Then one of us must go. Since 'tis my room and bed, I think we'll shave your head first thing after breaking the fast." He said it with just enough seriousness to bring a start of alarm to Raiven's face.

"I don't think . . ."

"No need to think about it at all," Quynn returned as if the matter were settled. He gave the tresses that lay between them like flaxen a considering look. "You have more than your share. You won't miss a hair or two."

"Now, wait one moment, milord," Raiven began.

"Tsk, tsk, we're back to milord again, are we? I thought we had become too friendly for that."

Raiven could feel her anger begin to build. "Friendly or nay," she snapped, "you're not cutting off my hair." She couldn't believe he would think of such a thing.

Quynn gave her a long look. "Then you mean to say I must go. I rather got the impression that you liked having me here. Oh, well," he shrugged, making to rise, "if you like your hair more—"

"Wait a moment," Raiven repeated. "I like you and . . . and . . ."

"And?" Quynn turned to her and prompted.

"And," Raiven tried to continue, her frustration mounting, "this is insane!" she burst out. "How did we get on such a stupid conversation?"

Quynn turned away again, but Raiven did not miss the telltale shake of his shoulders. When she realized he had been teasing her, she punched him, which only seemed to make him laugh harder.

Laying down, he grabbed her to him despite her struggles. "I can see 'tis going to be fun getting to know each other."

"Aye, for you perhaps," Raiven muttered.

Quynn chuckled. "Ah, Raiven, has no one ever teased you before?"

"Nay," came the surly response.

"Well, then 'tis high time someone did," he replied undaunted, "especially since you're so easy to tease."

"I don't like it," Raiven grumbled. "This teasing of yours is laughter at my expense."

"Have you also never laughed at yourself?"

"Have you?"

Quynn made a slight face. Without directly answering her question, he said, "I shall try to be more easy with my wit."

Feeling as if she had suddenly made a big issue over a small matter, Raiven mumbled, "And I shall try to develop a better sense of humor."

"Done," Quynn replied.

"Quynn?"

"Aye?" he answered lazily, his eyes closing.

"May I ask something of you?"

His eyes snapped open. "If I can grant it," he qualified, suddenly wary. Surely Raiven was not one of those women who felt that favors in bed should bring favors out of it.

Raiven colored slightly, uncomfortable with her thoughts and his intense stare. "This is difficult for me to ask yet again."

All the lightness of the moment fled. Quynn's eyes darkened. "Just speak it."

"Last night, eh, ehm." Raiven cleared her throat and tried again. "Last night you said I was all and everything, and then we, uh—and I never got to ask what that meant."

Quynn gave her a hard look. Was she asking him to tell her he loved her or something like that? Would it ruin what little they had when he couldn't do it?

His prolonged silence began to gnaw at Raiven.

"You said," she went on impatiently, "that some people speak with their eyes, some with their faces, and others with their bodies. Yet I am all. What does that mean?"

The tension left Quynn's body. He thought he'd

already explained that, but maybe he hadn't or perhaps she hadn't understood. Pulling Raiven closer in to his side, he tried to explain. "You do all three."

"How is that when I am unaware of it?"

Quynn continued as if she hadn't interrupted. "You ask things of my soul with those beautifully expressive eyes. You tell me of your feelings with your exquisitely lovely visage, and last, you wring every last shred of desire from me with the perfection of your body."

"Oh."

Suddenly it occurred to her that she was lying naked in his arms, and along with that realization came the knowledge that her position brought her no embarrassment. Only his words had made her aware of their position by starting a tingling in the pit of her stomach that she now knew was desire.

"Quynn," she called softly.

"Aye, Raiven?"

"Are my eyes, face, and body asking or telling you anything now?"

Quynn pulled her down and gently captured her lips with his, and like the night before, he enthusiastically answered her body's questions with his own.

The next time Raiven awakened, the sun was high in the sky. She opened her eyes slowly and lifted her head gently, remembering the pain it had caused her to move her head when Quynn lay on her hair. But her caution was wasted. This time she was alone.

And no wonder, Raiven thought, if the metallic sound she heard drifting through the window was what she thought it was. Jumping from the bed, Raiven ran to the window and looked out on the section of the courtyard where Quynn and his men went through their drills.

There, below her, proving that she had not been mistaken, Quynn's men practiced as they always did between the morning and noon meals. Remembering her nudity, Raiven moved quickly away from the window before someone saw her. She walked toward the garderobe to perform her morning ablutions, her mind dwelling on last night and the early morning. Had that really been her, making love with an abandon she hadn't known she could achieve? Feeling herself flush at the vivid memories, she realized that it was and she had. The strange thing was she had no clue as to what brought Quynn back to her bed. Certainly her bumbling efforts had not been the reason. He had made it seem such a natural thing, as if—nay! It couldn't be. Dear God, surely not that.

A lump of horror congealed in Raiven's chest, and she felt crippled under the weight of her thoughts. Was it gratitude for what she had done for Thomas? Had that brought him back to her? And if it did, did she care?

Feverishly running her hands through her tangled hair, Raiven realized it did matter. She had wanted him to be there for her and her alone.

Suddenly the world righted itself again as she recalled Quynn's asking her to want him for him. *That* had not been gratitude, of that she was certain.

Finishing her toilette, Raiven was about to go downstairs and seek food to satisfy her overwhelming appetite. She pulled open the door absently, her thoughts still full of Quynn, and was startled to see Ella on the other side, preparing to knock.

Raiven didn't know which was greater: her surprise at seeing Ella so unexpectedly or the fact that the woman had been about to knock when she had failed to do so at any other time.

For a few tense seconds, neither of them spoke. Finally, Ella cleared her throat, and using a tone Raiven had never heard directed at her, she asked, "I would like a word with you, milady, if you please."

Too stunned for speech, Raiven only nodded and stepped aside to allow her to enter. Once inside, Ella maintained her silence for so long that Raiven thought she must have changed her mind about speaking to her, and her discomfort grew. She knew she should not allow a servant to make her uncomfortable, but Ella always had the ability to unnerve her. When the silence stretched full measure, Raiven asked quickly, "How is Thomas? Did he pass the night well?"

Some of the tenseness seemed to leave Ella's shoulders at Raiven's words. "Aye, milady, that he did. That potion he was given by yer maid was just the thing. He sleeps now, but already I can see tiny spots of color in his cheeks."

Raiven smiled, genuinely relieved. "I am happy to hear it. Would you object, that is, would it be permissible for me to see him?"

Ella answered without hesitation. "Certainly, milady. 'Ere he fell asleep, he asked to see ye." Again the tension seemed to return to Ella's stance, and Raiven watched, puzzled, as the woman began to twist the front of her gown in her hands.

"Is there aught you wish, Ella?" Raiven prompted gently.

"Aye, milady." Ella bobbed her head once. "It has come to me that I've wronged ye greatly. I never gave ye the chance ye deserve. Why even when ye changed—I mean when ye made changes for the better in the hall," she amended quickly, her face reddening, "and others began to switch their favors, I held stubborn fast to mine. I never showed ye a courtesy and more than once showed ye the sharp edge of my tongue. Other ladies would not have stood for it and would have made the baron turn me out, but not only did ye not take action a'gin me, ye befriended my son and proved that friendship by saving his life at risk to yer own. I don't know the words, I don't have the words to tell ye how grateful I am for what ye have done. I can only say thank ye so much from the bottom of my heart and beg yer forgiveness for my earlier stiffness toward ye." When Ella finished her speech, she looked at Raiven pleadingly.

Raiven knew Ella waited for her to say something, but she was still in shock from what the woman had said. Ella unbending? Raiven had not thought she would live long enough to hear such an admission. Yet no matter about her unbending nature, Ella was extremely loyal.

Raiven knew if the woman declared you her friend, she never swerved. The same was true if she named you enemy. But here she stood not only saying with her lips, but with her eyes that she had been in error. It could be naught else but her overwhelming love for her son, and that love of family Raiven could understand. She had no children, but she would do anything for Jacques.

"I understand, milady, if ye cannot see yer way to forgive me," Ella said, misunderstanding Raiven's silence. "I just wanted to make sure that I told ye of my regret of my past treatment and my gratitude for what ye did for me and for Thomas."

"Nay, Ella, you misunderstand," Raiven hastened to explain. "It is naught for me to forgive. You were behaving with honesty, and I have always admired that. You are loyal to the baron, and I hurt him. I'm sure that there are many at Guirlande who would have reacted the same to him had they the chance. Rest easy, I bear no grudge, and your gratitude over what I did for Thomas is appreciated but undeserved. When I saw Thomas in the water, I did not think of you or the baron or anyone but myself, for that matter. All my thoughts were of Thomas. He has been my only friend since I came to England, and that he might die and how much I would miss him were my only thoughts. I was thinking of my loss. I am happy for you, but I am also glad that I have not lost my friend. Although you think you have done naught, in truth, you have. Indirectly you have given me Thomas, and I should be thanking you for that precious gift."

Raiven received yet another shock when she saw Ella's eyes gleam with tears.

"Milady, I don't know what to say. Thank ye for everything and please come and see Thomas whenever ye will." Then she rushed out the door before Raiven could respond.

Bemused by what had just taken place but not wanting to waste any more time standing about thinking about it, Raiven turned to leave, only to bump into the solid wall of Quynn's chest.

She bounced away and was glad of the strong hands

that reached out to steady her. When she'd righted herself, she raised her eyes to his, expecting to see amusement, but finding shadows within them instead. Thinking he had been disturbed by Ella's obvious distress, Raiven asked, "Did you hear our conversation?"

"Aye" was his short answer.

"Then you know the animosity between us has ended. What causes that darkness in your brow then?"

Quynn, knowing that Raiven possessed the rare talent of reading, placed a letter in her hands.

Looking down at it, Raiven slowly pulled away and stared down at the words her mind at first refused to comprehend. It wasn't lack of food that caused her world to sway as finally the meaning of the words slammed into her consciousness. Glancing back to Quynn she knew she fully understood the implication of what she had read. How could those few words—"His Royal Highness requests the honor of your presence at court"—cause such dread?

Panic clogged her throat as she asked, "Am I expected also?"

Quynn could read the terror she was trying to keep at bay. Giving an abrupt nod, he pulled her back into his arms, trying to keep her from seeing his own uneasiness over the summons.

"We leave for London by week's end."

# Chapter

# •19•

There was a sense of desperation about the hall over the next few days. Everyone tried to ignore it, behaving as if nothing had changed, but the feeling would not be allayed. On the surface nothing had changed, but there was a thick undercurrent of tension that could not be denied.

Raiven thought about it a great deal during the week before their departure. She thought she partially understood Quynn's disquiet. He was probably unsettled at the prospect of her meeting the king. After all, Quynn was only just beginning to know her. She was aware that he did not yet know her well enough to know how she would act when she met the king. The gravity of the situation forced her to admit *she* didn't know herself well enough to know what her reaction would be. Her feelings for Henry had not altered one whit. On the other side, her perceptions and feelings for Quynn had shifted. That coupled with the fact that Jacques remained a political prisoner left her vulnerable and uncertain.

Whenever her thoughts came to this point, Raiven pushed them from her mind. The only thing she could honestly admit under the circumstances was that she had no desire to hurt either Jacques or Quynn. Beyond that, she did not know.

For her dilemma, there was no answer until the moment came. Quynn's, however, was another matter, and the answers she received from her tentative queries were actually no answers at all.

When she had first asked him what was the matter, he had said nothing, pretending he had not heard. When she persisted, he had said only that going to court always made him ill at ease. He had tried to make light of the situation by saying he supposed he was not a courtier, but rather a country baron at heart, but Raiven was not convinced.

Perhaps had it only been his behavior, she would have been satisfied with his explanation, but then she noted the servants' strange behavior. From the moment Raiven had saved Thomas's life, the last vestige of resentment had disappeared. That change had lasted about a day. When the servants learned of their journey, they had changed again. Not in their behavior toward her, just in general demeanor.

Two days before their departure, Raiven was still pondering the situation when an answer came from an unexpected source. Needing to get away from the oppressiveness of the hall, Raiven went to visit Thomas to see how he fared.

Although he was still weak, his eyes lit joyously when she entered the cottage. After a few moments of quiet conversation, Raiven told him, "This visit will have to suffice for both of us for a while, Thomas. The baron and I leave for London two days hence."

Thomas's face instantly dimmed. "For how long, milady?"

Raiven studied his suddenly sad face. "I do not know," she answered slowly.

"Has it to do with Mama? She has told me that ye have patched bridges. She does not mind yer visits. She told me herself she did. She even said she was mistaken about ye." Thomas said this last with such astonishment that

Raiven couldn't help smiling. "Have ye crossed swords again?"

Raiven laughed outright, then leaned over to smooth back his bright red hair. "Women do not cross swords," she corrected mildly, "as if they were knights in a tourney or on a battlefield. We merely disagree."

"Is that it then?" Thomas persisted. "Have ye disagreed?"

Raiven shook her head. "Nay, Thomas. Your mother has made me feel very welcome, it is only that I have to go to London to see the king. He has requested that the baron and I come to him as soon as can be arranged."

Thomas sighed. "It might have been better, milady, if ye and Mama had cro—disagreed." He made the statement with such drama that Raiven was more amused than alarmed.

"Why?"

"On the cause that the baron hates court."

Raiven nodded. "I know. He has said as much."

Thomas looked surprised and relieved. "He has told ye why then?"

Raiven studied the youthful face before her, doubting that a ten-year-old lad would know the answer to that question.

"They hate him," Thomas said simply. "They hate him because of his great-grandfather. They hate him because of Havilland."

Thomas's face took on a look of agitation and Raiven tried to calm him. "Shush, Thomas. They do not hate him. Perhaps they just do not know him, but I'm sure—"

"They hate him, milady," Thomas avowed emphatically, "and no doubt they'll hate ye, too, on the cause that ye're his wife."

"Thomas—"

"They think he tried to kill the king."

Raiven's next protest died in her throat. She remembered when she first arrived in England, and Elaine had recounted to her an episode where the king's life had been threatened, but according to Elaine, Quynn had saved him. The tale Elaine told made Quynn the hero, not the villain. Thomas surely must misunderstand.

Thomas read her expression. "Ye do not believe me."

"Nay, it is not that," Raiven answered, trying to soothe him. "It is only that you are too young to understand and mayhap have not got the situation aright."

Little dots of red flared in Thomas's cheeks. "I am not too young, and I did not misunderstand. I heard Mama talking," he ended triumphantly.

"Thomas!"

Thomas grinned unrepentantly. "I know 'tis wrong to listen when others are talking and they are not talking to ye, but sometimes that's the only way to learn anything."

The look that Raiven gave him let him know she thought that was no excuse, but her disapproval was not as strong as it could have been. Despite herself, she was intrigued.

"Why does your mother think that they think the baron planned to kill the king?"

Thomas's grin faded slightly, and he admitted shamefacedly, "I do not understand *all* of it. I only know that Mama said that they think the baron planned to harm the king, but all did not go well and then the baron tried to save himself by pretending to save the king instead."

Raiven said nothing at first, considering Thomas's words. "I don't believe it," Raiven burst out. Quynn might be many things, but one who sneaks about in shadows to do under the cover of darkness what he lacked the courage to do in the day's light was not one of them.

"I am most happy to hear it."

Two guilty faces turned to the door to see Quynn standing there, watching them with disapproval etched on his face. He walked over to the bed where Thomas lay, and the boy's face suddenly paled again.

"I shall not lecture you on the value of holding one's tongue, lad, but know that no true knight carries tales of another, true or otherwise—especially tales that he discovered by dishonorable means."

"Aye, milord," Thomas squeaked, thoroughly chastened.

Quynn's nod was abrupt. "We'll leave now so that you may take your rest. When I return, I want to see a strong lad ready to resume his training."

Instantly Thomas brightened. "Aye, milord," he repeated with much more enthusiasm.

Raiven and Quynn left the cottage, walking in quiet through the gathering dusk. Quynn was lost in thoughts of his own, and Raiven, not knowing what to say, decided to do the wise thing and say naught.

Quynn had yet to say anything to her about her part of the conversation with Thomas, but surely he knew that she was not without blame. She had encouraged Thomas to speak what he heard.

They were nearly to the hall when he turned aside and began walking along the stone wall that enclosed the hall and a few other buildings. The silence between them continued until Raiven broke it by saying, "I'm sorry, Quynn."

He turned to her, and even in the descending darkness, Raiven saw his brow raise in question.

"I am sorry for my unpardonable curiosity that made Thomas speak of things he ought not. Most of all, I am sorry for the foolishness of your countrymen and the pain it has caused your family."

The intensity of his stare increased, but refusing to be discouraged, Raiven continued. There was more she had to say. She swallowed, then went on quickly. "I also apologize for what pain I have caused through my, er . . . uncooperative behavior. Knowing how it feels to have the home that has been in your family for generations threatened but once, I can only imagine how difficult a situation this has been for you. I wish I could say that originally I intended no harm, but I'm trying to be sincere, and I cannot say what I fear we both will know to be a lie. However, for whatever value can be placed on it now, I do apologize."

During her speech, Raiven's eyes had fallen away from him, and now when she looked back, the look in his eyes seared her through. Quynn just looked at her, saying nothing, standing as still as the stones behind his back.

Raiven was about to turn away, thinking her apology meant nothing, when he grabbed her in his arms and kissed her with a fierceness that, for just a moment, made Raiven wonder what she had done to bring out such desire in him. Her moment of consideration quickly cindered beneath the heat of his caress as she discovered the magic of making love beneath the stars.

When they were on their way once again, each having an arm wrapped around the other, a thought flashed across Raiven's mind that made her turn to Quynn with an accusatory glance.

"For one who heartily condemned a young lad for listening where he ought not, how is it you came to know the full nature of our conversation when you were not with us?"

Raiven could not be sure because of the darkness, but she thought she saw Quynn color before he answered, "I heard you."

"Oh, I see." Raiven paused. "What happens when Thomas realizes what I just have?"

Quynn pulled open the massive door to the hall, and as she passed him, he returned, "I hope to still be in London." He laughed softly at her expression as they entered the hall. And despite her slight pique with him, Raiven couldn't stop the smile that came to her lips.

The journey to London was pleasant, if uneventful, although Raiven had doubted it would be anything but. London was only a two days' journey from Havilland, but Quynn had several of his fittest warriors traveling along with them. They had covered only a short distance when Raiven had asked him why they needed so heavy an escort. She had eschewed riding in the wagon, preferring instead to ride astride Sunstar's back, and the countryside appeared peaceful. The large retinue seemed unnecessary.

"How much do you know of King Stephen?" Quynn asked.

Raiven shrugged. "Not a great deal. He was king before Henry. There were a few disturbances during his reign."

Quynn threw back his head and laughed. "A few disturbances, you say? How can anyone so intelligent know so little about the world around her?"

Raiven knew he was referring to the other time they had discussed a historical event and she had said William of Normandy "had felt a little cheated." Although there was no rancor in his voice, Raiven, not unnaturally, took offense to his question. "I know what I need to know. One does not have to be a monastic scholar to live a full and rewarding life from day to day."

The tolerant smile Quynn gave her made her bristle more.

"How much do *you* know of Eleanor of Aquitaine?"

"You mean, of course, Henry's wife, Queen Eleanor?" he asked.

"Is there aught other?"

"What should I tell you of her?"

"Anything you know," Raiven challenged.

Quynn gave her a sideways glance. "Let me see. Eleanor was born in 1122. I do not as yet have her date of death, but 'tis understandable since she lives still. She is reported to be a great beauty and much for courtly literature. She was the former wife of Louis Capet, divorced him and in a rather indecent amount of time married England's Henry, or so it's said. The lands brought to Henry from the marriage extend from the Channel to Gascony, from the Bay of Biscay to Île de France—"

"Enough!" Raiven interrupted, laughing and holding up her hand for him to cease. "Obviously some of us are monastic scholars. I apologize for my ignorance."

The glance Quynn directed at her was devilish. "Not a

moment too soon, for I do not know the lady's eye color nor slipper size."

They both chuckled. When Raiven sobered, she said, "You have yet to explain the need for so many escorts."

"Ah, aye, we did digress."

"We?" came the skeptical response, but Raiven's smile remained in place. She was enjoying everything: the beauty of the land and the day, but most of all she was enjoying the company of the man beside her. Quynn was doing his best to make the trip a pleasure, and the beaming expression on her face told of his success.

Quynn tossed a mock dark look at her. When he spoke, although his words were serious, he managed to say them in a way that made it appear to be ordinary conversation.

"King Stephen was a weak monarch. I say that with no disrespect. 'Twas a well-known fact. He allowed Mathilda, Henry's mother, not only to threaten his rule but briefly put an end to it for a short time. By the time he regained the throne, being an incompetent ruler even at his best, he could not reestablish his authority. Anarchy reigned instead of a king. There was no justice. Men took matters of law into their hands, and might made for right and the weak or weaker were not just your enemy. They became your prey. There did not appear to be a safe place in all England.

"With Henry in power, these things are slowly changing, but one cannot be lax. There remain packets of unsavory and unscrupulous men who feel the only law that exists is that of the sword."

They made camp later that night, and despite the rather shattering picture Quynn had painted of an England without order, Raiven fell instantly and deeply asleep.

When Quynn nudged her awake the next morning, she gave him a shy smile in answer to his query if she slept well. Ignoring him, Raiven quickly went through her abbreviated toilette and attacked her breakfast. She ate heartily and could blame it on naught but the fresh air and the vigorous activity of riding all day.

By noon, despite a full night's rest, she was drooping in the saddle. After watching her catch herself from falling at the last moment several times, Quynn reached over and pulled her in front of him on Khan's back.

Raiven did not make a word of protest. Instead she snuggled deeply into Quynn's arms, her only words being a request that he pull her cloak more firmly about her to ward off the chill.

When she awoke again, they were a short distance from London, as Quynn informed her in answer to her sleepy question. Then he asked one of his own.

"Are you feeling fit, Raiven?" he asked after studying her face.

"Very fit," Raiven responded immediately. "Of late I'm a little more sleepy than usual, but I have never felt better. Why do you ask?"

"'Tis naught. Your face is only a little pale, and when you slept so long and so deeply, I became concerned."

"Your concern is appreciated, but if there was aught the matter, I would say it."

A dubious expression crossed Quynn's face.

Instinctively, Raiven reached up and smoothed away his frown, pushing back an errant lock of black hair. "Truly, Quynn, I would tell you. Do you doubt my ability to pierce to the heart of the issue?" she asked teasingly, trying to lighten his mood.

Quynn's smile was derisive. "Never could I be that fortunate."

"Well, then, let's have no more of this talk. This is my first time to London," Raiven said, changing the subject smoothly, "and despite the shadows we cannot control, I intend to enjoy what I can of it. Contrary to my reputation as the village idiot, I have *heard* of London and its grandness. Is it as fascinating as 'tis told?"

Quynn shrugged. "Perhaps to one who has not been here before."

Raiven disliked the heaviness in his voice. "Come now, Quynn, are you not the least tiniest bit excited about being here?"

"Nay," he responded abruptly. "I do not like it.

Perhaps if I were someone other than who I am—mayhap a merchant or even a peasant trying to find a trade—but as things exist, this city holds nothing to fascinate me."

Immediately Raiven remembered all the suspicion that enshrouded him and wanted to kick herself for forgetting and trying to make light of the situation. Placing a hand on his chest, she whispered, "It appears again I must apologize. This time for my insensitivity to your circumstance. My only excuse is that to my mind it is too preposterous to consider that any could feel about you the way you say."

Too late, Raiven realized the implication of what she said. The tensing of Quynn's body beneath her hand indicated that he, however, had not missed the meaning behind her words.

"Why do you believe in me? You of all people should be ready to believe the rumors."

"Perhaps because of my circumstance I want to be the last to believe the rumors. If I believed them true, my situation would be bleak indeed." She shrugged. "I know I have not given you the best impression of me," she continued, ignoring his raised brow, "but my father taught me many lessons about people. He said 'twas important to know both your enemy and your ally. One can be forgiven for overlooking flaws in a friend; however, if you misjudge an enemy, there may not be given a chance to correct the error."

Quynn nodded. "Your father was a very wise man, and he reared a very wise daughter. Which am I to you, Raiven, ally or enemy?"

"At the moment, I have to say both," she replied with brutal candor.

"Never let it be said that you swell my ego," he muttered.

Raiven laughed softly. "I will always tell you the truth."

"Until I met you, I had always thought that to be a good thing," Quynn retorted.

"I assure you, you will again," Raiven promised, a deliberate look of invitation in her eyes.

Quynn lowered his head, about to accept her offer, when Raiven felt him tense again, this time his eyes staring over her head. She turned to see what had caught his attention and saw the riders coming swiftly toward them.

Before she could ask him who they were, Quynn shifted her, and Raiven noticed that he now had access to his sword. At that moment one rider broke away from the others to ride speedily toward them.

The tension left Quynn's body, and with one word, he explained his change.

"James!"

# Chapter
# •20•

James did not halt until he was beside Quynn and Raiven.

"What do you here?" Quynn asked, his pleasure at his seeing his brother evident.

"Greetings, Sister," James addressed Raiven. "I trust this cloddish brother of mine has not dealt too harshly with you."

"Not too harshly," Raiven returned with a smile. "I offer my greetings also. It is good to see you again."

"Likewise. The journey must have tired you. We can exchange further pleasantries at a later time. Now 'tis more important to see you settled."

Raiven, looking about the city they'd just entered, experienced disappointment. Although the city appeared colorful and prosperous with its many merchants and tradesmen bustling about and hawking their wares, it also seemed, to her eye, dirty and crowded. A lot of the wooden edifices had been replaced with stone, and some of the buildings merely looked confusing being part wood and part stone, as if the builder could not decide which he preferred. To make matters worse, try as she might to ignore it, there was an unpleasant smell in the air, and her stomach began an immediate protest. She was very happy to see the palace come into view.

"Is that the awesome Tower built by William the Conqueror?"

Quynn smiled at the skepticism and disappointment in her voice. "Nay. The Tower lies to the east. The king no longer resides there."

"It is a pity it lies vacant."

"People still occupy it—only not the royal family," Quynn corrected.

"Who lives there now? Do you think we shall get the opportunity to go there while we're here?" Raiven asked hopefully. Perhaps a visit to the place built by a Frenchman might enliven the trip. London so far was proving to be much of a disappointment. She was surprised when she heard James make a choking sound at her suggestion.

"I hope not," came Quynn's dry response. "I do not think the people there would be to your liking."

"Why not?"

"'Tis a place for prisoners now."

James was now chuckling outright. "Although I do not think there are more than a few who would wish us there, eh, Brother?"

Quynn grunted an answer, and Raiven said nothing at all. By this time they had made their way to the palace, and the great gates were opening to admit them. After entering, it was only a short time before they were inside the quarters arranged for them. And it wasn't too long after that that Raiven found herself alone in her strange new surroundings, Quynn having left with James to give their reports to the king.

Once the door closed behind them, Quynn avoided a preamble. "You could not state your reasons for being here in front of Raiven, but I'd rather know them 'ere we face the king."

"I did not wish to upset her," James offered.

Quynn nodded. "Aye, I knew the bend of your mind. 'Tis why I did not ask again. You have news of France." This last was an abrupt statement.

"Aye. 'Tis not as good as I hoped 'twould be," James began slowly.

"Speak," Quynn commanded brusquely. "You know I prefer words that are like my food, with very little seasoning."

James sighed, instantly recognizing Quynn in his role of baron of Havilland, one who would brook no deception of nicety.

"The king called me to court to give an accounting of the situation at Guirlande. 'Twould seem that word has reached his ear of the unrest there. Someone has informed him of the few unsettling events that have taken place since our arrival there a few months ago."

Quynn ignored the fact that James had not told *him* of those facts to concentrate on the more important information. "Who?" he asked tersely.

"I know not," James returned.

Quynn's brow furrowed. "'Tis unseemly that any at Guirlande would tell the king, so that leaves only the men with you, and none would go past you to tell Henry. It makes no sense."

James nodded agreement. "My thoughts took the same path. Nevertheless, I am here because of it."

Quynn shook his head. "Tell me of these incidents."

"'Tis naught overt. It has been more subtle than anything else with the exception of the death of Perevil's horse."

"The charger?!"

"Aye. 'Tis not necessary for me to tell you of his grief. For days, he did not speak."

"What happened?" Quynn asked, perplexed that anyone would kill a dumb animal, let alone so fine a piece of horseflesh as Perevil's charger.

"'Twas poison," James answered abruptly. "Someone gave the horse hay or oats that had poison in it. When I asked, naturally none knew of its occurrence."

Quynn rubbed his hand around his neck, loath to ask his next question, yet knowing he must. "What of Raiven's brother?"

"I have not seen much of him. He was, er . . . upset at

my arrival, but after the initial outburst of anger, he seems to have accepted it."

"That sounds about right," Quynn confirmed. Then in answer to James's look of surprise, he added, "If he's aught like his sister, that would be his reaction."

"Speaking of Raiven, how are things between you? She does not seem as hostile as when I left."

Quynn gave a wry smile. "Now, there has been a long road to hoe. Originally, I thought the woman was daft. When she wasn't ranting and raving at me, she was hiding away in her room like a scared doe. Then she was everywhere, making her presence felt"—at this Quynn's smile deepened—"in all parts of the estate. The woman had vowed to me that she was going to make her presence as little felt as possible. Then she promptly proceeds to turn my life upside down." Quynn laughed softly, not missing the growing confusion on James's face.

"For one who has had his life turned upside down, you appear to be faring well," James said slowly.

"Perhaps," Quynn said enigmatically as they moved on down the corridor.

They had walked a few steps when James asked, "Does your wife amuse you in all ways then, Brother?"

Quynn stopped and turned to him. "I do not know that I like the nature of your question, James."

James shrugged. "'Tis only, time is passing. I had hoped that since the news I bear is not pleasant, you would have something more appealing to say to the king."

Now it was Quynn who shrugged. "If Raiven is with child, she has not made mention of it to me. Perhaps 'tis too soon to tell. Perhaps she does not know yet herself. Nay, Brother. I'm afraid we both face the king with news that will not be to his liking."

Raiven was soaking in her bath in preparation for the evening meal when she would be formally presented to the king. Although she cared not one whit for the king or his opinion of her, she did not want to bring any sort of embarrassment to her family name or on Quynn. In just the few brief hours they had been there, there had already been a renewal of the unkind jesting to which, Raiven had to admit, she had done more than her part to contribute. One silly twit of a woman, Baron Rickhard's wife, had even had the temerity to knock on the door and beg admittance. Once inside, the woman had done naught but stare and gape until Raiven, losing her temper, had asked her to leave.

That episode had taught her much. It gave her a tiny glimpse of what Quynn had endured, and her heart softened toward him. In spite of all he had endured, he had still treated her with kindness.

Raiven rose from the now-cool water, drying herself quickly. She would have to hurry. Elaine had remained at Havilland. Therefore all that must be done she would have to do alone. Wanting to make the best possible choice, Raiven decided to wear a soft green bliaut over a chemise of the palest yellow.

Satisfied with her choice of attire, she turned to her next problem. Her hair. What could she do with it? Biting her bottom lip in concentration, she discarded in a trice the idea of attempting any of the intricate styles for which Elaine was famous. Simplicity was the answer. Pulling the heavy mass atop her head, she wrapped the length of it in a coil at the crown. Sparkling emerald pins adorned the base of the coil and enhanced the green gems glittering in her ears. She wore no other jewelry except that which adorned the handle of the dagger riding low on her hips, suspended by a golden girdle.

A quick glance in the shiny glass told her she looked as good as could be expected of a lady without a maid, and she settled down to wait for Quynn to escort her to the dining hall.

By the time he entered the room moments later, Raiven's nerves were nearly beyond control. She jumped up to face him, saying nothing, her color high in her cheeks.

Quynn studied her indolently from head to toe. "Nervous, sweet?"

Raiven would not allow him to see her disappointment over his lack of comment on her appearance. Smoothing slightly moist palms down the front of her bliaut, she said evenly, "You might say that."

"Why?" Quynn asked softly, walking toward her. "You look lovely. Your beauty will put the women in the shadows, and," he added teasingly, "that dagger you sport so naturally on your hip will put the men across the room."

A relieved smile crossed Raiven's face. "My thanks."

A quiet smile was his only response.

"Do you truly think I look beautiful?"

That question immediately halted his advance to the garderobe, and Raiven's mouth fell open in shock at her bold words. She recovered herself enough to close her mouth by the time he turned back to her, and she was happy for that because his expression was slightly sardonic.

"Seeking compliments?"

"Nay, nay, it is not the way of it," Raiven rushed to explain. "It is only that it is the first time I have done my own toilette—when it mattered. I do not wish to shame you," she added hastily, not wanting him to think her vain.

Raiven couldn't read the expression on Quynn's face as he came back to stand in front of her. When he stopped, she was already trembling, and it was then she noted his amazement.

Quynn was stunned. He had never thought to see her this unsure of herself. This was the woman who had married him with gnarled hair and a dirt-streaked face. In the few months since, he had never seen her even so much as glance toward a mirror or pout because a curl would not go just so—things he knew women did all the time.

Now, when he had never seen her look lovelier, she was worried about her appearance and not for herself, but for him. Leaning over, he gently clasped her face between his two hands and kissed her.

The casual embrace, begun only to give strength and encouragement, escalated in intensity. Quynn had to recall himself or he would be the one to bring shame by being late for the king. When he lifted his lips from hers, he looked into the green eyes that rivaled the artificial sparkle of the jewels she wore. For a moment he couldn't speak, and when Raiven reached up to lay tender fingers upon his lips, he couldn't think either.

Quynn shook his head and cleared his throat, trying to find his voice. The sound he finally forced out was a poor imitation. "You are truly the most beautiful woman I have ever seen. I had thought 'twas not possible for your beauty to be enhanced, but tonight there is a look about you that brings your beauty to such heights that it defies my most humble brain for description. Never fear that I would be aught but honored to be by your side."

Two large tears glittered in Raiven's eyes, not only for his words, but the emotion in his voice.

"Quynn, when you and I were wed, there was a bit of hypocrisy in the vows we spoke. Let it be known, here and forever after, that I do find you a fitting mate in spite of our differences. From this moment onward, I want to be your wife in all things, and I, too, find honor in being at your side."

Quynn's breath hissed through his teeth. "I find great joy in your declaration, but I lament the timing of it. I think I would have preferred hearing your avowal when I could have shown you the extent of my very deep appreciation. Alas," he intoned in a voice that belied the lightness of his words, "I can only say thank you and leave you with the promise of a later demonstration of my gratitude."

Raiven, beset by a different sort of nervousness, pulled away from him, well aware of the increasing current between them. "Although that saddens me beyond measure, 'twill have to suffice," she said sultrily, her eyes glinting.

Quynn laughed and moved away to prepare himself. Suddenly the evening seemed to stretch interminably before him and for different reasons than the ones that had occupied his thoughts upon entering the room.

Dinner went well. Raiven enjoyed the food—all ten courses of it. She could not recall when she'd ever eaten so much. Perhaps she was more relaxed than she had originally thought. The entire evening was a magnificent haze, starting from the time Quynn had come to their room.

At first there had been stares aplenty and even a few snickers and outright chuckles. Then the king had called them forward, and an oppressive silence had fallen. After her presentation to the king, Raiven sank into a deep curtsy, and it was Henry himself who helped her to rise.

"Reports of your fairness were not exaggerated," Henry began, only to end as Raiven stood erect, "neither were reports of your height. However, I shall show myself to be above all that, and I will not be intimidated. Nevertheless you will understand if I request that you remain seated in my presence?"

"Of course, Your Highness," Raiven demurred. "If I may say, sire, however, that one with a presence such as yours need never fear being looked down upon by any because all are too occupied looking up to your greatness."

If there was any sarcasm in her comment, Henry missed it.

"I like her, Havilland. You may keep her. Has all progressed well betwixt the two of you? Are my suggestions being met with eagerness?" Although he addressed the two of them, he looked at Raiven.

Raiven looked to Quynn to see if it was proper for her to respond, but Henry interrupted.

"Go on, girl. Speak your piece, or has Havilland terrorized you to the point where you can speak no thoughts of your own? The man has the very devil of a temper. He really should practice being more like me."

Deep silence fell at that pronouncement, for Henry's fits of anger were already legendary.

Casting a derisive glance around his court, Henry grumbled, "You may laugh. 'Twas but a bit of humor," at which much laughter erupted in varying degrees and sincerity.

Henry turned back to Raiven. "Now then, m'dear, do you still hate me? Speak, I am your king as well."

"I do not know," Raiven answered honestly, not sure of how much of the truth the king wanted to hear and unable to think of a speedy prevarication. To her surprise, she had answered wisely.

"Good. I detest liars and those that tell me aught but what they think I should 'ear. A king has more than his share of those. I shall retaliate by saying I no longer hate you either for your defiance." Not giving her a chance to honestly tell him that that was not what she had said, Henry ordered, "Let us eat."

With that, he held out his arm and escorted her to his table where she was seated between Quynn and James and across from the lovely queen Eleanor. Despite the eleven-year age difference between king and queen, Raiven still found them a striking couple. The queen's ethereal beauty complemented her more ebullient husband.

The meal had progressed uneventfully to its finish, and Raiven had been about to congratulate herself on not causing a scandal of any sort when strains of the conversation around her registered. She heard the name Fleurette Deveaux, and instantly her interest picked up. Looking about the room hoping to get a glimpse of the friend she had made during the journey to England, Raiven could not locate her. Leaning to her left, she asked Quynn what the furor signified.

"This woman, Fleurette, is to be executed in the morn," he replied distractedly, turning his attention back to the king and thereby missing the sudden loss of color in Raiven's face. Her strangled "Nay!" however, was enough to bring his eyes back to her face a moment before she opened her mouth and told the king of England, "You cannot! Father in heaven, you can't do such a thing!"

# Chapter

# •21•

All conversation ceased.

Raiven was unaware that she had stood until Quynn and James rose as one on either side of her. Whether their gesture was one of protectiveness or of restraint to prevent her from saying more Raiven did not know. Her eyes were riveted on the sharp gray eyes of the king, who, in turn, watched her with the piercing stare that had resulted in his being dubbed the Eagle.

For long, tense minutes no one spoke, and Henry, ever one for drama of the moment, allowed the silence to grow to painful proportions. Finally in a deceptively mild tone that softened his usually gravelly voice, he asked, "I take it you disapprove?"

Those few words were all it took for Raiven to remember exactly where she was and the tenuous circumstances that surrounded her, Quynn, and James. She lifted mortified eyes to Quynn's face and could detect no emotion there. In truth he was so still Raiven wondered if he still breathed. Swallowing, she shot a glance at James. The anger she had expected to see in Quynn's face was clearly defined on his brother's. His look said she had taken total leave of her senses, although he, too, was silent.

Knowing that it lay with her to try to extricate herself—and them—from this situation she had foolishly created, Raiven retook her seat and looked back to the king. "Sire, I offer my most humble apologies. It is only that I know the woman of whom you speak, and I cannot believe her capable of doing aught deserving of death."

Raiven knew the precise moment she lost the remnants of the king's approval. Blast her stupid tongue! On the one side she apologized, and on the other she had implied that the king's ruling was unjust.

"Would you care to know what she has done, madam?" Henry spat, his eyes flashing. Then, turning to include Quynn and James in his glare, he snapped, "Do sit down! None here will harm the lady—yet. She speaks in defense of her friend. Would you not do the same?"

Without waiting for an answer from them, he turned his attention back to Raiven. "The woman murdered her husband, Baron Gerhaldt, while he slept trustingly beside her. She deserves to die and she will."

Raiven did not miss the uncertain glance the queen gave her husband at his dire pronouncement, but Eleanor remained quiet. Raiven could not. Swallowing, she prepared to speak when she knew the king had dismissed the subject. "Your Majesty, I do not disagree with your justice, only the charge against the lady. Fleurette is not capable of such a deed."

Henry's eyes narrowed, and finally his voice was rife with true irritation. "On the contrary, madam, she did. No one else was there. The baron was alive when he entered and dead the next morning. Who but her?"

"I do not know, sire—"

"I *do.*" Henry's agitation was obviously growing. "I can applaud your loyalty to your people—to a point. From your view, they are naught but good. You may spare me the speeches, madam, for I have seen the other side. They are not pleased with me, and rebellion is all they deem my due." His eyes hardened. "I tire of the lot of it. The Deveaux woman will serve as an example that my hand will not be forever stayed and that"—here his eyes nearly bored Raiven through—"rebellion will not be tolerated."

Raiven understood exactly what the king meant, and she was not blind to his increasing displeasure, but if she did not speak for Fleurette, who here would? She was about to open her mouth again when she felt a pressure on her left hand. Turning to Quynn, who was staring instead at the king, Raiven tried again to speak.

The pressure on her hand increased, and finally Quynn spoke, his tone exceedingly normal, as if he was not crushing the hand of his wife beneath the table.

"My lady and I are both satisfied that in all aspects His Majesty will act justly. If you will excuse us, it has been a long journey and my lady tires easily. We bid your permission to leave, sire?"

Without hesitation, Henry waved his hand, and a second later Raiven was being half pulled, half escorted to her chamber by her furious husband.

If Quynn thought he was to be the first to speak, he was mistaken. No sooner had the door closed than Raiven turned on him.

"Why did you stop me? Fleurette is innocent of those charges. I know she is."

Quynn spared a quick moment to admire her loyalty to her friend, but then his anger boiled anew at her lack of both sense and loyalty to him. "She is worth so much that you would risk your head and mine by provoking Henry's ire? You expressed a desire to visit the Tower, well, madam, you very near got your wish. Have you no sense, woman? Why should the king believe her—especially on *your* word? He has lost a trusted baron and friend. There are few enough of either around. Rebellion does seem to be all your people know. I, too, am inclined to believe she did the deed," he finished savagely.

Raiven calmed in the face of his anger. She would do neither Fleurette nor herself any benefit by irritating the only man capable of helping her. She watched as Quynn began to tear off his clothing, and she experienced a moment of sadness that the evening that had begun so promisingly was ending so horribly.

"Quynn, I'm sorry, truly I am," Raiven began softly. "It is only, how would you feel if you were in a strange country around strange people who held the power of your life in their hands and who are already inclined to your death?"

"None here wants the death of a woman on his hands," Quynn returned, staring at her balefully. When he saw she was not quelled, he burst out, "What of Baron Gerhaldt? Who is to see that he is avenged from a premature end?"

"Are you interested in justice or the mere persecution of an available innocent?" Raiven snapped back, her anger coming to the fore.

Quynn glared at her, his fingers halted at the neck of his chainse. Then he sat tiredly on the end of the bed. "How long have you known this woman?"

"One week," Raiven replied weakly, knowing what his reaction was going to be.

"One week?" he growled. He opened his mouth to say more, but the words did not come as rage, the likes of which he had not felt in a long time, surged through him. Unable to sit under the enormity of it, he rose to pace it off, but still his fury did not abate. His anger fed voraciously off the magnitude of what his wife had nearly wrought—and all for a virtual stranger.

Quynn turned his back on Raiven, afraid of what he would say or, worse yet, do if he looked at her in his present state.

Knowing that he was losing the battle with his temper, Quynn furiously snatched up his tunic and turned to leave the room. He nearly made it, but she spoke. Father in heaven, the woman had no sense! Could she not tell now was not the time?

Raiven could tell. That Quynn undoubtedly would not believe her she understood as well, but that did not change the fact that despite all, Fleurette needed their help. That was why she called out to ask where he was going. She had seen his struggle for control. She didn't need the further demonstration of his back tensing like a drawn bow. It was not necessary for her to note the rippling of the muscle in his arm as he fisted his hands. She was prepared for his reactions, until he turned around.

Raiven had never in her life seen eyes like his. They were a frigid gray wasteland, seeming almost inhuman with the bright light of rage burning in them.

Quynn's face was rippling from the exertion not to shout, and his teeth made a horrible noise as they gnashed against one another. "Not . . . another . . . word," he ground out in a hideous voice. Then he turned and slammed out of the room, leaving Raiven alone and more afraid of a mere man than she had ever been in her life.

She didn't know how long she sat there, numbed by fear and lingering anxiety over Fleurette's plight. She heard the changing of the guard beneath her window. She noted that the palace had grown quiet as all sought their beds. Still Quynn had not returned, and Raiven was unsure she wanted him to.

The midnight hour came, and Raiven had not moved. She sat precisely where Quynn had last seen her when he reentered the room, halting short at the sight of her terrified and wounded expression.

Raiven noted that he was drenched in sweat, and his clothing looked limp and well worn from just the past few hours. A furtive glance at his eyes revealed that they had almost returned to normal. He had calmed somewhat, but the memory alone of his former rage prevented her from speaking.

Again Raiven was correct in her assessment of Quynn's demeanor, but what she didn't realize was that seeing her huddling on the bed, trying valiantly not to show her fear or shrink away from him, finally brought him true calm. He didn't know if he was in any better condition to hear what she had to say, but he was now capable of at least making an attempt to listen.

"How can you be so certain of someone's character in one week?" he asked, picking up the conversation from where it ended as if there had been no overwhelming explosion of rage and he had not stormed from the room hours before.

For Fleurette's sake, Raiven found her voice. She was not misled by Quynn's apparent air of calm. Gentleness was still the course to take, and so she quietly explained Fleurette's behavior and kindness. She told him that Fleurette had borne no ill will toward the English.

"Fleurette had the philosophical attitude that because a husband would have been chosen for her in any event, she was willing to make the best of the situation."

"Perhaps Henry married me to the wrong woman," Quynn quipped acidly.

Raiven swallowed, surprised at the pain his words caused. "I have no desire to argue with you, nor do I wish to hurt you," she said pointedly. "I only wished to show that Fleurette would not have murdered her husband. All during the journey here she encouraged me to pursue the course of mildness."

Quynn sighed. "Nevertheless, Raiven, there is naught that can be done." He turned away in dismissal, unable to bear the near pleading look in her eyes.

"Please, Quynn. Can you not at least go to her and hear her story? If she is guilty, 'twill not matter, but if she is innocent, 'twill make all the difference."

"Why is this so important to you?" Quynn asked in frustration, angry with her for her persistence and becoming angry with himself because he could feel himself weakening.

"Is it so easy a thing to dismiss someone's life?" Raiven asked with soft incredulity. "Quynn, I know you are not as hard-hearted as that. Above all else, I do not want Fleurette to reap what I have sown. She has done naught against your king. I have been the one to bring forth rebellion. I saw it in Henry's eyes when he said he would tolerate it no longer. He was talking about me, Quynn, but Fleurette is going to be the one to pay with her life. I cannot allow that to happen without doing all I can."

Quynn stared at her impassioned face a long time,

then once again furiously left the room without a word. Outside the chamber door he argued with himself a full minute before he angrily stomped down the hall, calling himself every kind of fool there was.

He knew they had not yet transferred Fleurette to the Tower, and feeling the need to get this fool's errand completed as quickly as possible, he marched hurriedly down the corridor that led to the dungeon.

Quynn stood for several moments outside the heavy iron door that opened to the rooms where prisoners were kept. Overcome suddenly by the futility of it all, he backed away before the guard, wherever he might be, espied him, saying to himself, "'Tis lunacy. Of what benefit is this?"

"Perhaps 'twill aid us both to get an eve's rest," said an amused gravelly voice behind him.

Quynn spun about, his hand automatically pulling his sword free to meet the amused face of his monarch.

"What do you here, sire?" he asked in surprise.

"Probably the same as you," Henry rejoined. A fleeting look of self-disgust was revealed on his face by the muted light of the candle. "I took note of your lady's determination, and I knew she was not one to let the dogs lie. By the by, I thank you for your prudence. 'Twould have pained me to send your lady to the Tower. In any event," he said, drawing back to the subject, "I knew she would not remain silent past the bedchamber." He seemed to be waiting expectantly.

Quynn laughed softly and confirmed, "Actually not past the door."

Henry nodded. "I thought as much. However, your lady is not the only determined one. My queen noted her arguments and found them sound. Her anger was greater because she felt she should have been the one to speak in the Deveaux woman's behalf, and yet it had taken your wife's courage to get her to see the right of it."

It was Quynn's turn to nod. Everyone knew of Eleanor's presence of mind. Quynn also understood why Henry had come himself instead of sending another. If, by any chance, Raiven and Eleanor were correct, it couldn't be said that the king had had his mind ruled by a woman.

Henry looked past Quynn's shoulder. "Where is the guard?"

"Inside the room, most like. All was as you see when I arrived."

Henry rubbed his chin thoughtfully. "'Tis strange. The baron's family set the guard themselves, not wanting to leave the matter to any other. I allowed this, but now, I do not like the look of it."

Neither did Quynn, a full dose of suspicion shooting down his spine. "Where is the woman?"

"If she is where she was previously, she is inside the inner room."

Placing the king behind him in a gesture of protection, Quynn advanced, sword still drawn to the dungeon door.

Not only was the guard absent on the outside, but the guard who was supposed to be stationed inside was missing as well. Quynn and Henry moved forward silently, cautiously approaching Fleurette's cell. As they drew near, voices made their way to them from within, and at the last moment, Quynn decided against calling out, instead inching closer to hear.

He recognized the voice of Gerhaldt's cousin Rolf speaking to the woman. "I really must thank you, m'dear, you and that oafish king who now sits on England's throne. Stephen may have been weak, but even he would not have made it as easy as this fool has done.

"Gerhaldt has long stood between me and what I wanted. The king merely granted me the opportunity to remove him. You will die for his death, and I shall live with his money and estates."

Quynn had heard enough. He was about to storm into the room, but Henry's hand stayed him. When Quynn turned back to him, he could see the gray sparks shooting from the king's eyes, but he signaled that they should listen further.

A soft feminine voice asked, "Why are you here? Is it not enough that I am to die? Must I suffer your presence and your taunts?"

Rolf made a sick laugh. "'Tis my story that you killed Gerhaldt as he slept because of his bedding you. I am here to ensure that you were touched. Nay, demoiselle, do not abuse your voice and my ears by screaming. None are here to hear it."

Impatiently Quynn turned back to Henry to see if the king had heard enough. At his nod, he charged into the room.

"So, murderer of old men and molester of innocents, try your hand at a true opponent. Draw your sword, Rolf, or I'll slit you through where you stand."

To Quynn's immense surprise, Rolf threw back his head and laughed. "I shan't draw a sword against you, Quynn, nor shall I stand idly by to be skewered. I am leaving. I trust you'll not waste your time running with tales to the king. Who shall believe you? The only witness you have is the condemned murderess. Who shall believe her? I will stand before the king with the strength of my family integrity and name behind me. What shall stand behind you? Who will speak for you?"

"Will I suffice?" Henry practically roared his outrage.

Rolf's face blanched a moment before he gathered himself, smoothly pulling his sword from its scabbard. His aim was for the king. It was the last thing he did. With the quickness of the panther everyone likened him to, Quynn struck, blocking the man's thrust and sending his sword through his throat. Rolf was dead before his eyes closed and he slumped to the floor.

The tiny woman who had sat huddled in the corner of the cell came forward and flung herself into Quynn's arms. Awkward with the situation, he nevertheless put his arms about her, recognizing and responding to her terror. His only other thought was that she was much too small.

Henry's chuckle turned Quynn to him. "Impressive, Havilland. Very impressive. But then I had no doubt. Slay a man with one arm, hold a lovely maiden in the other. Might I ever hope to have your talent?"

Quynn's anger began to ebb in the face of Henry's amusement and the cessation of threat.

"My arm is yours, sire. Besides, all know of Your Majesty's fitness."

"Hmm, well said," Henry answered, the amusement still in his eyes, "but for the moment I would say both your arms are well and truly occupied." Looking about, he went on, "Shall we leave our dismal surroundings? The lady seems done in. Oh, by the by, Havilland, I do believe now is the appropriate moment to inform her that you are already wed."

Henry's laughter boomed around the tiny cell as Quynn froze and Fleurette leaped away from him as if his body had suddenly become a hot coal.

Quynn took the opportunity to retrieve his sword, cleaning it on the front of Rolf's tunic, and then stood aside so that Fleurette could precede him from the cell.

Once up in the main part of the palace, Henry adjourned to his rooms, telling Quynn and Fleurette they would discuss all in the morning. Quynn, anxious to seek his own rest, hastily procured a chamber for Fleurette, with a guard—one of his own men—stationed outside. Henry would be the one to announce Fleurette's innocence. Until that time, however, the lady would need protection in case someone felt justice would be better served at their own hand. He gave the man strict instructions and was about to leave when Fleurette stopped him.

"M'sieur, I wish to thank you, and yet I do not know your name."

Quynn turned and, despite his fatigue, smiled at her, unknowingly raising a hint of envy in the small redhead's chest for the woman who was his wife.

"My name is Quynn St. Crowell of Havilland. No thanks are necessary. If you must thank anyone, it should rightly be my wife. She heralded your innocence almost to the cost of her own freedom."

Fleurette's delicate brow drew down. "Why would she do this for me? Do I know the lady?"

"Aye," Quynn averred. "You met on the journey to England, I am told. My wife is Raiven de Cortillion."

Instantly the confusion left Fleurette's eyes. "Raiven?!

She is *your* wife? She is here then? She is well, *non?"* The questions came out in rapid succession.

Quynn chuckled. "She is here, aye. She is well, and she is my wife. I'm sure she has much to say to you. Until tomorrow, madam."

When Quynn reentered his chamber, he was not surprised to find Raiven still up and about.

"What happened?" she asked without prelude.

Quynn decided to tease her a little. "What happened when?"

"Quynn, don't. Did you see Fleurette? Did she tell you what really happened? Are you going to help her?"

Quynn laughed softly, finally seeing the one thing his wife and the petite redhead had in common.

"Aye, I saw her. Nay, she did not tell me what happened, and there is no need for my assistance."

Raiven stared at him. "What do you mean, no need? Who else will help if you do not?"

"Henry."

"I do not understand," Raiven said slowly, sitting down on the bed.

Quickly Quynn explained what had happened, and Raiven listened attentively without interrupting. When he was done, all she said was, "There. Did I not tell you there was something amiss?"

Before he could respond to that rather immodest statement though, she flung herself from the bed into his arms. "Thank you, thank you, thank you, Quynn. A million times, thank you."

Raiven pulled back to move away, but Quynn's grip tightened.

"After an interminable day and through a grueling evening, do you think I will let you go when I finally have you in the place I have wanted you to be all the day?"

He did not leave her an opportunity to respond, kissing her thoroughly. Without breaking the kiss, Quynn picked her up high against his chest and carried her back to the bed to make beautiful love to her.

Later as they lay together, Raiven traced tiny circles with her finger on his chest, and she remembered his earlier statement and asked, "Do you still think Henry married you to the wrong woman?" Her nails dug a little deeper in his chest.

Quynn stiffened. "I apologize deeply for that, Raiven," he said, removing her nails from his chest and laughing at the unconcealed surprise on her face. "I should not have said aught so cruel. Am I forgiven?"

Raiven nodded, unable to find any words.

"Good," Quynn rejoined, rolling over to press her beneath him. "Since I've been allowed to speak my apology, you must now let me show it."

And he did just that.

# Chapter 22

The next morning Raiven rose as usual, going through her toilette and ignoring the queasy feeling that had plagued her for weeks during the morning. As she sat brushing her hair, she thought of things other than an upset stomach. She was too happy to be sick. Her happiness was based on the fact that her future no longer presented the dismal picture it once had. Last night Quynn had shown her a different side, actually, two sides. Raiven shuddered involuntarily as she recalled his rage, immediately pushing that recollection from her mind. That was not important—at least she was trying not to let it be. The important thing was he had shown that he was genuinely willing to listen to her. He was willing to concede her view. Although she knew this would not be a permanent condition, and she also knew she might again raise that monstrous temper of his, this new knowledge gave her more hope and encouragement than she'd ever had since coming to England. Perhaps he would be good for her people. After all, none could deny she'd needed a husband—a man strong enough to rule her people and control her impetuous nature and gentle enough to care about things other than his own interests.

Raiven stood quickly, eager to get to the morning meal

when, without warning, the world suddenly tilted and went black.

When she awoke she was lying on her bed, and Quynn was leaning over her. She started, disoriented with her surroundings.

"Easy, Raiven. Do not move just yet. I will call for the king's healer. I did not want to leave you until you regained consciousness." He rose from the bed.

Raiven quickly grabbed his hand. Although she did not feel the best, she did not want to see the healer.

"Nay, Quynn, it is all right. I am fine truly."

The look he gave her said she was being ridiculous. "No one who is fine faints," he argued.

Raiven's brow wrinkled as a heretofore unthought of possibility came to mind. Half to herself she muttered, "They do if they're *enceinte.*"

"If they're what?" Quynn asked impatiently. "What did you say? Raiven?!" Quynn was nearly shouting, but Raiven didn't care. She had finally solved the puzzle of her recent change in health, and to her shock, she was happy. She *wanted* this baby. She wanted Quynn's baby.

Suddenly she was laughing and crying.

Immediately Quynn sat back down beside her, clearly worried over her reactions, only to find himself being exuberantly hugged and kissed every place her lips could reach. Totally bewildered, he tried to pull away, but Raiven's surprising strength coupled with his desire not to use too much force and thus hurt her kept him where he was. Rubbing his hand on her thick blond hair, he asked in what he hoped was a voice that did not betray his deep concern, "Raiven, sweet, what is it?"

"I am with child!" she shouted, then started laughing and crying anew.

Quynn jerked back, staring at her for long minutes that eventually had a sobering effect on Raiven's euphoria.

"Are you not pleased, milord?" Raiven asked warily, unconsciously reverting to the more formal mode of address.

"Are you?" Quynn queried diffidently.

Raiven stiffened. "Could you not tell?"

Quynn shook his head. "I am not sure. Is your joy because we have fulfilled the king's order in the time allowed and now your home is spared?"

Raiven stilled even more. Until the moment he spoke the words, she hadn't given any thought to the king and his desire, which she still found obscene.

"Strange that you should mention that," Raiven began in a voice that was cooling quickly, "when 'twas the farthest from my mind."

"Do not scold, Raiven. 'Tis more of a surprise than aught else."

Raiven was not pacified. "You need not prevaricate, milord. Your reaction, or lack of it, was enough. I had forgotten for a moment the unholy bond betwixt you and your king. Never fear that I shall forget again. You may run along and tell your king that things are progressing according to plan." She turned away, appalled at the tears welling in her eyes.

Quynn reached out to gently take her in his arms despite her resistance. He turned her face up to his, wiping away the tears tracing down her cheeks.

"In truth I do not know what to feel. I only know I want you to be happy about it. I apologize that my cloddish reaction dimmed your joy."

Raiven sniffed loudly. "There is no need for pre—"

"Do not call me a liar again," he warned gently, his warning softened by his smile. " 'Tis only that a myriad of thoughts went through my mind, and regretfully I chose the wrong one to speak. I—" His voice stopped abruptly, and a look of horror crossed his face.

Instantly Raiven forgot her hurt. "Quynn, what is it?"

Slowly his gray eyes focused again on hers. "Last eve, we, that is . . . Oh, God! Do you think I hurt you or the babe?"

Suddenly the hurt was gone.

"From that tiny bit of sport?" Raiven teased. "Fie on you! Your child is cut from sterner cloth than that. Why, that little bit of play barely caused him a yawn."

Quynn's eyes gleamed wickedly. "Shall I try to fully awaken him then?"

"You are most welcome to try," Raiven answered softly, thinking to herself that the morning meal could wait. Heaven could not.

The meal to break the fast was well along when Raiven and Quynn joined the assembly. After asking a quick pardon of the king, they took their seats.

Raiven found she was ravenous. Instead of joining the conversation around her, Raiven paid diligent attention to assuaging her hunger.

Henry, who had been watching Raiven, posed a quiet question to Quynn. "Have you told your lady the news?"

Quynn smiled. "Aye, sire, and I received a bit of news myself. 'Twould seem I am soon to be a father," he said casually, making no reference to the king's order.

"Now that is good news," Henry said, beaming. "And there has been a sorry lack of it recently. 'Tis call for a celebration."

Before Quynn or Raiven could decipher his meaning, Henry stood and addressed the room. "As one and all know, we have attempted to unite our England with the region to the south. By means of such, 'twould make us a formidable power. To that end, several marriages have taken place between the good folk here and there, none so widely known as the marriage of Quynn of Havilland to Raiven of Guirlande."

There was an outburst of laughter at that, and Henry held up his hand for silence. "Since their circumstance is so well known, 'tis a pleasure to announce that their marriage is about to bring to the realm the first fruit of the union. The Lady Raiven, late of Guirlande, now of Havilland, is with child."

A loud outburst mixed with equal parts laughter and applause met the king's pronouncement.

Raiven wanted to expire from embarrassment. She had heard that Henry was a little coarse, but even she had not expected him to do something this vulgar. The only face she dared meet other than Quynn's was James's. At least his face reflected true happiness. To the rest of them, they were a source of amusement, like the newest court jester.

Her appetite fled, and she wanted nothing more than to leave not just the room, but London entirely and return to Havilland.

Quynn's hand gripped hers beneath the table, and that simple gesture imbued her with strength and the ability to endure.

Henry, not one to miss much, took note of Raiven's expression. He continued in his gravelly voice, "The lady is not pleased at my announcement. Perhaps because in our struggle of wills, mine has emerged victorious."

Raiven gasped, and Henry continued in a kinder tone. "Perhaps she will fare better when I say that we are only at a fair exchange. Because of her intuitiveness and persistence, a grievous wrong has been averted. The Lady Fleurette of Fairhaven was unjustly accused of the murder of Baron Gerhaldt. Lady Raiven's insistence of her innocence, in this very room, led to questions requiring an answer. Upon further scrutiny, I discovered the lady was innocent of the charges brought against her, and the guilty has already received his due." His gaze shifted to Quynn.

"As a reward, I am placing all lands and estates in the possession of Lady Fleurette under the stewardship of Quynn of Havilland. He was instrumental in saving the woman's life, and 'tis only fitting that he now continue in that role of guardian until she is wed. Before such an event can take place, approval must be gained by the baron and, in the event of a dispute, by me. 'Tis no less than he deserves, is it not?" Henry asked with a bit of a dare in his voice. If any had objections, none chose to air them.

Henry turned back to Raiven. "We thank the lady for her assistance, and we congratulate her on her speedy execution of her sovereign's wishes."

The applause now outweighed the laughter, and Henry smiled beneficently at Raiven who was still torn between outrage and admiration at the way he had made her both an enemy to be conquered and an ally to be admired.

Raiven had just decided that it would be the course of expediency to assume the latter when the loud slamming of the double doors claimed everyone's attention—especially Henry, who didn't like having the attention shift away from him.

"I hope Your Majesty will still feel as generous when he hears what news I bring from France."

Raiven looked toward the door to see a handsome man she had never seen before stride arrogantly toward the king, barely deigning to notice the other occupants of the room. She sensed more than felt the tensing of Quynn's hand over hers.

"Langford," Henry began somewhat crossly, "what do you here?"

The baron ignored the king's displeasure. "I have news, sire, that I trusted none other to tell." The baron cast a contemptuous glance to both Quynn and Raiven.

Without knowing why, Raiven braced herself for the man's announcement. She had never met him before this moment, but as the mongoose does with the boa constrictor, she knew her enemy, and when she looked into the frigid brown eyes of the man standing across from her, she immediately identified him as one. Looking about the room, she noted the expressions that alternated between shock and foreboding. Even James was uncharacteristically tense.

Baron Langford, satisfied that he now had the attention of all, proclaimed loudly, "Your Majesty nurtures a rebel in his bosom. That woman's brother, Jacques de Cortillion, has led the people of Poitou in open revolt against the king." Langford delivered the accusation with an exaggerated flourish, complete with quivering finger pointed at Raiven's head.

In the silence that followed, no one dared speak. Slowly all eyes turned to Raiven. Her reaction was not expected: she laughed. It was not a nervous, guilty twitter, but a full-bodied, amused laugh. Langford's face changing to an apoplectic red only increased her mirth.

Henry was, for once, at a loss as to how to proceed with this unexpected twist. Quynn, however, was not. Leaping to his feet, he stalked over to where Langford stood.

"What tales do you sprout now, Langford? If you have aught to accuse my wife or me, speak plainly."

Baron Langford did not match Quynn in size, but his temperament was sufficiently volatile.

"I carry no tales, Baron." He sneered the title. "I merely tell my king what he should know—all he should know. Your brother by marriage and the sibling of that half-wit—"

The rest of his words were garbled as Quynn grabbed him by the throat and began to squeeze off his breath.

Langford's face was quickly reddened and was rapidly changing to a horrid blue when Henry cried, "Havilland! You will cease this at once. I will not have one baron murdered by another for the morning's entertainment."

Raiven, who had rushed over to Quynn when he grabbed the baron, gripped his arms and pulled to no avail. His arm was as the iron gates that enclosed Havilland. Softly, she beseeched, "Please."

The sound of his wife's voice speaking that one word drew Quynn back from his rage. His hand opened, and Baron Langford fell gasping to the floor, struggling for air while trying to slide as far away from Quynn as possible.

Quynn was no longer aware of Langford. His attention was held by Raiven's gentle green gaze. Both were oblivious to the presence of the others.

"I shall have no more theatrics," Henry shouted, although the look on his face said he was enjoying himself.

Quynn tore his eyes from Raiven's. "Your pardon, sire, but I will allow *no one* to slander my wife."

"Understood," Henry nodded curtly, turning sharp

eyes to Langford, who still lay on the floor rubbing his throat, "I hope by all."

Langford's nod was short.

"As that is understood, rise, Langford, and cease to dust the rushes with your backside. Continue," Henry ordered.

The look on Langford's face showed his displeasure at the king's words and tone, but he held his tongue and stood unsteadily. "I have it," his voice croaked, "from the most trustworthy source that"—he glanced at Raiven—"the *lady's* brother has led their people in open rebellion. There have been attacks upon the good English sent there, and their very lives are in danger. Why, one of Havilland's own vassals was slain in the fight."

Henry's eyes bored into James. "Is that true?"

"Aye, sire." James stood and met the king's gaze unflinchingly. "As Your Majesty knows, I have told you this in my report."

"You did not say the lady's brother was behind it."

"I did not say it," James answered unhesitatingly, glaring at Langford, "because I did not know it. Your Majesty requested the facts and I reported them."

Henry strode back and forth. "Have you proof, Langford?"

"I need no proof," the baron replied audaciously. "The word of the man is enough, and," he continued with a sneer, "the death of another at her brother's hand should be proof enough that he spoke the truth. His blood is my proof."

Henry stopped pacing before Raiven. "Well, madam, what say you to these charges?"

Raiven looked from Quynn to the king, totally ignoring Baron Langford. "I do not know of this man of whose death the baron speaks. I am grieved at any loss of life. I, like the baron, have no proof of the things I avow. However, I know my brother, sire. Besides being only a youngling of ten and six, he would not, even if he could, do the things of which he is accused, for I am here among the English and he does not know what consequence it would bring to me. If, in the baron's case, the strength of the word of the man is enough, 'twould be logical to assume that the same rationale holds true for me. My knowledge of my brother and his love for me is my proof."

Henry stared at her a long time. "Well said," he murmured finally. Looking at Quynn, he said, "You have a rare treasure in that your lady is gifted with beauty and a methodical mind. Nevertheless, my admiration does not erase the fact that rebellion is brewing. I shall inform all of my decision anon." With that he left the room.

No sooner had he gone than frenzied whispers and suspicious glances began to be cast at Quynn, Raiven, and James.

Quynn felt the bite of impotent fury as the other barons who had just been applauding his bravery sidled to Langford, inquiring how he fared and commending him on his loyalty to the king.

Raiven, noting the wide berth they were given, wanted to challenge them all. However, there had been enough spectacle. Softly she asked Quynn if they could leave for their chamber.

Once outside the room, she said nothing, walking quietly between Quynn and James, her thoughts racing at a furious pace. Jacques was in danger. Even her compliance, although belated, with the king's demand had not saved her brother. She was not unaware of what fate befell traitors and rebels. Already her mind was picturing her brother with his neck in the hangman's noose or his head in the executioner's basket, and cold perspiration trickled down her back.

James left them at their room after agreeing to Quynn's quiet warning to watch his back, and Raiven and Quynn entered wordlessly, both oppressed by the strange twist the morning had taken.

Raiven watched as Quynn walked to the window that faced south and stared out. She knew he looked toward Havilland, and she, too, longed for the peace to be found there. Peace? At Havilland? She must be daft to think so. Yet no matter how outraged she tried to be, Raiven knew that Havilland was a haven for her, too. While it was true that suspicion had followed her there, it was suspicion based on the things she had actually done. Lord above, how had Quynn endured a lifetime of shadowed threats? In comparison, Ella's forthright disapproval seemed a blessing.

Glancing back to Quynn, Raiven was consumed with the desire to comfort him. He had said nothing after telling the king he would allow no one to slander her, but Raiven could feel his anguish and ire. It was there all about him, and it said quite loudly that he did not want to be approached. Nonetheless, things needed saying.

"Quynn." Raiven watched his shoulders stiffen, proving he had heard her call, but he did not turn. "Jacques would not do what they've accused. You know I spoke truly when I said he would not want the consequences to befall me, as I would not want the consequences of my actions to befall him."

"People change," Quynn stated tersely.

Raiven struggled to keep the tension from her voice. "Not that much. Would you endanger James or he you? He is all you have left, just as Jacques is all I have. We would never hurt or act in a way to bring harm to the other."

Quynn remained silent.

Feeling something horrible enter the room between them, Raiven went on. "I was right about Fleurette. Can you not trust me this one last time?"

Sighing tiredly, Quynn responded, "Your being right about Fleurette has little bearing on this."

The beginning of anger was churning in her chest at his attitude. "Are you telling me that I would know a stranger better than my own brother?" she hissed.

Finally Quynn faced her, and Raiven could see the anger in his eyes of which his voice had given no evidence. "What I say to you is that I know you love your brother and would do all to protect him. You have said as much."

"Oh, so now I lie? Is that the way of it?"

Quynn's jaw clenched. "Nay, you do not lie. 'Tis

worse. You do not reveal all the truth. You ask that I trust you. Well, I do not. The fate of Havilland and all my family has fought to maintain lies in the balance. I cannot betray that. So do not cloud the matter with the issue of trust, especially trust that has not been earned."

Raiven opened her mouth to confront his accusation, but his next words stunned her more. "I saw your eyes, Raiven, the day James was to leave. There was something you knew that you held back. You were too adamant in your avowal that your people would not accept James. Where then was this certainty that naught would be done by any here to endanger you? Why did you feel the need to write your brother? What was there to tell him unless you wished to dissuade him or encourage him in the rebellious path he has taken?"

The look on her face was answer enough as to the accuracy of his words. When Raiven could speak, she murmured, confused, "But when Baron Langford . . . you . . ."

"I defended my wife and my honor," Quynn explained shortly.

Raiven lowered her eyes. "Your honor. I see. 'Twas well and truly defended. However, in all kindness someone should explain that to Baron Langford. I would hate for the man to labor beneath the falsehood that he suffered so because of me. He should be warned 'ere he unknowingly make the mistake of besmirching your honor, thinking himself safe as long as he lays no tongue to me."

Quynn ignored the hurt and sarcasm of her tone, swinging back to look out the window.

Trying to set aside her hurt, Raiven said, "My brother has not done what they say, believe or not whatever else you choose, but know that one thing for fact."

"Can you not see what is before you? Why are you so blinded by loyalty?"

"Ah, milord, if I am blind at least it is because of a trait most admirable. What blinds you?" Raiven asked quietly before she walked away.

# Chapter 23

Why did you not tell me that Raiven's brother was at the crux of the rebellion?" Quynn asked James in a voice that had long since lost its edge. The vast amounts of ale they'd consumed had seen to that.

James shrugged. "'Twas naught to tell. All that exists are conjec—conjectu . . . rumors. Besides, I would have told you, but there was no time. How the devil did Langford discover that?" James's anger brought a moment of lucidity that the abundance of ale would not allow him to sustain. Almost as instantly as it came, his scowl disappeared to be replaced by a cheerfully insouciant grin.

"I know not," Quynn responded dryly. "'Tis a fine mess. I'll give you that."

"How so?" James focused hard on his brother. "It changes naught betwixt you and Raiven. You both seemed happy. The babe is coming. You were happy!" James shouted this last as if Quynn had denied his conclusion. "And now you are not," he went on in a comically sad tone. "I won't stand for it," he bellowed, standing abruptly and then sitting just as quickly.

"It has changed everything," Quynn countered sullenly, his expression morose. "This thing between Raiven and me was too new, too fragile. It cannot endure this sort of strain."

James eyed Quynn with bleak skepticism. "Is it the ale or did I hear a bit of the poet in those words?"

Quynn snorted but held his tongue. The ale had loosened it far too much for his liking. He had said enough. He wasn't that deep into his cups that he didn't realize what he was saying. Perhaps it was time to bid James good night. Rising unsteadily, Quynn looked down at James slouched in his chair.

"'Tis time for me to seek my bed. I shall see you on the morrow."

James nodded his agreement and made to rise from his chair. This time, however, he failed miserably and, giving up, waved to Quynn. It came to his mind that sleeping in chairs was a highly underrated pastime.

Seeing James make no move to follow, Quynn walked around to where he sat and tried to lift his brother from his seat. So simple a maneuver took longer than he expected and it was nigh an hour before Quynn was able to finally seek his own bed.

He dragged wearily into the chamber he shared with Raiven, unsure of his reception. They had argued bitterly with a harshness unlike any other since the days of their first meeting.

Quynn didn't understand why Raiven couldn't see that it was more than possible that her brother was guilty of the things they accused. She would not even consider the possibility, which, he thought petulantly, as he half ripped, half removed his clothing, was unfair. After all, he believed Jacques to be guilty, but he had at least spared a moment to consider the possibility of his innocence.

It made no sense otherwise, he argued fiercely to himself. Who else could rally the people to rebellion? First, it would have to be someone of rank and stature, for it was rare indeed for one peasant to follow another. Second was James's disclosure that the attacks were well timed and precise. Third, there was the issue of the location of the attacks. Each had been strategically located in a place to wreak the most damage and present the least danger to the attackers. Serfs and villeins did not have the capacity to initiate such offenses. It was ludicrous to think that his men had attacked themselves, and that left Jacques the only other capable one.

Moving through the still-darkened room, Quynn sat wearily on the bed, his elbows resting on his knees, his head hung in dejection. Raiven, who was otherwise so logical, refused to see this. And as surely as he felt his heart beat in his chest, he felt that she was keeping something about Jacques from him. He had been willing to let it alone because it was not worth the effort of the fight he had known would ensue. Now, everything was different. Surely she could see that keeping her silence was not the way to help her brother. However, this afternoon, when confronted with his suspicions, she had neither answered nor denied them.

Sighing deeply with the futility of it all, Quynn ached to lie back and sleep for a sennight. A tiredness that seeped from his bones weighed him down. Yet he was loath to lie in cold silence beside Raiven after the joy and warmth he had found in bed with her, and he hadn't consumed enough ale—a fact he now heartily lamented—to make himself oblivious to her presence.

Staring into the darkness, he felt his insides clench at the thought of the distance between them. He was so lost in the misery of his thoughts that he did not at first feel the touch of a soft hand against his back until gentle fingers glided around to caress his chest.

In astonishment Quynn felt the press of full breasts against his back and warm lips nuzzle his ear. He rolled toward her to take full advantage of her giving nature, sparing only a brief thought that he never expected Raiven to come to him when she knew his feelings about her brother. However, this was not the time to be lost in negative feelings when her lips were driving him crazy.

Growling low in his throat, Quynn decided to take a more active role in their loveplay. Fiercely, he wrapped Raiven in his arms. Bare flesh met bare flesh, making

Quynn instantly aware of three things: one, that the woman he held in his arms was not his wife; two, that he had best extricate himself as quickly and quietly as possible, sorting out this mistake later; and then three, that his wife was standing silently at the foot of the bed watching him cavort with another woman.

Quynn was so shocked at her sudden appearance when she should have been the woman in his arms he did not even think to have the woman cease nuzzling his neck. She no longer existed. All he saw was Raiven looking at him with unbelievable hurt, then anger, then nothing. For the second time that day, she walked away from him without a word, closing the door quietly behind her.

The door shutting with exaggerated quiet roused Quynn to action. Not sparing a glance at the woman he left in the bed, he dressed hurriedly and went to find his wife.

Raiven walked blindly through the outer court and past the palace gates. Anger and hurt gnawed at her until nothing else remained. She didn't see the somewhat dirty streets of London. All she saw was Quynn wrapped in a torrid embrace with another woman. She didn't feel the muck that sucked at her shoes. She felt only the burn of the pain of her betrayal.

She had been used. They had all used her. Henry had used her to gain his own ends. But Quynn . . . Quynn had used her in the worst possible way. He had convinced her that it was possible for their marriage to have meaning, and she had begun to believe him. Stupid fool she! The moment he knew she was with child, he sought his sport elsewhere. That fact didn't hurt nearly as much as his obvious contempt for her shown by his bringing his strumpet to their room. Either he had thought she'd be gone longer, or he hadn't cared if she knew at all. While he had stared at her, Raiven had seen by the dim light of the candle she held that the woman still kissed his neck. Obviously, he had seen no reason to stop her. Even now they were probably . . . She couldn't think of that. She wouldn't let herself. The pain would surely drive her mad. It was too sharp, too severe.

Exhaling slowly to lessen the tightness in her chest, Raiven walked on, oblivious to the shifting shadows. Her mind was too full with what had happened to notice the dregs of humanity who scurried through the streets, much like their four-legged, gray-furred counterparts, rummaging through trash and pouncing on any prey smaller or weaker than themselves.

She understood now the strange summons she had received. Quynn had not wanted to meet with her. He only wanted her out of the way. Again she saw the look on his face. He had not expected her to be standing there. His surprise had been clear.

Raiven laughed out loud in bitterness, making one of the shadows that had been approaching her stop and look about and then retreat with curious fear to the darkness. Unaware of everything, Raiven's only thought was that for once something had shocked Quynn enough to drop the inscrutable mask he usually wore, allowing her to read his expression. There was definitely a bitter irony in the fact that when she had finally seen the man behind the mask, it had been in the worst possible situation. Had it been only this morning that she had been so happy? Her discovery about the babe had brought none of the expected dread, only happiness. She could have done without Henry's announcement, but it had seemed such a minor thing.

Then Baron Langford had appeared, bringing a cloud of doom that lingered the entire day, ending with her finding Quynn with someone else. The pain of betrayal cut so deeply it scarcely seemed real. Yet it was the feeling of helplessness that left her crippled, the knowledge that there was nothing she could do and nowhere for her to go.

Raiven looked about with awareness for the first time since she left the palace. Immediately, she recognized the danger she should have, and would have, noted before had she not been so stunned by Quynn's betrayal. The pain had driven her to behave rashly, and she cursed her foolishness.

Uttering a small prayer of thanks that nothing worse had happened, and including a request for safe passage back to the palace, Raiven began to walk back. Fortunately, she had not wandered too far afield, and the palace, though distant, was still in view.

The sound of an approaching horse made her draw to the side until she recognized Khan and her husband seated on his broad back. Raiven did not slow. When he drew abreast of her, she kept walking toward the palace gates, not deigning to acknowledge his presence. She did not attempt to avoid his arm when he reached down to pull her onto Khan's back. She didn't bat an eyelash when he muttered, "Little fool. Have you lost all your senses? Have you no ken of the danger?"

Raiven's voice was ice. "I can imagine the depth of your concern. 'Twould do no good to have the broodmare maimed 'ere the birthing of the prize foal."

Quynn's arm tightened reflexively, but he made no comment as they reentered the palace grounds.

Once back in their room, which was now empty, Quynn grabbed her arm as she moved to the garderobe. Raiven looked down at his hand and then up into his eyes, her green eyes flat and lifeless.

"Aye?"

Quynn gritted his teeth. "We must talk."

Raiven shrugged. "I do not think there is aught to say, milord. The picture you presented spoke well enough."

"I thought she was you," he said simply, quietly.

Nothing.

"Did you hear me? I said I thought she was you."

A brief spark lit Raiven's eyes, then they became dull again. "I understand that for you that must be either a compliment or an explanation. Forgive me if I can accept it as neither."

Quynn struggled to hold his temper. He tried to imagine how he would feel if the situation had been different, and he realized Raiven's reaction was by far the tamer. Still, her stubborn refusal to accept his word left him raw.

"I understand your feelings." He ignored Raiven's raised brow and went on. "But the truth is that nothing happened, nor would it have happened from the moment my arms enveloped the girl. 'Twas then I knew it was not you I held in my arms."

"Very well then, milord. As you claim. You thought 'twas me, and my untimely return had naught to do with your forbearance," she said in a toneless voice that called him a liar more forcefully than the words could have done. "Please excuse me. The day has been hard and fraught with discoveries. I need to rest."

Raiven pulled her arm from his grip and turned away, ignoring Quynn's clenching fists.

"I give you the truth, Raiven. I do not lie."

Her step did not slow. "So you have said."

Quynn watched her disappear into the garderobe, her back stiff and straight, and he would have received another shock of the day had he been able to see the tears she could no longer stave off roll down her face. All he saw was her stubborn refusal to accept his word. His hands clenched so tightly the knuckles whitened, and after he made the conscious effort to unclench them, deep half-moons were visible in his palms.

Knowing that he would get no further with his wife and deciding that time was what was needed—for both of them—Quynn slammed from the chamber.

A knock at the door broke into Raiven's thoughts. The intrusion was both welcome and a bother. She didn't want to see anyone, yet she didn't know how much more depressing solitude she could endure. Turning from the window and the overcast skies above the dismal gray of the city that had been her view, Raiven called a distracted, but impatient "Enter."

A moment later her dark thoughts scattered, and impatience fled at the sight of the bright head peeking around the door.

"Fleurette? Is it you?!"

Fleurette's petite figure filled the doorway, and her smile warmed the room.

"But of course, my dear friend. Did you think to avoid seeing me?"

Raiven shook her head hesitantly before joy freed her from immobility. Rushing forward to Fleurette as the slim girl ran to her, they embraced enthusiastically, tears of happiness falling from their eyes.

It was Raiven who pulled away first, looking her friend up and down. "You are well then? No worse for wear after your stay in Henry's dungeon?"

Fleurette wrinkled her pert nose. *"Mais non.* Of course I have bathed at least a score and more times since my release, but other than trying to remove the stench from my body and the fear from my mind, I am well. What of you? How do you fare being married to that gorgeous man to whom I owe my virtue and my life?"

Raiven used the distraction of sitting down to avert her eyes and answer noncommittally, "It goes as well as the circumstances allow."

"Are you happy?" Fleurette pressed.

*For a moment I was.* "As happy as I can be," Raiven replied evasively. "Enough talk of me. What has befallen you since we parted?"

Fleurette stared into the fire that burned cheerily in the hearth. "I was married to a wonderful man, Raiven. He was kind, and I think he had begun to care for me."

Raiven's brow wrinkled in confusion. "Did I misunderstand? I thought he died on your wedding night. I do not mean to be indelicate, Fleurette, but how could you know the man so well and he know you if he was killed shortly after the ceremony?"

Fleurette smiled, still staring into the flames. "You must remember, Raiven, not all who sailed with you had the same stipulation. We were allowed time to know our future husbands or wed immediately, as each baron deemed fit. Gerhaldt decided we should wait.

"We spent much time together, and I came to know

and care for him. By the time of our wedding, I wanted him as much as he wanted me. I really thought"—Fleurette's voice caught—"that we would have been happy together."

Raiven thought of Quynn. Her anger at him was based on his blatant betrayal, not any deep emotion. He gave hope and then dashed it away. 'Twas that alone making her feel such hurt at his seeking another woman. She did not care for him. Bringing her thoughts away from Quynn after having promised herself not to think of him anymore, Raiven heard only the end of Fleurette's question.

"I'm sorry." She smiled sheepishly. "I did not hear you."

Fleurette nodded. "Were you thinking of your husband?" The look on her face and the tone of her voice told Raiven that Fleurette totally misunderstood her preoccupation.

"It is not what you think," she said stiffly.

*"Non?* Then explain it to me. He seems to be a good-hearted person."

Raiven grimaced, then, remembering herself, quickly smoothed away the expression. It was too late; Fleurette's eyes darkened with worry.

"What is it, Raiven?"

"It is too complicated, my friend. I am just happy that you've known happiness, despite my sadness at its brevity."

Fleurette refused to be waylaid a second time. "Tell me," she insisted. "I seek your happiness just as much—probably more now." She reached out and grasped Raiven's shoulders in her tiny hands, studying her face. "I would not have thought it possible . . . ," she said absently as if she spoke her thoughts aloud, "but is he cruel to you, Raiven?"

*Aye, he is. He gives me flashes of hope and of a life that could be, and then he snatches it all away.* "Nay," she whispered.

Fleurette's brows puckered.

"I am with child, Fleurette."

The frown between the delicate brows increased. "And you are not happy about it? Is he not happy?"

Raiven shrugged. "I suppose he is happy. He has no wish to lose his home," she said bitterly.

"Raiven?" Fleurette paused long enough for Raiven to raise her eyes. "Have you told him of your desire for peace? Did you tell him what you told me?"

Raiven shook her head.

"Why?"

"I do not know," Raiven replied softly, looking away.

"Surely you know 'twould make all the difference?"

"If he were another sort, mayhap. With circumstances being what they are . . ." Her voice trailed away, and two large tears slipped down her cheeks. "I'm sorry," Raiven sniffed, wiping them away. "'Twould seem it is my lot of late to burst into tears over the least of things."

Fleurette rubbed Raiven's shoulders comfortingly. "Your happiness is not the least of things. I just cannot believe that things have turned so badly for you." Her brown eyes dimmed in retrospect. "When your husband burst into the dungeon to save me from Rolf's attack, he looked to me like one of the ancient gods of Greek lore. I recall thinking that even had we met under less dire circumstances, I would have perceived him in the same way.

"I was overjoyed when I learned that this man was your husband. Now, I find that I cannot rejoice because of your sadness. What is it, Raiven? Can you not tell me?"

Raiven eased out of Fleurette's grip and moved back to the window to resume her blank stare at the city below. There was nothing in the view that met her eyes she found captivating, certainly nothing to rival the beauty of Havilland, but the dismal vista took her away from Fleurette's disconcerting gaze. The more she stared, though, the less she saw of the busy city. Instead before her eyes she saw Quynn and herself. She saw the uncertainty and terror of her first days in England. She saw Quynn's temper blaze over an injustice dealt to one of his people. She saw Quynn bending low to teach

Thomas the correct positioning of his arm to launch his arrow. She saw Quynn and Khan galloping across the green meadows of Havilland with her and Sunstar traveling apace. She saw the light in Quynn's eyes as he talked of his home, his plans, and Havilland's future. She saw the spark that lit his eyes just before he kissed her.

Her visions then entered the realm of sensation. Raiven felt his hands on her body, the imagery so clear that even now her senses responded. She heard him whisper words with passionate intensity in her ear. And the tears that flowed down her face were for the loss of all that once was.

"Aye, beloved," she whispered softly, unaware of the endearment she used, "perhaps Henry did wed you to the wrong woman."

Fleurette, whom Raiven had forgotten, heard the gentle utterance and the sadness in it. Seeing that Raiven truly needed to be alone, she rose quietly from her chair and let herself out of the room.

Not even the gentle click of the door registered in Raiven's consciousness as she continued to stare sightlessly outward, seeing only the inner pictures of her mind's eye and all the glimpses of what could have been.

Quynn was helping James prepare for departure when over his brother's shoulder he caught sight of the petite redhead determinedly making her way toward him. He straightened fully from the coffer he'd been about to load onto the cart when Fleurette stopped in front of him. He was surprised to notice the brown fire leaping in her eyes.

James, who had turned to see what captured Quynn's attention, stepped aside just as the tiny redhead, who reached no higher than his brother's chest, said, "Milord, I need to speak with you."

Quynn nodded curtly, slightly amused by the warlike demeanor of the small woman.

"It is a difficult subject for me to broach. I feel a certain indebtedness to you because you saved me from Gerhaldt's odious kin. However, I feel more deeply the bond of friendship that Raiven and I have forged. What have you done to her?" she demanded bluntly without further preamble. "What is wrong?"

Quynn stiffened immediately, all amusement gone. "You have seen Raiven?"

Fleurette nodded.

"Then surely if you have seen Raiven, she has told you what she feels you ought to know."

She did not miss the censure in his voice, but Fleurette chose to ignore it. "Milord, I have no desire to overstep my boundaries despite your seeing it otherwise. It is only that Raiven is my friend and she is miserable. If there is aught that I can do to help her, as she has helped me, I will."

A slight relaxing of his posture was the only evidence Quynn gave that he heard her words.

James chose that time to speak. "Quynn, perhaps—"

"Should you not be readying for your journey, Brother?"

Fleurette turned to face James for the first time. Her calm, "You are James St. Crowell?" did not reveal the sudden lurch of her heart or the thought that struck just as abruptly that he was as handsome as his brother—probably more so.

James nodded, totally captivated by the tiny slip of a woman who dared to charge so aggressively against his brother.

"I am Fleurette Deveaux. The king has told me that I shall accompany you back to France. He feels it best since your brother now has stewardship of my estates and is now my guardian."

James bowed deeply. "'Tis a pleasure, madam." The long look he gave caused Fleurette to blush delicately.

At last Quynn spoke. "If you are to leave with him, should you not make haste? He leaves on the evening tide."

Fleurette tore her eyes away from James to stare back at Quynn. "There is no need for concern, baron," she stated quietly. "What you see is all I have. A condemned prisoner is not allowed much in the way of personal possessions."

Quynn looked away from her direct stare, slightly uncomfortable with the fact that he had inadvertently reminded her of her recent plight. He didn't know what to make of Fleurette. She reminded him of a butterfly, yet after the way she had accosted him, she appeared more of a butterfly with wings of steel. He did not want to be angry with her, but her questions put him on the defensive. He just wanted her to go away, but she showed no sign of obliging him. Instead, she turned back to James and said, "Would you think me terribly rude if I begged a moment with your brother?"

Without sparing Quynn a glance, James said, "I could never think such. Excuse me, milady, Quynn," before walking away.

Fleurette looked to Quynn, and again he was reminded of a butterfly, this time a determined one.

"Baron, I know you must think me forward and ungrateful. In truth in any other situation, I would share your opinion, but there are things that must be said, and I fear Raiven is too stubborn to say them."

The brown eyes she raised to his were hopeful, and Quynn could not resist their plea. "What things, madam?"

His tone was abrupt, but Fleurette smiled nonetheless. He could have dismissed her, but he did not, and that was a favorable sign.

"Do you know aught of France? I do not mean to lay insult upon your intelligence, it is only I know not where to begin and that seemed a likely place."

Quynn nodded. "I know something of the country."

"What of Aquitaine?"

"Aye, madam," Quynn said with a sigh, allowing a bit of impatience to creep into his voice.

Fleurette swallowed, her nervousness increasing. "It is a most unique place. As in England, there are many lords, barons, earls, and the like. However, unlike England, in Aquitaine the countryside is divided into portions that are almost completely ruled by the baron, viscount, or what have you of that region. It is a difficult situation since there is much distrust and dislike among those of different areas. Émil de Cortillion, Raiven's father, was a unique man. He ruled over two provinces, that of Poitou and Gascony. It is too long and unimportant to describe how this came to be, but suffice it to say that beneath his strong rulership these two provinces flourished and knew peace.

"Émil was unique in another aspect: he knew that his daughter—not his son—was the one to continue the peace and prosperity. Despite the unusualness of such a thing, he left total control to Raiven. She did not want it, but neither did she want to betray the confidence her father had in her. 'Twas difficult at first, because neither province accepted Émil's decision."

Fleurette shrugged. "I do not know if times were difficult because the people tested her fitness, but there was one crisis after another since her father died six months ago."

"Six months?" Quynn did not hide his surprise. He knew Raiven's father had died after her mother, but he had not known it was so recent. Then that meant—

"She was still mourning her father when she received word of her upcoming marriage to you," Fleurette finished his thought for him.

Quynn's face reflected his shock, but Fleurette went on as if she did not notice. "Raiven had only just begun to gain the respect of her people when she was ordered by Henry to turn stewardship over to you. Perhaps under other circumstances she would have been overjoyed, but this felt too much like betraying her father's trust. She could not meekly hand over her family's estates. Could you?"

Quynn looked hard at Fleurette, and for the first time he saw the quiet intelligence in the soft brown eyes.

"I believe you already know I could not," he stated quietly.

Fleurette nodded, unable to deny the things she had heard during her brief stay at the palace. When Quynn said no more, she continued. "When I met Raiven, she was tired and rather lonely."

For an instant Fleurette lost her audience as Quynn's

eyes grew unfocused, and as if it were taking place before him again, he saw a blond-haired queen perched on a throne of a wooden stool while a young boy raked hay and again he heard her tale of loneliness and fright. Forcing himself back to the present, he concentrated on Fleurette's words.

"I remember thinking I had never seen anyone work so hard to hide their fear—and that I had never met anyone that willful. Then one day, a few hours after we docked, she let down her defenses enough to tell me of her fears. The only thing she wants, milord, is peace."

Quynn ran his hand through his thick hair and made a rude noise, causing Fleurette to laugh.

"Truly, Baron. It is all she wants. However, she feels that it is quite impossible. She said to me that conflict is all she's known since her father's death, and her deepest grief was not being able to grieve for him properly. She has had to endure and continue. Do you ken, Baron, her biggest objection to your marriage?"

"Without doubt," Quynn responded dryly.

Fleurette looked at him through narrowed eyes, accurately reading his thoughts. "Nay, milord. 'Twas not you. 'Twas the fact that the union would not allow her any peace."

Quynn's gaze, which had wandered, riveted back to Fleurette. "She told you such?"

Fleurette bobbed her head. "The day we arrived. I have prayed every day since our parting that she would find the peace she sought. I cannot say how it saddens me to see she has not."

For a long moment Quynn studied Fleurette's face, gauging the sincerity of her words.

"Why do you tell me these things, madam?"

Fleurette shrugged. "If Raiven were to know, she would not thank me or agree that it is necessary. Instead, she would be angry, but I feel that you are the man that can give Raiven the peace she seeks so desperately. You can give her peace and so much more. I also feel she can give those things to you, if—pardon my bluntness—you both would stop being so blind about each other."

To Fleurette's surprise, Quynn threw back his head and laughed. When he sobered slightly, he murmured, "A butterfly with a stinger."

"Pardon?" Fleurette asked, confused.

"'Tis naught." Quynn shook his head. "Did anyone ever tell you that, for such a small person, you possess a large quantity of courage?"

Fleurette smiled. "Because I dared speak to you?"

"Because of that," Quynn said with a chuckle, "but even more, because I have the feeling you speak thus to Raiven. Anyone who can do that must have great courage," he said with exaggerated emphasis.

Fleurette's laughter fell between them. "Thank you for your compliment, milord, but I would be more grateful if you would give thought to what I've said. Please, Baron."

The look he gave her was considering. "Raiven has chosen her friends well. I will give thought to your words."

As Quynn promised Fleurette, the similar promise he had made to James flooded his memory. He turned to walk away when a sudden thought occurred to him. "Madam, have you perchance ever met my wife's brother?"

Fleurette's delicate brow wrinkled. "Nay, milord," she answered slowly, not liking the darkening she saw in his expression, but before she could question him, he was gone.

# Chapter 24

Quynn slipped quietly into the room, his eyes immediately searching for Raiven. He was about to call out to her when he saw she was asleep in the bed. Crossing over to it, he stared silently at his wife while she slept. Even her sleep did not bring true rest, for she twitched and moved as though disturbed.

Quynn thought he detected the faint path of tears on her cheeks but immediately discarded the idea. Raiven was not one to cry. Throughout all she had endured, with the exception of their bleak wedding night and her joy at the babe, he had not seen her give way to tears. Never having been one to tolerate them, Quynn now found himself strangely annoyed instead of relieved that Raiven did not cry as other women did.

Sighing, he turned away from the bed, annoyed and amazed that whether asleep or awake, Raiven had the ability to confuse and irritate him. He let himself out into the corridor, and when he turned, he nearly knocked over the woman who had come up behind him.

Instinctively, Quynn reached out to keep her from falling and was surprised to see the woman flinch away in rejection of his assistance and fall unceremoniously to the floor. His eyes narrowed at her strange behavior. From her dress he could see she was a servant, but there was no need for her to recoil from him. He was not one of those barons prone to smite a servant merely for daring to be in his path and not having the good sense to move out of it quickly.

Understanding her fear, Quynn slowly reached out to help her to her feet and was shocked to see her slide from his reach, eyes wide in fear. Righting himself slowly, a frown of confusion on his dark brow, he asked, "What ails you, girl? I mean you no ill."

Despite his words, the girl's expression did not change, and Quynn took a step back while trying to smooth his expression. In a voice he hoped was non-threatening, he asked, "What do you here? If you have come to aid my wife, she is sleeping. You may return later."

When the servant continued to stare, saying nothing, Quynn grunted in disgust and finally turned away.

"Baron?"

It was surprise that made him turn back.

The girl was now standing, and Quynn absently noted her remarkable height at the same time it registered that although her body still trembled, some of the fear had left her eyes.

"Aye?"

"I am Teris, milord," she stated, making it sound more like an admission than an introduction.

Quynn began to frown in confusion, then remembering her fear, asked blandly, "Should that have meaning for me?"

Teris smiled shakily and clasped her hands together. "I am—was the girl in your room—bed last eve, milord."

Quynn's eyes blazed, causing Teris to retreat from him, but at the moment he did not care.

"What do you here, girl?" he repeated his former question, only this time, harshness was rife in his tone.

Teris swallowed heavily. "I came to explain, milord, and to set things aright." Teris watched Quynn's face, and seeing no encouragement, she continued, but her earlier consternation had returned and her words were garbled. "I wished . . . only . . . to explain—"

"So you have said." Quynn studied the girl, and her nearly palpable fear eased some of his ire. "Why do you fear me so?"

"I feared your temper, milord. I ken you have the right. 'Tis only this morn that I learned you did not send for me as I was told."

"Told by whom?" Quynn asked, immediately interested.

Teris's shrug was disappointing. "I know not. The word was passed among the servants that you, uh . . . wanted a bed partner. Many wanted to come, but I was the only one having done my chores."

She waited expectantly for Quynn's reaction to his obvious appeal, but when he said nothing, it was she who experienced disappointment. Her last hope that what she'd heard this morn was a mistake died in her breast. It was not unusual for a lord to request a partner other than his wife, and it was also not unusual for that lord to deny it, should the tryst be discovered. But from the time last night when the baron had pulled away, leaving her naked in his bed without a backward glance, Teris had known something was wrong.

Then this morning as the servants prepared the meal to break the fast, gossip had been flowing back and forth about the trouble between the baron and the lady. The baron, it was rumored, slept elsewhere, and the lady—the things being said about the lady, considering she had caught her husband with another, were not kind. Some even thought she deserved it for her haughty ways. In spite of all that, Teris had felt a niggling guilt. She didn't like her part in it, and although under other circumstances, she would have gladly shared the baron's bed, she didn't like the darkness that pervaded the entire situation. That was why she had waited outside their room to speak to the baron, but he had entered the room so quickly she did not get the opportunity to call to him. She had gathered her courage enough to knock when he had exited abruptly and knocked her to the floor.

Having come this far, she had to make things right despite the baron's fearsome countenance.

"When I heard—" Teris stopped and cleared her throat. "When I heard," she began again, "that there was trouble brewing between you and the lady, I came straightaway. You did not call for me or anybody else. I ken that. I'll be happy to be telling your lady as well."

For the first time, Quynn smiled at her, and upon seeing the renewed brightness and suggestion in the girl's eyes, he made his words more curt than he originally intended.

"'Tis very good of you. My wife is taking her ease, but later upon arising, I am sure the news you bear will be pleasing to her."

Teris nodded happily, not put out in the least by Quynn's tone. She walked away, belatedly remembering to give her hips an extra sway. If the baron was watching, she wanted to give him something to remember should he change his mind in the future.

She could have spared herself the effort. Quynn was staring, true, but his stare was for the thick portal that separated him from his wife, and his gaze narrowed apace with the darkening of his thought. Although the anxiety he felt over the situation was reduced, to his surprise he was not relieved. He tried to tell himself it was only that it had yet to be settled and that was the reason for his discomfort, but that rationale did not help. Of a sudden he wanted to find Teris and bring her back immediately. Without being able to explain why, he felt an urgency that had no substance.

Reentering the room, he walked over to where Raiven lay sleeping and watched her for a long time. When he left the room again, the feeling he'd tried to shrug off as nonsensical returned even stronger.

"Bah," he scoffed. "Have I become an old woman to dream of night visions and shadowed specters? Enough!" he ended forcefully, striding down the corridor. There was no need for further worry. This was at least one problem in his overburdened life he was capable of solving.

Quynn's "solution" was a bit premature. Later when he rejoined Raiven so they could take the evening meal together, the dinner guests were all abuzz. It would appear that this visit to court was supplying them with more intrigue than any imagined. First there was the incident with the Deveaux woman, then the disturbance caused by Langford as he all but accused the baron of Havilland of aiding a treasonous spouse, and now there was the mysterious death of the servant girl. Nay, none could say that this visit to court had been less than stimulating. Why, even the king was riled, and Henry riled was something to see.

It was quite natural that one who possessed boundless energy such as the Plantagenet, was rarely still even under the most calm circumstances. There had been evenings when the guests dining with Henry had had to take their meals standing because the king, refusing to sit, paced to and fro. Naturally if he did not sit, neither could they.

Now Henry alternated between sitting and standing, or, as one baron put it, "sitting or wearing a path in the rushes."

When Quynn and Raiven entered the room, Quynn took in all the excitement, and immediately the hackles rose on his neck. Something was wrong. Usually, when he or James was at court, the gossip centered around old intrigue, with one or another baron conveniently remembering his family history. This visit had been no different, and with Langford's dramatic announcement yesterday, Quynn had been certain that any meal following would be a difficult ordeal. Yet with the king requesting their presence, staying away was impossible. Only James had been excused, and that was because he sailed for France on the evening tide.

Quynn spared a quick glance at Raiven, who had been unusually docile, and he noted that she too sensed the undercurrents. When he first came for her, he'd thought that Teris had somehow managed to speak to her, but then he noticed the coldness beneath her manner, and he knew the girl had not. Deciding to leave his explanation until later, he'd silently escorted her to dinner only now to see that she was not as oblivious about what was going on around her as she'd tried to appear.

Raiven's eyes were darting from one end of the large room to the other, and finally she raised them to meet Quynn's stare, a question clearly expressed in their green depths.

"I know not" was the tense response.

Shifting her eyes back to the occupants of the room, Raiven tried to compose her features. She had expected everyone to stare at them from the moment of their entrance. However, the way they were being ignored seemed more ominous.

Quynn led them to their place at the table at the precise moment that Henry's voice boomed out, "Havilland, what insult is this in your lateness again?"

Raiven felt Quynn's arm beneath her fingers tense further.

"My lady was resting, and I did not want to disturb her due to the delicacy of her condition."

Henry's sharp gray eyes narrowed. "Who was with her while she rested?"

Before Quynn could speak, Raiven responded. "I slept alone, sire. No one else was there."

By this time all in attendance had turned to hear what Raiven and Quynn had to say to the king and, more importantly, what the king had to say to them.

Raiven did not like the sudden silence, and she did not like the look in the king's eyes.

"Your pardon, sire, I did not know 'twas necessary to have—"

"I saw her asleep there myself, Your Majesty," Quynn interrupted forcefully.

From somewhere within the room a voice sneered, "And of course we all know the value of *his* word."

The arm beneath Raiven's fingers became so stiff that

Raiven thought that with the least bit of pressure from her it would snap. But to her surprise and admiration, Quynn said nothing. He did not even bat a lash at the sarcastic comment; instead he asked the king, "May we know why the nature of our whereabouts is the cause of such interest?"

Henry grunted before turning away to resume his pacing. "Your location was not in question. Many saw you with your brother helping to load the cargo."

"Then, sire, why was my wife's location of import?"

"The serving girl Teris has been found dead."

Quynn's eyes widened.

Henry did not miss the first reaction his baron had shown. "Then you are acquainted with the girl?"

"Aye. I am. However, milord, I doubt that Raiven is."

"How come you by such certainty, Havilland? She would have reason . . ." Henry let the insinuation hang.

Raiven struggled to maintain her silence. She realized the blunder from which Quynn's interference had saved her. She didn't care to repeat the mistake, but who was Teris? And why should they think she would have aught to do with the girl's death?

Quynn finally looked away from the king. Staring deeply into Raiven's eyes, he answered her unspoken questions. "Teris was the girl you saw in our bed last eve. Obviously someone has decided the time she spent among the living had sufficed."

Raiven looked from Quynn to Henry back to Quynn. "And they believe I had a role in her death? Why?"

It was Henry that spoke. "All know what happened between your husband and you, milady. When the girl was found today after no harm had befallen her 'ere now, 'twas a natural conclusion. It wouldn't be the first time a wife took a situation by the reins when she discovered her husband's infidelities."

Bright red flooded Raiven's cheeks. She didn't know what the source of her blushes was: her overwhelming anger or her mortification at having so private a thing discussed so publicly.

"I do not mean to cause you deliberate discomfort,

milady. But the fact is that a person has been murdered and questions, no matter how unsavory, have been raised and must be answered."

Raiven finally moved away from Quynn's side to walk up to Henry. From the corner of her eye she could see men clear their swords as if she posed the greatest threat to the king. She also knew that Quynn saw it, and he stood prepared to protect her at all costs.

One overzealous young baron rushed forward only to be halted by Henry's hand, Raiven's direct stare, and Quynn's drawing of his sword and stepping forward. Although which of the three things actually halted him, none could say.

After smiling brilliantly into the suddenly pale face of the young man, Raiven turned her attention back to Henry. To the surprise of all, she bowed low before the king and asked humbly if she could speak as a servant of the crown.

Henry appeared to be more in shock than any other present. Bemused, he bent down and lifted her erect. "Speak."

"Sire, although it is only our first formal meeting these few days past and despite the fact that the circumstances have been a bitter draught, I have known of you long before I came to your attention. In France, in spite of my countrymen's lack of enthusiasm for your rulership, your strength, your integrity, and most of all your justice are spoken of often and in the most praiseworthy tones.

"We all heard of the state of England before your reign and we all heard of the anarchy that pervaded here, although perhaps some of us knew it better than others," Raiven added with a quick glance at Quynn. "It is said that not only does the Eagle fly swift, but true as well. Since my arrival in England, I have seen evidence of this. Now, more clearly than ever, I see your interest in fairness and justice when most would simply claim 'twas naught but the death of a serf. You, however, sire, are showing that you are king of all England, be that the great or the small. It is before that king that I deliver myself, giving my solemn word that during the afternoon

I passed the time in my chamber, either entertaining another recipient of your justice, my friend, Fleurette Deveaux, or else sleeping. I do not know the time of the unfortunate girl's demise; I can only say," and Raiven raised clean white palms for Henry to see, "that these hands had no part in ending her life. I vow it."

Despite himself, Henry was moved. Reaching out, he grabbed her hands and then faced his assembled barons and other guests.

"Let it be known that I believe her innocence. The matter of Raiven of Havilland and the death of the servant girl Teris is at an end."

Only Baron Langford dared to speak. "What of the serving girl, milord? What of the person who did the deed?"

"I did not dismiss her death, only the Lady Raiven from among those under suspicion," Henry answered.

"There are no others," Langford cried.

"Then I suggest, Langford, that you find some," Henry snapped. Facing Raiven again, Henry said, "I've told Havilland before of the rareness of a woman of your breed—beauty, grace, and an indomitable sense of logic. Truly a treasure indeed."

"Your Majesty is kind."

Henry tilted his red head as if giving her words consideration. "Kind? I do not think it. 'Twould do a monarch no value to be kind. However," he added, a twinkle in his eyes, "if one or two of his subjects believed it thus and expressed it from time to time, he would not object overly much."

By the time Henry returned her to her place at the table, he was speaking freely to her. "By God, Havilland, did you know your lady knows quite a bit about horseflesh? And not just which way the saddle goes?"

Quynn nodded. "Aye, sire. I have been made aware of her talent in that area."

"And others, no doubt," Henry added with great insinuation, but with such a playfulness Raiven could not take offense. "Well, 'tis time you shared your good fortune with your king. My Eleanor is not present this eve, and I have a need for female companionship that is more than beauty."

Instantly Quynn's face darkened, and his hand reached out.

"Sire," he began in a tense tone, only to be cut off by Henry's burst of laughter.

"Rest easy, Havilland. I only want your lady as my dinner partner. I do believe Eleanor would have my liver if I took a paramour this soon in our marriage."

Quynn instantly eased his aggressive stance, although he did not totally relax. He and Raiven were among their enemies, and he would not forget. Casting a glance around the room at the hostile and envious faces, Quynn knew that forgetting would be impossible. No one would ever allow him to.

The hour was late when the king gave Raiven and Quynn leave to see James off. They walked in quiet to the stable where Khan and Sunstar stood, already prepared.

The docks were not far, and as Raiven rode alongside Quynn and his knights, she realized how foolish she had been to set out alone at night by herself.

It wasn't that the streets were deserted. Far from it. The streets bustled with activity. A person could disappear within the bustle, and none would notice nor likely care with all the activity. There were many shops still open that sold wine and practically everything else, and there were painted women strutting their wares in brilliant costumes. And above it all was the activity taking place on the ships as they were being made fit for sailing or docking.

Raiven felt like a small child as she gaped in unbridled curiosity at all that was taking place around her.

"Greetings, Sister," a deep voice rumbled. "'Tis pleased I am to once again see you come to bid me adieu."

Lowering her eyes to James's sparkling ones, Raiven smiled.

"'Twould seem all we do is say good-bye."

"I prefer something less final," James returned.

Raiven looked across the Thames. "How long will you be gone this time?"

"Quite a while, but I do not wish to think of that. Come, there's a friend who wishes to speak to you 'ere we sail."

"Friend?" Raiven's brow puckered. "I know no one on your vessel."

"Raiven?" called a familiar voice.

"Fleurette?" In an instant Raiven was off Sunstar's back and headed for the plank of the ship. After an exuberant hug, Fleurette pulled back, eyes moist.

"I go home now. Is it not wonderful?"

Raiven could only nod, trying to control the spurt of envy she felt.

"Do not be sad. We will meet again soon, I am certain. After all, your husband has stewardship of the estates left me by my father, and he has to approve of whomever I eventually wed. Since I do not intend to remain the 'virginal widow'—"

"Fleurette!" Raiven interjected.

Fleurette was not repentant. "It's true. Besides, 'twill give us the chance to be together in the future. For now, I am to spend some time at Guirlande, then later the baron's brother will take me home."

Raiven's face tightened at the mention of her home. Now Fleurette did apologize.

"I am sorry, Raiven. I should not have said that."

The effort it took for Raiven to compose herself was evident. Finally she said, "Nonsense. It is only a bit of homesickness I did not know was still there." Raiven linked her arm through Fleurette's and walked away from where James and Quynn stood making last-minute preparations.

"Fleurette," she began, switching to French, "I have a request to make of you."

"Anything I can do, you know I shall, Raiven."

"Good." Raiven nodded. "I need someone to talk to Jacques for me. I cannot communicate with him otherwise. Tell him I am fine. Tell him he must—"

"Honestly, Quynn," came James's deep voice from directly behind them, "you would think I never sailed before. All will be well. Ready, madam?" he asked Fleurette.

A quick glance was all Fleurette could give Raiven in assurance before she turned to James. *"Oui,* m'sieur. I am ready."

James's eyes darted back to Raiven, and she thought she read a warning in them as he stepped back, giving them a moment more. However, Quynn's gaze rested penetratingly on her, and Raiven dared not continue. Instead, she hugged Fleurette fiercely. When they pulled away, their eyes were glistening.

Before Raiven recovered from her farewells, she found herself swept up into James's strong embrace and heard in flawless French the same words she had whispered to him before he had left for France.

"Take care, little sister."

Raiven pulled back. "You speak French, James?"

He shrugged, and his words were light, but the message in his tone was heavy with warning. "I manage. One cannot live among people and not learn from them."

There was no response Raiven could make to that so she merely gave him a sisterly kiss on the cheek and moved to Quynn's side.

Within moments, James and Fleurette had boarded the ship, and the anchor had been lifted and the ship began its slow lumber out into the Thames.

On the way back to the palace, Quynn and Raiven maintained their silence, but once inside their room, Quynn's voiced stopped her on the way to the garderobe.

"Raiven, we must talk."

Raiven did not turn to face him. "I am tired. The day has been long and wearisome as it seems every day has been since my coming to England."

"Be that as it may, we still must talk." Quynn's voice was quiet but implacable. When Raiven still did not turn to him, he barked, "Face me when I speak to you."

Slowly Raiven swung about. She finally looked into Quynn's eyes but said nothing.

"Have you nothing to say?"

"If memory holds, it was your suggestion that we speak. Therefore I think it is your place to supply the words," she replied in a calm, toneless voice.

Quynn's jaw twitched. "Give not a hair's breadth, is that the way of it, Raiven?"

For a moment, her eyes fell from his. Quynn reached out to pull her gaze back to his. An interminable moment passed in which Raiven felt as if his eyes were attempting to ferret out every emotion she longed to hide.

*I must be strong. I cannot allow you to hurt me more.*

Things had not changed. The image of Quynn wrapped in another woman's arms was all that was before her eyes. It was all she could allow herself to see. Pain hardened her heart and the expression in her eyes.

A brief emotion flickered in Quynn's eyes before he dropped his hand and walked away. Raiven almost called out to him, but the picture of him entwined with that girl on their bed stilled her tongue, and then the moment was lost beneath the quiet click of the door shutting behind him.

It was a long time before Raiven fell asleep that night, and still Quynn had not returned. She repeated to herself over and over that she wasn't going to think of where he could be and with whom. She would not allow herself to think of it. Yet, her mind contradicted itself by not allowing her to think of anything else.

Just as Raiven was falling into a troubled sleep, Quynn let himself into an empty chamber. This evening had not ended the way he'd envisioned. He had wanted to explain to Raiven that he did not hold her responsible for her brother's actions. After spending last night in solitude, he had wanted to pass the night in peace and warmth, which he was beginning to suspect only Raiven could bring him.

Now he was sleeping alone, and this time he felt her absence more keenly than those nights at Havilland when he had stayed away. A chasm existed between them that was daunting. He knew that she felt that everything she had thought would come to pass had indeed occurred.

How things had gone so miserably awry, Quynn could not fathom. Thoughts of past events made him rise to slide the lock of the door in place. He needed no more unwelcome company.

Trying to remember some of the brief bliss he and Raiven had shared did not work. All he could see was the look in her eyes before he walked out of the room or the hurt she hadn't been able to conceal yestereve before the frost had swallowed all the warmth from her eyes.

Quynn slid beneath the pelts on the bed as a chill breeze swept the room. Too weary to rise and build a fire, he turned his mind instead to a few days hence when they would journey home, and his thoughts were of how the chill might affect Raiven. It was going to be a cold trip.

Before his eyes closed, Raiven's frigid face appeared again in his mind's eye. Aye, it was going to be cold indeed.

# Chapter
# •25•

The gray, cloudy sky reminded Raiven of the day she arrived in England. Her spirits were no higher now than they were then. Nay, that wasn't quite true. Her spirits were lower.

Rising from the chair where she had collapsed after her knees refused to continue to support her, Raiven paced furiously back and forth. One by one, her agile mind thought of different plans to extricate herself from the mess her life had become. One by one, each plan was rejected. There was no way out, and with each day, her circumstances seemed to worsen. All the promise and hope that had been her and Quynn's companion on the journey to London had withered beneath the ferocious flame of distrust and betrayal. Quynn believed he couldn't trust her or her brother, and Raiven knew she couldn't trust him. She needed no more evidence. Her eyes had seen it. They still saw it. The only time the image faded was when it was replaced by the image of the king questioning her about the girl's death.

Raiven grimaced in reflection. Surely it was those images that had made her lose control with Quynn and strike him when he had come to her to try once more to smooth the situation between them. Her reaction was as much a shock to her as it was to Quynn, revealing how truly unprepared she was to discuss his infidelities. It had been too soon for discussion. The hurt was too acute, the pictures in her mind too vivid.

Regardless of the images flashing relentlessly through her mind, there had been no mistaking the crackling blaze in Quynn's eyes. Moments after Raiven's hand connected soundly with his face, he had her in a grip of unyielding, unbreakable steel. The fury in his gray eyes seared wherever it touched her. Raiven had never seen such anger or heard such venom in his voice as he snapped softly, "Madam, you carry my child, and I pray 'tis a son you will bear, and know 'tis that and that alone that stays my hand." He had paused and took a deep breath, his nostrils flaring, giving mute evidence of his tremendous struggle for control.

"Perhaps, lady, when our son is of an age of manhood and his honor and respect for you runs high, he will allow you the liberty of assaulting his person. I, however, am not your son, and my mother lies cold in her grave. Do not ever again mistake the issue and stand warned: *Do not ever raise your hand to me again. Is that clear?"* he ground out.

Raiven had barely nodded when he released her. The walls still shook from the sound of the door slamming to its rest.

Remembering Quynn's fury, she nearly weakened again, and Raiven had to pause in her frenetic pacing. Nay, things were definitely worse than they had ever been between her and her husband.

When Quynn had first entered the room, he had informed her that they would be leaving for Havilland on the morrow. It was ironic that had that announcement come just two short days ago, Raiven would have rejoiced. Now she felt no joy, only a bleak sort of expectancy that could not be willed away despite her efforts. It was not as if there was anything in this cold, gray place she found endearing, she just didn't want the enforced solitude with Quynn that the journey back to Havilland would produce. However, there was no alternative. The more she tried to think of one, the more confused her thoughts became.

With tired resignation, Raiven lay down on the bed that had been the scene of both unbelievable laughter and joy and of unbearable pain and despair. Last night she had slept here alone. She didn't know where Quynn had sought his rest, and she tired of telling herself she didn't care. But she didn't. Truly she didn't. Perhaps, Raiven thought with another grimace, if she continued to say it, she would believe it enough to convince him of it by the time she next saw him.

The sky was no brighter as they departed the next morning and neither were Raiven's spirits. The only benefit the gloomy skies afforded was that they, combined with her not totally false plea of fatigue, enabled her to ride in the cart rather than astride Sunstar.

Raiven could tell that Quynn was still very angry with her. When she made her request to have the cart modified, he agreed abruptly and then turned Khan away. Gavin had seen to the modifications and her comfort. It was Gavin who rode beside Quynn. The only consolation that brought was the fact that from the expression on the knight's face and Quynn's sharp answers to the few questions that were put to him he was no more enjoying himself than she would have had she been riding beside him.

Raiven groaned, rolling to her side as the cart hit a rut in the road. Instantly one of the knights asked, "Milady, is aught amiss?"

Biting her lip to still its tremor, Raiven managed to respond in a voice that she hoped hid her misery. "A little soreness is all. My thanks for your concern." She tried to give him a small smile, but her facial muscles refused to obey.

The knight, Cedric, she believed he was called, smiled reassuringly and moved away. Raiven closed her eyes, relieved he had not persisted, and attempted to seek what rest she could. Yet despite the many men in their party, the loaded wagons, horses, and other necessities of travel, there was too much silence. The jovial camaraderie that had been present on the trip to London was glaringly absent. It was as if the men sensed the trouble between her and Quynn, and they were observing a sort of mourning for the death of the happiness the lord and lady had shared.

Raiven turned again, trying to wipe out the sounds of silence, trying to still the tiny voice that said the morose atmosphere was her fault.

It was not her fault! Had she put that woman in Quynn's bed? Nay! Had she accused herself of her death? Nay! Had she accused her brother and herself of treason? Nay! It was all their doing. They forced her into this defensive posture, and she would not allow herself to feel guilty. Silence be hanged!

As she rolled over yet again, careful this time to make no sound, she opened her eyes for a brief moment and then widened them as she stared into her husband's cool gaze. Before she could gather herself or think to ask him why he was there, he spoke.

"Cedric seems to believe you are having difficulty." His tone implied that he did not share his knight's opinion.

"Cedric is kind," Raiven stressed, and Quynn's eyes flared slightly, "but he worries for naught. It is only that I am seeking to find my rest."

Quynn inclined his head. "Then I shall leave you to it," he said, galloping off on Khan's back before she could say another word.

Raiven eased herself further onto her side, wincing when the cart bumped through yet another hole in the road. How was she ever going to endure two days of this? She didn't know if she questioned more her ability to endure the ride or to bear the horrible situation between her and Quynn.

About an hour from Havilland the gray clouds that had followed them from London withheld their watery tribute no more. With a suddenness and intensity that made Raiven gasp, the clouds released the water in a rainy sheet that instantly obscured vision and immediately soaked the travelers through.

Raiven could hear Quynn giving hurried orders, although with the heaviness of the rain, she couldn't see him. Suddenly he was before her, lifting her onto Khan's back. No sooner had he settled her there than he wrapped the material they'd used for their tent around her, effectively protecting her from the downpour.

It took Raiven a few minutes to surface from the "tent" he had made around her. The second she stuck her head out, Quynn tried to push it back.

"Wait," Raiven cried desperately.

Her call made him pause.

"Aren't we going to stop? How can we continue in this rain? Shouldn't we make camp?"

Quynn's expression beneath his plastered hair was grim. "Are you daft, woman? Where would we camp? The ground is already soaked as are the blanket rolls the men used to seek their rest. There are only three tents; even if they survived the wet of the ground, not all would fit beneath such scanty shelter. Furthermore, Havilland is an hour's ride away. Better to be wet and moving and gain the warmth and comfort of the hall than to sit motionless, seeking meager protection."

He grunted as he slapped the end of the material back over her head with a finality that Raiven did not dare ignore.

Offended by his condescension, even though she herself had thought the very same thing after having asked the question, she began to mutter in ire. "First I'm jostled about in that horrid cart," she grumbled, totally forgetting it was her own idea to use that means of transport. "Then I'm smothered in tent material and hauled about like a sack of grain, and *he* has the temerity to be annoyed? What gall!"

If Raiven had known that Quynn was listening and could hear every mumbled word, she probably would have held her tongue. Certainly if she had seen the reluctant smile creep across his face, she would have been tempted to jab her elbow into his ribs. However, since she was blissfully unaware, she continued her irate murmurings until she finally exhausted herself and fell into a fitful sleep.

As finely attuned to her as he had been to nothing else before in his life, Quynn knew the moment the storm in his arms had passed. His grip on her immediately tightened, and he smiled again.

When the welcome gray walls of Havilland came into view, his smile was still there.

"Elaine, do stop fussing and come to rest. You are beginning to remind me of an irate goose." Raiven's smile removed all the sting from her reprimand, which she doubted Elaine had heard in any event.

"Oh, but, milady, 'tis soaked through you are, and what with the hall being drafty and damp, a cold is what you'll be catching sure as sure."

Raiven raised her eyebrow. Elaine had spoken as Ella or Mildrede might have.

"Have you become an Englishwoman in my absence, Elaine?" Raiven asked with dry humor and just a hint of seriousness.

The answering expression on Elaine's face was priceless. Forgetting all somberness, Raiven immediately burst into laughter, causing Elaine's outrage to grow.

Drawing herself rigidly erect, which to Raiven's mind only made her seem more English than ever, Elaine stared at her lady. "'Twas no need for insult, milady. I was merely offering my concern for your well-being."

Raiven would have laughed again, but a thundering voice calling her name gained her instantaneous and undivided attention.

"Raiven," Quynn bellowed, his voice shaking the foundation of the hall as he advanced menacingly upon her. "'Tis no longer necessary to question your wits, madam, because as of this moment, I am certain you haven't any."

Raiven drew herself up stiffly. She was about to tell him precisely what she thought of him and his opinion of her wits or lack of them when he reached out and with a ferocious grip pulled her to him.

"What do you here, madam? Standing about exchanging pleasantries whilst turning blue from the wet and cold?"

Raiven attempted to jerk herself away from him, but her bid for freedom only caused his hand to increase its pressure. Realizing that he had no intention of releasing her, Raiven stood very still, not bothering to mask the scorn in her eyes or her tone.

"If you will be so good as to unhand me, I was about to withdraw abovestairs to change my clothing and soak away the chill in a warm bath. What you saw," Raiven continued, "was the warm welcome exchanged between two who care for one another and had been forced apart. Elaine herself was curtailing our reunion until she could see to my comfort. Your concern was not needed," she spat out contemptuously.

Quynn stared down into the yellow gold blaze of her eyes. His soft response was totally at variance with his still aggressive stance.

"Or wanted?"

Raiven dropped her eyes from his. She didn't want to see anything more in his eyes than disgust, and she didn't want him to see anything in hers but her contempt. This time when she drew back, he allowed her to go.

Squaring his shoulders when Raiven stubbornly refused to answer him, Quynn said, "'Twas my concern for my heir that I expressed, madam. Your feelings about whatever I can offer you have been made clear," he retorted sharply, rubbing the jaw where Raiven had slapped him.

They both ignored Elaine's gasp of surprise, but that sound saved Raiven from making a scathing retort as she remembered they were not alone. Although her eyes still shot sparks, her lips remained tightly closed, and she turned toward the stairs, not looking back or speaking another word.

Quynn stood below, staring after his wife's stiff back

until she disappeared through her bedchamber door. He forgot Elaine still stood there staring at him when he slammed his fist onto the table, cracking the thick wood through the center and uttering a fervent "Blast!"

The muffled noise, part fear, part shock, recalled him to his senses, and he turned to stare at Elaine's pale face, oblivious to the blood streaming from his abused hand.

He may not have noticed it or cared, but to a trained healer like Elaine, his battered hand could not be ignored. Her fear instantly gone, she had disappeared from his view only to return clutching the pouch he had seen her carry when she was intent on healing one of the people on the estate.

Without a word, she reached out and took his hand, examining it. Quynn watched the back of her small dark head bent over his hand, and although he couldn't see her face, he knew she was frowning. He also knew that if he weren't lord here, she would be fussing at him as he had heard her do with his men—and his wife also for that matter.

As with any healer, Elaine detested damage done to the body, most especially deliberate, uncalled-for damage. She bristled silently, cleaning his hand and wishing she had the right and courage to box his ears.

"Let it out," an amused voice said above her head.

Elaine stood so quickly that Quynn didn't have time to move his head, and the back of hers collided with his chin, causing him to bite his tongue soundly.

He was about to swallow his censure, pressing his tongue against the roof of his mouth in a bid to ease the pain, when he saw the look in her eyes. The wench was actually pleased.

Quynn's eyes chilled. "Is there aught in this situation to please you, mademoiselle?"

Quickly, Elaine masked the look in her eyes. "Nay, milord," she whispered.

Immediately Quynn regretted intimidating her. This was the first time she had looked at him with something other than wariness, and he had terrorized her. The girl had committed no crime. In fact, had Ella been present, there probably would have been great amusement at his behavior, and it wouldn't have been silent.

A bit of a blush suffused his face when he thought of how childish he was behaving, and aye, he thought ruefully, he could see the humor in that.

Tentatively, he extended the hand Elaine had unconsciously released when he'd quelled her with his glance. He genuinely smiled at her, an attractive twist coming to his lips as the smile reached his eyes, and he silently cajoled her into taking his wounded hand.

"Contrary to the impression I have given, I am past the age of swaddling. My apologies for my behavior."

Elaine took his hand and bent her head back to her task, but not before he saw the return of the twinkle in her eyes.

"'Twas not my intent to insult, milord. 'Tis only my fondness for incorrigible boys and their temper tantrums. At the time, you reminded me of one."

Quynn grunted.

"But 'tis truth," she went on, darting a quick glance up, carefully avoiding his chin, "that despite my fondness for those sorts of lads, I also feel an almost irresistible urge to box their ears."

Elaine's hand tensed on his, while she waited for a response.

His tone had not lost its amused quality, but the implacableness of his words was clear. "I would heartily recommend such resistance."

Elaine's head bobbed, and her hand relaxed. "So noted, milord."

Raiven was soaking in a hot bath by the time Elaine entered the room. The heat of the water was second only to her anger, which had not cooled one whit. Nay, if it was possible, it had grown. Her first words to Elaine were a cross, "Where have you been?"

Elaine eyed her mistress warily, deciding that discretion and distance were needed. She had already had her share of mercurial people with quicksilver tempers.

"Belowstairs," she answered, offering no more.

"Hmph! Did you not know that I needed you here?"

Elaine looked about, and Raiven read her expression as clearly as if she had spoken. Raiven was also aware of the fact that her accusation was unfair. Normally, she dressed and bathed herself. Elaine more or less took care of her clothes and her room when she was not in them. It was unfair to berate her for a service she had never demanded. But Raiven didn't care about fair. She knew only that she was angry, and besides Elaine was supposed to be there for her to talk to, not belowstairs.

Raiven had not missed the loud bang coming from the main hall just after she closed the door to her room. It also had not taken much to discern what it had been. And, Elaine, traitor that she was becoming, had probably stayed below to fix the damage he'd inflicted on himself.

Elaine still stared at her incredulously, and Raiven could feel her anger wane. She was never one to hold onto anger when it wasn't justified.

"I apologize, Elaine," Raiven finally said with a sigh, only to wonder at the reason for Elaine's sudden smile.

Elaine shrugged, not answering the unspoken question in Raiven's eyes. "'Tis more than your condition making you so cross." Carefully folding away the clothing Raiven had taken with her to London, Elaine asked, "I did hear the baron correctly? I did not misunderstand?"

Raiven's answer was barely audible. "Nay, you did not."

True joy sparkled from Elaine's eyes. "'Tis a good thing, is it not?"

When Raiven did not reply, Elaine said, "When you left for London, things seemed—"

"Things change," Raiven interrupted bitterly. Before she could stop herself, and because there was no one else, Raiven found herself telling Elaine about their disastrous stay in London, leaving out nothing. By the end of it all, she was crying almost uncontrollably.

Elaine helped her from the bath and in a short while had Raiven snug in her bed. Then she sat beside her, wiping her hair back from her brow. Despite their being the same age, there were times—like now—that Elaine felt so much older.

"You must put it behind you, milady. Things happen. Perhaps all 'twas not the way it appeared."

Raiven bolted upright. "I *saw* him, Elaine. I saw him. I wish I had not. I wish a thousand times I had not, but I did."

"What did you see?" She held up her hand when Raiven was about to speak. "I understand, truly I do. I would tear any alive who dared hurt you, but the baron does not seem to be a deliberately cruel man. I just think 'tis more than what is there."

Elaine studied Raiven's face, taking in her mistress's surprise. In truth, Elaine had surprised herself at her feelings, but they were there, strong and undeniable. The problem was Raiven was thinking too much with the cold, methodical mind her father had so loved. That mind was now making it difficult for her heart to do its job. But there was something in Raiven's eyes that gave Elaine the answer to her next question even before she asked it.

"You love the baron, do you not?"

Raiven, whose thoughts had been winding along a similar path, refused to answer. She had run from that truth for days. She would not make the admission out loud when she had refused to admit it to herself. It would destroy her. Yet it clamored inside, bursting to be said.

"Do you not?" This time Elaine's voice was coaxing.

Raiven's head did a slow nod as tears made a new course down her face. "Aye," she cried, dropping her face into her hands, crying out her torment. "Aye, I love him, but there is no joy in the loving. Oh, God, what am I to do? What am I to do?"

# Chapter 26

The days passed slowly and at the end of each one, Raiven's despair increased. She loved him. She loved him! The words continued to reverberate around in her head until it seemed she could hear no others. At least she no longer wept her misery. God's truth, she didn't think she had any more tears to shed. During the past days she wept enough to flood the Channel. Elaine had not known what to do, never having seen her in such a state. That first day she had acknowledged her feelings, Elaine had merely bade her rest and sat with her as she cried herself to sleep. The next morning when Raiven awoke, she had been violently ill, and she wasn't sure whether her illness had been brought about by her condition or her emotional upheaval.

As the days went by and the crying ceased but the sickness did not, Raiven realized that it was due to the child she carried and the adjustments her body was making. That thought brought none of her earlier joy, so she pushed it from her mind. She didn't want to face the reality of the baby yet. There had been too much change in too little time. Her mind refused to grasp it.

However, despite the dictates of her mind, her body continued to make her take notice of its changes. Each morning she arose later and later, trying to wait for the feeling of nausea to pass, and each morning she failed. The sensation subsided only after she emptied her stomach of its meager contents.

Elaine encouraged her not to fight the feeling. "The sooner you empty your stomach, the sooner you will be relieved."

Raiven merely rolled her eyes at that bit of enlightenment.

Elaine also encouraged patience, saying this stage would soon pass. However, she said this when Raiven was bent double, retching into a chamber pot, and she was not inclined to believe her or want to wait for some time in the future for permanent relief.

It was during this particular time one morning, about two weeks after their return, that Quynn chose to visit her.

Raiven was surprised to see him, for he had steadily stayed away from her since their return from London. The only times their paths crossed were when it could not be avoided. He never sought her out. And although Raiven drank in his presence at those rare times she saw him, she maintained her cool facade, wanting him to think his absences did not matter.

She could not tell if her insouciance affected him. All she knew was the strain of pretending indifference was definitely wearing on her. The tension between them had enveloped everyone at Havilland.

If the ride back to Havilland was awkward, day-to-day life in the hall was sheer torture. Their former fleeting happiness whispered in haunted corners, mocking them, making the present situation even more unbearable. Servants tiptoed around the hall, all but trying to disappear into the stones, and Quynn's knights fared no better. Before their journey to London, sparring with Quynn was considered to be an honor, sought by both the seasoned and unseasoned. Now the men drew lots—sometimes two or three times if the unhappy winner felt the draw had been unfair or was unwilling to accept it—to see who would have to endure the rigor of training with him. Mealtimes were a silent, sullen affair to be gulped down no matter the dish's taste or temperature. More than one knight had risen from the table with a burned tongue, silently endured, because of not wanting to gain Quynn's attention. From the highest-ranking knight to the lowest serf, all prayed for a reconciliation between the baron and his lady. All wanted to see a return to the happiness that had so briefly warmed Havilland. All wanted to see the return of Raiven's smile and, more, the departure of the chilly gleam from Quynn's eyes.

Which was why when Quynn barged in unexpectedly on Raiven, Elaine was not the only one secretly applauding the moment, however much she might have wished he had chosen a better time. They needed to be alone, and she couldn't leave.

Raiven herself was also wishing Quynn had chosen a better time. But there he stood at the foot of the bed with that blank expression, waiting for her to acknowledge his presence, which, even had she wanted to do, she could not. She couldn't acknowledge his presence without opening her mouth and could not open her mouth without being ill. Until now, she had been able to keep these disagreeable episodes from him. It was prideful, she knew, but she didn't want to seem weak. And most definitely, she did not want him to see her in the embarrassing position of bending over a chamber pot while her stomach emptied its contents. So, she lay there, watching him, inwardly begging him to leave.

Her silent pleas were of no avail. Quynn did not move. He barely seemed to blink as he carefully watched her facial expression. Raiven knew he did not like the grim set of her lips by the reflexive tightening of his own. She could also tell from his stance that what he had to say she was not going to care for either. She saw the precise moment he decided she had ignored him long enough.

Catching Elaine's eye, he absently inclined his head toward the door, his face registering momentary surprise when she did not immediately do his bidding.

"Milord, I cannot—"

A slight narrowing of his eyes changed the servant's mind about the wisdom of continuing, and casting an apologetic glance toward Raiven, she rose to leave just as Quynn walked over to the right side of the bed.

Raiven's alarm rose apace with her gorge as she saw Elaine leaving. Opening her lips slightly, she called, "Elaine, wait—"

"I wish a word with you, madam, and I asked your servant to leave," Quynn stressed unnecessarily as if Raiven had not seen his actions. He looked pointedly at Elaine, who had hesitated at Raiven's call.

Raiven raised a weak hand, wishing she could yell his ears off for his autocratic manner, but mostly she still wished he'd leave before she disgraced herself in front of him.

"Very well, milord," she said between her teeth, "what is it you have to say?" She swallowed heavily and closed her eyes, waiting for him to speak.

"First, you will do me the courtesy of looking at me."

Raiven kept her eyes closed. Let him think what he would. The nausea was more bearable with her eyes closed, and she certainly was not going to inconvenience herself any more than she already was.

"I assure you that although my eyes are closed, my ears are not," she bit out.

The soft hissing of Quynn's breath was her first warning that she had gone too far. Hurriedly she opened her eyes to keep him from grabbing her as she knew he intended, but it was too late. Her agonized "Quynn, don't" came out at the same moment that his hands jerked her into an upright position.

So much for control. Raiven knew she had precious seconds to make it to the garderobe before she was sick, but Quynn refused to release her. She struggled with increasing violence as she realized she was about to be ill in the bed and still he wouldn't let go.

"I'm going to be sick," she finally managed to murmur.

Instantly his hands fell away, and Raiven rushed to the garderobe.

The retching was worse this morning than ever, and somewhere in the middle of it, she felt a tear or two slide down her face as she wondered agonizingly if it would ever end. She was so miserable that at first she didn't notice the cool cloth being pressed to her forehead or the soft words being uttered in her ear or the gentle arm supporting her as she heaved unrelentingly.

As soon as the spasms decreased in intensity, Raiven became aware of all of those things. When they ceased altogether, Quynn gently washed her face and then carried her back to the bed. Raiven lay there limply, too exhausted to care that he had seen her have one of her worst bouts of morning sickness ever.

"Why didn't you tell me you didn't feel well?" came the soft question.

Raiven closed her eyes and made a feeble shrug, which was the only answer she felt capable of giving. To her surprise, he sat gently on the bed and began to massage her temples gently, stopping only to smooth back the blond hair that had fallen into her face.

It felt so good an involuntary groan of satisfaction escaped her as she felt herself relax. She was almost drifting off to sleep when he spoke again.

"I came to tell you that we must leave for France soon."

Raiven's eyes flew open. France? They were going to France? Why? Quynn hadn't said "I," he'd said "we." Why? When just three months ago, she was not even permitted to send her brother a letter.

Quynn read the question in her eyes, and he simply said, "Henry wants the child to be born in France on Poitevin soil. None can deny it then."

His calling the baby "the child" stung. It made it seem to lack importance. Raiven jerked away from his solicitous fingers and snapped, "Please leave, milord."

A stunned expression on his face, Quynn pulled away, his hands instantly ceasing their soothing motions to fall beside her head. "What ails you now, woman? I thought you'd want to journey to France. Is there never to be any understanding of what goes on in your head?"

"For your knowledge, milord, my people will accept *my child* whether or not it is born on Poitevin soil. You nor your king have aught to fear."

Quynn's smile was nasty. "I doubt if there is aught to fear in France that a strong hand cannot repair. However, the birth is not the only reason Henry is desirous of our journeying there. He is tired of the unrest and the rumors of revolt. I tire of them also. He wants me to go there as 'tis fitting, since the holdings there are now mine."

Raiven inhaled sharply at his stressing of the word *mine,* but he left no time for comment as he finished, "and he wants me to quell either the rumors or the rebellion or both, depending upon what I find."

Not unnaturally, Raiven took this as a direct attack on her brother and her people. The color was beginning to return to her cheeks, and her eyes sparkled angrily as she spat out, "There is no rebellion."

Quynn appeared entirely undisturbed by her vehemence. "There is. The only question remaining is who is behind it and why, but 'twill not be difficult to ascertain and prove."

"Well, why bother with this mockery of a journey to France for justice," Raiven hissed. "Why do you not send the men for my brother's head now and be done. The king has what he desires. You have what you want," she ended in a whisper that was at once furious and forlorn, placing her hand on her stomach.

She saw his hand jerk as if he just stopped himself from touching her, and despite her stony expression, inside she was pleading, *Nay, do not stop. Touch me, Quynn, touch me as you did that night many nights ago. Touch me as if you want me and not the heir or the lands I bring.*

All around them was intensely quiet, leaving them both to struggle with their wills. His hand moving back to his side was the end of the sweetly poignant moment. Raiven lowered her gaze, and slowly Quynn stood.

"I suggest you make preparations as soon as possible for the journey. Henry left the time of departure to me, but I do not wish to delay."

"Heaven, help us should that happen. 'Twould delay my brother's date with the executioner by a day or more."

Quynn's eyes began to warm under her barbs. "I have not once mentioned your brother. However, 'twould seem I am not the only one with doubts—if your hasty assumptions are any indication."

"My brother is innocent!" Raiven fairly screeched.

"I did not say otherwise," Quynn retorted, turning for the door.

Raiven watched him walk away with hot eyes that should have been able to bore a hole through his back.

At the door, he turned to look back at her, and his voice was as flat as the expression in his eyes. In a quiet tone he asked, "Do you never tire of the battle, Raiven?" He stared into her shocked face for a moment, then turned to leave without waiting for her to stumble through an answer.

Raiven sagged with relief when the door shut behind him. What on earth did he mean, did she never tire of the battle? She was so tired of the battle she could weep with exhaustion. Yet her feelings did not matter. They never had. From the time Henry had set her upon this path, no one had given a moment's thought to how she might feel. Everything was supposed to be bigger than she was. Do it for Guirlande, her people, Jacques. They were more important. Do it for England. Do it for a life free from strife. There was a jest if ever she heard one.

Now when things were not going as smoothly as the king and Quynn expected, the blame was placed again before her, as if she planned this fiasco. What did they expect her to do? She had complied as best as she was able. She had even tried making England her home—of sorts. But when her brother's character was maligned, when he and her people were accused falsely, she had to show herself strong for them, didn't she? She had to be the support for them, didn't she? Quynn could claim

Guirlande all he liked. It would not change the fact that it was hers. Her father had left it to her, and though she might surrender its ultimate control, her heart and the hearts of the people—even the heart of the land itself—knew who the true ruler was. And she would continue to be that until she ceased to breathe. That was only right, wasn't it?

Yet no matter how loud the logic of her mind, which tried to convince her that she had been right to behave the way she had, something in the quiet blankness of Quynn's stare and voice kept telling her that she was wrong.

# Chapter

# •27•

The time Quynn had set for departure—one moon—came and went, and still they had not left for France. Raiven could scarcely complain because, during the delay, the persistent morning sickness had eased. Now each of her days began with a spark of energy that she found invigorating and welcome. It was certainly a pleasant exchange for the lassitude and nausea of the past month.

However, the abatement of her sickness was the only relief. The tension between her and Quynn was still there with a healthy, vibrant life of its own. Quynn had long since ceased trying to explain what had happened the night she had found him with Teris, a fact that left Raiven with mixed emotions. She wanted him to have an explanation, yet she couldn't truly accept that there was one for what she saw. There were times when she consoled herself with the thought that his silence on the matter might bring the ability to forget. Then, during the other times, she was angry that he didn't try to convince her. *Figure that,* she thought to herself on more than one occasion since their return. To her mind, if he cared one whit for her sensibilities, especially since she carried his child, he would make a more fervent attempt to explain despite her apparent lack of belief.

Staring out at the lower bailey, Raiven couldn't help the smile that curved her lips at her own inconsistencies. It seemed that her ability to think rationally diminished apace with the increase in her girth as the babe grew within her. Placing her hand gently on the tiny, yet firm mound of her stomach, Raiven experienced a feeling of such warmth and love she was practically moved to tears. But her eyes remained dry. Thankfully, her almost uncontrollable as well as spontaneous bouts of weeping had passed along with the morning illness.

Aye, a lot had changed in the last month. Once the shock of loving Quynn subsided, the babe had taken on new and precious dimensions in her heart. Gradually the circumstance of its conception ceased to be troubling. It was her child and his, and she loved it with all her being. She was able to recognize and admit that part of the overwhelming love she felt for the babe stemmed from the feelings she had for Quynn. She didn't try to decipher those feelings as she had tried to figure out everything since meeting Quynn, she merely accepted them and tried to rise above her circumstance. She was even trying to rise above what had happened in London, but that was a thing more easily spoken than accomplished.

Perhaps if Quynn would come to her and apologize, seeking her forgiveness instead of an understanding she knew she'd never give, she would be able to put the episode from her mind. He had not done that, and Raiven knew with a clarity that blotted away all doubt that an apology was what she needed to hear. She would be able to forgive him then, and everything would not seem so hopeless.

Sighing over the whole situation, Raiven left her room and the hall, heading for the stables. Of late there had been no time for riding Sunstar as she had been occupied in making preparations to leave. Because they had not left and Quynn had not told her of their new departure date, she decided to resume as many of her old activities as possible. This being the first warm day, the temptation was too great.

Selkirk, the stablemaster, seemed surprised to see her walking toward Sunstar's stall, but aside from a brief nod and curious glance, he said nothing. However, when Raiven turned to ask the usually helpful stablemaster whether or not Sunstar had been exercised, she found she was alone. Shrugging, she turned back to the white horse, stroking her neck absently while looking about for a saddle. Once that task was done, she climbed onto the mare's back and eagerly led her out into the bright sunlit yard.

It was a beautiful spring day, and Raiven looked forward to galloping across the meadows and forests of Havilland. Her pulse began to beat with excitement of the ride, and she began to smile in anticipation. Even nature seemed to share her enthusiasm, as the shrill whistle of a bird sounded and Sunstar's ears twitched in acknowledgment.

"Ready, girl?" Raiven asked softly just before she gave the command for the horse to break into a full gallop. To her surprise though, Sunstar would not move. Raiven nudged her again, but the mare stayed still, making Raiven's brow furrow in puzzlement.

"What is it, girl? What's the matter?" Raiven patted the horse's neck soothingly, her eyes searching the path ahead to see if there was an obstruction that would make the horse balk. There was nothing.

When she prodded the horse a third time with no better results than the former, she slid from its back. The moment her feet touched the ground, she heard, "'Tis the smartest thing I've seen you do this morn."

Raiven spun about to see Quynn standing at a distance behind her. His voice had the same effect on her as whatever it was that was affecting Sunstar. Raiven stood very still. Despite the fact that he was not close and his features were obscured in the shadow of the tree he stood beneath, she knew he was angry.

It was amazing that she knew that because he gave no evidence of it. His stance was indolent, his arms folded across his massive chest. He hadn't raised his voice or spoken with an edge to it. Yet as surely as she knew her name, Raiven knew Quynn was furious.

Feeling slightly off center by his attitude, Raiven decided to try for neutrality. "I did not see you there."

Quynn began to approach slowly. "'Tis obvious, that."

Raiven was beginning to feel stalked, and she didn't like it. "I was about to go for a ride," she said unnecessarily, a defensive note in her voice.

Quynn was close enough now for her to see his brow raise. She felt compelled to continue. "But something is wrong with Sunstar." Her voice was weak, and she used her concern for the horse as a reason to turn away from her husband.

Quynn's continued silence was truly beginning to grate on her nerves.

"Haven't you heard what I said? Have you no care for the horse? Something is wrong with her. She won't move."

Finally Quynn spoke. "There is naught wrong with the horse. Indeed she shows more wisdom than her mistress." The sharpness was now in his tone.

Raiven spun back to him. "What do you mean, she shows more sense than her mistress? She—"

"I ken," he cut her off abruptly, "she does not move. She does not move because I told her not to. You, madam, should be half as wise."

"When did you . . . ? How? I did not hear you speak 'ere a few moments ago." Raiven did not try to hide her confusion.

A grim smile crossed Quynn's face. "Aye. But you did hear this," and then he made the sound of a shrill whistle, and instantly Raiven recalled hearing it when she and Sunstar had first left the stables. She had mistaken the sound for a birdcall. She remembered Sunstar's ears twitching in what, even to her, had appeared to be acknowledgment.

Forgetting their situation and his anger, Raiven gave

him a beautiful smile. "It was you. It is incredible. Are all your horses so trained?"

Stunned by the beauty of her smile and the warmth of her voice, Quynn could only nod slowly.

Raiven turned back to place her hand on Sunstar's mane. She spoke to Quynn over her shoulder. "No matter what command I gave, she wouldn't move. Such training is marvelous. Is the call to release the same? Nay, it must not be," she answered herself, her growing fascination apparent. "Because you just did it again, and she has not moved. But then again I have not tried to ride her either."

Raiven was so taken with her new discovery, she missed the return of darkness to Quynn's brow.

"Perhaps I should test it and see," she concluded, putting her foot in the stirrup, only to find herself lifted totally off the ground and held fast against her husband's chest.

"Put me down!" she cried out in surprise. "What ails you?" When she turned her face to show him her anger, she was met with the blaze of anger in his.

"Are you truly this daft, woman, or do you only seek to test the limits of patience?"

Raiven stared at him blankly, not knowing what had caused his ire. His eyes touched on her stomach, and understanding dawned. When he looked back into her eyes, he saw it.

"Finally a candle is lit in your head. I did not," he bit out, "halt Sunstar to impress you with my training of her. I knew your tendency to ride at incredible speeds and thought only to see to the safety of my child." He did not add "since its mother did not," but it wasn't necessary.

Raiven bristled beneath his accusation. Couldn't the man see she was using a saddle—something she had not done before?

"If you know of my 'tendency,' milord, then surely you can see that I have thought of my condition."

His expression was now baffled. Quynn realized she

thought she had made a telling argument, but he did not see it.

"The saddle, milord. Do you not see the saddle?" She said it with such conviction, he immediately knew she was serious.

She thought . . . a saddle? Quynn couldn't help it. Immediately from the depth of his chest came the laughter. He rocked with it while still holding Raiven securely in his arms. When he calmed enough to speak, he looked down at her now angry face with a smile that grew increasingly unsteady.

Raiven knew he was having to struggle to keep from laughing at her again, and that knowledge only made her seethe more.

"Am I to take it then that you do not want me to ride at all?"

That sobered him completely. "Aye."

Raiven went totally still in his arms. She searched his face for signs that he was jesting and saw none. Even though she knew it was no use, she whispered, "Why? I cannot believe you are serious."

He showed no reaction, not even that irritating little quirk of his eyebrow.

"Would you please set me down?" Raiven asked woodenly. "I can assure you I will make no further attempt to ride."

Quynn stared into her face a long while. "Is it so difficult to accept my concern, Raiven?" The question came out softly, and it would have been difficult to say who was more surprised.

Raiven quickly lowered her eyes, staring instead at the slow steady pulse beating at the base of his neck. Why was he making it appear that she was the one being difficult and intractable? She had tried. She had wanted him. God's truth, she still did. She just wouldn't allow herself the luxury of giving in to her feelings. That resistance had not been by choice. Quynn had forced her into it. Where was his concern for her when he sought someone else?

In a voice more chilled than ever, Raiven asked to be released.

Without a word he set her down, and she began to walk back to the hall. She didn't glance back. She couldn't. Because if she did look back, it would not be with her eyes, but with her heart.

Later that afternoon as Raiven sat in the room where she and Quynn and James had shared their first meal together, she tried to calm her still frayed nerves by practicing the stitches her mother had tried to teach her as a child. She was determined to learn to sew. She wanted to make clothing for the babe, but today her stitches were more of a jumbled mess than usual, and the relaxing sensation that accompanied sewing evaded her.

She was about to try to repair the mess she'd made of the fabric when a shadow fell across her hand. Looking up, she was surprised to see Ella standing over her. Immediately her hands moved to cover the mess. Judging from the not unkind smile on Ella's face, she hadn't moved quickly enough. With her characteristic forthrightness, Ella launched into the subject.

"Would milady like some help with her sewing?"

Raiven's face colored. "Since you've already seen my attempts to do it myself, I am not allowed to give the prideful answer of nay."

Ella's smile widened. "There is always something that one does not do well. I wouldn't know which end of the arrow to aim at my target."

Raiven laughed; however, she was still ill at ease. Ever since she had pulled Thomas from the water, Ella had softened toward her. There had been no effusive conversation, but Raiven had definitely recognized the olive branches of tentative friendship Ella had been offering. This by far was the most open, and it surprised her, coming especially at this time. All here were aware that things were not the best between her and Quynn. Before, when she and Quynn had experienced difficulties, it was assumed by all that she was to blame, and they treated her accordingly.

Raiven hadn't expected anything different now. But to her amazement, the servants, serfs, tenants, and knights still treated her with quiet respect and admiration.

Looking directly into Ella's eyes, which reflected warmth, Raiven momentarily forgot her line of thought and gasped, "Thomas has your eyes!"

Ella blushed becomingly. "Actually, milady, 'tis the only feature of mine he does have. His looks are exactly those of Thomas—my husband."

"How wonderful that must be for you then. It is almost as if he is still with you."

Ella nodded and added shyly, "Perhaps milady will soon be blessed in the same way."

Raiven looked away, her fingers unconsciously tearing at the material in her hand. "Perhaps" was all she could bring herself to say to that. It wasn't that the thought of having a child who looked like Quynn dismayed her. It was just that there had obviously been love between Ella and her Thomas, whereas her relationship with Quynn was barely civil. The two did not compare.

"You wished to see me, Ella," she prodded, switching the subject. "I'm sure that although it is desperately needed and I thank you for it, you did not come to give me assistance with my stitchery."

Once again Ella smiled. "I am not known for beating about the bushes when something needs saying." She paused to gauge Raiven's reaction. When Raiven's only comment was a brief, but wary smile, she went on. "'Tis about the baron and ye. First, milady, I know 'tis not my place to broach the subject, and I feel a bit of the traitor myself, but I feel ye should know. The baron sent me but only to tell ye of yer departure at week's end."

For a moment she watched Raiven for reaction, and after noting her mistress's stiffening and kneading of the now useless cloth in her lap, she spoke further. "Having told ye that, I can honestly tell the baron I have done as he asked, but for my own part, I feel I should tell ye why ye've not gone till now. Don't ye want to know?"

Raiven did indeed want to know. It was not like Quynn to delay following an order Henry had given.

Nodding again, she waited for Ella to continue. But she was unprepared for the answer.

"'Twas because of ye, milady, and the wee one," she said, pointing to Raiven's stomach. "The baron knew ye were faring poorly with the morning sickness, and he sent word to the king that he would not force you to travel in such a condition. The king was not pleased, but when the baron refused, saying he'd not risk your life and the child's, the king relented."

Raiven was too stunned by what Ella was telling her to answer. All she could think of was Quynn standing up to his king for her. Then all she could think of was his question this morning: "Is it so difficult to accept my concern?" Accept it? She'd practically thrown it back in his face.

But why? Why had he done this?

"I think ye know the why of it in yer heart," Ella replied in response to the question Raiven had not realized she uttered aloud.

Abruptly, Raiven stood and went to stare into the flames of the fire. "I do not know."

She could hear the smile in Ella's voice as she said, "As ye wish, milady."

Without turning around, Raiven asked, "How do you know this?"

Ella understood what Raiven wanted to know. "I happened to overhear the baron and Douglass talking. The baron has always spoken freely in front of me," she rushed on so Raiven would not think she was naught save a gossiping eavesdropper. "He knows I do not speak what I hear."

"Until now."

Ella nodded, unashamed. "Aye. Until now."

"What am I supposed to do with this knowledge?" Raiven asked softly.

Ella moved to stand behind her mistress. "Perhaps naught, perhaps all. For now 'tis enough only that ye know."

Raiven listened to her walk away, and still she did not move from her place. For a long time she remained quietly staring into the fire, listening to its crackling. As she continued to stare, feeling the heat from the flames, she felt a heat from within. A heat whose source sprang from a burning flame in her heart—the same flame that refused to be doused despite her many attempts. It refired with the knowledge Ella had given her, gaining intensity, greedily devouring the dispassionate logic of her mind as inexorably as the fire of the hearth consumed the wood.

Finally the day they were to leave arrived. Raiven awoke feeling refreshed and excited. Throughout the week she had refused to allow herself to feel any excitement. She kept telling herself it didn't matter—only because it did so much.

Disappointment had almost become a way of life for her and she didn't want to depend on the fact that she was going home. But the day had dawned clear and bright, and they were on the ship, readying to sail on the evening tide. She was going home to France! After being gone nearly half a twelvemonth, she was going home! She would get to see Jacques and all the others at Guirlande whom she loved.

Thoughts of Jacques caused her smile to dim just a bit as she remembered the accusation that had been made against him. That day long ago in London when Quynn had said he didn't totally believe in her brother's innocence, because she did not, he had not been far from the truth.

Although Raiven strongly believed that Jacques would do nothing to harm her, unfortunately she kept remembering the look of hatred in his eyes as she had left. Then there had been so little time. She could not speak to him as she would have. If Jacques were leading the rebellion, and Raiven, for her own peace of mind, stressed the *if*, then he was doing it in retaliation for what he felt was done to his sister and his home. In that case, she would show him that was not what she wanted.

Had Quynn allowed her to write to him, all of this could have been avoided. Now Raiven felt a desperate chase with time, and she could only pray that it had not run out.

"What ails you, milady?"

Raiven turned from the ship's rail to face Elaine. Not wanting to discuss the nature of her thoughts even with her most trusted servant, she posed a question of her own.

"What do you here, Elaine? On the journey here you could not raise your head from the bed."

"On the journey out I neglected to bring my herbs and potions with me. I was able to gather enough to last until we return home. Among the ones I brought is the garden herb that soothes nausea. Besides, milady," Elaine ended, waving her hand toward the ship, "we have yet to sail."

Raiven ignored that last as two things struck her. Elaine had called England home, and, two, she had known of an herb that alleviated nausea, yet she had allowed her to suffer days on end with the condition.

"Elaine, am I to understand that you knew of an herb for nausea, and yet you did not give it to me when I suffered?"

"Aye." At Raiven's almost betrayed expression, Elaine rushed on. "I could not. 'Tis very strong, and the other effect is not pleasant. I do not know enough of it to take the chance and give it to you while you are with child."

Raiven's brow cleared. "What is the unpleasant effect?"

Elaine smiled. "Let us say, milady, that upon taking enough of this herb, one should not stray far from the chamber pot."

Raiven nodded vigorously, her smile returning. "Elaine," she asked slowly, "do you like England?"

There was a long pause as Elaine stared in the direction of Havilland. "I do not much know if I like England, milady, but I have come to have a care for Havilland and the people there," she said, darting a quick look at Raiven to see her reaction.

This time Raiven's nod was slow, reflective, as she considered her servant's words.

"May I ask why you wanted to know, milady?"

"'Twas something you said a moment past. You referred to England as home. I would have thought you'd think we were going home now."

Elaine moved closer to Raiven, and they both faced south, toward France. "Milady, one of the best things about being in your service is that I was able to learn from you and those that taught you. 'Tis funny," Elaine said, her tone dry, "the other servants in both England and France think I speak too much like my betters. None seemed to understand that 'tis the only way I know how to speak. For the most part I have been with you. With the exception of the art of healing that I learned from my mother, I have learned what you learned. Maybe another servant would have 'cocked up their toes and died' as Dara the cook back at Guirlande said when she learned I was going to England. But Dara was not with you to hear your father say things like 'Home is the place you build with your heart' or 'Never value mortar and stone above flesh and blood.' If she had been, perhaps she would have been able to adjust as I have done. My home is where those that love me are. Right now, milady, I guess that makes this ship my home."

On impulse, Raiven reached out and hugged her servant and friend. She couldn't help but think that perhaps she had made it difficult for Elaine. What man of her station would want her with what he would surely see as a mind above her class? Then she pushed that thought away. Ignorance was what bound a person to his or her station, and only a person good enough to know that was good enough for Elaine.

Elaine left her shortly after they set sail to see to their cabins, and as it was when she arrived, Raiven watched the shoreline of England recede in the distance alone. A touch on her elbow brought her about sharply to stare into the chest and then the eyes of her husband. How had she not heard him approach? How could a man so large move so silently?

"Elaine has told me the cabin for you is prepared. You should seek your rest."

Raiven nodded, pushing away from the railing. Of late she hadn't known what to say to Quynn. His concern for her left her unbalanced and feeling uncharitable. Even now he held her arm solicitously to ensure she did not slip.

The feeling that she should say something continued to grow, but the words would not come. When she finally thought of something to say, she was glad Quynn held one arm because, in the joy of her discovery, she almost clapped her hands in childish happiness.

"How long until we arrive in France?"

"Anxious?"

"Nay," Raiven answered evenly, aware of double meaning in his question, "just curious."

"Two days."

"Two days?!" Raiven hadn't meant to screech, but his answer disconcerted her. She had spent a week on the ship when they were traveling to England.

Adequately reading her expression, Quynn reminded her, "When you came, the ship had many ports to make. Do you not remember you were not the only female and not all were from Poitou?"

His answer made sense, but Raiven was more amazed at his uncanny ability to read her thoughts. She had heard that there were people who did that, but she did not believe it.

Quynn chuckled softly. "Nay, I cannot read minds, not even yours. I enjoy jesting with you and perplexing you by speaking out loud what I know you to be thinking, but the answer is simple. I read your face, not your mind."

They had reached her cabin, and Raiven, though loath to say good night, knew she could not stand in the companionway, especially if she had naught to say. However, to her surprise, once Quynn opened the door to admit her, he followed in behind her, leaning back against the door, to close it with finality.

Raiven's eyes shot to his. "Was there aught else?"

"Nay."

His gaze settled on her in a way that made her

uncomfortable, and Raiven quickly turned away, looking around the cabin. Compared to the cabin she'd shared with Elaine on her journey to England this one was luxurious. Elaine would be . . .

"Where is Elaine?"

"In her cabin."

"I am to have this cabin to myself?"

"Nay."

His abrupt answers increased her discomfort. Time stretched between them as Raiven waited for him to say something more. When he did not, she blurted, "Are there any other cabins aboard?"

"Aye."

"Are they filled?"

"Nay."

Raiven's control snapped. "Will you cease saying either nay or aye?"

Quynn smiled slowly. "What would you prefer I say? Would you like me to answer the question I see in your eyes?"

Hot color rose in her face. "Nay," she mumbled. When his brow quirked in question, she clarified, "I do not think so."

Slowly, Quynn lifted himself from the door he leaned upon and walked over to Raiven, taking her arms into his hands. "Why do you not just ask me why I am here with you instead of all this prattle about other cabins? I can see you want to know."

Raiven opened her mouth to deny it, then closed it.

Quynn gave a soft chuckle, shaking his head briefly at her stubbornness. "I am here because 'tis where I wish to sleep. You are my wife, and 'tis where I should be."

Gathering her courage, Raiven asked, "Is that all we'll be doing—sleeping?"

Instant flame leaped into Quynn's eyes. "Do you want aught else?"

"Nay, nay," Raiven responded hastily.

The light in his eyes dimmed. "Very well then. We shall both rest and save our strength to fight something other than ourselves when we arrive in France."

# Chapter
# •28•

Raiven's awakening was complete and abrupt, with no languorous transition between the world of sleep and consciousness. Realizing that it was not yet morning, she was about to go back to sleep when she became aware that she was alone and that was what had awakened her. Casting that feeling off as foolish, she tried to summon satisfaction from her solitude and shifted over onto her side, closing her eyes. It was no use. Her mind stayed fully alert, repeatedly showing her Quynn's eyes and the look in them when he had spoken in a resigned voice that she still heard.

Giving up her attempt to ignore the voices and images of her mind, Raiven let herself out of the cabin and walked out onto the deck. She didn't pretend she wasn't looking for Quynn, and her eyes immediately sought him out.

He was standing at the ship's rail looking out at the expanse of water, which to Raiven's mind resembled a black carpet with a thousand twinkling stars embedded in its surface.

The chill of the night made her clasp her robe more firmly to her at the same instant she noted that Quynn stood chainseless, the wind caressing his bare chest and causing the midnight blackness of his hair to billow out on its current.

The feeling that had driven her from the cabin drew her to him and the picture of solitude he presented. She walked over to stand beside him, not looking at him but staring ahead.

"Could you not sleep?"

"For a time I did, but then . . ." Quynn shrugged, letting the sentence die off.

"You seem troubled," Raiven blurted unexpectedly. "Is there aught the matter?"

For a long time he said nothing. Just when Raiven thought he would not answer at all, he spoke. His words were not a response, rather a question of his own. "Are you happy to be returning to France, Raiven?"

There was more meaning to his words than the simplicity of the question. Raiven sensed it. Speaking very carefully, she told him, "I am always happy to return home."

Quynn spun around to her, pulling her to face him and taking her in his arms, his embrace so tight it was nearly painful. His impassioned words, though whispered against her hair, were clear. "You have a home—in England with me."

Raiven stiffened, and she knew Quynn felt it because his arms tightened further. She tried to pull back, but he wouldn't allow it. When he spoke again, his voice was weary, lifeless, sounding much as it had earlier this evening when he had told her they would only rest in their cabin.

"You are right. We do not have a home. We have an entrenched battlefield where the French meet the English. I tire of the lot of it. I am wearied beyond the telling of divisions in my hall. I had wanted so much more. I thought we deserved so much more. I want peace in our home, true peace between us. We cannot raise our child successfully under conditions as they now exist."

Quynn's emphasis of the child as *ours* and not *yours* or *mine* solidified a nagging thought that had worried

Raiven ever since he'd told her they were going to France and why. When she had stressed the child as belonging only to her, she had been trying only to show him that her child was going to be genuinely loved and not be valued only as a political gamepiece. And if she were truthful, she had been trying to hurt him.

Yet when she saw what she had thought was pain flickering across his face, she had felt no satisfaction. Instead, guilt had plagued her until she convinced herself the moment had been too fleeting, and she couldn't be certain what it was she had seen. Now there was no more running from the truth. She had hurt him with her sharp tongue.

It was in her mind to pull away so her apology would be given to his face, but still Quynn wouldn't relent in his fierce grip.

"Raiven," he said before she could speak, "I want us to try. We can begin now, while we're on neither English nor French soil."

At last he allowed her to move back so that he could look deeply in her eyes, which were clearly illuminated by the full moon beaming brightly overhead. His eyes asked again the words he had just spoken, and Raiven didn't know what to do. Her heart said aye. She loved him. That meant there was no choice. But was that enough? He had not mentioned love. Would it be wrong to read more into his words than he had said?

Raiven closed her eyes against the searing heat in his, leaning her forehead against his chin. Her arms ached with the effort of not touching him. Her lips trembled with the need to say the words he wanted to hear and more. Above all, though, her entire body throbbed to be with him.

An eternity passed that was counted in mere minutes. Raiven did not know what made the decision for her. Perhaps it was Ella's words about his concern, perhaps it was Quynn's impassioned plea. Perhaps it was the night, whispering that it was right. Perhaps it was all three. In any event, she slowly, very slowly, raised her arms to his neck and lifted her head. Gently she kissed him, molding her body to his. It was the first voluntary embrace she had ever given him, and the results were devastating.

Quynn's arms tightened around her again, and he groaned like a man in the throes of the most acute pleasure. Wordlessly, he picked her up and took her to their cabin.

In minutes they were both naked, lying side by side. Raiven's fingers were trembling as they traveled over Quynn's face, drinking him in through her senses as if just seeing him was not enough. When he tried to grab her hands to cease her exploration, she groaned.

"Nay, let me, please. Let me know you, love you. It is all I ask, Quynn. Whatever our difference, whatever may come with the dawn, tonight I want to hold out selfishly for me. Take what I give and know it is my gift to you and what I give no man may command or take."

Quynn was glad of the enveloping darkness. He would not have wanted her to see the unmanly amount of emotion in his eyes. Gathering her to him in a kiss that brought ecstasy a mere breath away, he gave her his acceptance of her plea.

When he released her, Raiven pulled away slightly. As one without sight, she explored the length and breadth of him, and what her hands felt, her lips kissed and her tongue laved with love.

Quynn could endure no more. In a grip that was almost savage, he pulled her beneath him. It was then that he noticed how far the growth of his child in her womb had progressed. Some of the feral light went out of his eyes. Bending low he kissed her stomach in warm possession and awe. Then he gave the same attention to each breast with as much warmth but far more passion.

"I will take care that no damage befall our child," he said gruffly as he slid into her.

Raiven cried out, pleasure so acute that her climax was instantaneous. Quynn, who had been planning an erotic extended loving, lost control at her cries and immediately released his seed deep in her womb.

Despite the overwhelming desire to collapse atop her, he pulled himself to her side and drew her to him.

Harsh breathing gradually slowing was the only sound in the room for a long time. Just when Quynn thought she had finally drifted to sleep, her soft voice called, "Quynn?"

Reflexively he hugged her tighter. "Hmm?"

"Is this all?"

His eyelids popped up. He had been almost asleep himself, but that made him instantly alert.

"All?" he repeated, thinking she surely didn't mean what he thought.

"Aye. What do we do now?" Raiven buried her face in his chest, embarrassed, forgetting that he could not see her expression in the dark.

"We—that is, I mean, you—have always been able to make me feel special and wanted when we're abed, but out of it, there was naught. I do not want to return to that."

Quynn smiled. "Neither do I. I would like us to be friends."

"Friends?" Her dissatisfaction with that notion was evident in her tone.

"Aye, the best of friends—out of bed that is," he whispered, "and in bed—the best of lovers."

"I'd like that," Raiven replied in a voice that stammered only a little. "However, aside from my desire, I would make a poor friend. I know naught of you."

"Then we shall talk. You shall tell me of yourself, and I will tell you of me," he said, rolling to his back and pulling her to his side.

Raiven lay beside him quietly, too happy with the moment for words. A few seconds later Quynn nudged her.

"I thought we were to be talking?" he teased. "Very well then, since you are too dazzled by my charm to speak, I shall begin."

And then he proceeded to tell her of his life. He shared with her, and through the telling of his life he got to know her better. He loved her sensitivity. She wept for his tragedies. She rejoiced in his triumphs. When he spoke of the time he, at thirteen, took over the running of Havilland and described himself as only "bewildered," Raiven hugged him tighter, placing a light kiss on his chest.

It occurred to her to tell him that James had already told her some of it, if only to keep him from reliving the entire painful episode, but she held her tongue. Quynn was sharing, truly sharing, with her, and she wouldn't have stopped him for the treasures of the kingdom.

Suddenly he became silent.

"Quynn?"

"I had begun to think I had bored you to sleep." Even though Raiven could not see his face, she could hear the embarrassment in his voice.

"I was not bored, only listening attentively," she said, hugging him again.

After a brief chuckle, Quynn returned her embrace. "Now 'tis my turn to listen attentively."

Raiven hesitated, unexpectedly reluctant to tell him of her past. She had not lived an orthodox life, as many people—especially men—had been quick to point out to her. When faced with finally telling Quynn, she didn't want him to think she was too unusual.

"It is not much to tell," she began.

"Why do I have difficulty with that as truth? Come, Raiven. Have we not made a new beginning this night? Hmm?" he asked sensuously, his lips nipping at her ear and neck.

Suddenly it became difficult to breathe, and Raiven's thoughts scattered.

"Are you ready?" Quynn asked in a deep voice that revealed he wasn't unaffected by what he was doing to her and her reaction to it.

"You wish to talk . . . now?" Raiven breathed.

Quynn laughed, and even his laughter had a seductive quality. "Nay, wife. I wish to listen. 'Tis your turn to talk and tell me all of you."

Raiven was about to tell him that he hadn't told her everything. He had skimmed over the period when his parents and sister died, merely saying they died when he was three and ten and he began to oversee Havilland. Raiven decided to follow his pattern.

"My mother died when I was a child. I do not remember much of her. All I can recall when I think of her is the sound of her laughter. She was a happy person. I remember that. I also remember her trying to teach me all the things she thought important, things that were in direct opposition to the things my father taught."

Raiven smiled in the darkness. "It is strange that although I grasped my father's lessons more readily, I do not recall her becoming upset or discouraged with me.

"There are times, Quynn, when it becomes very important to me to remember her face," Raiven said almost desperately. "I try and I try and I cannot. I should be able to think of something, of some feature, but I cannot."

Quynn, sensing her agitation, began to draw soothing circles on her back with his fingertips. "Be calm, Raiven. You were a small child. You remember enough. You recall the important things."

Raiven made an indelicate snort. "The sound of her laughter?"

"The warmth of her love."

A stunned silence fell between them as the warmth caused by Quynn's heartfelt declaration raised different reactions in each of them. Quynn, for his part, was feeling uneasy with the words that were coming from him almost of their own accord, but Raiven could not think of a time when she had felt more secure. She was about to tell Quynn of her feelings when he interjected gruffly, "What of your brother?"

Raiven did not detect any suspicion or veiled accusation in his voice despite the roughness of his tone. That lack enabled her to answer him more comfortably than she had ever done since coming to England.

"He's three years younger than I. He is tall, nearly as tall as you are, Quynn. His smile is quick. His temper is slow, and his heart very loving. It is strange that these past months since my father died, I thought I was taking care of him. It was only when Henry separated us that I realized that I needed him. I leaned on him almost as much as, perhaps more than, he leaned on me. It is the one thing that excites me about going to Guirlande. I cannot wait to see him again. I want you to see him, to come to know him as I do."

The note of hope in her voice was clear. Quynn could not tell her he still harbored thoughts of Jacques's guilt, so he held his silence on that and deftly changed the subject.

"'Tis the one thing that excites you?" he questioned skeptically.

Raiven's mouth dropped open as she realized what she'd said and its implication. Making an attempt of her own to shift the subject, she said mischievously, "Other things excite me, but you said you'd rather we talked."

Quynn did not allow her to prevaricate. In a determined voice he asked, "What meant you by that, Raiven?"

Raiven held her tongue a long time, and Quynn patiently waited. Finally, she said, her tone reflective, "I suppose I must have heard more of my father's teachings than even I had originally thought. Mayhap it was Elaine's reminder earlier. I cannot say."

"What reminder was that?" Quynn prodded gently.

"To never value mortar and stone above flesh and blood."

Quynn's brow lowered. "Meaning?"

Raiven could see he was going to be relentless about this. She had the opinion that he knew what the words meant, but he wanted to hear her say it. So be it.

"'Home is a place built with your heart' was one of my father's favorite sayings. He would always end by saying, 'Never value mortar and stone above flesh and blood.' I knew from his words that in spite of the love he had for Guirlande, he loved us more and that we, my mother when she was alive, my brother, and I, were all it took for him to be happy and at home. I think he wanted me to learn to imitate the sentiment."

"Have you?"

"Without knowing it," she said, her voice husky. "I must have because I've never felt more at home than I do at this moment."

A deep moan came from the back of Quynn's throat. He reached for her as a man compelled, kissing her fiercely. It was he who pulled away, squeezing her tightly, breathing deeply, trying to regain control of his runaway emotions.

"Before I answer that statement the way it fully deserves, I want to ask you to clear up a myth for me."

Raiven, whose senses were still befuddled by his potent kiss, repeated absently, "Myth?"

"Aye. 'Twas rumored—and now that I have seen your face, I know it for the lie it was—that you kept your face veiled. 'Twas said it was done because you were so unsightly that none could stand to look upon you. Of course, this cannot be true, but I have wondered many times how such a rumor developed."

To his surprise he felt Raiven shake within his arms a moment before her sweet laughter rang out.

"Raiven, do not laugh. I had never seen your face to know the truth of it. How could I know such a rumor to be a vicious lie?"

"But it was not," Raiven managed between chuckles. "I did wear a veil."

Quynn was totally perplexed. "Why?"

"Because of my father. He knew from early in my childhood that he was leaving Guirlande to me. He said he saw from the time I was half a score that I would be beautiful." She said this last as if she did not believe it. "He said that men in the presence of a woman—especially a beautiful one—thought with their loins instead of their heads. He wanted me to have the confidence to know their opinions stemmed from the reaction to my thoughts and not my face. He also said it was a protection."

Quynn laughed softly in admiration. "Your father was an extremely wise man, as I've thought more than once. Just in the event that you doubt the wisdom of his words, come a little closer so I may show you which part of me is reacting to you now."

When he pulled her beneath him, Raiven did not resist. She was as ready and unhesitant as he. Their joining was wild, uncontrolled, and totally satisfying.

It was only when it was over that Quynn remembered her condition. Instant worry assailed him. He had been so careful of her state before, and now he was afraid he'd hurt her. Touching her stomach gently he apologized.

"I'm sorry, Raiven. I did not mean to be so undisciplined. Did I hurt you?"

"Nay. It was what I wanted also. I rather liked your lack of discipline—ah!" she gasped, and Quynn didn't have to ask what had caused her surprise. He had felt the fluttery but strong movement beneath the hand he still had on Raiven's stomach.

There were no words to describe his fascination. The sense of possession and tenderness he felt for the small form nurtured so securely in her womb was overpowering. He didn't recognize his voice when he asked, "Was that the first time he stirred?"

Raiven nodded. "Aye."

Quynn's laugh of satisfaction and joy rang out. "What say you to that, Wife?"

Raiven was glad for the concealing darkness so he could not see the sudden rush of tears that filled her eyes and spilled down her cheeks.

"I say he has shown the wisdom of both his father and grandfather."

The aura of happiness that surrounded them stayed the remainder of their time on the ship and throughout the journey inland to Guirlande. Their faces beamed with it and their joy in finally finding each other. There were no more ghosts. Raiven herself had brought up the question of Teris and why Quynn had sought her out, and when he answered, she listened, really listened, to his words. And she believed.

It was a happy pair riding ahead of their escort that

approached the riders coming from Guirlande to welcome them. One look at James's face and Quynn knew something was very wrong. He had to fight the impulse to jerk the reins of their horses about and head back to England at the fastest pace. But Raiven had already seen them, and her face was shining with expectancy.

Shrugging aside his unrest, Quynn told himself he was being ridiculous. They already knew of the trouble. Even had it escalated, it would not be unbearable news. Straightening to his full height, he drew up, waiting for James to approach.

"Greetings, Brother," James said, glancing quickly at Raiven and then looking away. He went on without further preamble, "I bring ill news. I must say it quickly for the unrest here is great." At last he looked at Raiven and fully met her gaze. "I apologize with all my heart, Raiven, but I'm afraid your brother has been grievously wounded. He may not live the day."

Raiven did not hear Quynn's strangled "By whom?" The world was starting to slip out of focus and tilt alarmingly. Suddenly there was blackness before her and around her, swallowing her completely in blessed oblivion.

She was unaware that Quynn's arms had caught her. She was unaware of the turmoil that Quynn couldn't hide as he thought not only of what this would do to their fragile beginning, but the pain it would bring his wife. As he knew nothing else, he knew Raiven loved Jacques. He was no mortar and stone. He was flesh and blood—her flesh and blood. His voice filled with rage and pain, he asked again, "By whose hand?" only to blanch all the more when James replied, "By mine."

# Chapter 29

The news that Quynn thought could not be worse worsened. His stare was penetrating as he searched his brother's face. There was more here than the wounding. Quynn could feel it, yet he knew James would offer no excuses, only await his decision.

"You do not look well, James," Quynn said slowly. "Is it the ill news you bear that causes this strain about you or is there yet more?"

James's expression was grim. "There is no more. I am tired of late."

One of the men riding with James interrupted. "But your head—"

"You will be silent!" James snapped in a tone Quynn had never heard him use before.

Quynn looked from his brother to the man and back again to his brother. "'Tis not the time to discuss matters. I must see to Raiven. 'Twas not good—the shock she had. It may harm the babe." He looked down at the woman in his arms and asked James, "Why could you not have waited?"

James too cast a glance at his sister-in-law's face. "I would sooner cut off my right arm than cause her pain, but you have always taught me to tell you of circumstances and their possibilities before aught adverse can occur. The hall is practically at war against itself since last eve."

"He was wounded last eve?" Quynn interjected incredulously.

"Aye." James's nod was curt. "We have had to be ever wary. Two of our own have had their throats slit this morn. To those who seek vengeance, your throat presents the more valuable target. I could not hold my tongue."

Suddenly James swayed.

"To the hall!" Quynn ordered sharply, no longer giving James the opportunity to deny his ailment.

Without another word, they turned to Guirlande. Despite the turmoil in his heart, Quynn was struck by the beauty of the place rising majestically from amidst the verdant countryside. The hall itself was a pale gray edifice surrounded by bushes of budding roses and other colorful flora. It was huge, square in shape. From his angle, Quynn could see that the stone wall running around the perimeter had notched spaces atop to accommodate archers. From that vantage point, they could methodically annihilate their enemies in relative safety.

The place had the look of one that normally buzzed with activity, but today, it was ominously silent. No one came out of the hall to greet them.

Quynn cast an uneasy glance to James, at once sensing the urgency about the place. It was a sad irony that something so beautiful and peaceful in appearance would emit such awful tension.

"You see my meaning, Brother." It wasn't a question.

"Aye," Quynn muttered. "To your backs, men," he called out over his shoulder, and immediately the men behind him tightened ranks. During his conversation with James, his and Raiven's escort had arrived, and now they entered the outer courtyard as one quiet, tight throng.

Quynn immediately handed Raiven to one of his men who had already dismounted. Wasting no time, he vaulted from Khan's back, took his wife's still limp form, and entered one of the most beautiful halls he had ever seen. Yet the beauty was haunted, for the place was deserted. When a quiet voice said, "Milord, if you will follow me, I shall lead you to your chamber," Quynn almost started at the sound that broke the oppressive silence.

He turned to look down into Elaine's tear-dampened eyes, and he knew she had been told.

"I am sorry, Elaine," he said, surprising them both, but once the words were out, he realized how much he meant them.

Elaine stared at him, and he knew the intensity of her gaze sprang from her desire to plumb the depths of his sincerity.

Quynn had never had a servant look at him in such a way. However, he felt no anger, not even irritation. It would seem that distrust was the precept of the day. Allowing her to look her fill, he nodded when a slow smile crossed her face and then followed as she led him to Raiven's chamber.

After laying Raiven gently on the bed, Quynn stood back while Elaine saw to her comfort. He barely spared a glance to the quiet, elegant beauty of the room. All he wanted to see was Raiven open her eyes. He wanted that, and at the same time, he did not. Upon her awakening, there would be pain—a pain he was acquainted with well. If he was to help her cope with the pain, he needed answers. He didn't want to think of how unendurable her agony would be if he could not supply the answers to her questions, especially when she learned his brother had done the deed.

Suddenly James appeared in the doorway. "Has she regained consciousness?"

Quynn shook his head.

"But she has been unconscious for so long. I have never known a swoon to last more than a few minutes. Surely this cannot be good for the babe."

"I know," Quynn returned bleakly. "James, 'tis the truth I give. I care not for the babe if the cost is Raiven's life."

James touched his brother's shoulder. "She will be fine, Quynn. She is strong."

Quynn watched James closely, taking in his general unsteadiness and pallor. "Seek your ease now, James. I would hear a full account, but it must wait until I know Raiven is improved."

"'Tis why I am here," James said softly. "I know you would prefer her awakening with answers."

Quynn could not control his surprise at the astuteness and maturity James was showing. "Aye, 'twould be my preference, but I can see you are not totally fit."

James shrugged but lowered himself into one of the chairs by the window. "I need only a few days to recover. What is happening here, Quynn, I am not sure we can recover in a few days or at all."

His expression grim, Quynn took the chair opposite. "Tell me."

James was quiet a moment, gathering his thoughts. "You know the disturbances Langford announced to Henry and the full court."

Quynn grimaced.

James smiled slightly, taking that for a positive response. "'Tis odd. That is all they were—disturbances. Some larger than others but not outright rebellion. After the first few weeks here, the people were beginning to warm to us. Perevil and I discussed it with some relief. 'Twould seem that 'tis their nature to be generous and warm.

"Things changed, however, after my trip to England. Upon my return, the attacks were more devastating and damaging. There was a viciousness behind it that I would not have believed possible previously. 'Twas almost like hatred, Quynn, instead of disapproval. I know it sounds strange, but that was the way of it."

Quynn nodded, then remembered something Langford had said. "What of the man who died?"

He did not say any more. It wasn't necessary. He and James were so attuned to each other that James knew the bend of his mind and to what he was referring.

"I never completely understood that. The man was a

simple patroller. His duty was merely to observe and report back. He was found stabbed through the heart at the edge of Guirlande's boundary. I do not know if he saw aught for which he needed to be silenced or if he chanced upon a roving band of miscreants. I cannot say."

Quynn sighed, perplexed by the unsolved riddle. Rubbing his hand wearily across the back of his neck, he sat back, bracing himself for what was to come. "Now tell me of Jacques."

He cast a glance over to Raiven, but she had not stirred. Looking back to James, he nodded, surprised to see a slow, sad smile cross his brother's face. When he spoke, his words were tinged with amused disbelief.

"I imagine I found Jacques as much a surprise as you found Raiven. Initially, he was hostile, and I understood and respected it. I would certainly have not just handed over Havilland on the word of another. Yet, Quynn, I tell you that as time proceeded, I thought I was winning him 'round. He was stubborn and headstrong, true, but he was not a simpleton. He once told me he had tried to discourage his sister's rebellious course. I asked him if he felt that he made an error in judgment. He looked me square in the eye and said his answer would have to depend on the type of men we proved ourselves to be. I was shocked by his bravery but even more so by his wisdom. He did not speak as a lad of seven and ten."

"I thought him to be one year less," Quynn interrupted.

"It has been several months, Quynn, his day of birth has passed."

Quynn nodded, absently wondering why Raiven never mentioned that. It was not too strange, he supposed, in her circumstances, and he put it from his mind to concentrate again on what James was saying.

"There is not much more to tell except shortly after that Jacques became more and more quiet, then he disappeared altogether." James's face showed his bewilderment. "Then he sent word that he wanted to see me. I went to meet him. There were others with him, but I did not fear attack. Jacques had shown himself to be honorable. He was about to speak when an arrow shot past my ear and killed the man to his left. Things happened too quickly after that.

"Suddenly, instead of talking, we were fighting. I remember the look of betrayal in Jacques's eyes just before we engaged swords. My heart was not in it, Quynn. He was just a lad. I tell you 'tis the first battle I ever fought that I wanted to lose. I recall admiring his skill and then nothing more until Perevil came across us. I must have been struck from behind. When I awoke, all was quiet, and Jacques lay wounded at my feet, my sword just below his heart."

The strangled sound coming from the bed caused both their eyes to turn toward it. Raiven sat up, her magnificent blond mane flowing about her. She had never looked more beautiful, Quynn thought, or more in pain. Her eyes sparkled, but there were no tears, only the heightened light that told of darkest pain.

"You did this to my brother?" Raiven's strangled voice was barely recognizable as her own. She stared at James, unwilling to believe what she had heard while she lay quietly listening and even more unwilling to believe its obscene implications. While she had been cuddling up to the Englishman, his brother had been trying to kill hers.

Raiven shook her head slowly in an attempt to keep the savage pain at bay. "Oooo, nay," she moaned, unable to bear it. "Nay, nay, nay. It cannot be. *Nay!*" she screamed, launching herself from the bed to attack James with violent fury.

James did not defend himself against her, and Raiven had landed a few telling blows before Quynn was able to pull her away.

"Raiven, cease!" he ordered.

"Nay, I will not cease," she snarled. "It is only sorry I am I did not think to use a sword instead of my fists." She panted and strained against the arm he had beneath her breasts, her eyes the violent gold of vengeful fire.

Then as suddenly as the rage came upon her, it ebbed,

and though her eyes were still hot, her voice was filled with unbelievable sadness as she asked, "Why, James, why? Could you not see it in your heart to protect him? Throw him in the dungeon, banish him, but this? Oh, God, why?"

Raiven's eyes searingly searched his. Through the curtain of grief clouding her vision, she was certain she saw something in his countenance before he looked to Quynn.

"I shall leave. My presence here is upsetting her, and 'tis not good in her condition."

Quynn nodded brusquely, and despite the fact that Raiven no longer struggled, he could still feel her underlying tension, so he did not relax his grip. "I will be down anon."

James turned to Raiven to say something, but her venomous words stopped him.

"Do not speak another word to me—ever."

He was going to try again when he saw Quynn shake his head. He left without another word.

Raiven slumped against Quynn, not realizing how rigidly she had held herself until she sagged against him. Her voice had a lifeless chill in it when she said, "You may release me. Your craven brother is safe."

The slur was not lost on Quynn, but given the situation, considering the circumstances, he chose to ignore it. He spoke slowly. "Raiven, 'tis a tragedy what has happened, but we must not allow it to affect us. Could you not hear James's pain as you lay there feigning unconsciousness?"

Her astonishment was clear.

Quynn's lips twisted in a parody of a smile. "Did you really think I believed you unconscious for so long a time? Or that from the corner of my eye, I did not see you wave Elaine away? 'Twould have better suited your ruse had you allowed Elaine to stay. Your trusted servant would not have left your side had you not been recovered."

Raiven's shock evaporated quickly. So what did it matter that he knew she feigned unconsciousness? She had needed to hear what really happened without any pretense. She had not wanted carefully tailored stories. She had wanted the whole truth, not realizing how much additional pain that truth would bring. Now Quynn had the temerity to speak of "us." Was the man mad? There was no "us," and there never could be again. His brother's sword had done more than wound her brother and jeopardize his life—it had ended theirs.

Of all the injustices she could forgive, did he really think this would ever be one of them?

In a voice harder and colder than a block of Nordic ice, Raiven said, "There is no 'us.' The only 'us' that could have ever been died when your brother's sword plunged below my brother's heart. I do not know how you dare to ask me if I heard his pain. His pain? What of mine, Quynn, or is my pain so easily shunted aside? He has nearly killed my brother," Raiven ground out.

Although awed by her contained rage and pain, Quynn still tried to reason with her. "He does not know precisely what occurred. He said as much, or do you discard what you do not want, to hear only what you want?"

"Nay. I discard nothing," Raiven spat out. "I also saw the look in his eyes when I confronted him. You were always one for telling me of body speech and the like. Or now did you not see that there was more to the telling than he gave? If he was so innocent, why hold back? Why not tell all? If my holding back was enough to condemn me and my brother when you confronted me at Henry's court, why does the ruling now change because it is your precious brother's hide you seek to spare?"

Quynn stood staring at her for a long time as he quietly accepted the logic of her arguments and something else that he found even more overwhelming. He loved her. He did not know where the knowledge had been all this time, but it suddenly struck him between the eyes as he watched her rant about his brother. His love, he knew, was the most vital reason he wanted her to see James's innocence. He acknowledged the fact that as long as she believed his brother guilty, he would never have her, and the thought was unbearable.

He knew James would never act dishonorably, but it was not enough. He knew that honor was all the St. Crowells had left and that James would never betray that. But that was not enough. In truth, he realized that it had never been enough in his entire life. He needed proof to give to the enraged woman before him. He had needed proof to give to his detractors throughout his life, only then, it had not mattered. This mattered more to him than his life. So, until he had that proof, there was nothing for him to say.

Raiven had quietly watched as Quynn's face became more and more closed, until finally the shuttered mask he habitually wore fell back into place. Her heart, having long since renounced pride where he was concerned, cried out to him not to do it. She needed him, although she could never say it. She did not need him to turn his back on her, choosing the honor of his name instead of recognizing her pain. However, it seemed that the choice was not to be hers.

Dropping her eyes from his face, she turned away in final dismissal, not knowing which prayer was more fervent: the one she uttered that he would stay or the one for him to go.

Long moments dragged out, and finally Raiven heard him move behind her, and her body tensed, waiting for his touch or the sound of his voice. Except there was no touch, and the only sound she heard was the quiet click of the door as he shut it behind himself.

She refused to feel the pain that threatened to drive her insane with its intensity. She would feel neither the pain of losing what little chance for happiness she had with Quynn nor the pain from the threat of the death of her brother. Thank God there was no time to ponder either. She must be strong. Jacques needed her—now more than ever.

# Chapter 30

Quynn swung sharply to his left on Khan's back, hearing the crisp sound as of a branch breaking beneath a weight in that direction. Both horse and rider relaxed when they realized the sound had been caused by nothing more dangerous than the sentry who patrolled this area approaching on foot. The man looked as tired as Quynn felt. These past weeks had been harrowing for them all. The one benefit Quynn had thought would come from Jacques's still-unsolved—for him—wounding would be the easing of hostilities. If he was the leader of the rebels, then they had temporarily lost their guidance.

The very next day after Quynn and Raiven's arrival proved how futile that assumption was. The man sent to patrol the western border was found dead. Two days later one of Guirlande's tenants was found hanged in apparent retribution. The situation grew from there to the point where Guirlande seemed to be the army camp Quynn had once described to Raiven, with the French and English deeply entrenched in opposition to each other.

There seemed to be no ready answer. To the English, the French were the ones causing the trouble, killing the man on patrol, and the tenant's death was explained as a roving band of bandits who had chanced upon him. Naturally the bandits were French.

To the French, the tenant had been killed in a petty act of revenge because of the death of one of the English sentries. Who killed the sentry? To their minds it could have been anyone as long as that person was not French.

Quynn had tried amassing the people together, French and English, to speak to them. One look into the blank stares of the residents of Guirlande and the angry stares of his men and he knew he would have no success.

The only recourse left was to double the patrols and the men riding them. No sentry was ever alone, and at regular intervals, they had to make their reports. If a report was delayed, then they rode out as they were doing now.

Quynn barely listened as the sentry, a man named Jonas, made his report. He was exercising extreme self-control to keep himself astride Khan's back. His every impulse was to hurl himself at the guard and beat him senseless. With all that had been taking place, the man actually wanted him to believe that he was delayed in reporting because of assisting two peasant girls?

The guard had stopped speaking, waiting for Quynn's response, and Quynn grated his teeth together in an effort to calm himself. Why, the thickwit did not even realize the blatant inconsistencies in his story or the fact that his mail was on backward!

Quynn's grip on the reins became punishing, and Khan snorted his disapproval of such treatment. He reduced the pressure and took a deep breath.

"And where is Gilberk?" he asked in a rigidly controlled voice one octave lower than thunder.

The sentry before him actually blushed, and Quynn was certain his rage would explode him into a thousand fragments when he heard the man's coughed-out answer.

"He was still . . . uh, helping . . . uh, assisting the other young girl, milord. I came ahead to make the report."

Quynn's brow rose. "Afoot?"

"Uh, aye, milord, my mount is—"

"With Gilberk, who is still giving assistance." Quynn had had enough. Aside from his genuine anger at the man, he had weeks of frustration with trying to deal with Raiven. He needed a release. This sentry had been foolish enough to provide him with one.

He was about to let loose a blistering tirade and a sound thrashing when James placed a restraining hand on his arm. Quynn froze and looked from the hand on his arm to his brother's laughing face.

In a quiet voice that none other could hear, James said, "Do not be angered with him, Quynn, for seeking a release from the situation—a release, I might add, you yourself were about to indulge in, in a less pleasurable manner."

Immediately Quynn lost some of his ire. James spoke truly. They had all been tense and under tremendous strain. He glanced back at the rest of his men and saw the smiles on their faces—the first real smiles he had seen in a while—and the remainder of his anger evaporated. Still, he could not allow himself to lapse totally from discipline. Turning back to Jonas, he admonished, "I shall expect a full accounting of this incident on the morrow."

Quynn couldn't decide whether the man looked more ecstatic or chagrined as he murmured, "Aye, milord," and turned to go back the way he had come.

"Jonas," Quynn called.

The guard turned.

"Is it a long walk back?"

"Nay, milord," Jonas replied, his distress obviously increasing as Quynn once again referred to his absent mount.

Deciding to lighten the man's mood some small whit, Quynn called out again. "When you give your account, don't make it *too* full. Understood?"

Jonas's face was split by his smile. "Aye, milord." He turned, walking away jauntily, whistling, and Quynn could not help but laugh.

"We ride for Guirlande!" he called to his men in the

most jovial tone they had heard him use since coming to France.

James looked at him curiously, asking a silent question.

"Jonas has just given me a wonderful idea."

Despite his lightened mood, Quynn still approached Raiven cautiously. He found her in the sewing room and was happy that for once she was not ensconced in the room with her brother. Her constant vigil over him and the fact he seemed not to improve despite all care were taking their toll on her. There were faint smudges beneath her clear green eyes, telling of her lack of rest. She immediately looked away from him, but that did not cause him dismay. She was sitting with the rest of her ladies, which he would use to his advantage. She would show her silent disapproval, but she wouldn't voice an objection in front of the women—or so he hoped. As always, where Raiven was concerned, he was not sure. She was too unpredictable.

Raiven had heard his return and upon his appearance in the door of the sewing room, her heart had jumped. She knew he could be there only for her. Involuntarily she had looked up to see him and then looked away, confused. Her heart adamantly refused to give up on the love she had for him, but her mind demanded that she give no more.

When his shadow fell across her lap, she was no more clear on the conflict between her mind and heart than she had been weeks ago. Yet she could not deny the tiny thrill she experienced when he said, "Raiven, I would like a private word with you."

Glancing to her ladies, who had grown silent on Quynn's arrival, Raiven was about to dismiss them when he spoke again.

"There is no need to send them away. I would like you to accompany me."

Instantly wary, Raiven wondered what he wanted to discuss that could not be done where they were. Then she looked down at the misshapen lump of fabric in her lap, which was supposedly a nightshirt for the babe, and wondered wryly, *What does it matter?* It wasn't as if she was accomplishing her purpose here. Sighing inwardly, she admitted defeat. She would have to leave the making of garments for the babe to the women. They had already completed several during the time it took her to mangle one.

Rising from the chair, she followed Quynn without another word of protest. When he led her to the room she knew he slept in, she stopped. "Why are we here?"

"I said I wished to be private. No one dares enter here."

Raiven gave him a curious glance, wondering at his tone, then stepped inside the room. The moment she stepped inside she understood the slight sarcasm in his words. While the room was not filthy, it was far from the sparkling condition of the rest of the hall. Raiven turned surprised eyes to his.

Quynn shrugged. "I suppose they are too busy. I never mastered the art of room cleaning, but I manage to keep it just short of a sty."

"Why didn't you speak of this?"

"I did not think it would matter. I am a warrior, Raiven," Quynn added, frustrated that they were drifting farther and farther from the reason he had brought her here. "I do not need much in the way of comfort. In truth, my needs are few."

Something in the way he said *needs* made Raiven's eyes snap to his disbelievingly. He couldn't be referring to what she thought. However, one quick glance at his smoky gray eyes assured her he was.

"You must be jesting," she burst out.

Quynn leaned back slowly against the door, firmly shutting and barring it with his huge body. "About my needs? I assure you, I am not."

Raiven was intrigued and revolted at the same time. She allowed revulsion to gain the upper hand. "After what has been done to me and my family . . . ? If you think I'll readily bed down with you, you are insane!"

Quynn sighed. "Nay, Raiven, I do not think 'twill be done readily despite my hopes. However, it will be done before either of us leaves this room."

"Then we shall never leave this room," Raiven retorted, "because that's how long you will have to wait until I will readily give you anything."

The smile that crossed his face told her he didn't believe that, and he knew that she didn't believe it herself. "Did I say I was going to wait?" he asked smoothly, his sensuous smile growing.

Raiven didn't like the way her senses were responding to his mere smile. As much to deter him as to convince herself she said stiffly, "It will be force then."

Quynn straightened away from the door. "Nay, never that."

"Then what do you here?"

"'Twill not be force, Raiven, and well you know it. I have come to the end of my patience with fighting wars within my own home and especially my own bed."

"This is not your home."

"Nay, it isn't," Quynn agreed, "but I fully intend to make it so." He began to approach her slowly, and Raiven panicked. He had not even touched her yet, and already she wanted him.

"How can you want this at a time like this?" she blurted.

Quynn stopped. "What time is it?"

"It is a time of unrest, wounding, and near death. Your people kill mine." Raiven lowered her face and her voice, shame at wanting him overwhelming her. Her whispered words were a bid to make herself remember something she was appalled she nearly forgot in his presence. "Your brother wounded mine."

"Raiven," Quynn began in a warning tone.

Raiven looked up, eyes hot and dry. "He did," she repeated with quiet fire.

"James himself is not sure of what took place, and he was there. How can you be so certain?" Quynn could feel his anger rise at her unwillingness to be just. He was bending over and back to make allowances for the many slights and injuries he and his men had sustained, and she was tenaciously holding to her ill-supported opinions.

"Even if he did wound your brother, 'twas not an unwarranted attack as you would like to see it, but self-defense. Or would you rather my brother be the one lying near death now? I can see why those here are blind. How can they be aught else when the one who claims to lead them is as blind as the winged creature that haunts the darkest caves?"

"What more is there for me to see? As you say, it is my brother lying more dead than alive."

Quynn's frustration mounted apace with his temper. Breathing deeply, he strove for calm. Ignoring her last statement, he said, "Raiven, can you not see or at least allow that the treatment I and my men receive is similar to the way my servants and people treated you in England?"

The resemblance was too glaring to deny, even if she had not seen Quynn's room. She nodded jerkily.

Quynn eased a bit. "Did you not once say to me that perhaps my people were reacting if not by my direct order, then from my obvious feelings, thus showing their loyalty to me?"

Again Raiven nodded.

"Then could it not be that the same took place here? Jacques left the hall, Raiven. Why? He was living among those known to be hostile to the English. Why?"

Raiven's eyes burned. "My brother is struggling for his life now, Quynn. There are no answers to the questions you pose."

"I know." He sighed. "I only wish you to see that it was probable that he did what was said and that even after his wounding, his people, your people, still carry on with what they thought or think he wants them to do."

Raiven's face looked to be carved from ivory. "Very well, Quynn. I see it. I concede it. I can even progress a step further. My brother was not only angry and hostile, he was furious. I saw it in his eyes when I left. It was the main reason I asked you to allow me to write to him. I wanted to dissuade him from any course of rebellion because I had done enough harm. However, I was not permitted to write. Whether or not my brother followed the path of rebellion, I do not know. I never saw him or was allowed to hear from him again, and now he cannot tell me," Raiven said, her voice catching. "Nevertheless, if he did, then he is paying the supreme cost—with his life.

"As for my people, they follow no leader, near dead or alive. I have spoken to Simon, the man who was steward before James's arrival. I believe not only his words, but the truth I see in his eyes. So, if a word of advice from an accused rebel rouser is of any value, I would look elsewhere, milord, to find the person that has nurtured such malice toward you."

Quynn studied her face, then nodded. They had talked and solved nothing. He tired of talking. He knew Raiven thought their conversation had turned his attention from his true desire, but she was soon to find out it had not.

"Raiven, I tire of all this talk of hatred and death. I prefer to think of what could be, of the life that is soon to come into the world. I prefer to dream the dreams we spun that night aboard the ship."

"It is too late for that. That ship sailed past, taking any dreams we foolishly harbored with it." She spoke sharply because all too quickly she remembered everything about that night. It stood out in stark contrast to every night since when she had been alone and wanting.

"Were they foolish, Raiven?"

"Please, Quynn, do not do this. I beg you, don't do this. Allow me to—"

"To what?" Quynn asked softly, coming near. "To lock yourself away from life, from me? To separate me from you? Where does that leave me and my child?" He touched her rounded stomach gently. As had happened the night on the ship, the babe moved gustily. "You see," Quynn went on, a tender note in his voice, "my son does not want it so. I do not wish it so, and even his mother does not. I do what I do for you as well, Raiven. You cannot lock yourself away. Feel the life within you, not just in the babe, but in your heart. Feel the joy we can bring to each other."

Quynn bent and captured her lips in a nonthreatening kiss. When Raiven groaned in protest, backing away, he murmured, "Just *feel.*"

That last coercion was all she could endure. Feverishly Raiven returned his passionate kiss, pressing herself fully into his arms. Their clothing seemed to melt away, and soon their bodies were straining together, both desperately searching for the oblivion that passion alone could bring. Their movements were not languid or careful. It was as if both knew this was only a moment and, because of its brevity, one to be cherished.

Raiven clung to Quynn, deliberately not thinking, only allowing feeling and sensation to register in her mind, hungry for him in ways she had not known possible. She could have wept at the sheer piercing joy of being in his arms. When the bliss of their joining was upon her, she cried out his name and her love. So enthralled was she at the unadulterated beauty of the moment, she didn't realize that Quynn stopped abruptly at her cry to stare down into her face.

What he saw there coupled with her words brought him immediate release, a release so keen and shattering that he closed his eyes in wonder as ripple after ripple of pleasure rocked his body.

Despite the strength-sapping experience, his mind was alert with boundless joy. She loved him! Raiven loved him! It was no mere passion's talk. The truth of her words was echoed in the emerald clarity of her eyes.

Quynn felt exultant. There was no battle he could not win, no foe he could not defeat. He would find out the truth about the happenings here. He would do it for them and for their love, which he was going to tell her about as soon as he stopped this unmanly trembling.

He could have saved his words. When he opened his eyes to declare his undying love and his unrelenting quest to find the truth, he found his wife had succumbed to her passion and exhaustion. She was asleep.

* * * *

A rainy night had fallen when Raiven awoke, momentarily disconcerted by her unfamiliar surroundings. Then memory came flooding back, and she was grateful that she was alone. She would not have been able to face Quynn just then. She knew he would not understand. After the fire of her response and her declaration of love, he would not understand the ice that once again settled around her heart with the fading of passion's heat.

*Traitor!* her mind accused. His brother had nearly killed hers. Even while she lay writhing in decadent pleasure beneath the brother of the man who had done the deed, Jacques could have breathed his last. While he might have been gasping out his final breath, she had been gasping words of love to the man just as responsible for the deed as if he had done it himself. Wasn't it bad enough that she had not been able to tell him she wished his brother had been wounded in place of hers, unable to bear hurting him that way? Wasn't that betrayal enough? Nay, she had gone on to do the unforgivable.

Raiven came from beneath the covers that she knew Quynn had placed over her body. It was strange that after the warmth of the pelts, she did not feel the chill. Instead she stared blankly at her stomach, well rounded now with Quynn's child. She tried to summon some feeling—any feeling—but all she felt was a curious detachment from everything.

Once dressed, Raiven walked silently, almost trancelike, from Quynn's room. She didn't go below to join the others for the evening meal, nor did she go to Jacques's room as she had for so many nights now. She didn't think she would be able to bear seeing his pale, lifeless features after what she had just done. Instead, she went to her own room, and as she had done too many times to recall, she went over to the window and stared out at the lushly sculpted rear gardens. Unlike those other times, however, this time there was no contentment. There was nothing.

Raiven stood there a long time. The direction of the rain shifted, and the cold drops pelted her, wetting the front of her gown, but she didn't notice. She didn't feel the cold. She just stood there. Watching and seeing nothing. Shivering and yet feeling nothing.

And that was the way Quynn found her. He had entered the room without knocking, certain that she would not have answered had he observed that propriety. Seeing her standing so perfectly still, he knew his assumption was correct. Her dejection was a palpable thing, and he cursed himself for leaving her alone.

He had not made a sound to announce his presence, but Raiven knew he was there.

"Please go away, Quynn," she said without turning.

Quynn swallowed, experiencing a chill from the frost of her voice. "Nay, I cannot."

He walked up behind her, and with each step, Raiven tensed further. When he reached for her, she jerked away.

"Do not. Please. I could not bear it if you touch me. Not now." Her voice was fragmented as if she would break at any minute, and its lifeless quality turned Quynn's chill to fear.

"Raiven, cease such talk. Come away from the window. You shall catch a chill if you do not."

Raiven completely ignored him.

Deciding not to ask again, Quynn reached for her and spun her about. Immediately she began to struggle, attacking him in much the same way she had James the day she had heard of Jacques's fate.

"Raiven, stop!" Quynn ordered, trying to subdue her without hurting her while seeking to protect himself. When Quynn finally had her under control, they were both breathing heavily.

One look in Raiven's eyes though, and Quynn forgot all else. The expression, or lack of one, in their desolate green depths was colder than any northern breeze, freezing his heart within his chest. Her eyes were bright. Too bright. And dry. It was then that Quynn realized that Raiven hadn't shed one tear over her brother. She had pushed the grief back, and now it was eating away at her soul. Pulling her stiff body to his, he held her fast, trying to infuse some of his warmth in her nearly frozen body.

"Cry, Raiven," he whispered against her hair. "Let out your grief before it tears you to pieces."

Nothing. She stared unblinkingly at the wall beyond his shoulder, and by not so much as a twitch did she acknowledge his presence, let alone his words.

"Raiven, please. You cannot continue in this manner."

Still nothing. If not for the small shallow breaths she took, it would be difficult to tell if she was alive at all.

When Quynn lifted her in his arms, Raiven did not resist. She had expended all the energy she had. Now she felt—empty. She had spent too much of the days past swinging from one volatile emotion to the other. First anger, then hurt, but beneath it all there was the pain of loving Quynn. When first Raiven heard of Jacques's attack, she had felt the agony of helplessness, that she could do naught for him. Today she felt as if in addition to all she couldn't do for him, she had betrayed him in deed and in words. Under the weight of the other emotions, she had been able to function slightly. However, the weight of the guilt she now felt left her empty, and she couldn't go on. The cold lump in her chest was growing to the point where every function of brain and body brought pain. Even breathing was a chore.

So when Quynn peeled off her wet clothing and put her to bed, she had no resistance left. Yet when he climbed in beside her, she found the strength to fight, clawing him with her nails and pummeling him with her fists.

Conquering her struggles was no easy task, and when he looked into her wild eyes, he saw that despite her exhaustion, she was prepared to fight him anew should he release her.

"Raiven, what is it? Tell me."

Raiven let her eyelids drop. She could not tell him she was afraid for him to touch her. Afraid for the intimacy with him that she couldn't seem to resist, which brought her a comfort she didn't deserve. It would kill her to betray Jacques that way again.

"Tell me," Quynn repeated, his voice soft but stern.

Raiven kept her gaze focused on his chest. When Quynn pulled her against him, she stiffened, preparing to fight him again, but his words came almost as if he read her turbulent thoughts, stilling her.

"Be easy, Raiven. I ask nothing of you. Since you will not talk to me, I shall speak to you." He paused a moment. When he spoke again, his voice was softly comforting. "I am sorrier than I can say at the pain you are suffering. To grief I am no stranger, and I would give anything that you not know its bite."

Raiven did not tense for further battle, and neither did she relax. She merely lay within the circle of Quynn's arms, convinced for now that all he wanted was to hold her.

Quynn began to rub her hair and temples, maintaining the soothing tone that was in harmony with the gentle movement of his fingers.

"My parents died when I was three and ten. They were a"—he paused—"an unusual match," he ended carefully. "My father did not seem to communicate well with his children, but the love of my mother was constant. My mother . . . my mother was everything a child could wish for. I adored her. She was my sun in day, and her gentle wisdom was my moon at night. She softened my father's harshness, guided me, protected me when she could, loved me always. I never knew how greatly I depended on that or my father, for that matter, until they both died of the fever."

The next few minutes were filled with nothing save silence, then Quynn continued, his voice now distant. "I cannot describe the feeling, nor have I ever tried. The pain and emptiness were almost unbearable. Too soon Darrielle contracted the fever. She did not linger as they did. Perhaps, being younger, her body was not as strong. She was dead within a week."

Raiven could hear the sadness the death of his family still brought him. It was almost as if he was speaking not only for her, but for himself as well.

"Then James became ill." His voice grew hoarse with

remembered terror. "I was beside myself. Ella was there to help. All I can remember is staring at him and praying that he not die." Again a pregnant pause.

"For the longest time I thought the pain and the fear would never cease. Even after James recovered, the fear lingered that he would be taken from me, and 'neath the fear was the pain that threatened me every moment of every day. The pain lasted so long I felt it had become me, that there was naught inside but the pain.

"Ella took me aside one day and told me that although my strength was commendable and despite all my father's rigorous lessons about the value of a man's strength, I would have to let the grief out. She said it was tormenting me because it wanted to be set loose, and I was preventing it. She declared that until I did, it would haunt me night and day and eventually it would win. She told me without embellishment that I didn't have the strength to fight such a mighty foe, and that didn't make me weak or less of a man, only human. And, she added, being human was not such a bad thing."

Quynn chuckled in memory. "She said the rest of creation muddled through being human all their lives and that surely I could survive being so for a few moments."

For a long time he continued to hold her, saying nothing. Then, "Can you not be human, too? Talk to me, Raiven. Really tell me of your life here. Tell me of Émil, Genevieve, and Jacques."

Each name was a sharp blade, stabbing at Raiven's defenses, tearing at her resolve to be strong. She didn't know if it was that pain, his impassioned speech, or the overwhelming need to speak as he had said before the grief became all that she was.

She began haltingly, telling him of her mother and father and of the things she had done as a child.

Finally, she spoke of Jacques, saying his name aloud for the first time since the day she found out he was wounded. The reminiscences came slowly at first, then more fluently. Somewhere between the tale of her cutting Jacques's hammock string as he slept and the tale of his pouring the ink bottle over her head, she began to cry. No great sobs, just gentle, steady tears. Her voice broke when she told of Jacques's strength and his youth.

"If he dies, I would have killed him," she confessed in a tiny voice. "And I've failed my father. My father entrusted me with the care of the land, the people, and my brother. I have done none of those things. The land is torn by strife, the people by dissension, and Jacques is dying."

Raiven cried quietly while Quynn held her and soothed what he could of her hurt.

"If I could bring my brother to full health, I would give you the land."

Quynn's hold on her tightened as he told her he didn't want her land. Raiven, too lost in the pain of sorrow, didn't hear.

"Nothing is worth this, nothing. Had I known the cost, I would have given in to Henry's demands without a struggle." Weeping openly, she beseeched, "Why, Quynn, why? He could have caused no great harm."

Quynn gathered her closer to him until the torrent of tears ceased. When he thought she was calm enough to hear, he spoke.

"I do not know the why of it, Raiven. Yet I give you my solemn word I intend to find out. I know at this time you do not hold James's honor in high esteem, but I know him. Raiven"—he tilted her face to his—"I know he would not harm a young boy without justification. And even if justified, he would have tried other means. I will find out who did this terrible thing to your brother and caused you so much pain and also who has darkened the St. Crowell name as one who maims children. I do not ask that you believe it now, nor do I ask that you believe in James's innocence. All I ask is that you trust and believe in me."

The sheen of tears lent a jewellike sparkle to the green eyes she raised to him. "Why? Why should I believe and do as you ask?"

"Because you love me and you're not foolish enough to love a man you cannot trust or one who has no honor.

There is also another more important reason for you to do what I have asked."

"What is that?" Raiven asked softly.

"Because this man who has no proof of honor aside from his word happens to love you with all his heart. Is that not reason enough?"

Raiven nodded, then she laughed, and then she cried.

# Chapter

# •31•

The court of justice seemed to drag on forever.

The court was something Raiven had told Quynn her father had begun so that all would have a chance to have their grievances settled in a fair way. When they had initially reinstituted the practice, no one had appeared for the court, not trusting the judgment of the Englishman, especially in light of what had been done to one of their own. However, as time passed and although Jacques did not improve, neither did he die, and there was a visible lessening of tension between the lord and the Lady Raiven, gradually more and more came to test Quynn's fairness of rule. The trickle of people had become a virtual stream, and Quynn was seeing more of the tenants and serfs than even he wanted.

Today, for example, he had settled disputes ranging from the unlawful attack upon a serf by the tenants who had suspected the lad of stealing to the argument over the ownership of a chicken.

Raiven, who usually sat with him, had pleaded exhaustion and absented herself from this session. Quynn had readily agreed, thinking she did look tired, and the heavy burden of the child she carried seemed to press more upon her recently.

Now, however, he selfishly wished she had stayed so he could glance upon her beauty and the warmth of her smile, which told him he was doing well and treating all fairly as person after person appeared before him.

Finally the stream of people slowed to a halt. He was about to breathe a relieved sigh when a tenant entered, looking warily about the near empty hall. The man was peculiar looking, to be sure. He had the look more of a friar than a tenant. Despite the warmth of the day, he had on heavy woolen garments of a nondescript color, and the cowl of his tunic was pulled far over his head, obscuring his features. He was of medium build, and nervousness added an unsteadiness to his movements.

It was not necessarily his shrouded appearance or his agitated motions that placed Quynn on guard. It was when the shadowed face in the cowl settled on him and then approached cautiously. Quynn eased some as he noted the man carried no sword. His only weapon was a short blade at his waist.

Putting a casually bland expression on his face, Quynn gave a quick thanks that Raiven was not present, then turned his full attention to the man, who now spoke.

"I wish a private audience, milord." For all his apparent skittishness, the man's voice was clear, with no tremor.

"What is the nature of your crime?"

"I have no crime."

"Your complaint then, your grievance," Quynn added sharply.

"Milord, I mean no disrespect, but if ye will grant me private audience, ye will hear all my words and render judgments as to whether the bigger dilemma be yers or mine."

Quynn stared harder at the man, trying to see his features in the shadow of the cowl. The man took a quick step back.

"Who I be is not the thing of import. I bring news for ye and yer ears alone."

"Then at least let me hear the subject of this news that is for my ears alone."

Quynn thought he heard a sound like a laugh come from the cowl.

"Do ye not have trust? I cannot inflict much damage with this short blade I carry."

Quynn laughed. "I would have been dead long 'ere now had I learned to trust only what my eyes beheld."

The cowl nodded slowly. "Ye have the wisdom my father said ye did."

Quynn's eyes sharpened. "Who is your father?"

"I will reveal all, milord, in private, for yer ears only."

The silence stretched out long between them as Quynn studied what he could of the man in the well-worn hose and tunic. "Allow me to view your face," he said finally, "and I will do as you ask."

"Milord, I will gladly bare all to ye, but 'tis most urgent and I fear my life forfeit should I not proceed with extreme care."

Quynn nodded abruptly. "Very well."

He walked to the room where the ladies usually sat doing their sewing and exchanging bits of news from near and far. After asking the ladies to leave, he deliberately stood aside and allowed the man to enter the room first.

The man looked from one place to another much in the same manner he'd used when he first entered the hall.

Quynn's voice was mocking. "'Twould seem your trust of me is no greater than mine for you."

A short negative shake of the head was his response. "'Tis not ye I do not trust. Terrible things have been happening here at Guirlande of late. Despite the fighting taking place in other areas of France, we have always enjoyed peace. Yer English king Henry tore us apart. 'Tis no peace to be found in the land, only treachery and the suffocating decay of betrayal."

The man did not speak as a mere tenant, and his diatribe was not just another in the many against Henry and all things English. He spoke with a sincere sorrow that was plain to see. Suddenly Quynn knew who he was.

"Speak, man," he said in the friendliest tone he'd used

since the man approached him. "I do wish to hear what you have to say."

As if the friendlier tone was the signal for which he waited, the man reached up, pulling off his cowl. Quynn hissed in recognition at the same time the man said, "I believe ye know my father, Simon. I am known as Reynar."

Quynn nodded, not needing the man to introduce himself. Reynar was a younger version of the ex-steward of Guirlande, Raiven's beloved Simon.

"'Twas you he sent then?"

"Aye. He needed someone he could trust, and after hearing of what happened to the lady's brother, I wanted to go. It was that and his words of how important this was to the Lady Raiven that swayed my mind long 'ere he told me of yer and yer brother's suspicions. He said one of yer own men would not do, because if as ye suspect, there be a traitor among ye, the one to find the knowledge must be someone unknown. I have not been around since yer brother's coming."

Reynar studied Quynn. "My father spoke rightly about ye. Not many men would look to their own to find a Judas. 'Tis too easy to blame another."

Quynn's insides clenched at Reynar's statement. He managed to keep his voice emotionless when he said, "I merely followed a piece of sage advice given me by a wise woman. You have news?"

Reynar's "Aye" was drowned out by the door being swung open.

Then several things happened seemingly at once. Perevil's voice called out to him, and Quynn noticed Reynar's eyes widen an instant before he heard Perevil scream, "Rebel," and felt something whiz by his ear. Turning quickly to combat the threat, he found none, only Perevil standing behind him with a grim expression. Quynn spun back to see Reynar, who had been upright moments before, lying still on the floor, Perevil's dagger embedded to the hilt in his chest.

Quynn quickly ran over to him, trying to see the full extent of his wound. Perevil's aim had been true. The blade had found the man's heart. Still kneeling over him, Quynn looked back to Perevil.

"Why?"

Something flickered in Perevil's eyes that Quynn did not read. "The man was a rebel. No doubt his intent was to murder you. 'Tis relieved I am and you should be also that I came in from the drills when I did. I knew something was amiss when I saw the ladies wandering about the main hall. When I asked, they told me where you were."

Perevil's tenseness eased a bit. He laughed lightly, although the sound was somewhat forced. "That makes twice I have saved your miserable hide. The other was when your father—"

"Perevil," Quynn interrupted with somber stillness, coming to his feet, "how did you know this man to be a rebel?"

Quynn, who was watching him closely now, saw Perevil freeze, then swing about, tensed as the string of a pulled bow, and still he forced himself to keep his neutral stance. Even the dangerous feral gleam in the dark blue eyes was not enough to mobilize Quynn as his heart began to ice over in his chest at the realization his mind was forming.

"Why?" Quynn asked again, and they both knew what he meant.

"Why not?" Perevil sneered. "What right did you have to any of it? Your family betrayed England, mine gave its land and its wealth to support her. Why should you be rewarded? Did you truly think I did not know? That I had not heard of the way your great-grandfather hid behind your great-grandmother's bliaut to keep Havilland safe? 'Twas all the talk, especially at our home—what was left of it," he said caustically. "'Twas that and the loss of our family's resources that most embittered my father. He never approved of our friendship. He said I would become weak as all the St. Crowells. Only I did not listen. I did not support my own father, and he died an embittered and broken man. On his deathbed he made me vow to avenge the wrong done to England and the Dunkirks not by marauding Normans, but by those claiming its heritage. Those who called themselves sons of England. In that way I could right the wrong done and regain what my family had sacrificed nobly while your family hid behind cowardice to maintain."

Perevil was practically snarling when he finished speaking, and still Quynn just stood looking at him, showing no reaction.

"'Twould seem what my father said was true. 'Tis twice I have called the St. Crowells cowards, and still you have not drawn your sword. What does it take to make men out of any of you, or is it a task hopeless to all?"

The numbing pain that had enveloped Quynn's heart when Perevil first began to speak was beginning to crust over, making him impervious to the insults Perevil hurled at him. Although it was one of the hardest things he had ever done, he had to push aside any thought other than gaining the truth. The pain would be there.

"You attacked Raiven's brother." It was not a question and Quynn really didn't need Perevil's curt nod.

"For what cause?"

"I did not trust him. The lad was too clever by half. When he began to stay away from the hall, I suspected he knew more than I was safe with him knowing. However, I could not find him. When he found James, 'twas too good an opportunity to let pass."

"And if he lives?" Quynn asked with quiet intensity.

"He won't," Perevil promised.

A flash of anger showed in Quynn's eyes, but anger was an emotion, and the numbed state of his heart would not allow him to sustain it. Besides, he wanted—needed—to know all of it.

"You were the one telling Langford all he wanted to know." Again it was a statement, not a question.

"Aye." Perevil smiled cruelly. "However, I alone sent Teris to your room and then to her Maker."

The anger was there again. This time it was a little stronger, faintly reflected in Quynn's eyes.

Perevil shrugged. "The stupid wench actually wanted

to go to you and tell you the truth. She claimed some nonsense about not wanting to hurt either you or the Lady Raiven. I could not allow that. I was not supposed to be in England. She said she would not speak of my part in it, as if I would actually take the word of a serf."

"She held to her word."

For the first time Perevil looked surprised.

"I saw her. She told me she did not know who had spread the word that I needed a bed partner. She was to come back and tell Raiven, but, alas, she met you." He spoke as if these events had nothing to do with him. He merely put together piece by piece a puzzle that had long plagued him sorely, not allowing the shock of the amount of blood on Perevil's hands or his betrayal to register.

"The attack on Henry and later on the tenant—by supposed French rebels—that was you also, or at least at your instigation." It amazed him that he could say these things to the man who had been like a brother to him and feel nothing. "Did you perchance have a hand in Gerhaldt's death as well?" he asked in an almost conversational tone filled with sarcasm.

Perevil laughed. "How else was I to sow trouble for you? Murdering a king is a treasonous business," he actually sounded amused, "but then you saved him and all I had to content myself with was further suspicion. You were always too quick. When you arrived at the tenant's cottage, it was all my men could do to get away. The curses in French, of course, were deliberate. I couldn't have you and your wife finding accord too quickly—if at all. As to Gerhaldt, there are other problems in the world beside your own." All humor was gone from Perevil's voice, and his smile was nasty. "Although it did distress me when I learned that you had benefited from that."

Quynn nodded. "Why did you not kill James as he lay unconscious?"

Perevil's smile turned uglier. "Ah, Quynn, have you not yet discerned that I wished to make you suffer and then watch you die? 'Twas never my intent to kill you, only to make your life miserable so that when Henry came to his senses and ended it as he should have done years ago, you would have died an embittered man as my father did. That is true vengeance.

"Although this is not nearly as much suffering as I would have wished, I shall settle for the joy of killing you now."

Reflex alone made Quynn pull his sword from its scabbard. "You shall not succeed, Perevil. Your trail is too wide and too bloody. Justice will be served."

"I think not, but in any event"—Perevil shrugged again—"you shall not be here to see it."

The harsh clang of steel upon steel rang out as they engaged each other. All the while they fought, Quynn kept repeating to himself that this was his enemy and this fight was for his life. Here at last was one of the nameless, faceless people that had taunted and sullied the house of St. Crowell. Yet, with all those thoughts running through his mind, he found himself unable to attack, only to defend himself against the punishing blows that Perevil tried to inflict.

They fought around the room, turning over tables and chairs, until finally with a lightning-fast maneuver, Quynn twisted Perevil's sword from his grip, sending it flying. Quicker than a blink, he had the tip of his sword against his former friend's throat.

"End it now, Quynn. Show some honor and kill me here," Perevil panted.

Quynn lowered his sword and stepped away. "You wanted all of England to see, and they shall. I leave you to Henry's justice and not my vengeance. The crimes you have done are against him also."

He turned away to call his men to take Perevil away and was surprised to see Raiven standing in the door. In the frenzy of the fight, he had not noticed her. Then he noted the fear in her eyes. His battle instincts came fully to the fore, and he turned, sword still in hand, to greet Perevil's distorted visage, which immediately smoothed.

The short blade Perevil held in a tight grip clanked to the floor and he fell not long behind it, Quynn's sword protruding from his back.

For a long time, Quynn stood looking down on the lifeless body of the man he had loved like a brother, dead by his own hand. There should have been grief . . . guilt . . . pain, but there was nothing. Even the faint stirring of anger he had felt was gone. The protective shell that had surrounded his heart would not allow him to feel anything—until Raiven laid her hand gently upon his arm.

Quynn turned to her as a plant turns to the sun—automatically seeking warmth and sustenance.

Raiven was afraid of the dark, haunted look she saw in his eyes.

"Quynn?" she called softly.

There was no reaction. He continued to stare at her. Not knowing what else to do and having heard everything, Raiven took Quynn in her arms and held him.

It was a long time before his arms returned the embrace.

"It is as if I have killed my own brother," he finally whispered in a husky voice thick with the pain Raiven had seen swimming in his eyes.

Even knowing what the hideous man lying dead on the floor had done to her brother, Raiven couldn't help but respond to the pain in his voice. "I know," she replied in soft consolation. "It is why I could not bring myself to thrust my dagger in his back when it was presented to me. I know the agony I felt when I thought your brother had wounded mine; I could not subject you to the same."

Quynn pulled away slightly. Staring deeply into his eyes, Raiven saw a lessening of the pain.

"I love you, Raiven," he said solemnly.

"I know that, too."

# Chapter 32

Scream, milady, if you must."

Raiven, drenched in sweat and gripped in the most horrendous pain she had ever experienced in her life, weakly, yet stubbornly, shook her head.

"Nay," she gasped, falling back to the bed as the contraction passed.

It had been a long labor, and throughout Raiven had not made a noise above a loud groan. Elaine, nearly as worn as her mistress, looked down at her, too exasperated to argue. She tried to reason instead.

"'Twill not make you weak. Many women scream. 'Tis only a release. You've suffered half a day and an entire night. 'Tis no shame."

Raiven's eyes snapped open, the green orbs surprisingly clear considering the grueling toll of a near twenty-four-hour labor.

"I do not consider it suffering to bear my husband's child. I want it more than anything on earth. Anyth—" Her words were cut off by a gasp as another hard pain hit. When it passed, she looked at Elaine's dubious expression.

"I cannot believe, milady, you have the strength to be stubborn even in the pangs of childbirth."

Raiven panted through another pain.

"Truly, Elaine, it is not stubbornness. I fear if I give in to the urge to scream, I will not be able to cease. 'Twill worry Quynn and Jacques, and he is only beginning to mend, and it cannot be good for the babe and I already fear—ughhh."

Another pain seized her, and Elaine instructed, "Gently, gently. The pains are hard upon you. This means the child will be coming soon. 'Tis no need for fear, milady. First babes are unpredictable and oft take their own leisure entering the world. I am sure the baron knows this."

Raiven relaxed back, while Elaine examined her. "How much—"

". . . more, James?" Quynn asked, straining to hear any sound from the room abovestairs. "It has been nearly a day since Raiven's labor began. I did not expect it to be a hurried process, but this is much too long for my liking. Surely," he continued, his worry evident, "even one with her strength cannot endure the agony of childbirth much longer."

Panic seized him as he thought that perhaps she hadn't endured this long. Maybe she had died, and no one ventured forth to tell him.

James accurately read the expanding dread on his face. "Quynn," he said steadily, breaking through Quynn's rapidly mounting disturbing thoughts, "she fares well. I do not know how much longer 'ere the birth, but all will be well."

"How do you know this?" Quynn demanded, anxiety sharpening his voice. "Have you heard a sound from the room? From what her ladies led me to believe, women scream with the pain, and when I heard her cries, I should not fear. None mentioned a silent birth, as if . . ." Quynn trailed off.

James fell silent, and he looked to Jacques, who, though still pale from his ordeal, had asked to be brought down to await the birth of his niece or nephew. In just the short time he had come to know his sister's husband, he could feel the love he had for her. In light of the happiness he could see would be Raiven's, he could and did forgive everything. These were honorable men. What had occurred was not their fault. He tried to offer Quynn comfort, thinking to himself how much like Raiven he was.

"She is strong, Quynn," he said softly, ignoring the slight shiver of dread he had felt himself at Quynn's pronouncements. "Raiven is not like other women."

"There is no difference in this," Quynn asserted stubbornly, watching the young man who so favored his wife. He was, as Raiven had described him, gentle, kind, and even tempered—very unlike his sister, he thought with a weak smile. His thoughts turned back to Raiven as he resumed his pacing. "She feels pain as all the rest. She can di—" His eyes widened, and he bolted from the room without finishing the thought.

When he burst into the bedroom, it was just as Elaine was exhorting Raiven to push one more time. Elaine ignored him, too absorbed in what she doing, as he walked over to the bed.

Raiven lay still on the bed, her eyes closed, her face devoid of all color. Quynn felt his heart lurch.

"Raiven, my love, if you hear me, open your eyes please." It was the first time he had ever used that word with her, and his tone was the softest Raiven had ever heard. She opened her eyes slowly, immediately finding his.

Quynn was forced to bend to the edge of the bed, so relieved that she was still alive, his knees weakened.

"Milord," Elaine said crisply, "if you must be here, then you give assist. She is much weakened. Lend her your strength. Push her up. 'Twill make the pushing easier. She must push now."

Quynn did not take offense at being ordered about by his wife's servant. Instantly he sat at Raiven's head and lifted her to lean against him. He was surprised when she stiffened and tried to pull away.

"You should not be here to see me like this," she whispered weakly.

Quynn pulled her back. "Why should I not? 'Tis my child you struggle to bear. If I can be there for its making, I can be there for its birthing. Now, do as Elaine says and push, love. Lean on me. Borrow my strength."

Fortified by his words and the unmistakable love in them, Raiven gathered her waning strength for another push. She totally ignored Elaine's pleased smile, smiling only when Quynn kissed her temple gently and whispered, "Well done."

At the start of another pain, it was Quynn who urged her, "Push, Raiven. That does it, bring us our joy. Give us our child."

Mustering the very last reserves of her energy, Raiven pushed and was rewarded with the rushing feeling of the child being expelled from her body. She collapsed back against Quynn as Elaine cut the cord and cleaned the babe.

"What is it?" Quynn asked anxiously, for the child had not made a sound and Elaine worked silently.

Elaine finally looked up from her task, her face beaming. "You have a son, milord, a fine, healthy—"

The babe chose that time to make his presence known to his father and mother by screaming forcefully.

"—and loud son."

She brought him to Quynn, and he eased Raiven onto the pillows before Elaine slipped the babe into his arms. She moved away to hurriedly see to the task of expelling the afterbirth, sighing with satisfaction as she examined it and her mistress. When she looked up, relief wiped all exhaustion from her face, and she smiled again.

"The child has done no damage, albeit his large size."

She could have saved her words; Raiven did not heed them, and Quynn did not hear them.

"Quynn, how is he?" she asked in a voice already regaining strength.

Quynn had to swallow twice before he could speak, so overwhelmed was he by the poignancy of the moment. He had never known so instant and overpowering a love.

"He is a fine babe, Raiven, with a thatch of raven

wing's black for hair and eyes a peculiar shade that I feel will match the green of his mother's."

Elaine had finally finished, and immediately Raiven reached for her son. Quynn lowered the babe to her arms.

For a long moment, she just stared at the babe that lay resting in her arms. A tremulous and unexpected smile shaped her lips as he stared back at her.

"Can he see me?" she asked in wonder.

"I do not know, milady, but 'tis certain he knows you're his mother."

Raiven nodded, then at last tore her eyes away from her son to stare at her husband. "Are you pleased?"

Quynn smiled. "Aye. I am pleased. I am more than pleased."

A sudden dark thought clouded Raiven's eyes. "I'm sure Henry will be satisfied," she murmured.

Quickly Quynn's gaze found Elaine's, and at a nod from him, she left hastily.

"Raiven," Quynn began after the door shut behind the servant, "we have never discussed Henry or you and me. While 'tis very true that were it not for Henry's machinations, we would not have learned of one another, 'tis equally true that Henry's influence ended there. Henry could control only our coming together, not how we feel about one another. I have told you that I love you. 'Tis not Henry who said that. 'Twas not of his design. Our loving one another was not a part of Henry's order. We did that of our own hearts' urging. No man alive could make me say the words were it not true. I have naught and all to gain by saying them to you.

"I have naught in that I do not want your lands or your many halls. I hope to gain all in that you have never really spoken of love aside from once in the depths of passion."

Raiven dropped her eyes from his. She remembered that time. Did he think it just mere passion talk? How could he not know? Not see it? She fastened her gaze back on him when he began to speak again.

"I once thought that the loss of Havilland would mean all to me, that above all things the tradition of it must continue. 'Tis what my father believed. 'Tis what he taught incessantly." Quynn's eyes took on a faraway look.

"I do not believe I ever pleased my father. He always demanded more and yet more again. His marriage to my mother was to produce heirs, and his heirs were for Havilland. I do not know if he ever felt any more for us than a satisfaction that the St. Crowell line would continue. Perhaps the deeds that stained his grandfather's life blotted his life as it did that of Perevil's father. I cannot say. All I know for a certainty is that you have taught me something I did not know I needed to learn. You have taught me 'tis not wrong or a weakness to live for people rather than a block of stone and a patch of land. 'Tis the loving of people done within the block of stone that makes a place precious.

"I still love Havilland and I will still fight to keep it, but it is no longer all for me."

"Mortar and stone," Raiven whispered, her eyes misting.

"Aye," Quynn averred. "My treasure, all the wealth I ever hope to possess, is within this room. Your bearing my son has given me the moon and stars. All my world needs to be complete is your giving me the sun of your love." He lifted her hand to his lips and pressed a warm kiss in her palm. Then his gaze intensified. "And I give you my solemn word I shall never ask aught else of life."

Tears flowed down Raiven's cheeks. "I do not know what to say, Quynn. I never dreamed that the horrendous plot Henry began would end as it has."

She was referring to his loving her. He assumed she was speaking of the attack on her brother.

"Raiven, I am more grieved than words allow about what has occurred. This I have said before. I know 'tis no solace to you now, but Jacques has been avenged. If I had known before the deed what end would have come, I would have done more. From the things I have learned of him, he understands. He gets stronger with each day's passing, and he would not want you to be tormented by guilt. 'Twas not your fault. If you must lay blame, place it on me."

"You have no blame here. You did not nearly kill him."

Quynn's brow arched derisively. "Did I not? I sent Perevil here. I trusted him. 'Twas my miscalculation of his character that caused all this."

Laying the babe on the bed, Raiven took hold of Quynn's face in her hands. Staring deeply into his gray eyes, streaked with the pain of his betrayal and guilt, she said, "You cannot take the blame for this. You, too, have been a victim. Perevil was distorted. He had allowed his hatred of your family to eat away at his soul. There was naught any of us could have done. He allowed his hate to consume him until there was naught left. His crime against you was nearly as heinous to my mind as what he did to Jacques. I have come to know your mind, and to see Perevil fall at your feet was as painful as if it were James. You have suffered, and yet, you had no control over the situation.

"If, however, I had not proven stubborn, Henry's ire would not have flared and perhaps Jacques—despite his mending, he is far from well—would not have had to suffer as he has. My list of misdeeds extends to the wrong I have done your brother in thinking him to be an attacker of children. Not only did he forgive, but he insisted there had been no offense to forgive."

It was agony for him to see the pain, which was never far from her gaze, return and to discover the source of the pain was not unfulfilled vengeance, but unremitting guilt.

"Shall we not say we both have suffered, thus that is another strand to bind us together. In any event, we should not speak any more now. Elaine would have my hide if she knew I kept you from your rest this long to talk of things so unpleasant. Rest. I will take our son—"

"I will rest better if he stays beside me," Raiven protested.

Quynn nodded, and without saying more, he left the room.

Later that night when he returned to see how she fared, Raiven was awake and nursing the babe. Immediately he tried to withdraw, thinking she might feel slightly awkward, but Raiven beckoned him in.

Neither spoke. Quynn sat gingerly on the side of the bed, watching her as his son suckled, his own contentment and happiness so keen it pierced him.

When Raiven finished, she burped the babe, then set him aside, and Quynn asked, "How are you faring?"

"Well. My joy in our son grows with every minute," she added, looking down on the sleeping babe.

"That is good to hear," he said in a rather stilted manner.

"Is there aught the matter, Quynn?"

The thing closest to his heart, for which he longed with all his being, he could not bring himself to ask for, so he shook his head and stood.

"Nay. All is well. Good night, Raiven. I shall see you on the morrow."

Ever since coming to Guirlande, he had slept in a different chamber. Initially, it had been their differences that sent him there. Then, despite their semipeace, he had remained there out of fear for her and the child. Now despite his knowing it to be highly improper, he wanted to sleep beside her. If their relationship had ever had a normal moment, he would have just done so. As things were, he waited for Raiven to suggest it, but apparently all seemed fine to her as it was.

Her voice stopped him at the door.

"Quynn, I have something I wish to ask of you."

He turned back. "Name it."

The moment had come. Raiven had rehearsed her speech ever since awakening. She wanted him to stay with her. She had wanted him to be there during her pregnancy, but their circumstance was so strained. She tired of waiting for him to take charge in his usual forthright manner. He was taking too long. But now that the time was at hand, she couldn't remember the words she had practiced.

Gathering her courage, she met his gaze in the candlelit room and said baldly, "Stay with me. Hold me now. I have waited all day to feel your arms around me."

"Is it allowed?" he asked hesitantly despite his wanting to accept her offer before she changed her mind. She had been forced enough. He wanted from her only what she was willing to give.

Raiven laughed. "In our house it will be."

Needing no more urging, he came around the bed and, slipping out of his clothes, slid in beside her. Quynn was content just holding her, but Raiven startled him by speaking.

"I cannot forgive what Perevil has done, but I can understand being prodded first by the fear of loss and then the spur of hate. For the longest time, fear and hate controlled my actions. I hated Henry. I hated England. Before I knew you, I hated you. I blamed Henry for ripping away what remained of my world. There was precious little of it left after the sudden death of my father."

Raiven smiled slowly. "Although it pains me to say it, I owe Henry a debt. True, he tore away the rest of my world, but all that had been there was worry and anxiety of caring aright for the responsibilities my father left to me. When you entered, the fear grew to proportions unreal. I thought I'd never find my way back to my world."

She fell silent.

"And did you?" Quynn prompted.

"Nay," she said simply, surprising him with her blunt answer. "I was forced to learn to live in another one. But in this world, there was peace—if I was willing to take it—peace, contentment, happiness, and then love. It was the world you built for me, Quynn, laying it before me as an irresistible prize just for being alive."

"I will rest better if he stays beside me," Raiven protested.

Quynn nodded, and without saying more, he left the room.

Later that night when he returned to see how she fared, Raiven was awake and nursing the babe. Immediately he tried to withdraw, thinking she might feel slightly awkward, but Raiven beckoned him in.

Neither spoke. Quynn sat gingerly on the side of the bed, watching her as his son suckled, his own contentment and happiness so keen it pierced him.

When Raiven finished, she burped the babe, then set him aside, and Quynn asked, "How are you faring?"

"Well. My joy in our son grows with every minute," she added, looking down on the sleeping babe.

"That is good to hear," he said in a rather stilted manner.

"Is there aught the matter, Quynn?"

The thing closest to his heart, for which he longed with all his being, he could not bring himself to ask for, so he shook his head and stood.

"Nay. All is well. Good night, Raiven. I shall see you on the morrow."

Ever since coming to Guirlande, he had slept in a different chamber. Initially, it had been their differences that sent him there. Then, despite their semipeace, he had remained there out of fear for her and the child. Now despite his knowing it to be highly improper, he wanted to sleep beside her. If their relationship had ever had a normal moment, he would have just done so. As things were, he waited for Raiven to suggest it, but apparently all seemed fine to her as it was.

Her voice stopped him at the door.

"Quynn, I have something I wish to ask of you."

He turned back. "Name it."

The moment had come. Raiven had rehearsed her speech ever since awakening. She wanted him to stay with her. She had wanted him to be there during her pregnancy, but their circumstance was so strained. She miraculous one, and he wanted to savor it, recounting his many blessings.

Rest could come later. For now he merely wanted to hold his love within his arms close to his heart, feel her warmth, and bask in the sun that brightened his world despite it being the darkest of night.